the

CHERRY
ROBBERS

ALSO BY SARAI WALKER

Dietland

the

CHERRY
ROBBERS

SARAI WALKER

HARPER PERENNIAL

NEW YORK • LONDON • TORONTO • SYDNEY • NEW DELHI • AUCKLAND

To my sister, Michelle

And to all the women throughout my life who have been sisters in spirit

hell must break before I am lost;

before I am lost,
hell must open like a red rose
for the dead to pass.

— H.D.
  From "Eurydice"

CONTENTS

THE CHAPELS

Belinda Holland Chapel (*born 1900*)   Henry Chapel (*born 1893*)

Aster Chapel (*born 1930*)

Rosalind Chapel (*born 1931*)

Calla Chapel (*born 1933*)

Daphne Chapel (*born 1935*)

Iris Chapel (*born 1937*)

Hazel "Zelie" Chapel (*born 1939*)

The Violet Notebook

August 3, 2017 — Abiquiú, New Mexico

When Lola went to San Francisco last year, she bought me what she thought was a sketchbook, one small enough for me to slip in my pocket and take on my early evening walks through the hills surrounding the village, when I might see hollyhocks I want to draw, or a desert cottontail, or any number of things. I never know where my walks will take me or what I'll see. The destination isn't what's important but the light, best in late afternoon. Artists chase the light.

The book is bound in faux leather and dyed a brilliant shade of bright blue, almost turquoise, one of the reasons Lola chose it for me. It was gray and gloomy the whole time she was in San Francisco, and when she saw the blue, it reminded her of the sky at home, and the sky reminds her of me. Lola once described our life together like this: Picture taking off in an airplane from a city where the weather is too bleak to bear. The airplane climbs and climbs and finally breaks through the clouds where there's nothing but light and blue sky. That's my life with Sylvia, she said. That's how it feels, and that's how it looks. At an elevation of more than six thousand feet, the sky here is somehow bluer than the sea.

Lola always brings me gifts when she travels. It's part of our ritual, our little courtship dating back decades. She sometimes travels for work, taking a couple of big trips a year. I stay home, interested only in what's around me. The world to me is not *out there*. But Lola, like most people, doesn't see it that way; she ventures out, then returns home with small tokens to let me know she'd been thinking of me while she was away. I loved the blue book as soon as she handed it to me; I could imagine her buying it in a bookstore on one of those vertiginous San Francisco streets, she in a simple skirt-and-sweater set, silver-black hair pulled back into a low knot, a simple chain around her neck. No lipstick, never anything like that. Lola doesn't need adornment.

The blue book was wrapped in plastic, and when I opened it the next morning after Lola had gone to her study, I discovered it wasn't a sketchbook but a diary with lined pages. I decided not to tell Lola about the mistake she'd made, that I hated those lines that looked like bars on a cage. I see in flashes and impressions, color and light, not in words snaking across and down a page, that deep cavern of writing, which I rarely choose to enter.

I put the diary on the bookcase in my study and hoped Lola wouldn't mention it again, never suspecting that one day I would need to write in it with a sense of urgency.

That's not what I'm writing in now, that beautiful but disappointing blue diary. I *will* write in it — after today that is a certainty — but I have to warm up to this diary-writing business first.

I'm writing now in a Moleskine notebook I bought years ago in a bookshop in Taos. It's a radiant violet color, with an attached elastic band, also in violet, that wraps around the notebook from top to bottom. There were so many colors of Moleskines stacked on the shelves at the shop, and I picked through them, pulling out the violet one on instinct, thinking of Wordsworth: "A violet by a mossy stone, half hidden from the eye!" I tend to see colors as flowers. I bought the notebook thinking I'd use it to make shopping lists, to-do lists, the sorts of prosaic things I'm not good at doing, but true to form, I've never used the Moleskine except to press a sprig of lavender inside the front cover, a sprig now flattened but still pungently fragrant.

I suppose I could call this notebook a diary, but I'm not going to do that. That raises expectations.

I've turned to this notebook now because Lola isn't here and I need someone to talk to. The truth is I have no one else.

I've never wanted to leave a trail. That might seem strange for someone in my position — an artist, and a rather famous one. I've certainly left a trail of paintings behind me going back decades, highly personal in many ways but really only breadcrumbs. People know my art but not me, and I always intended to keep it that way.

But today something happened that I wish I could say I'd dreaded for a long time, though that wouldn't be true. I was caught, as they say, *off guard*. That might be the downside of not writing in a diary, of leaving no trail. The diary isn't the point so much as what the lack of one reveals. I've been too willing to forget.

After lunch today, I walked to the post office, taking the usual route down the dirt road that runs around the edge of the village (I've always preferred edges), wearing my wide-brimmed sun hat that hides my face. Lola is in Brazil for about a month teaching a course on the art of perfumery at a prestigious institute, the name of which eludes me. When she's home, we take this postlunch walk together and chat about what we'll be working on in the afternoon until we meet again for dinner. (There's no talk of work allowed during meals, house rule.) Walking on my own, I was left to think about my afternoon and the large blank canvas that's been sitting on the easel in my studio for weeks, untouched. I've been dancing around it, not ready yet to approach it, so I spend my time doing sketches. The anticipation is delightful.

There are always letters in the post office box for me, almost none of them with my address. They are simply addressed to Sylvia Wren, Abiquiú, New Mexico, 87510. Only a handful of people know my full address, but in a village of around two hundred residents, the letters still find their way to me. It's kind of people to write, but the mail does pile up quickly and it begs a response even if the writers don't ask for one.

I employ a woman in Santa Fe as my assistant of sorts, one of those New Age white people who flock there dripping with turquoise jewelry and smelling of sage. I'd prefer to hand off all the letters to her. It's her job to turn down requests for whatever I'm being asked to do, whether it's interviews or speaking engagements or, God help me, commencement addresses. She's been my assistant for more than a decade now, and we meet for the occasional lunch when I go to town. I've never invited her to my house, though I know she's dying to visit. She jokingly refers to herself as the Mistress of Refusal and will probably write a memoir about me after I'm dead, titled something dreadful like *In the Shadow of Sylvia Wren*. I see her making mental notes every time we meet in the restaurant at La Fonda.

But I never give the fan letters to my assistant since Lola prefers to read and respond to them herself via a special postcard she had printed up. She's always loved reading my fan mail; when we were younger, I think it turned her on a bit, all those people clamoring after me, and she the only person in my bed.

I grabbed the letters from the PO box, darting in and out of the building in mere seconds; anything longer invites conversation. Back home, I struggled to open the gate, the only entry point in the low stucco wall that wraps around the property. We leave the gate unlocked during the day if we're home but always lock it at night and when we go out. No amount of oiling the lock has ever been able to fix it for me; Lola doesn't struggle with it like I do. I have a theory that the house doesn't like me to leave it, that when I do it punishes me, makes me fight for reentry. We are bound, the house and I, as much as any pair of lovers. I've lived and worked for decades inside its walls. Someday I'll die in them too.

• • •

My study is at the back of the house, my desk positioned in front of the window that overlooks the flower garden and the hills, with the Cerro Pedernal in the distance, a mesa that looks like a neck with no head. The rocky hills behind the house are red, almost Martian in appearance; they deserve to be called "otherworldly" when so few things described that way actually do.

I sorted through the letters, fighting the urge to dump them somewhere. I have to make an effort at practicality while Lola is gone; she's the one who normally handles that part of our life — paying the bills, doing the shopping, calling the plumber. I removed the electric bill from the stack of letters, then separated what was clearly fan mail, the air mail envelopes from Japan and South Africa, and the more familiar American envelopes, almost all of them with feminine handwriting. It's mostly girls and women who write to me — I'm not an artist, after all, but a *woman artist*. There were two more letters that I would pass along to my assistant, both on professional-looking stationery, the addresses typewritten; one from the University of Nebraska, the other from a woman in Greenwich, Connecticut, both almost certainly requests for something I would refuse to do. But I at least peek at some of the letters so I'm not completely out of touch. The letter from Connecticut was the obvious choice.

I tore it open and pulled out the sheets of slightly pebbly pale-blue stationery. On the first page, printed at the top, it said: ELIZA L. MORTIMER, JOURNALIST AND DOCUMENTARY FILMMAKER.

Dear Ms. Wren, the letter began. *I'm a great admirer of your work.* I groaned. Eliza, surely you can come up with something better than that.

> *I've been desperate to get in touch with you. I'm a freelance journal-*
> *ist and documentary filmmaker covering the art world. I called your*
> *agent, hoping to connect with you, but he said you won't talk to jour-*
> *nalists under any circumstances and refused to even forward my let-*

ter. Finally, after working through many of my contacts, a friend of a friend was able to get your mailing address from a gallery owner. (I'm sure you'll understand that I don't want to say who it was.) I hope this letter has actually made its way to you. I understand that you don't want to be bothered, but . . .

On and on she went about how she loves my work and how she has a framed poster of *The Purple Iris* hanging in her bedroom. I didn't like the thought of my paintings as posters, as postcards, and likely as coasters and magnets and key chains. Why had I ever agreed to that? Accessibility, my lawyer had said when I'd signed the licensing agreement. "Art should be accessible to the masses." She'd implied I'm a snob, which is not the case. With my success, I could be living in a villa in the South of France, surrounded by acolytes and attending fancy parties, but instead I live in a modest adobe house and drive a fourteen-year-old car, finding pleasure not in the world but in my work, engaging each day in the ritual communion that produces it. I don't think it's too much to ask that this work not be turned into tacky trinkets destined to clog up a landfill.

I was about to abandon Eliza's letter since it was obvious her flattery was building up to an interview request, but my eye caught the start of the next paragraph: *At a recent luncheon at the Sandler Museum, I was seated next to a woman who grew up in Bellflower Village, Connecticut . . .*

I inhaled quickly — a stabby breath of panic.

Her name is Pauline Levasseur and she's an art collector who splits her time between New York and Paris. She keeps a rather low profile and isn't flashy the way so many collectors are. Her maiden name is Pauline Popplewell. When I told her I'm based in Greenwich, she told me she grew up nearby in Bellflower Village. She recalled her childhood there fondly, saying she lived on St. Ronan Street in a big Victorian painted robin's-egg blue that according to her was the prettiest house in town.

I'm wondering if any of this sounds familiar to you?

I laughed audibly, more like a scoff of confusion, alarm. *Why* would it be familiar to me? I'm Sylvia Wren, an artist who lives in Abiquiú, New Mexico. I was born and raised in Illinois and now I'm a New Mexican. I know nothing of New England. Or at least that's what I tell people.

But I kept reading the letter because Bellflower Village, the Popplewells, and the house in robin's-egg blue are not actually unknown to me — or rather to the person I used to be.

I don't mean to be coy, Ms. Wren, so let me get to the point: Mrs. Levasseur had a bit too much champagne at lunch and let slip that she knows a secret about you.

I folded the letter and put it back in the envelope. If I pretended I hadn't opened it, maybe I could keep whatever it portended from happening. It's not possible to rewind time, but I was willing to try. I stuffed the envelope into the stack of letters, closed my eyes, and imagined I had just returned home from the post office, sat down at the desk, and hadn't opened a thing.

The dishes in the kitchen sink had begun to accumulate, so I set about washing them. I pride myself on doing housework since I was helpless in domestic matters until I met Lola, and I couldn't even boil an egg until age twenty. Now that Lola and I are getting on in years, we pay a young couple who lives nearby to do the more strenuous tasks for us, the mopping and scrubbing, the odd jobs that need doing, even the garden now, although I still do the watering and pruning.

I occupied myself with chores for a while, chopping up vegetables for a salad and cutting long stems of rosemary from my herb garden to put in a vase on my desk. I tried to keep busy, but it turns out you really can't rewind time. The letter and its tease of a secret were planted in my brain, a tiny seed that had sprouted green shoots of curiosity. Ignoring it wouldn't make it go away. I sat down at the desk again and continued to read.

The rest of the letter is enclosed.

When I pressed her on the secret she claimed to know about you, Mrs. Levasseur told me that like her, you grew up in Bellflower Village. She said your real name is Iris Chapel, not Sylvia Wren, and that you were an heiress to the Chapel Firearms fortune. You had many sisters and all of them died, but no one quite understood what had happened to them. Apparently, Iris ran away when she was around twenty years old, in the late 1950s, but she was never forgotten. Mrs. Levasseur said no one of that generation in Bellflower Village could ever forget the Chapel sisters. Back in the seventies, a few people in the village saw a photo of Sylvia Wren in Life *magazine and they knew she was actually Iris Chapel. But they've kept the truth to themselves, feeling protective of her, a daughter of Bellflower. She'd had such a tragic life; who could blame her for running away from the fate her sisters had suffered, which could have been her fate too?*

I told Mrs. Levasseur that I wanted to look into her story to see if it's actually true. She was horrified, so please do not blame her — she didn't realize when we spoke that I'm a journalist, though I did tell her so when we were introduced. (She's a bit hard of hearing now, at her age.) I've begun digging around and I think Mrs. Levasseur might be right about you, so I'm reaching out now in the hopes that you'll talk to me.

I understand that you're a world-renowned recluse. I read that a biographer tried to write a book about you but gave up after a frustrating year. "Sylvia Wren is a ghost," she declared, and turned her attention to Edna St. Vincent Millay. A recluse, a ghost — I'm sure you have your reasons, but I believe your story deserves to be told. I've been speaking to editors at a couple of major magazines about writing this piece. Your cooperation would be invaluable.

Will you please reply to this letter, send me an email, or give me a call? I'd love to talk to you. You can find my card enclosed.

Yours sincerely,
Eliza L. Mortimer

I set the letter on my desk, then brushed it away and watched it sail to the floor as a toddler might. My hollyhocks waved just outside the window, trying to cheer me, but I wasn't in the mood.

The letter disturbed me, there's no question about that, but she would never discover the true story, which is impossible for anyone outside the Chapel family to know. And who is left of the Chapels to tell it? No one.

On one of the postcards Lola uses to respond to my admirers, which is printed on a thick ivory stock with a black-and-white photograph of the Abiquiú sky on one side and delicate blue bordering on the other, I wrote my message.

>*Dear Ms. Mortimer,*
>
>*I have received your letter, and while I admire your tenacity, I'm afraid I'll have to disappoint you. I am not Iris Chapel.*
>
>*Yours,*
>*Sylvia Wren*

I stuck a stamp on the postcard, hoping to feel that I'd vanquished Ms. Mortimer, but I felt no such satisfaction. On the contrary, I was certain that everything was about to unravel.

August 4, 2017 — Abiquiú, New Mexico

I went to the post office after breakfast, not waiting for my postlunch walk. On the way there, I couldn't enjoy the cottonwoods or the cloudless sky, and I resented how thoroughly Ms. Mortimer had disrupted my daily rituals. They may seem silly, but for me, they're a necessity, especially when Lola is away. I didn't sleep well last night and that's always how things start to go wrong.

I slipped the postcard into the outgoing slot, then discovered a new envelope from Ms. Mortimer in my own mailbox. I waited to open it until I was back home in my study. Inside was a photocopy of a newspaper article with a green sticky note at the top.

It's Eliza again. The Bellflower Village Historical Society finally reopened after the volunteer who runs it returned from her summer vacation. In looking through their archives, I found this article and wanted to send along a photocopy. Looks like Iris Chapel didn't just run away in the late 1950s but escaped in quite dramatic fashion. I'd love to discuss this with you.

The Greenwich Observer
August 19, 1957

MISSING HEIRESS

The Connecticut State Police seek the public's assistance in locating Iris Chapel, 20, of Bellflower Village. Miss Chapel absconded yesterday from the psychiatric wing of the Seward Hospital. She did not have permission to leave the facility and now the police are searching for her.

Miss Chapel's doctor, Raymond Westgate, advises the *Observer* that Miss Chapel is unlikely to be a threat to the public, but she might be in a state of confusion and in danger of hurting herself.

Henry Chapel, president of the Chapel Firearms Company, is offering $1,000 for information regarding his daughter's whereabouts. If you have any information, please contact Sergeant Wilkins at CSP headquarters.

Ridiculous. I rarely thought about Iris Chapel; she was, as far as I was concerned, dead. (Poor Iris.) But nevertheless, certain things were unforgettable. Yes, she was once briefly a patient in the psychiatric unit of the Seward Hospital (no shame in that), but she hadn't *absconded* from the hospital with the police in pursuit. Confused and in danger of hurting herself? Outrageous. I read the article again, stunned at the stories that had circulated after Iris had disappeared.

I began to wonder if Eliza Mortimer was really who she claimed to be. Was this even a real article? Anything can be faked nowadays, but regardless, I wondered if Ms. Mortimer was looking for a payout to keep quiet. Someone as famous and wealthy as I am is most certainly a target. My lawyer had warned me about that.

My thoughts immediately went to Lola. She'd know what to do. I wanted to call her, but I didn't know what time it was in Brazil. She taught her classes all day and had events in the evening so I hated to interrupt her. She'd taken her laptop and that was the only computer in our house since I'm not a fan of technology. I had no way to research my concerns. I considered calling my agent, but he's obnoxious. (Lola claims I just don't understand him, and he's really her problem anyway since she handles most of my business affairs.) Since this was a potential legal matter, I decided to call my lawyer in New York, the only one of my representatives who doesn't drive me completely up the wall. I had to be careful how I framed the situation. Rebecca, like most people, knew very little about me, and I intended to keep it that way unless things with Ms. Mortimer escalated.

When we connected, she searched online for me and verified that Eliza Mortimer was indeed a journalist and filmmaker based in Greenwich who covers the art world. "I'm looking at her website now," Rebecca said. "Interviews with Judy Chicago, Johnnie Marquis, Zaha Hadid. A documentary about the Glasgow Girls. She looks legit to me."

"I'm not so sure."

"Sylvia, you must receive interview requests daily. Why the panic over this one?"

"I'm not *panicked*," I said, covering the receiver with my hand to take a steadying breath. "This alleged journalist is claiming to know secrets about me. Isn't that blackmail?"

"Has she asked for money?"

"No, nothing like that. She wants to interview me."

Rebecca started to laugh but attempted to turn it into a cough. "That's what journalists do. It's not criminal."

"I don't like her snooping around."

"All right," Rebecca said. "You know I'm here to help. What secrets is she claiming to know? Anything damaging? I can always send off a threatening letter if she's telling lies about you. The good old *cease and desist.*"

I didn't answer; my mind wandered, and I thought to myself: *Sylvia Wren is a ghost,* repeating the line from Eliza's letter. What a terrible thing, to be a ghost while still alive. Yet the assessment wasn't wrong. If women had family crests, a ghost would certainly be on mine.

I was aware of the silence on the line, the ticktock of the hourly fee, not that I cared. "Sylvia?" Rebecca asked, as if calling a cat that had wandered outside. "Are you still there?"

"I'm here," I said. "I'd like to get a restraining order against Eliza Mortimer."

"A *restraining order?* Sylvia, what's going on? Is Lola at home?"

I hung up the phone. A few seconds later, it rang and I didn't answer it. It rang all afternoon but I ignored it. I threw away the newspaper article and Eliza's note, and spent the rest of the day working in my garden. As the sun set behind the red hills out back, I sat with a glass of lemonade, content in the August breeze.

Middle of the night

I hated everything about Eliza Mortimer's letter, but being called a "world-renowned recluse" bothered me as much as being called a "ghost," and I lay in bed awake, fixated on it. I've so successfully blocked out the world beyond the borders I've set for myself that it's startling to be reminded of what I've become and how other people see me.

I never wanted to be a recluse. I wish people could know that about me. If I were going to respond to Ms. Mortimer in any meaningful way, I would tell her that I don't think it's in my nature to be reclusive. Growing up with five sisters, I felt like we were one being, like a Hindu goddess with many arms and faces. Becoming a recluse would have required a sense of individuality that was impossible for me to possess as a child, and don't those formative years shape everything that comes after?

It took time and effort to become what I am now, this *ghost,* this *world-renowned recluse* — all code, I know, for *weirdo.* My reclusiveness has become a key aspect of my biography, this thing I never wanted to be. It's long been assumed that I've been making some sort of feminist statement by refusing to be interviewed, for being entirely absent from public view, with only my art representing me. Women are raised to be accommodating, so I suppose a woman who draws clear lines that others are not allowed to cross becomes remarkable for that fact alone.

It's never been easy for me, this disappearing act. We have to adapt to our circumstances, whatever they are. Nuns adapt to their cloisters, and birds to their cages, and I had to adapt to my way of living, pretending to be someone else and keeping anyone from finding out the truth. I was forced to be evasive, but it eventually became second nature. I'm not pretending to be Sylvia Wren anymore. I've become her.

And yet for all my talk of becoming Sylvia Wren, I know that's not the whole story — or rather that's overly simplistic.

Some years ago, I read about a Las Vegas show tiger, a docile creature that performed nearly every night for more than a decade, jumping through rings of fire for the amusement of the crowd. Then one night in the middle of a performance, for no apparent reason, the tiger turned on its trainer and swiped at his neck, severing an artery with one of its massive claws. The man bled out on stage before help arrived, a scarlet pool spreading around him to the horror of the audience.

When you live in defiance of yourself, you can adapt to your circumstances, but remnants of who you are at your core remain. A bit of wildness that can't be tamed.

Tap tap.

This is how it starts. I was afraid this was going to happen. I hadn't thought about Iris in a long time, or her sisters, or the hospital, or her running away; I'm not surprised that poking those dormant memories caused a response.

I heard the tapping, sat up in bed, and turned on the lamp; I'd given up on sleep anyway. The curtains were closed, but I knew what was beyond them without having to look: the deepest darkness, endless fathoms of it, as black as outer space and as vast and unknowable.

The downside of living in middle-of-nowhere New Mexico is the night. That's why we keep a rifle under the bed, to make sleeping easier. The rifle is loaded and I know how to use it. I pulled it out from its hiding place and climbed back into bed with it. The gun brings me peace, an irony that only Lola would understand. When I have moments like this, when the darkness suffocates me, I need to hold on to something more powerful than myself.

I stayed still in my bed, waiting for the tapping to resume. The gun wouldn't help, I knew that, but I clung to what I had. The tapping on the glass is always the first sign of what's to come. It never happens when Lola is at home. My visitor only comes when Lola is away, when everything I've submerged rises up to the surface.

Tap tap.

"Here she comes," I said aloud. "Don't be afraid."

asphodel grows
in the underworld
of my mind

— calla chapel

THE BLUE DIARY

Volume One

Bellflower

1950

I.

Later, once the tragedies began to happen, one after another, the children in the village made up a rhyme about us.

> *The Chapel sisters:*
> *first they get married*
> *then they get buried*

It didn't help matters that we lived in an enormous Victorian house that looked like a wedding cake. If this were a novel, that detail would push the boundaries of believability, but that's what our house looked like and I can't change reality. Our home, on the west side of Bellflower Village, was a foremost example of the so-called wedding-cake style of architecture. It was one of the most photographed private residences in Connecticut; I'm sure even now you can find a picture of it in a textbook somewhere.

The house, with its cascading tiers and ornamental details, looked as if it were piped with white icing. The eyes are drawn first to the central tower, looming and Gothic, perched above the rest of the house and circled with tiny dormered windows. (You could imagine Rapunzel tossing her braid out of one of those windows.) Below the tower, the sloping mansard roof banded around the top of the house, punctuated by third-floor windows, which looked miniature from the ground. A prominent widow's walk and balustrade marked the second floor, then there was the ground floor, with its bay windows and portico, curlicues everywhere, and tall stalks of flowers ringing the base.

It looked like something out of a fairy tale, that's what everyone said. If you could have sliced the exterior of this wedding-cake house with a knife, you would have found inside six maidens — Aster, Rosalind, Calla, Daphne, Iris, Hazel — each of whom were expected to become a bride one day. It was the only certainty in their lives.

Dearly beloved.

Dearly departed.

2.

Aster went first. As the oldest, she was used to going first, so I suppose it's fitting this story begins with her walking down the aisle into what came after, what my mother called the "something terrible." Someone had to go first, and since Aster was always the kindest and most responsible, I'm certain she would have seen it as her duty to light the way for her sisters even if she hadn't been the oldest. As it was, she didn't know she was the beginning of a story. Only the younger among us would live to see it through.

The summer before Aster's wedding was the last normal summer. That's when she met Matthew. As much as I don't want to think about him and all that he wrought, there wouldn't have been a wedding without him.

That summer in 1949 we went to Cape Cod as we did every year, staying in a suite of three rooms at the hotel on Terrapin Cove, which was located at the elbow of the Cape. These two weeks in July were the only time of the year my mother and sisters and I traveled away from the wedding cake. Our summer vacation was our annual airing out, when the dome placed over us was lifted and we, choosing from any number of metaphors, scurried away like ants, flitted into the breeze like butterflies, scattered on the wind like petals.

Since we were used to being confined at home, we didn't scatter far and usually spent our days on the beach spread out on an assemblage of blankets. My father, never one for leisure, stayed at home during the week so he didn't have to miss work. He joined us on weekends, but even when he joined us, he wasn't really there, staying in the hotel for most of the day with his papers and ledgers. He'd come outside occasionally, looking out of place in his unfashionable brown suit, squinting into the sun, his hand a visor on his brow. He'd look for his wife and daughters, an island in the sand, and once he'd spotted us, he wouldn't wave or smile, only turn and go back inside, secure in the knowledge we were there. I assumed he had this scheduled on his calendar: *11 a.m., family time.*

My sisters and I sat with our mother on the beach in front of the hotel every day of our vacation, encircled by open parasols. Belinda (I'm going to refer to her by her name as much as possible; she was her own person, after all, not simply our mother) always held a parasol over her head at the beach, as she did when she worked in her garden at home. She wore white linen dresses, her long white hair (it had turned white in her mid-forties) looped into a bun like a Victorian's with just enough at the sides to cover her missing earlobes. Like the wedding cake, she seemed to exist outside our time. She looked like the austere, melancholy women in Julia Margaret Cameron's photography — wide downcast eyes, an oval face with prominent cheekbones and a subtly aquiline nose, and pale skin lined like a sheet of linen paper that had been lightly crinkled then smoothed back out.

She liked the beach; it calmed her in a way home never could. She didn't swim, didn't partake in sunbathing or any other merriment, but she liked walks. Mostly, she read books, which she stacked neatly next to her canvas chair, Emily Dickinson's poetry or a novel by one of the Brontës. Her nostrils would flare as she read, inhaling the salty breeze. It was as close as she'd get to *taking the waters.*

My sisters and I, pale-skinned like our mother but with dark hair, would each claim a blanket and parasol for ourselves. We'd take our places after breakfast, each of us in modest swimsuits, and there we'd be most of the day, eating lunch from a hamper supplied by the hotel, usually quite a decadent feast, with little pots of foie gras, thick slices of ham and Emmental cheese, a French baguette, and an apricot tart. I would occasionally swim with my younger sister, Hazel — Zelie, everyone called her. We were only allowed in waist-high water. If the waves began to creep in, inching their way toward our nonexistent bosoms, we had to move back to the shore or our mother would call our names and embarrass us.

"How about a walk to the cove?" she asked Zelie and me one weekend afternoon (it had to have been a weekend since my father was in the hotel). We, as the two youngest and least cynical daughters, were the only ones willing to consider such an excursion. Zelie used this to bargain.

"Can I bring a turtle back to the hotel?" she asked.

"You know you can't," our mother replied.

"Then can we get a snow cone?"

The three of us trudged off, Belinda with her parasol, Zelie and I racing ahead of her to look for terrapins down the long stretch of marshy grass and sand, luxuriating in our mother's attention. We spotted only a pair of them that day, their diamond backs and speckly skin a delight, making it worth the walk.

Belinda, as always, was more interested in the greenery. "Those grasses are halophytic," she said, pointing to what looked like a vast green lawn edging into the sea. "Do you remember what that means?"

"Plants that grow in salty soil," I said quickly, before Zelie had a chance.

"That's right," she said, looking pleased. She knew everything about plants.

After a while, we made our way back to the beach, Zelie and I slurping raspberry snow cones. The rest of the family hadn't moved while we were away. My two oldest sisters, Aster and Rosalind, read magazines and sunbathed and gossiped away their days. Aster was slightly plump and Rosalind was long and lithe; in swimsuits the contrast was more apparent, but regardless of shape, both their bodies glittered with the sand dust that had stuck to their sun cream. That's what I remember most about how they looked on the beach that summer, their limbs the color of sugar cookies still baking in the oven, a coating of sandy brown sugar all over them, making their skin a confectionery.

"They'll be engaged by Christmas," Rosalind said to Aster, as we approached, the two of them deep in conversation about some friend or other. "She's making a dreadful mistake. Do you remember that *awful* tie he wore to her birthday party?"

"You can't judge a man's character by his choice of tie," Aster said, swatting Rosalind on the arm with a rolled-up copy of *Glamour*.

"You most certainly *can*."

"Be serious, Roz. I think he's nice."

"You *would* think that, wouldn't you?" she said, only half teasing.

My middle sisters, Calla and Daphne, each sat cross-legged on a blanket nearby, absorbed in their projects. Calla scribbled poems in her notebook, shielded at all times from the sun by her parasol *and* a sun hat. Daphne kept herself busy with her watercolor set and sketch pad, and would usually eat an enormous amount of food, going through several foot-long hot dogs and bags of popcorn in the hours after lunch.

They worked side by side companionably, only occasionally erupting into argument. "You dripped purple paint on my toe," Calla said, shoving Daphne away. "I look like I have gangrene."

"Don't you find gangrene romantic?" Daphne flicked more paint onto Calla's foot. "All that withered flesh. Tennyson must have written about it."

"Whitman, I think," Calla said, nibbling on her pencil. Musing on this seemed to calm her.

Belinda reentered this scene reluctantly, sitting in her chair with a sigh and picking up her book.

"What on earth happened to you two?" Rosalind said, looking at Zelie and me, appalled.

"Your mouths are bright red," Aster said.

"We ate snow cones on the walk back," Zelie explained, as I wiped my mouth with my beach towel.

"You look like you bit the head off a seagull," Calla said. "It's disgusting."

The conversation descended into bickering from there, over what I can't recall, but then a roaring splash interrupted us. A creature had emerged from the depths of the ocean, having burst through the surface of the water like a submarine, or at least that's how I remember it. We hadn't seen him go in, but suddenly, where nothing had existed before, there he was, a bare-chested thirty-year-old in snug striped trunks, blond tendrils stuck to his forehead.

Until then, I hadn't realized men could be beautiful. I didn't necessarily feel an attraction to him, but I was drawn to his force, the way he throbbed with life, his skin the color of golden syrup, the muscles that rippled across his abdomen like a flag of flesh. Later we would find out he'd been a bombardier during the war, a hero who just four years earlier had sailed through the skies over Japan raining down fire on the people below. Sea or air, it didn't matter; he was a master of the elements.

He stumbled onto the surf, a male friend in tow. They were laughing and ribbing each other and not looking where they were going, and within a few seconds, the sea creature had almost stumbled onto our island. He quickly came to a halt and stared down at the seven female faces looking up at him.

"Ma'am," he said to Belinda, suddenly serious. He nodded at her. "I'm sorry. I hope we didn't disturb you."

"It's fine," she said, setting down her poetry, her face cloaked in the shade of her parasol. She looked beyond him to the sea. He didn't mean anything to her, not then.

"Ladies," he added, nodding at my sisters and me as we pulled our towels around us and tried to tuck in our arms and legs. "I'm Matthew Maybrick," he said. I couldn't take my eyes off the symmetry of his red nipples.

Mother looked back at him, clearly annoyed that he was still there. "Mrs. Belinda Chapel," she said.

"Chapel? Not the firearm Chapels?"

She winced, as she always did when the guns were mentioned. Her daughters turned to her instinctively, and Aster spoke up before something awkward could happen. "Yes, the firearm Chapels," she said playfully, glancing at Rosalind.

And with that, Aster, fresh off her nineteenth birthday, seemed to come into focus for Matthew. He smiled down at her in her orange-skirted swimsuit, a monarch butterfly stitched across the chest. She pulled the towel tighter around herself, her legs folded modestly beneath her, and brushed the dark curls from her shoulders. Matthew continued to stare and eventually she met his gaze, her face as round as a scallop, eyes sparkling and eager, beglossed lips closed into the shape of a tiny pinched heart. Matthew took her in rather brazenly, observing what was visible, probably imagining what wasn't, letting his eyes linger where they wanted, then turning to his friend, who had stayed a few feet behind. "Hey, Arnie, this is the Chapel family." He made one of his hands into a gun and shot it. Arnie waved shyly.

"I'm one of the Maybricks," Matthew said to us, the name laid over us like a blanket. It was clear his name was supposed to mean something to us, just as our name meant something to him. Matthew's family owned Maybrick Steel, which surely Belinda had heard of; most of the trains in America ran on Maybrick steel, and most of the skyscrapers in New York were constructed with it. The company had been founded by Augustus Maybrick, the most ruthless of the nineteenth-century robber barons.

But if Belinda recognized the name, she didn't give any indication. She didn't care about notable families and their scions. Normally, a family like ours would be in demand on the Cape, invited to sprawling seaside estates and lavish parties, but we lived our lives at a remove from everyone else of our class, and that's the way our mother preferred it.

"Is Mr. Chapel here?" Matthew asked, perhaps assuming he'd have more luck impressing him.

"He's working in the hotel," Aster said, prompting Rosalind to jump in.

"He's working on *business matters* in his *room*," she said. "He's not a bellboy."

Matthew laughed and turned to his friend again. "We'd love to meet him, wouldn't we, Arnie?"

"It'd be an honor."

"*It would?*" Zelie said, and I elbowed her to be quiet.

We never gave our father much thought, so it was easy to forget how others saw him. Like our mother, he preferred to live at a remove, and even at my young age, I knew he wouldn't have cared about impressing Matthew Maybrick and his friend. My father was one of the wealthiest men in New England, and our family name was emblazoned on guns that were sold around the world. It was something to be feared, the name Chapel. A man like my father, who manufactured a product that was a bridge to *the other side* — didn't need to impress anyone.

Belinda frowned at all this talk of guns and her husband, neither of which she had any affection for, and stood up from her beach chair and brushed the front of her dress. "Come along, girls," she said. "Your father will be wondering what happened to us." This was a lie, but we stood up anyway, knowing she didn't appreciate this intruder.

Matthew Maybrick was apparently unaware of the oddness of our family. Most people in Bellflower Village thought of Belinda as a madwoman, but it didn't seem as if her reputation had spread to New York City, where the Maybricks lived. Matthew, not realizing he was upsetting Belinda, not seeing himself as an intruder, made a gesture as we walked away. "I was wondering," he called after us. "Would your two older daughters —"

"Aster and Rosalind," I said, speaking to him for the first time. He winked at me in the way one winks at a small child.

"Would Aster and Rosalind like to have a drink with my friends and me before dinner?" When Belinda glared at him, he added hastily, less confidently: "My parents and sister will be there too."

Belinda turned without a response and continued to the hotel with Daphne, Zelie, and me in tow; Calla had already raced ahead to the lobby. Only Aster and Rosalind remained with Matthew, and half an hour later, they joined us in our suite of rooms, bouncy with excitement. They explained to our father that they'd been invited for drinks with Matthew Maybrick and asked for permission to go.

"Leland Maybrick's boy?" He seemed taken aback and removed his glasses, setting them on his legal pad. Glasses were for work, and this was a family matter, something he wasn't normally bothered with. "What does Matthew Maybrick want with you?"

"Daddy!" Rosalind practically shouted. She was the only one of us to call him by the more jovial-sounding *daddy,* as if she could cajole him into being that kind of man. "Why *wouldn't* he want to invite two charming girls like us for a drink?"

"I see," our father said, as Calla and Daphne and Zelie and I watched from the sidelines. Our mother had taken to her bed.

Aster had graduated from high school a year earlier and had gone on dates with young men whose families lived in the village or whom she'd met through their sisters at school, all from wealthy and respectable families, but a Maybrick was in a different league. "Please," Aster said, her robe wrapped tightly around her, face flushed from a day in the sun. Aster was of legal age, and Rosalind nearly so, but they wouldn't have presumed they could do whatever they pleased.

"Very well," our father said, putting his glasses back on and taking up his pencil. The Maybricks were probably too flashy for his taste, but like Mr. Bennet in *Pride and Prejudice,* a novel our mother read at least once a year, he had many daughters to marry off, and exceptions had to be made.

It was all arranged, and that evening I sat at dinner with my parents and three of my sisters in the hotel dining room while Aster and Rosalind mixed with the Maybricks on the terrace. There was a buffet in the restaurant every night, and I would make a dinner of hors d'oeuvres — shrimp cocktail and deviled eggs and potato puffs — and Zelie would copy me, which I hated. Our parents paid no mind to what we chose from the buffet, so Daphne loaded up on slabs of pink prime rib and crab claws and repeated helpings of duchesse potatoes, and we sat and looked at the ocean while we ate so we didn't have to look at one another.

We could see the terrace from our table, with the ocean just beyond, and I watched Aster and Rosalind, their glasses filled with our favorite drink: club soda with a splash of grenadine syrup and a mint leaf, girly drinks; they were basically still girls. They mingled with the sea creature and his ilk, he in a pastel yellow button-down shirt and trousers. Aster and Rosalind wore the strappy sundresses they'd bought for the trip; the colors escape me now, but I remember their lovely bare shoulders in the evening sun, the honeyed seaside light drizzled over them. I picked at my food, too distracted to eat. I knew this signaled a break in our story, a change already underway.

And, in fact, Matthew Maybrick, war hero and heir to the Maybrick Steel fortune, would ask Aster to marry him five months later. The intruder was inside the gates.

3.

Nearly a year after that first meeting on the beach, Aster and Matthew were set to wed. I'm trying to summon that week leading up to the wedding so I can describe it for you (*you* — who exactly are you?). But I've pushed that time down into what my sister Calla would call the "underworld of my mind." Imagine it: a cold and lonely place, asphodel growing through cracks in the concrete, the sound of distant dripping water, a creaking door.

Emily Dickinson wrote that it's not just houses that are haunted but that the "brain has corridors." Indeed. And mine are overflowing. The underworld of my mind — all those haunted corridors, however you want to describe it — contains shards of broken glass scattered all over the ground. I pick up a shard and describe what I see, then set it down.

This story is jagged, could cut a deep wound. It isn't a story I can tell with a thread and a needle, stitching in clean lines. It's shards or nothing.

4.

So let me try again. The week leading up to the wedding.

School had ended for the summer. Zelie and I were free to run wild through the grounds around the house, which were as big as a city park. Many wealthy people lived in Bellflower Village, which was only a twenty-minute drive from Greenwich, which was itself only a short train ride from New York City, but none of the other homes were as enormous as ours.

A vast expanse of grass stretched from the house to the street, sloping and rolling as gently as a brook, and behind the house, there were flower gardens and a terrace, and farther behind that, a frog pond and a meadow. Across the street and to the north of the house, there was nothing but deep forest. Next to the house on the south side lay the family plot, enclosed by a pointy iron fence and a canopy of maple trees. When I was a little girl, there were only three graves there, my grandparents and a stillborn who had preceded my father. The rest of the plot had yet to be disturbed.

At home during the summer, Zelie and I usually spent much of our time outside; we liked to escape the dark gloom of our house and our noisy, bossy older sisters. As long as we stayed on the property, no one minded what we did. They wouldn't have been able to find us if they'd come looking, which they rarely did anyway. Our names were often merged together, *IrisandZelie,* as if we were one.

Where are *IrisandZelie*? This question wasn't asked often enough.

But that summer, the summer of Aster's wedding, was different. I didn't feel like our usual hijinks. It was incredibly hot that June, with temperatures regularly reaching the upper nineties. As miserable as that was, worse still was that I, at thirteen, had recently started my monthly bleeding. Aster had shown me how to use the belt with the pads, an awful contraption, but it was all we had back then. When the bleeding started, I knew my days of running free were over. I didn't understand much about what was happening to me, but I knew it was a secret. We weren't allowed to wear pants, so I checked my bare legs all day for signs of exposure.

I suggested to Zelie that we go on nature walks and look for ladybugs and butterflies. I took a sketch pad and pencils with me. We didn't talk about my bleeding though she knew. It wasn't something that was discussed openly even among my sisters; I hadn't even told my mother, not that she would have cared much. But the bleeding and the heat laid a pall on that summer even in its early acts. If I mixed a palette for June 1950, I'd start with vermillion, then add hematite, then a deep russet brown, the shades of my cotton pad the filter of my memory.

I'm sure we went to church that Sunday, my father and sisters and I. Back home, I tried sketching Zelie at the frog pond. She would have been chatting incessantly about the wedding in that long-ago little-girl voice just on the cusp of puberty: "Isn't Matthew dreamy?" She loved to call boys that. "I can't wait until we get our flower-girl dresses." She loved talking about the dresses too, which she called "princess dresses." They still weren't finished, which worried Aster — two items she couldn't check off her list.

She would have continued chatting, and I would have tried and failed to sketch her. She was far beyond my talents at the time, a raven-haired pre-Raphaelite shrunk to the size of an eleven-year-old. She and Aster, the two bookends in our row of sisters, A to Z, looked the most similar. They shared a ripe roundness, which today would likely be described as fat in the negative way fat has come to be spoken about, but in those days, things were different. Aster and Zelie looked as if their skin couldn't contain what was inside them, as if I could press my finger against Zelie's arm and the juices would come spilling out. I can taste that juice, a tangy peach. I think of that poem by Christina Rossetti, the sisters and the goblin men: "Come buy, come buy." My sisters and I loved that poem; we'd no sense then of its eroticism.

Soon after that, we walked back to the house for water and food, and spotted Belinda in her garden, a slim figure in her long white dress, head obscured by a pink parasol in full bloom like a dahlia; she was surveying the flowers, a swath of purples and pinks and yellows.

The flower garden was next to the terrace at the back of the house, and it was Belinda's domain entirely; the groundskeeper did much of the work, but she directed all of it. Her flower garden was the only thing about her that was neat and organized, with its rose-entwined trellis, hydrangea bushes, and tidy sections of petunias, salvia, and zinnias. Utterly different than her mind, a jumbled thicket of fear and sadness locked behind a gate only she could open. I can't imagine sunlight ever penetrating that mind of hers, not the kind of luxurious light that bathed her flowers.

"Mother!" Zelie called excitedly, and Belinda turned. She watched us approach, and I could tell by the tight set of her lips that she didn't want to be disturbed, but she smiled anyway.

Unlike our sisters, we were always happy to see her. We didn't see her often, usually only at mealtimes and other stolen moments. I was never entirely sure how she spent her days. She consulted with Dovey about the running of the household, tended to her garden, wrote in her spirit journal, did a bit of needlework and sketching. She'd nap in the afternoons since she never slept well at night. It's difficult to see how those activities added up to entire days, but her life unfolded mostly out of view.

"Look at the two of you," she said with concern, cupping her hand under my chin and turning my head to one side, then the other. "You're both as red as radishes." She put her free arm around Zelie and gave her a squeeze. "It's too hot to be outside today."

"*You're* outside," Zelie said. This was notable, as Belinda didn't normally come outside during the heat of the day.

"Hmm," she replied. We stood with our arms wrapped around her waist, her body cool despite the weather. She smelled of Violet Fleur, her favorite perfume, a re-creation of Empress Joséphine's favorite scent. The perfume wasn't marred by the smell of sweat, and Belinda's face was freshly powdered. She hadn't been outside long.

"Are you going to make a bouquet for Aster's wedding?" Zelie asked.

Belinda glanced at her but didn't respond. She'd had no involvement in her eldest daughter's wedding, showed no interest in it at all. In retrospect, perhaps that should have been a clue of the trouble to come.

"I came outside to check on my flowers — they're struggling in this heat. I'm worried." She freed herself from us, handing me her parasol as she bent down, rubbing her thumb across the petals of a sagging purple petunia, then a sweet pea. I couldn't help but feel a twinge of jealousy.

Belinda had an intimate connection to her flowers, as a baby does to its mother through an umbilical cord; her flowers fed her life. After a long winter, she came alive at the sight of petals in her garden blooming like lights turned on after months in darkness. But now it was only June and they were fading.

"My flowers are dying," she said, which wasn't true; they were lagging like the rest of us, but like the rest of us, they were still alive at that point.

"They're not dying, just sunburned," Zelie said, placing a hand on Belinda's back as she leaned over her flower bed. "They'll be all right."

"I fear they won't be." Belinda stood up, and we both inched closer to her under the shade of her parasol and wrapped our arms around her waist again. We looked up at her, but she said nothing more, offered no comforting return of our gazes. Her eyes moved along her flower beds, taking in their slightly withered flesh.

"You better go inside, petals," she said, and released herself from our embrace again. She was slippery like that. "I'm going to lie down for a while. I have a headache." She pulled a white handkerchief from her pocket and I thought she was going to wipe her brow, but she held it to her mouth and nose instead, and breathed in. "Go into the kitchen and get some water. Go on."

Dismissed, we reluctantly left her in the garden. We plodded through the grass around the side of the house, wounded by the sting of maternal rejection. When I turned around, hoping for another glimpse of her, she'd disappeared through the door in the courtyard.

Dovey corralled us at the kitchen table and we drank two glasses of water each. "You girls," Dovey said, shaking her head. "Likely to faint in that sun. Just look at you with that water, like two thirsty spaniels."

She must have been around fifty then, the same age as Belinda. She'd been in America for a little more than twenty years, having somehow found her way from Ireland into the Chapel family's employ soon after my parents were married. Her official title was housekeeper, but she did much more than that.

"We saw Mother in her flower garden," Zelie said, water spilling down her chin, drenching the front of her dress.

Dovey frowned a little, not caring if we noticed, and refilled our glasses from a pitcher. "The sun'll do her some good." She wore a plaid skirt and white blouse, her shabby blond hair permed into a crown of tight curls. Miss Edna Dove was her full name, but we all called her Dovey, and if she minded, she'd never said so. She lived in the third-floor servants' quarters, which were empty except for her. The cook and the maids lived out.

On the kitchen table there were paper bags of Jordan almonds, and spools of ribbon, and tiny gauze pouches in gold. There were pretty things all over the house, all for the wedding. "Can I have one of those?" I asked, attempting to pick up one of the pouches of almonds, but Dovey swatted my hand away.

"No you don't. I've been working on those all morning." She took our lunch from the icebox, a platter of ham and mustard sandwiches on white bread, and a bowl of strawberries with shredded coconut sprinkled on top.

"Ham and mustard again?" I said, taking one of the sandwich halves.

"If you don't like it, take it up with Mrs. O'Connor."

Mrs. O'Connor was the woman from the neighboring village who'd cooked all our meals since before I was born. After her son was killed in the war, she missed two months of work, and when she came back, our father forbade us from complaining about her food. "No thanks," I said.

"She's not here anyway," Dovey said. "She's gone home. Aster is cooking the dinner tonight."

"Aster doesn't cook," Zelie said, and we both laughed. The thought of Aster cooking anything was hilarious.

"She's going to start. She'll be running her own household soon enough, and she'll have to cook for her husband, won't she?"

Zelie stuck out her tongue at the thought and picked up a sandwich half, then another. "I better eat up . . ." She took a big bite of her sandwich, and dots of mustard oozed out from between her lips.

"Try to be supportive of your sister," Dovey said. "It's not easy running a household. I should know." She opened the icebox again and stood in front of it, moving it open and closed like a fan. There were sweat stains under her arms. "I don't want you two going outside again this afternoon — the newspaper says it'll be dangerously hot."

Dovey stepped in on a daily basis to make sure Zelie and I didn't perish of thirst or hunger, heatstroke or frostbite, even though it wasn't her job.

"Go find your sisters now, it's my afternoon off and I'm going out," she said, shooing us away. "Tell them I'll leave lunch in the dining room."

. . .

We had our own wing on the second floor of the wedding cake — the girls' wing, as it was called, three bedrooms and a sitting room. Despite the enormity of the house, we'd always been confined to this wing, two girls to each bedroom. The walls of the bedrooms were covered in flowers. Our mother had painted them when we were young, inspired by a French book of botanical drawings, swirls of petals and leaves, a garden in each room, and each one at the edge of a dark forest.

Aster and Rosalind's bedroom was painted with asters and roses, but there were far more asters. Belinda had never been fond of roses, and even the name Rosalind sat slightly askew from its origin, an attempt at honoring her mother, Rose, without giving in fully to a flower she hated. But asters were her favorite. She'd painted the asters as if they were stars; *aster* is Latin for "star" — each bloom purple with pointy rays and a golden center. When I was little, Aster would take me onto her lap and point to the wall of aster stars, and say, "Make a wish," and each time I would wish for something different, something more spectacular than before. After Aster was taken from us, I sat in front of the wall of stars and wished for her to return. "I wish, I wish," I would say, my eyes squeezed shut. I wished for her to climb up through the dirt in the family plot and come back to us.

In Calla and Daphne's room, Belinda had painted calla lilies in a vase next to an open window — she was afraid of the toxicity of lilies, which she claimed could cause asphyxia if placed in a closed room. For Daphne, there were pale pink daphne blooms and a laurel tree standing in isolation. Our mother told us the story of the naiad Daphne, who had vowed to remain untouched by a man but was pursued through the forest by the amorous Apollo. Daphne ran from Apollo, screaming for her father, a river god, to protect her, so he turned her into a laurel tree before Apollo could catch her. I didn't think this was fair, that Daphne should become a tree. It was Apollo who deserved to have his greedy hands frozen into scaly branches that would never know the embrace of true love. But even at that age, I knew that it was often women who suffered the consequences of men's actions.

In the room I shared with Zelie, irises were spread out as a carpet of purple, similar to the constellation of asters, but these flowers were firmly rooted in the ground, extending into a vast distance, leading to a dark forest. For Zelie, there was a wall of witch-hazel blooms, the spidery yellow flowers not at all beautiful despite our mother's efforts. This is perhaps why Hazel became Zelie soon after she was born; the name Hazel didn't seem to fit our youngest sister, who was as round as a peony.

The girls' sitting room at the end of our long hallway continued the garden theme. It looked like a greenhouse, with windows all around; the windows were framed with green curtains that puffed out in the breeze like a frog's throat. All the fabrics were verdant, with sofas and chairs in nile green, and ceramic pots of ferns in the corners, walls covered in hand-painted ivy vines. The only thing that didn't fit was the portrait that hung over the fireplace: Annie Oakley with a Chapel rifle slung over her shoulder. The portrait was a gift from Annie, who had used Chapel rifles in her Wild West shows with Buffalo Bill. She had visited the house on multiple occasions when my father was a boy. The painting had hung in his den for years before he decided we should have it.

Zelie and I found our four older sisters in the sitting room. Thanks to the heat, they were in various states of undress, their long white arms and legs sprawled on the sofas and chairs, their delicate fingers twirling strands of dark hair. They rested their heads on sofa arms and velvet pillows, the pale cylinders of their necks stretched out. The climate in the room was humid, but I didn't mind the smell of their sweat. They were mesmerizing to look at, the four of them languid and beautiful, like swans in a marsh.

It took a moment for them to notice us in the doorway. "The little ones are here," Rosalind said in her rasp of a voice nearly the octave of a bee's hum. She'd picked up her head for a moment to look at Zelie and me, then set it back down again on a pillow wedged against the sofa arm. "Close the door, darlings. We don't need anyone looking in."

"My heavens, you two look rough," Aster said in dismay at the sight of Zelie and me. "What have you been doing since church?" She was lying on the sofa at the opposite end from Rosalind, their ankles entwined in the middle. There was a Baedeker guide to Paris on the floor in front of the sofa, pages folded down to mark the places Aster and the sea creature would visit on their honeymoon. "Whatever will happen to you when I'm gone?" she said, her cheek resting on the sofa arm as she peered at us.

"You're here now and look at the state of them," Daphne said. "Practically feral." She reclined on another sofa, one of her lurid paperbacks in her lap, *Vixen* or *Sin on Wheels*.

"You must pitch in after I'm gone," Aster said to Rosalind, Calla, and Daphne. "*All* of you."

Calla, curled in a chair near the fireplace and staring blankly out the window, reluctantly turned to look at Zelie and me. "They don't look so bad," she said, then turned back to the window.

"That's the problem," Aster said. "None of you take notice."

"We notice," Daphne said. "We just don't care."

Rosalind sat up and summoned me to sit next to her. I left Zelie at the doorway and slid carefully onto the cushion, worried I might leave a bloodstain but too embarrassed to say anything. Rosalind removed the ribbon from my hair, releasing it from its ponytail. She made an attempt to untangle my shoulder-length hair, tugging at a few strands, pulling at a knot, then giving up with a sigh. "Might be easier just to cut it all off," she said, flopping back.

"Rozzy, what will you do when you're married," Aster asked, sitting up so Zelie could sit next to her. "Children will be expected or have you forgotten?"

Rosalind considered this. "I'll have a well-behaved daughter," she said. "Just the one. And if it turns out I'm not the motherly type, I'll put her in a Moses basket and leave her on someone's doorstep."

"That's horrendous, even as a joke," Aster said. "The things you *say*, Rozzy."

"I wish our mother had done that with us," Daphne said.

"It's an interesting thought," Calla responded, appearing taken with the idea. "To imagine what other fates we might have had."

I didn't like this discussion of marriage and children and fate. It was bad enough Aster would be leaving us soon; I didn't like to think of Rosalind also leaving. "I don't want you to get married too," I said to Rosalind, nestling into the steamy crook of her arm, which she then wrapped around me. Aster's trunks had been stacked in the hallway for months while she'd filled them, her "trousseau," as she called it. When she'd finally finished, they had been taken away.

"Don't get married? And stay in this house forever? *No thank you.*" Rosalind picked up her glass of lemonade from the side table and held it to her cheek. "There's only one way out of this house, girls. Our Aster is leaving first, and I won't be far behind."

"Is that so?" Daphne asked. "What's his name?"

"Don't know yet," said Rosalind, biting her bottom lip. "But I'll be gone by next summer, you can count on that. I don't care *who* he is." She turned to Daphne. "And what about you, Daph? What kind of man do you plan to marry?"

"How about no kind of man," she said, exchanging a look with Rosalind.

"Marriage seems so dull," Calla said. "So *tragic,* in a sense. Look at our mother."

"Our mother was tragic before she ever got married," Rosalind said.

"Yes, but it certainly didn't help matters." Calla picked up her notebook and pencil from the table next to her. "Her womb is probably shredded like cabbage, poor dear. Just think for a moment about the utter destruction of the female body over the course of a woman's life, of the female *soul,* and for what? To perpetuate the human race when just a few years ago all of humanity was almost obliterated." She shook her head in disgust and wrote something in her notebook.

"Golly," Aster said, as Daphne laughed. "Is that what you envision is about to happen to me when I get married, Calla? My utter destruction?"

Calla looked up from her notebook, tapping her pencil on the armrest for a moment. "Perhaps," she said, without any emotion. Then she went back to writing.

Aster looked demoralized, so Rosalind jumped in to smooth things over. "Just ignore them, Aster dear. They're rotten with jealousy."

I twisted the rings on Rosalind's fingers, topaz on one finger and a coral cameo on another. First Aster, then Rosalind — they'd all leave eventually. I could see the aftermath: Zelie and I alone in the house with our parents, the silent hallway of the girls' wing, the empty bedrooms, the tedious dinners. "I hate being the youngest."

"Second youngest," Zelie corrected me, refusing to give up her place at the tail end. I pulled at the coral cameo, slipping it over Rosalind's knuckle before she snatched her finger away.

"It's not so bad," she said, readjusting the ring. "When we're old women, you and Zelie will still be young — or at least younger."

"I don't want to be younger."

"Come now, you're being unreasonable," Rosalind said.

Zelie rose from the sofa and went to the fireplace, taking a peacock feather from a vase on the mantel and holding it out in front of her, using it to fan us, its blue and green eye swaying hypnotically.

"They need a nanny," Aster said, watching Zelie in her damp dress, her toes and sandals brown with dirt.

"Absolutely not," Daphne said. "Our father will bring in another bossy Irish girl who thinks she can tell *me* what to do and I don't need looking after."

"Nor I," Calla said, as Zelie continued to fan us. Our last nanny had fled years ago and hadn't been replaced.

"Well, someone has to look out for them after I leave," Aster said.

"They *do* have a mother," Rosalind said, and the older girls, even Aster, began to laugh.

5.

Our mother thought our house was haunted. That's one of the reasons she was a figure of ridicule. She'd told us many times that on the day she first stepped into the wedding cake she felt the chill of a house paid for by death. She heard voices. She saw things. She had always believed in ghosts, from her earliest days, before she ever met my father and became his wife. From the start of her marriage, she knew the wedding cake was full of spirits and that they wanted to talk to her and her alone.

Our house *was* paid for by death, which couldn't be denied. My father had inherited the house from his father, whose own father had built it in the 1870s with the profits he'd made from the Civil War. That's how our family made money, after all: war, murder, suicide, animal slaughter. As macabre as it was, the Chapel rifle was nevertheless a treasured American icon, and my father had photos of himself with General John J. Pershing and President Franklin D. Roosevelt. The Chapel factory, which employed hundreds during peacetime and thousands during war, was located just outside the village. The workers, who couldn't afford to live in the area, were bused in from elsewhere, then promptly bused out again every afternoon at four o'clock.

The Chapel factory had a global reach, and that was a source of local pride. During the war, many of the women in the village worked in the factory, and the rifles they helped manufacture were shipped to the troops in Europe and the Pacific, where they were used to gun down Nazis and Japanese soldiers.

But my mother wasn't like everyone else. For her, there was a cloud over Bellflower Village thanks to the Chapel factory and the weapons and ammunition it produced, a cloud of moral pollution. As a girl, I didn't understand why Belinda hated guns so much; like my sisters, I thought she was just strange — embarrassing even. She didn't feel proud of the Chapel conquests — wars won, territories claimed — when seemingly everyone else did.

She had little to do with village life and never spent an afternoon on Main Street in the village shopping for housewares and eating éclairs with the other wives of her class. It was possible to live in the wedding cake as if marooned on an island. Maybe that was part of the problem. (The "problem." Where Mother was concerned, we were always in search of the root problem — a fruitless endeavor, I should know better by now.) No other signs of life could be seen from the house, not even through binoculars. Belinda professed to hate the wedding cake, yet she rarely left it, staying inside, cut off from the world, roaming the hallways in her long white dresses, living in a world of daughters, flowers, and spirits.

As a girl, I knew there was something wrong with my mother, but I didn't quite know what. I assumed that other mothers didn't wake up screaming in the night as she did, claiming she'd seen or heard a ghost. I assumed they didn't spend their mornings writing about their ghostly encounters in a notebook. She wrote in a notebook, a book like I'm writing in now, because her family didn't believe her stories.

I wondered why she couldn't behave normally, and drive us to school like the other mothers did, and stand with them at the gates as classes let out for the day dressed in a colorful frock with a matching handbag and shoes, hair perfectly rolled. But she never came to our school and was noticeably older than my classmates' mothers — taller too, at five foot nine at least. (Were you imagining her small? She wasn't small.) She was quite thin though, elongated, and with her white dresses and shock of white hair, she might have resembled a cotton swab from a distance.

Since none of us believed her stories, we weren't afraid that our house was haunted. We were more afraid of Belinda and the power of her imagination; we pitied her, my father and sisters and I. As far as we were concerned, it wasn't the house that was haunted but Belinda herself. I grew up believing our mother was haunted, and since my sisters and I had each lived inside her for nine months, I wondered if we were haunted too.

6.

With her life as a housewife in the New York City suburbs imminent, Aster set about cooking our family dinner that evening. Mrs. O'Connor had been sent home, and our mother couldn't be expected to provide any oversight. She'd taken no part in preparing her oldest daughter for married life.

Without any other assistance, Aster received help from her new Betty Crocker cookbook, which Mrs. O'Connor had labeled an abomination. Aster chose to make pot roast for us that night with mashed potatoes and green beans. It was far too much for her, even more so on a sweltering summer evening, but it was Sunday and our father expected a Sunday dinner.

It didn't seem as if Aster had any idea what she was doing. Rosalind, who'd offered to help, was nowhere around. "What a catastrophe," Aster said, dabbing her forehead with a dish towel. She wasn't talking to anyone in particular. Zelie and I watched from the kitchen table, with strict instructions not to get in the way.

After freshening up in her room for far longer than was necessary, Rosalind finally appeared. "I see things have gone downhill since I nipped upstairs," she said, as she walked in.

"You've been gone for *ages*."

"Have I? Mea culpa," she said. "In my absence, you've gone and gotten mashed potato all over that stunner of a diamond." Rosalind, seemingly shocked at Aster's disheveled appearance and the state of the kitchen, led her to the sink to wash up.

"I don't know if the roast is done," Aster said, as she dried her hands with a fresh towel.

"Gosh, don't ask me." Rosalind plumped her hair, the dark wavy pageboy that Aster had trimmed for her the night before. The sides were pulled back loosely and fastened with tortoiseshell combs, revealing tiny hoop earrings. She picked up the cold bottle of beer that was meant for our father and took a swig. When she was done, she shook her head rapidly, as if braced. "Call Mrs. O?"

"I have to do this myself. Mrs. O'Connor won't be living with Matthew and me."

"I should hope not," Rosalind said. "That doesn't sound like much fun, does it, girls?"

Rosalind was the froth and fizz in the family, the rest of us having sunk to the bottom of the glass by comparison. She's the only one of us who carried the spark of our firearm legacy. I often wonder what would have become of her if she'd been born into another family. I can see her as a lady pilot in a Luscombe 10 doing somersaults over the Atlantic, or in a hot-air balloon over a field of red poppies in the South of France, or climbing a snowy peak in the Andes. Rarely do I see her tethered to earth. As it was, she seemed wasted on us, all that boundless energy and heat locked in the chill of the wedding cake, with marriage the only way out she could imagine.

Rosalind opened the oven to check on the roast, then turned to us behind Aster's back, her expression a silent *Eek*. "The poor little fella looks kind of dark. Is that smoke I see?" Rosalind coughed and moved away from the oven, fanning the smoke from her face. Aster, armed with pot holders, pulled the roasting pan from the oven and set it on the stove top.

"Oh no," she said, almost tearful. "It's burned."

"I'm sure it's fine on the inside." Rosalind flicked the charred crust with her scarlet fingernails. "Chin up," she said, placing a hand on Aster's shoulder. "After you're married, you don't want Matthew coming home from work to find you in a state like this, do you?"

"Of course not. But I have to learn to feed him."

"Heavens, he's not a German shepherd," Rosalind said. "Listen, he's managed to keep himself alive for what — thirty years? The man has flown bombing raids over Tokyo, for crying out loud. He can survive a burned roast, a burned chicken, and whatever else you might burn in the future."

Aster looked around helplessly at the wreck of a kitchen, the mixing bowls strewn all over, the pots rattling on the stove, spitting out water and steam. "Your reaction is all that matters," Rosalind continued in her most soothing voice. "What would Katharine Hepburn do in this situation? She'd laugh it off with a cocktail."

"Katharine Hepburn? Rozzy, that's not helpful." Aster went back to her potato mashing, and Rosalind, chastened, tried to help by taking the bread rolls out of the pan and putting them into the breadbasket for the table. "These rolls look wonderful," she said, sniffing one. "Well done."

"Mrs. O'Connor made those," Aster said without looking up from her bowl.

"Oh." Rosalind turned to Zelie and me, mouthing *Oops*.

We Chapel girls had very little experience with domestic chores. A house like ours was so large that it needed to be run by a staff, and a woman of my mother's social standing wouldn't have been expected to slave over a hot stove and mend clothes. For women of our class, learning to run a household meant learning to manage the other women who did the actual work.

Aster and Matthew wanted a different kind of life. "Modern," as Aster described it. Matthew rejected his parents' offer of a townhouse on the Upper East Side and instead used his own money to make a down payment on a colonial in Rye within walking distance of the commuter rail to Manhattan. Matthew would take the train into work every day, as senior vice president of Maybrick Steel, and Aster would stay at home, where she would cook, perform light cleaning (a maid would visit a couple of days a week to do the rough stuff), and eventually care for the children she and Matthew were eager to have. She didn't want to live in a castle, she said, describing our life in the wedding cake, and Matthew didn't want his parents' life, his mother's martini-soaked evenings, his father's affairs, their endless arguments.

"You've done all you can, Aster darling," Rosalind said. "À table!" She untied the apron from Aster's waist and began turning the dials on the stove to the off position.

Aster sent Zelie and me into the dining room with the drinks. Rosalind brought the basket of rolls and the bowl of mashed potatoes. Our father and Calla were already seated at the table, linen napkins on their laps. They weren't speaking to each other since Calla was reading a book of poetry by Tennyson and ignoring him.

As Zelie and I began to pour the drinks, Daphne came into the dining room in capri pants and a sleeveless gingham shirt tied in a knot just above the waist, her hair in a stubby ponytail. Our father looked up as she made her entrance, then looked down without acknowledging her. He didn't approve of pants on females nor the sight of belly buttons. Any of the rest of us would have been sent upstairs to change, but Daphne wasn't worth arguing with.

"Where's dinner?" she said, while I filled her glass with lemonade. We ate every evening at 6:30 and dinner was already ten minutes late. She resented any extra time spent at the table with our parents.

"Let's be nice about the dinner," our mother said, as she came into the dining room, sitting down in her usual place at the opposite end of the table from our father. "I'm sure Aster has worked hard on it." She looked tense, as she had in the garden earlier.

As I took my usual seat next to her, we heard a calamity from the kitchen, and Aster's voice: *"Oh no!"* Daphne laughed mid-drink. Rosalind went back to see what had happened.

Our father poured himself some beer. We hadn't seen him since church. Whenever he was home, he was working in his den. "What did you do to-day?" he asked Zelie and me. He loosened his collar a bit but hadn't removed the brown suit jacket he'd worn to church despite the heat.

"Iris sketched me at the frog pond," Zelie said.

"Do you have lessons this week?"

"We have our piano lesson on Monday," I said.

"And I have ballet class on Friday," Zelie said. She sat stiffly in her chair, only relaxing once it appeared the questioning was over. His questions were usually anodyne, but it was best to be on guard.

"And what about you, Calla?" he asked. "What are you reading so intently that you can't look away even at the table?"

"'The Lady of Shalott,'" she said, and began to read aloud: "She lives with little joy or fear. Over the water, running near, the sheepbell tinkles in her ear. Before her hangs a mirror clear, reflecting tower'd Camelot."

"Yes, thank you," our father said, raising his eyebrows and straightening the cutlery next to his plate. "I've never been one for poetry."

"No," Calla said. She set down the book and picked up her water glass, sipping from it delicately. She had beautiful plump lips, but their resting position was a frowning pucker. It sort of ruined the effect.

At last Aster and Rosalind arrived with the roast beef and green beans. The slices of roast beef, on a white platter, smelled pleasant but were unadorned. Mrs. O'Connor usually added a flourish of salad greens to the platter or some sprigs of parsley and orange slices, but Aster hadn't done that. The meat sat in an oily liquid, as if it had been dropped into a rainy puddle. We each hid our distaste as we used the fork to lower slices onto our plates.

Daphne began to eat before everyone else was served, attempting dramatically to cut the meat with her knife before picking it up and eating it

with her fingers. Our father observed her, then turned away in disgust. Aster looked around at the rest of us, awaiting our verdict. At dinner she was
usually freshly coiffed, but tonight she was ruddy-cheeked, hair as frazzled as
Albert Einstein's, with a splatter near the collar of her white dress, the palest
of pink blood, likely from the raw piece of meat she'd handled hours earlier.

"You'll never guess who RSVP'd today," Rosalind said, having returned
from the kitchen with the forgotten gravy boat. She took her seat next to our
father, ending the unbearable silence. He turned to her, sipping his beer, unwilling to play a guessing game.

"Samuel Colt," she said. "Samuel the fifth or sixth or who knows what
number they're on now. He's the younger one, around twenty, I think."

He set down his glass and considered this. "Who invited him?"

"We did, of course," Rosalind said. "Daddy, you approved the guest list."

"Did I?" His mind often seemed to be elsewhere, on more important
things.

"All your gun people are coming," she said.

"They're not *my* gun people," he replied. Most of the gun manufacturers
in America were based in Connecticut and Massachusetts — Colt, Smith &
Wesson, Winchester, the Springfield Armory, Mossberg, Ruger, Remington
— but he and his brethren in bloodshed were, for the most part, competitors,
not friends.

Our father made an attempt at the roast as Aster watched nervously. He
sliced off a hunk, put it in his mouth, and nodded at her as he chewed.

Belinda's plate contained a single slice of roast beef and a scattering of
green beans, but it was clear she had no intention of eating them. She buttered a bread roll and chewed it absentmindedly, staring out at the forest to
the north of the house through the window that was behind her husband.
Sometimes, when she was feeling particularly stressed, she radiated the kind
of spaciness that was typical of someone who'd been medicated, staring into
the void, then snapping back into conversation. But I didn't think she was
actually drugged. The doctor rarely visited our house, and on the occasions
I snooped around her bedroom or used her bathroom when the one in the
girls' wing was in use, I never saw any pills besides aspirin. Belinda didn't

seem to have any vices — didn't smoke cigarettes or drink coffee or alcohol; she faced every day head-on, defenseless. As a result, she seemed to shrink away from life; as if she were staring into the sun, she couldn't help but turn away.

"The Wessons are coming too," Aster said. "Elvira Wesson and her mother."

"We would have invited Annie Oakley and Buffalo Bill if they were still alive," Rosalind replied in jest, and our father grunted in agreement.

The wedding had ballooned into a huge affair, thanks to the Maybricks. They'd invited hundreds of people, nearly all of whom had accepted, so the reception was moved from our house to Wentworth Hall, an estate near Greenwich used for society weddings and other grand events. Our side had far fewer invitees. Our father was an only child and his parents were dead. Our mother's parents were also dead. She had a half brother with his own family in Boston, but she hated him; we had no contact with him at all. A handful of prominent residents in Bellflower Village had been invited and some of the New England gun manufacturers, but that was it.

"The thing is —" Rosalind began.

"I . . ." Belinda said suddenly, this single word drawing our collective attention. We all turned to Mother, but the rest of the sentence wasn't immediately forthcoming. She kept staring out at the woods, her eyes vacant. We waited for her to snap back to attention, and when she did, she continued her thought: "I have a feeling something terrible is going to happen."

There it was finally. She had opened the door to all that would come after.

"What I mean is . . ." She set down her roll on the edge of her plate. "The wedding is going to bring about something terrible. I don't know what exactly, but I think we should consider postponing."

Mother's odd behavior was like the smell of fresh paint. You noticed it at first but then you got used to it. I wasn't yet old enough to know for sure when something she did or said was truly noteworthy, but this certainly seemed to qualify. Her announcement was soon followed by the sound of silver clanking against china as my father and older sisters set their cutlery on their plates and turned to her in various states of alarm.

Our father was the first to speak. "My dear, what are you talking about?"

"Mother?" Aster asked in a nervous voice.

Belinda had uttered only a couple of sentences in the softest tone of voice, but they knew what she was capable of. Her propensity for drama was endless. "I have a terrible feeling about it and I simply don't see the rush," she said, reaching for one of her jagged earlobes and caressing it slightly.

"The rush? I'm twenty years old." Aster sounded panicked. She was so close to getting out — less than a week to go — and now this.

"That's right. You're still young," Belinda said. "You have no understanding of what marriage is really like. How you'll belong to a man once you marry and cease to be yourself."

"Oh Mother," Rosalind said, rolling her eyes.

"There's no need to rush into it," Belinda said. "I didn't get married until I was twenty-nine."

"Yes, but you —" Aster said quickly, loudly, her voice more high-pitched than usual. Rosalind elbowed her, and Aster paused and took a breath.

"You didn't *want* to get married, Mother," Rosalind said. "Aster does, so you see, there's the difference."

Our father picked up the saltshaker and shook it over his green beans, all the while staring at Rosalind, waiting for some kind of acknowledgment that she'd made a faux pas, but she was oblivious. It wasn't a secret that Belinda hadn't wanted to be married. No need to dance around it.

"Most of my friends are married or engaged," Aster said. "That's what I want, to be a wife and mother."

"There's plenty of time for that. I had Zelie when I was almost forty."

"Forty!" Rosalind said. "Mother, you do say the most astonishing things. Who wants to wait to have a baby until they're almost forty?"

"My point is that she could stay in college for now. At least until this bad feeling subsides."

Aster had attended Darlow's Ladies College for a year but wouldn't re-

turn in the fall now that she was getting married. Rosalind, having just graduated from high school, would be starting in September. Darlow's Ladies
College wasn't a college so much as a finishing school for well-off young
women. The more academically minded would have gone to Wellesley or
Smith to bide their time until marriage, the less well-off to secretarial school,
but our father wouldn't have allowed any of that. A Chapel girl didn't need a
college education, he said, since she would never need to work for her living.
He'd allowed Darlow's Ladies College because Aster couldn't very well sit at
home all day between high school graduation and her eventual marriage. She
needed to better herself, to learn social graces and how to run a household.

"I plan to stay in college for as long as I can," Daphne said. "I want to go
to art school in Europe."

"I'm not paying for any art school," our father said. "Put that out of your
mind."

"I'll pay for it myself," she replied, and the thought was too ridiculous to
prompt an argument.

"Why should I stay in college?" Aster asked. "So I can study to become
a teacher or nurse?" She said "teacher or nurse" in the same tone she might
have said "hobo or prostitute." She looked to our father for assurance. He
nodded his head.

"Nothing is being postponed," he said.

"Matthew certainly wouldn't wait for her," Rosalind said. "A man like
Matthew doesn't wait."

Mother sat back in her chair, defeated. She'd been foolish to think she
could postpone the wedding. She'd never used much of a guiding hand with
her daughters, had never tried to steer us in any direction, since most of
her energy went into her own day-to-day survival. Her girls had progressed
through the normal stages of life, and now one of them was at the marriage
stage and it was too late to set a different course.

"Something terrible is going to happen," she said again, mostly to herself. My sisters glanced at one another. Our father looked down at his plate.
Belinda was full of strange ideas, but I couldn't remember her ever sharing a
premonition with us.

"She wants me to end up like Millie Stevens," Aster said. Millie was the most tragic figure in our village. She was unmarried at twenty-eight, having earned a law degree from Columbia, where she'd gone only because Yale Law didn't admit women, and after graduation, she'd had the door of every law firm in New England slammed in her face. Defeated on practically every level, she lived with her parents on Birch Street and gave piano lessons to earn money. Her other part-time job — inspiring horror in Bellflower Village's female population — went unpaid.

"I've always liked Millie," Belinda said, and it was true. Millie came to our house once a week to give Zelie and me our piano lesson, and our mother occasionally engaged her in conversation, which she rarely did with anyone else.

"I suppose you'd prefer to have Millie for a daughter?" Aster said, having crossed the line into histrionics.

When Belinda didn't reply, Aster stood up from her chair and tossed her napkin onto her dinner plate. She pushed in her chair, then stilled her trembling hands by gripping the back of it. "I haven't said anything all these months, Mother, but —"

Our father attempted to stop her. "Please don't, dear."

"I'm sorry, but I must. I've been carrying this inside me and I have to express how I feel." Aster turned to our mother. "You haven't shown any interest in the wedding. For my friends' mothers, their daughters' weddings are the highlight of their lives, but not for you. It couldn't be more obvious that you don't really care."

I looked down at my lap as Aster spoke and wished I could disappear. My sisters and I talked about Mother behind her back all the time, but none of us had ever confronted her to her face like this.

"I don't know what's wrong with you, Mother, and I never have." Aster seemed to be emitting some kind of scorching heat with her words; we were baking in it. "But I'm not going to let you ruin this for me."

"I'm not in the habit of ruining things," Belinda replied calmly, though I knew she was anything but calm inside.

Daphne snorted. "That's practically *all* you do."

"Enough," our father said. He told Daphne to go to her room, to which she replied: "Hallelujah."

Aster followed Daphne out of the dining room, her stint at cooking dinner apparently not extending to the cleanup afterward. Rosalind dabbed her lips with her napkin, then tucked it under the side of her plate and left as well.

My parents, Calla, Zelie, and I were left at the table. At some point during the discussion, Calla had picked up her poetry book again and was reading to herself, having pushed aside her dinner plate, which had been cleaned of potatoes and green beans, leaving the single piece of grayish meat, like a tiny mouse corpse, to rest on the white china.

In the silence, she began to read aloud, apropos of nothing but capturing the mood of the room: "A pale, pale corpse she floated by, Deadcold —"

"Stop," our father said.

"Deadcold, between the houses high, Dead into tower'd Camelot."

"Enough," he said, and Calla left the table, taking her Tennyson with her.

Zelie looked from Mother to Father, her eyes filling with tears. Such open warfare had never broken out at our dinner table before. Disagreements usually happened behind closed doors, in hushed voices.

"I don't want something terrible to happen," she said, waiting for someone to do something or say something that would make everything all right.

"You can't believe your mother," our father said to Zelie. "Nothing terrible is going to happen to anyone." He pushed his dinner plate away, half his meal uneaten, and stared down the table at his wife. "I hope you're pleased with yourself."

"It had to be said."

"Did it really?" He finished his glass of beer, then directed Zelie and me to go upstairs.

I hesitated to leave our mother alone. Zelie, as was her custom, waited to see what I was going to do. I wasn't afraid my father would strike our mother or shout at her. He was never violent, would never even yell. He ruled over a house of women without ever raising his voice. Still, I didn't want to leave her. She needed an ally. She rarely had one.

"Did you hear me?" he said.

I stood up, a coward, and pulled Zelie along. Belinda looked down, seemingly too ashamed to meet my gaze, so I leaned over and whispered in her ear: "I believe you, Mother."

I didn't know if I actually did then. But she would end up being right, of course. Something terrible *was* going to happen, and later on, after it had, I wondered how it was possible that she had foreseen it.

The Headless Bride

1950

I.

In the weeks before Aster's wedding, my mother began to smell roses. Belinda smelled roses when there were no roses to smell, when the closed windows blocked any scent from the garden, and when there was no one around wearing rose-scented soap or perfume. Rose fragrances weren't allowed in our house, so there was no chance the smell could be coming from inside.

When she began to smell the roses in the lead-up to Aster's wedding, Belinda knew not to bother looking for the source. The first time this had happened to her — the mysterious scent of roses — it was twenty years earlier when she was pregnant with Aster. She hadn't yet known she was pregnant; she and my father had just returned from their month-long honeymoon to Europe, and she had stepped into his house for the first time. It was a faint scent at first, probably a floral arrangement or sachet, she thought, and though she had never been fond of roses, she wasn't alarmed until she realized she smelled them everywhere, even in the bathtub, even in her own bed. She asked her husband what he thought and he said he didn't smell anything and didn't seem interested. She looked everywhere for the source of the smell and couldn't find it. The doctor told her the phantom scent was a side effect of pregnancy, like cravings for pickles or sardines. He assured her it was nothing to worry about. She held her nose to block the scent, breathing through her mouth, but it made no difference. The rose scent, she soon realized, was coming from inside her.

When she woke up each day, she smelled the roses on her breath, and the smell grew so intense that it made her retch and vomit. The doctor told her it was morning sickness, but Belinda knew it wasn't. She knelt before the toilet and it filled with the floral scent, leaving the bathroom smelling like perfume. The doctor said it would subside after three months or so, but it continued on, month after month; he was no help so she stopped calling him, accepting that she was on her own.

Her daily torment became so unbearable and unrelenting that she screamed and clasped her head and banged it against the wall, trying to force the smell out. She screamed so loudly that her throat hurt and her head throbbed. The pain dulled the scent a little bit, or distracted from it, but it wouldn't go away. The doctor came again and tied her to the bed and that's when her husband began to wonder if she was crazy.

Belinda's mother's name was Rose, and Rose had died giving birth to Belinda in 1900.

Rose's mother, whose name was Dollie, had died giving birth to Rose in 1873.

Dollie's mother, whose name was Alma, had died giving birth to Dollie in 1857.

Belinda, a motherless daughter, whose mother had also been motherless, as had her mother's mother, had in the process of being born killed the person who would have loved her most in the world. She had never met her mother but had lived inside her most intimately; they were intertwined, Belinda and her mother's shadow, an uneasy companionship.

When Belinda had first begun to smell the roses, she wondered if her mother Rose was trying to warn her, but it was such a frightening thought that she dismissed it. Yet as the smell consumed her, she became certain that her maternal legacy was catching up with her — she was about to die.

She didn't want to spend the final days of her life tied to a bed like a patient in an asylum; she had already lost so much of her dignity — marriage itself had turned out to be the greatest indignity, the way her husband had used her body to pleasure himself and was slowly killing her with this pregnancy. She was certain she had little time left, and she wanted to preserve whatever freedom she could. So she stopped screaming and endured the scent in silence. She was released from her restraints and pretended everything was normal for a few days, waking early to eat breakfast with her husband before he left for work and chatting with him amiably when he returned home at the end of the day, balancing a bit of needlework on her belly as they conversed while she stitched something for the baby's nursery. The scent was nauseating, but she hid her reaction to it; she was good at hiding things. Once she had convinced everyone she was fine, not only her husband but his parents and the watchful housekeeper, they stopped following her every move and she was able to leave the house one morning with a chair and a piece of rope and walk deep into the woods north of the house. She set the chair on the forest floor and rested for a while, caressing her eight-months-pregnant belly before doing what she knew she must do.

She stood on the chair and lassoed a tree branch, knowing that many people would consider what she was doing to be a grave sin, killing herself and her child. But Belinda's father, a scientist, had always told her there was no such thing as God, and Belinda had never doubted him. What kind of God would have let her kill her mother? And if there was no God, no punishment awaited her. She and her child would live in a world of spirits, like fireflies in a meadow on a midsummer night — Belinda liked the thought of that.

As she fashioned the rope around her neck, she considered the possibility of letting herself die naturally in childbirth so her child could live. She would have been willing to die an agonizing death for her child; she had never wanted it, but since it had begun to grow inside her, she'd become protective of it. But she knew that letting the child live would mean leaving the baby with her husband and his parents in that wretched wedding cake of a house. If she could barely endure that life, how could a child?

When Belinda didn't appear for luncheon that afternoon, Dovey went looking for her. The Irish immigrant, prematurely middle-aged, wearing her usual cardigan and plaid skirt with thick cream-colored stockings on her legs, trudged into the forest and spotted Mrs. Chapel standing on a chair, a rope hanging from a tree branch, the noose around her neck.

"Jesus, Mary, and Joseph!" she screamed, clutching the gold cross that dangled from her necklace. She must have realized as soon as the words left her mouth that it wasn't a good idea to startle Mrs. Chapel, given her precarious position.

Belinda, suddenly frightened, nearly lost her balance. She was surprised that her overwhelming instinct was to fight for survival, and as the chair wobbled beneath her feet, she clawed at the rope around her neck. It was touch-and-go for several seconds, the door to the afterlife swinging open and closed before her like the door to a saloon that was loose on its hinges. Open, closed. Open, closed. She saw glimpses of eternity as she continued to wobble on the chair, awaiting her fate, clawing at her neck. She would later say that she'd never felt more alive than in that moment.

Two days later, Belinda gave birth to Aster without incident. The baby had been born at dawn, and Belinda cradled her in her arms as the sun came up and shined on them both through the bedroom window. For months she'd been so sure that she was going to die, but she hadn't. She drank it in, this feeling of being alive. She inhaled it, like she did the perfume from her garden, the lilies and carnations — but not the roses. The rose scent, like the baby, had been pushed out.

She was the first mother in her maternal line to survive childbirth in eighty-nine years. She marveled at the miracle of Aster, at her tiny fingernails and eyelashes. Belinda had defied the death her mother had forewarned, and now, faced with this vulnerable baby, she grew overly protective of her. She kept the baby with her all the time, wouldn't allow the nurse to take her, and had the crib brought to her bedroom. She and her husband slept in separate rooms in their wing, so he didn't resist and even seemed pleased at the close bond Belinda had with the baby, given what had happened during her pregnancy. When he and his parents wanted to visit with Aster, Belinda made them come to her sitting room where she could watch them, all of them awkward with the baby, straining to love her as they strained to love anything, cradling Aster as if they were holding a ham. Belinda took meals in her sitting room, baby in her arms — she even held her as she bathed. On the few occasions her husband came to her room at night, seeking again the pleasures of her body, Belinda left Aster in her crib next to the bed.

For three months Belinda kept Aster close, and then one day the roses returned. The scent was as strong as it had been at the end of her previous pregnancy, but now she tasted them too, heard the sound of their petals rustling in her ears.

She was pregnant with her second child, that's what the roses were telling her. She was ill from the start this time, the roses causing her to retch and vomit almost constantly, weakening her so much that she often crawled between the bathroom and the bedroom. She was unable to care for Aster in her state and surrendered the baby to a nurse, heartbroken when her daughter cried for her and she was unable to hold or feed her. But she wondered, in the dark hours of the night as the roses continued their assault, whether Aster needed to get used to being motherless. The second baby might be the one to kill her.

But Belinda once again survived, and after the birth, she thrived. She decided to name her second daughter after her mother: Rosalind, an offering she hoped would ease her mother's concern and the toll that came with it.

There was a break after Rosalind, and Belinda hoped she'd somehow reached the limits of her fertility. Her husband continued to come to her despite her pleas that she couldn't survive another pregnancy; he said it was un-natural for her to refuse him. Yet six months passed, then a year. She'd been afraid to grow too close to Rosalind, but with time, in the absence of roses, she relaxed.

Another year went by and Belinda grew more confident until one morning the scent returned and enveloped her, announcing the torment of another pregnancy. Calla was born in 1933, then Daphne came in 1935. Each time was worse, more torturous than before, and it was impossible to recover once the babies were born. The first four babies had left their weight in her body; she felt as if her insides were pressing down, that if she didn't keep her legs squeezed tightly together part of her might fall out. And so she held herself rigid.

Still, her husband came to her. In 1937 she gave birth to me, and two years later Zelie came along when Belinda was nearly forty. She was confined to her bed for the entirety of her last pregnancy. Zelie was a thorny baby, Belinda said, and she felt the thorns pierce her placenta and tear at her internal organs on the way out.

Her other daughters came to visit her in her bedroom every day after lunch, having grown accustomed to her constant sickness. It didn't bother them, and this worried Belinda. During their visits, they chattered endlessly and ran around teasing one another, pulling hair, and shouting, "Mother, look at me!" but Belinda didn't have the energy to look. She'd produced six of them, and they all hung on her, wanted things from her she was unable to give. Their care had largely been handed over to a nanny.

By the time Belinda had Zelie, she was weaker than she'd ever been, but she was content in the knowledge that she would never have another baby. That, she knew, would be impossible. She'd heard an old wives' tale that baby girls steal their mother's beauty; she'd never been a great beauty, but each of her daughters had stolen from her; along with her husband, they depleted her, taking her health and vitality, her life. She had offered up six perfect pearls, and at last she was a shell; she was empty.

Belinda wondered if this is what her mother had been trying to warn her about. Maybe her mother had been trying to warn her not that she was going to die but that she was going to live a life she'd never wanted, a life she couldn't bear.

2.

Growing up, we knew about the roses that assaulted our mother during her pregnancies. We understood them as ghosts in another form — as our grandmother, Rose, haunting our mother while she was pregnant, always a dangerous time for the women in our family. We were used to hearing about our mother's ghosts in whatever form they took, and so for us, it wasn't startling or scary. We'd grown up with our father dismissing all of our mother's stories as the work of her imagination.

Once, when I was still very young, we were all playing outside when Daphne plucked a rose from Belinda's garden, inhaled its scent deeply, and exclaimed: "Help, I'm going to have a baby!" We all thought it was hilarious. After that, the roses were nothing more than a joke.

Perhaps for that reason, Belinda didn't tell us that she had begun to smell the roses again in the weeks leading up to Aster's wedding. We didn't see her on the Monday after the disastrous dinner. It was clear that her warning was going to be ignored, so she closed in on herself, a bloom at night. Dovey took trays up to her room at mealtimes, but otherwise the door to her sitting room in the wing my parents shared remained closed.

Whenever I passed by the darkened hallway that next day, I wanted to ask her questions about what terrible thing she thought was going to happen if Aster and Matthew were married. Aster and my other sisters had completely discounted the warning, coming to various conclusions — she wanted attention, she just hated marriage and wanted to ruin Aster's chance for it — but Rosalind was the most forceful with her theory, declaring simply: "She's crazy."

I accepted that my older sisters knew Belinda better than I did, but I feared that something was different now — Belinda had never warned us of anything before. We'd never had any sense that the spirits she saw, the visions that haunted her, could somehow hurt us too. If she'd said to me, "Iris, don't go out to the meadow tomorrow, something terrible is going to happen," I would have stayed inside, afraid. I worried it was a mistake not to be afraid now. But I knew how my sisters would react if I told them how I was feeling, so I kept quiet.

Still, Belinda's warning followed me. On Monday afternoon, Zelie and I had our piano lesson. Seeing Millie Stevens only reminded me of what had happened the night before. Zelie, of course, couldn't keep quiet about it.

"We talked about you at dinner last night," she said to Millie, as the three of us walked together to the music room at the back of the house. "About how you're not married."

I grabbed Zelie by the arm and dug my fingernails into her skin; she glared at me. Millie, her dark hair in a high ponytail, wearing a plaid dress, smiled to hide her embarrassment and kept walking, entering the music room ahead of us and setting up her sheet music at the piano.

"Our father asked about our lessons, that's all," I said to Millie, as I sat down on the bench next to her; she smelled of gardenias. "We told him how much we enjoy them."

Zelie, who lounged in a chair near the window, didn't pipe up to contradict me.

"I'm flattered that you'd mention me to your father," Millie said quietly. I thought I'd smoothed things over by lying, but I felt awkward with Millie for the rest of the lesson, remembering how cruel Aster had been about her. Millie's life didn't seem so bad to me — teaching, playing music all day. To her, maybe that was preferable to being a housewife and taking care of babies.

When my thirty minutes were up, I was glad to let Zelie, the more serious music student, take my place. I went upstairs to the empty girls' wing, passing again by Belinda's darkened hallway. In the girls' sitting room, I sat on the window ledge and worked for a while on a sketch of a robin that I'd started earlier in the day. After a while, I heard Aster call for me.

"Iris," she said. She sounded distant, as if she were in her bedroom.

I didn't look up from my drawing, annoyed at being interrupted, at never getting to be alone. "What is it?" I called back.

"Iris, I need you."

This time her voice sounded almost like a vibration, something I could feel in the floorboards. I could smell her, too — Yardley's English lavender, her signature scent. I set down my pencil and went to her bedroom. But no one was there.

"Aster?" I checked the other rooms, but they were empty. I stood in the middle of the hallway, baffled. I'd heard her voice as clear as day and smelled her perfume.

Zelie arrived a few moments later, fresh off her lesson, to find me standing in the hallway looking lost. "Where's Aster?" I said. Nosy Zelie, better than I, knew the comings and goings of everyone in the house.

"She's out furniture shopping with Matthew."

"No — she can't be. I just heard her calling me."

"All the way from New York? Your hearing is as good as Wonder Woman's," she said, and fell into a fit of laughter.

"Cut it out," I said, embarrassed to have been caught imagining things. I shook my head. Aster, and Belinda's warning, had been too much on my mind.

Aster was supposed to cook for us again that night, but she stayed out with Matthew, perhaps worried she'd have to face Belinda. Mrs. O'Connor prepared the macaroni and tomato casserole with green salad that Aster had planned to make. It turned out that Aster hadn't needed to worry about seeing our mother that night — Belinda's place at the table remained empty, and while I would have thought the mood would be lighter without her there, it wasn't. The previous night's dinner, and the warning about the mysterious terrible thing, continued to shadow us.

Although we didn't see Belinda at all on Monday, that night we heard her, her solitary shriek piercing the night, a sudden puncture in the protective layer of silence and sleep that enveloped us. I opened my eyes briefly, then rolled over in bed, slipping easily back into sleep. We were used to our mother's screams; they didn't come every night, but I heard them often enough that the sound didn't alarm me. Our mother's terror was our lullaby. My sisters had always told me to ignore it.

On Tuesday, I saw a sign of Belinda in the kitchen, the remains of her lunch tray that Dovey had gone to collect from her: a chicken wing with the meat nibbled off, and an empty bowl of something sweet — rice pudding, perhaps.

I picked up the wing off the white china plate, putting part of it in my mouth and sucking on it. Zelie came into the kitchen and ran her finger around the empty bowl to lick off the sweetness. As the two youngest Chapel girls, we were used to our mother's scraps.

"Let's go to her room," I said, setting down the chicken wing. Zelie followed me upstairs to our parents' quarters. Our mother had two rooms to herself, her bedroom and a sitting room. The door to the bedroom was open and I peeked inside. I could never resist. The room was ascetic, painted white with no pictures or wall hangings. The blanket on her bed was simple Belgian linen in an isabelline shade, and the furniture was chestnut, all solid lines with little adornment. On one of the nightstands, there was a collection of candles in jars; Belinda said the bright light from the lamps hurt her eyes at night. On the other nightstand, there was a tiny stuffed wren, its feet glued to a polished piece of wood. Her bedroom couldn't have been more different than the colorful floral scenes she'd painted in the girls' wing. Belinda, an ancient name, means "serpent." Once when Zelie and I were playing in her bedroom — Belinda was away from home on one of the rare appointments that took her from our house and Bellflower Village — I noticed a snake painted on her wall behind her wardrobe just above the baseboard. It was a looping snake in dark verdigris, with spots and round brown eyes. Her secret snake, to represent her name; unlike her daughters, she wasn't a flower.

She wasn't in her bedroom, no surprise. She did nothing there but sleep. I knocked on her sitting room door.

"Come in," Belinda said, and Zelie and I found her sitting on the sofa, holding a cup of tea.

"Oh," she said at the sight of us. "I thought you were Dovey." She set her cup and saucer on the side table next to a hobnail vase of yellow calla lilies. Only one of the drapes was open, revealing a slender bar of light. Her sitting room was more decorated than her bedroom, and even with the dim light, I could see the creamy Japanese chrysanthemums on the wallpaper, her writing desk, and the display cabinet filled with curios she'd collected over the years, most of them from travels with her father when she was young. In spite of the closed drapes, the room was stifling hot.

"Close the door, Iris," she said.

"But —" I pointed to the calla lilies.

"Dovey bought these for me in town this morning, aren't they nice?"

"But you said never to place lilies in a closed room. You said they'll poison the air, and —"

"And what?" There was an odd tone to her voice, an aggressive annoyance.

"You've been sitting in here with them all day."

"Close the door."

I did as she asked, shutting the door gingerly. Zelie sat on the sofa next to her, neatly poised on the edge of the cushion, careful not to plop back, limbs astray, as she normally would have done.

"Where are your sisters?" Belinda held her handkerchief to her mouth.

"Downstairs," Zelie said, leaning toward Belinda to get a better look at her face. "Why are you covering your mouth?"

"I'm not feeling well." She stood up from the sofa with some difficulty, apparently wanting to get away from Zelie's examining gaze. She went to her writing desk in front of the window, picked up her pencil, and began to draw.

"Mother?" I said.

Her back was still to us. "What is it?"

"What did you mean when you said something terrible is going to happen if Aster gets married?"

"I have a bad feeling. I don't want to talk about it."

"But is Aster going to be all right?"

She kept drawing, avoiding my question, which I could only assume meant the answer was bad. I frowned at Zelie and motioned for her to stand up so we could leave. It had been my idea to find our mother, and now I wished we hadn't.

As I waited for Zelie to tiptoe toward me after having been distracted by a trinket on the coffee table, I noticed the spirit journal on the side table with the teacup and calla lilies. I went to pick it up, surreptitiously opening it and flipping through the pages. Maybe in the journal I would find a clue. I turned to the most recent entry, dated from that morning.

> *2:40 a.m. little Indian girl, right side of her head missing, bloody, standing at the foot of my bed, crying for her mother*

I had not been expecting to read something like this, and I felt shaken by the gruesome description. I should have set the journal down, but I flipped the pages again, drawn to this window into my mother's mind. I had always thought of her ghosts as amorphous floating creatures, translucent like jellyfish, shimmering and white. In my mind, they were romantic somehow, like characters out of Calla's poetry, the lost pair of lovers who haunt the moors. Not bloodied and suffering.

> *3:22 a.m. the little Indian girl continues to wail. Where is her mother? I wish she would leave me alone*
> *4:04 a.m. pounding on the door, a male voice: "I need to see you, let me in."*

I set the journal on the table. *I need to see you.* Those words gave me a chill. This encounter and the others were so specific that it was difficult to believe she had made it all up.

Belinda said the spirits that visited her had been killed by Chapel firearms. She felt our family was in some way responsible for their deaths, that the spirits were looking for us, the Chapels, since our name was on the guns that had killed them, and they were drawn to Belinda in particular because she was the only person who could see and hear them. I wondered why the ghosts were looking for us rather than the person who had shot them, but I'd never asked Belinda that. As always, my older sisters had said to ignore her. Even Calla, who in temperament was most similar to our mother, curled up her nose in disgust at Belinda's antics, which she found to be an embarrassing display of "female hysteria." Calla chose to channel her thoughts about spirits into poetry, a much more suitable medium, she said, than journals and screaming.

Belinda rose from her desk, and I stood up and went to the door. "What's the matter?" she said, watching me as she returned to the sofa, walking with the creaky movements of a much older woman.

"Have you seen visions of Aster?"

Belinda sat down and took up her cup and saucer. "What a strange question," she said. "What do you mean?"

"Like the visions you have of dead people."

Belinda drank from her teacup, wincing slightly at what must have been the bitterness of the tea leaves. "They're not visions. The spirits are with us in this house."

"Did the spirits tell you that something is going to happen to Aster?"

"I told you, it's a feeling. I don't know exactly what it means." She looked at me for a few seconds before resting her head on the back of the sofa and closing her eyes. I could tell from that look that there was something she wasn't saying.

"I'm tired," she said, starting to drift off. "You girls go outside and play."

"Mother?" I whispered several seconds later, hoping the flowers weren't getting to her. There was no answer.

I opened the door and waved for Zelie to follow me. I shut the door behind me, then opened it a crack to let out the poisoned air.

3.

After we left our mother, Zelie wanted to join our sisters downstairs, but I told her I was going to the girls' wing. She followed me even though I didn't ask her to. "It's hot in here," she complained, as we entered our sitting room, which was bright and inviting compared to our mother's.

"Then go downstairs," I said, as I sat on one of the green sofas. I would have preferred that she did. We were all paired off — it was just my bad luck to be paired with the sister who never stopped talking.

"Iris," Zelie sang. "What are you doing?" She twirled in front of the bank of windows that overlooked the trees behind the house.

"Zelie, *be quiet.*" I groaned and lay back, closing my eyes, wanting to think in silence for once. I could hear Zelie rustling around in the room, and when it was clear she had no intention of leaving me in peace, I opened my eyes to see her sitting on the windowsill, the window open to allow for any scrap of breeze to come through. She was reading one of her Nancy Drew novels, but every few seconds she looked up at me.

"Do you think our mother is crazy?" I said. Zelie, eager to dump the book, set it down next to her on the windowsill without even bothering to mark her page.

"Everyone else does."

"That's not what I asked you." I already knew that. "What if everyone else is wrong?"

"What do you mean?"

"What if Mother is right and something terrible *is* about to happen? Shouldn't we do something just in case?"

"What could we do?"

"What if we got Aster to postpone the wedding somehow? Just until Mother's bad feeling passes and we can be sure she'll be okay."

This was too much for Zelie, clearly; she looked dumbfounded. If I was going to act, I'd need to take the lead. "Come on," I said.

The girls' library, just off our wing, was where the wedding things were stored. Neat white boxes were stacked along one of the walls, ready to load into the car on the day before the wedding. Some of the boxes contained wedding favors, one for every place setting, including the pouches of Jordan almonds, cigarette lighters engraved with *A & M,* and packets of aster seeds hand-painted by Daphne. There were also tiny boxes of champagne truffles, but they were stored in the cellar so they wouldn't melt.

Other boxes were filled with place cards for the reception tables, handwritten by a professional calligrapher, and the seating chart that Aster had worked on for months along with Matthew's family. One box contained gifts for Aster's friends who had helped in some way with the wedding preparations. She would have only her sisters as bridesmaids and flower girls; since there were so many of us, it didn't leave room for anyone else. But she'd wanted her friends to feel included and they'd helped out here and there. For them and for us, she'd bought blister-pearl compact mirrors and bottles of White Shoulders perfume.

Along two other walls there were long folding tables covered in ivory tablecloths where the wedding gifts were displayed. Packages arrived daily, and Aster unwrapped them and placed the items on the tables, the crystal candlesticks and vases, the china place settings she and Matthew had selected, the silverware and framed artwork and pewter serving platters that probably wouldn't fit in the modest colonial where Matthew and Aster were going to set up home. They'd need another house just to store it all.

As alluring as the gifts were, they were overshadowed by what was displayed in the middle of the room: Aster's wedding dress, standing upright, looking exactly how I'd pictured Belinda's ghosts — disembodied white figures floating through the room. The dress had been made from the most luxurious silk, yards and yards for the long sleeves and high collar, the basque-style bodice and the bell of the skirt. It was almost medieval in appearance, a picture of elegance and grace. The regal train was spread out on the floor, encircling the dress completely, like Venus's scallop shell, the dress rising above it.

The gown wasn't really floating, of course; it was fitted to a dress form, a mannequin without a head. The dress form was almost completely hidden under the voluminous fabric of the dress; only the slender white neck extending above the collar by an inch or two was visible. Above that, there was nothing, as if the bride had suffered the same fate as Marie Antoinette. The bridal veil, for which this figure would have no need, was laid out on its own folding table at the back of the room. It was made of imported French lace and had orange blossoms sewn into it.

Zelie and I, though eleven and thirteen years old, were not allowed in the room with the headless bride. We would always be the little sisters, always children no matter our age. Aster worried we might break something or muss the dress somehow with dirty hands or chewing gum. The closest we were allowed to get was the doorway to the library, where Zelie would stand several times each day to gawk at the gown, her princess fantasy come to life.

I left the girls' sitting room, Zelie following close behind, and went to our old playroom near the girls' library. Now emptied of toys, it was a storage room, and there I found our family's luggage, which we only ever took on our summer trips to Cape Cod. I picked up two large canvas duffel bags for myself and handed a small suitcase to Zelie. She followed me out of the playroom to the girls' library, but she remained in the doorway as I ventured inside.

"Iris!" she whispered. "What are you doing? What if Aster comes upstairs?"

"Stop being such a baby," I said, opening one of the white boxes that was stacked against the wall. I scooped out handfuls of the pouches filled with Jordan almonds and dropped them into one of my duffel bags, then moved on to the cigarette lighters. Zelie watched as I continued emptying the contents of the boxes into my bags, the perfume, the seed packets, all of it.

"Go down to the cellar," I said. "Put the boxes of champagne truffles in the suitcase, then meet me outside by the shed."

"Why?"

"Just do it, Zelie!" I said in a whispered shout. She dashed away. Sometimes she was afraid of me and I took advantage of that now. I had never harmed her — Daphne was the one who inflicted punishments, pulling our hair or pinching us when we displeased her — but I suppose, to Zelie, all older sisters carried the same potential for menace.

I loaded my bags with all of the wedding favors, the gifts, the place cards, the seating chart. There was room in one of the bags for a few more things, so I grabbed the crystal candlesticks and one of the vases, and somehow managed to smash everything down and zipper the bag closed. On my way out, I grabbed a china plate and wedged it under my arm. I tiptoed down the stairs so my sisters or Dovey wouldn't hear me, all the while straining to carry the heavy bags. I slipped out the door into the courtyard and found Zelie waiting for me at the gardener's shed with her suitcase. Mr. Warner wasn't there, but he'd left the doors to the shed unlocked. I dropped my bags on the ground next to Zelie, then placed the china plate on top of them; the sight of the plate made her eyes go wide. Ignoring her terrified look, I went into the shed and grabbed two shovels.

We carried our bags and the shovels and the single china plate into the forest. "What are we doing?" Zelie kept asking, as she trailed behind me. "Iris, we're going to get into trouble." I continued to ignore her, forging ahead with confidence. Although I hadn't really thought things through, I didn't want Zelie to know that.

It was somewhat cooler deeper in the forest, the red maples and black birch trees shielding us from the blaze of the afternoon sun. Looking up, I could see the brilliance of the sky, the blue of it shining in lacy patterns through the treetops. When we were younger, our mother took us on occasional walks in the forest when she wasn't too tired; she would teach us about moss and ferns — our grandfather had been a botanist and she learned all about them from him. We'd return home from our walks with leaves and flowers, and she'd help us press them in old books.

But as I walked with my bags, I traipsed over the leaves and didn't give a thought about what they were called. I turned to make sure Zelie was still following me, that she hadn't run back to the house to tell on me. She hadn't, but she was lagging far behind.

We must have walked for nearly ten minutes, each of us huffing and puffing, and when we reached a small clearing far enough away from the house, I stopped and dropped everything I was carrying onto the ground, unable to continue. "We can dig here," I said. "We each need to dig a really big hole."

"But why?" Zelie dropped her suitcase and stomped her feet, making me wish I hadn't brought her. "I'm not digging until you tell me why," she said, as I broke ground with my shovel with only my small sandaled foot to press the blade into the earth. This was going to be harder than I thought.

I dug for a few minutes, with Zelie watching me, but I had nothing resembling a hole, just a modest amount of upturned earth among the twigs and branches and scattered leaves. "We need to bury everything that's in these bags. Get going."

I rested for a moment, looking down at my legs for signs of blood. Zelie still hadn't made a move. From the glare she gave me when I glanced at her, I knew she was only getting angrier.

"Zelie, come on. You heard what Mother said — something terrible is going to happen to Aster. We need to postpone the wedding."

I could see Zelie wrestling in her mind with the ideas we'd always held about Belinda's grasp on reality, with her fear of upsetting Aster and ruining the wedding, but also with the possibility that Belinda was right — it seemed that this was what finally pushed her to action. She picked up the shovel and tried to help though she barely made a dent in the ground. Her efforts were useless and I told her to join me in digging my hole instead. We worked for a while in silence, and soon we had a hole large enough to bury something small, a bag of flour or a kitten. We were making progress but had a long way to go. The exertion and the heat and my menstrual cramps had all left me nauseated. I longed for water but hadn't thought to bring any. I needed a moment to steady myself and used the shaft of the shovel for balance. My distress, clearly visible to Zelie, offered a window for her doubts to creep back in.

"This is silly. Nothing's going to happen to Aster. Let's go home and put everything back. It's not too late."

"But if something does happen, we'll feel guilty that we didn't do anything to save her."

"Save her from what?"

"Mother won't say." I started digging again, this time with renewed energy. I was getting the hang of it finally, the earth softening once I'd dug a bit more, darker and more fragrant the deeper I got.

As we dug, we heard the chirping and cawing of the birds punctuated by our shovels slicing into the ground and our grunting. Zelie was sickly pink, the dark coils of her curls stuck in sweaty clumps around her neck. We had never worked this hard. Our exploration of the forest was usually more leisurely, and in physical education class at school, we played tennis or walked around the gym but never did anything too strenuous. We were like two china dolls preserved in a display case, saved for some future purpose. It felt good to dig, to grunt like an animal, to feel my muscles burn. We were getting deeper, and I welcomed the challenge, wanting to see how deep I could go, but then something startled me, a flash, a vision, and I screamed and threw my shovel aside.

"What?" Zelie asked in terror, as I backed away from the hole. "What is it?"

I'd seen something in the hole. I continued to back up, stumbling slightly, until I hit the trunk of a tree. I steadied myself, back against it, and struggled to catch my breath. The hole before me was empty, but for a moment, I thought I'd seen the headless bride lying inside it.

"Iris?"

"I thought I saw something." I shook my head. "It's nothing."

"What did you think you saw?"

"A snake," I said without thinking. Zelie became afraid and I had to assure her there was no snake in the hole.

I knew I'd imagined the headless bride, but it bothered me that she had looked as if she were really there, in a grave. This was my mother's fault. She'd put morbid thoughts into my head. I placed my hand to my chest, waiting for my heart to slow down. I steadily returned to normal and slipped into big-sister mode, not wanting to dwell on what I'd seen.

"I'm fine," I said to Zelie, and while she knew me well enough not to believe me, we both started digging again until I announced we were finished.

"It's deep enough. Let's bury everything."

She opened her suitcase and I unzipped my duffel bags. I turned the first bag upside down, and the almonds and cigarette lighters and bottles of perfume tumbled out and landed in the hole. "Can I eat one?" Zelie asked, as she bent over to pick up a pouch of almonds. "I'm hungry."

"Go ahead," I said. She crunched on the hard pastel as I dumped my second bag into the hole, then took the pink boxes of truffles from her suitcase and tossed them in as well. Lastly, I threw the china plate onto the heap.

"Poor Aster," Zelie said, as we stared down at the wreckage, the tangle of spring colors and shimmery gold and silver, at the cracked bottles of White Shoulders perfume wafting bergamot and peach up at us. The sight of the destruction I had caused took my mind off the memory of what I'd seen earlier, the headless bride in a grave. She'd been replaced by these pretty things.

"I don't know how this is going to stop the wedding," Zelie said, as I began to fill in the hole. If I was really honest with myself, I didn't know that it would. All I knew is that we had to try.

4.

That night, I awoke with cramps. I was curled in bed around the hot water bottle Dovey had prepared for me, but the pain shooting through my abdomen wouldn't cease; the bottle only made it harder to sleep given the heat of the bedroom.

I got up from bed and limped down the hallway, not wanting to wake my sisters. In the bathroom, I closed the door without turning on the light and stepped into a massive spider's web of silk. I flipped the switch, and the blast of the bulb whited everything out for a moment, then I could see — I'd walked into stockings and bras, all the things my sisters had rinsed out before bed and hung up to dry on the thin cords that were affixed to both sides of the bathroom. I batted them away as I tried to find my way to the sink through the webs and dangling branches, a damp feminine rain forest. I took two aspirin from the medicine cabinet and swallowed them using my hand as a cup for water, then gripped the cool sides of the basin to wait for it to take effect.

I didn't want to go to the toilet, not wanting to see the swirl of blood in the water. At that time of my life, I didn't understand the mechanics of what was happening inside me, and I worried I was leaking blood from some unseen wound, like one of those dead animals hung upside down until it's drained. I squeezed my legs together, hoping to stem the flow.

As I continued to grip the basin, I thought I heard footsteps in the hallway, the soft creak of the floorboards. I turned off the light and opened the door, but my vision was blotchy. "Hello?" I whispered, expecting to see one of my sisters waiting for the bathroom. No one was there.

When my eyes began to focus in the darkness, I thought I saw a white figure walking away from me toward the girls' library at the front of the house.

Disturbances in the night weren't uncommon in the wedding cake; occasionally Belinda wandered into the girls' wing, confused and frightened, and one of us would have to lead her back to bed. I suspected this was her now, but it was odd that she was quiet. I hesitated in the doorway of the bathroom, thinking back to the afternoon, to the forest and the headless bride in the hole. The quiet was getting to me.

I decided to follow the white figure. My older sisters had always told me Belinda's ghosts weren't real and that it was silly to be afraid. The figure had stopped in front of the doorway to the girls' library and was staring inside. As I approached, I recognized who it was, but recognition only made my body become tense.

"Mother," I whispered. "What are you doing?"

She didn't seem to hear me. She wasn't herself. I hadn't known her to sleepwalk, but with Belinda, anything was possible.

"Mother," I whispered again. I nearly reached out to touch her shoulder but then pulled my hand back, worried that if I touched her she'd scream. She was transfixed by the headless bride, who was illuminated ever so slightly by the moonlight. Belinda stared at the dress, eyes wide and unblinking. I let out a faint whimper. It scared me to see her this way. "Mother? What do you see?" She continued to stare into the library, fearful, the way I thought she must look when she encountered one of her ghosts. "It's all right. It's just Aster's dress."

No response. It was as if she hadn't seen or heard me. "Mother?"

Finally, she looked down at me, her eyes like a doll's, like dark beads lacking any spark of life. "They're coming for us, Iris. *Run!*"

5.

I did as she commanded, racing back to my room and hurrying into bed. I pulled the covers up over my head and didn't sleep for the rest of the night, listening for footsteps in the hallway, for whomever was coming for us. But there was nothing.

I arose before dawn and put on one of my sundresses. In the girls' library, the headless bride greeted me, calm and demure in the blue morning light, not ruffled by the night's events as I was. I'd brought another duffel bag and looked around, deciding what to take next. If Aster had come into the library, she probably wouldn't have noticed anything amiss. The white boxes that had held the wedding favors were still neatly stacked against the wall. The gown and veil were still in place, and only a few of the wedding gifts were missing from the tables.

I didn't dare touch the dress or the veil. Even I knew that in a room where everything was off-limits to me those were the most off-limits. I imagined for a moment taking the gown off the dress form, but that's as far as I got in my fantasy. The thought of touching the dress made me sick to my stomach. I'd have to stop the wedding without ruining that.

I looked over the tables and decided on the wedding china. How could I not? The creamy white porcelain was decorated with pink apple blossoms. Not roses, of course; Aster knew better than that. It must have been a challenge to find a floral-patterned china without roses. There were stacks of the Wedgwood dishes — plates, bowls, cups, and saucers, eight place settings in all. I carefully loaded the dinner plates into the duffel bag first, wishing I could run back to my bedroom for some clothes to wrap around the dishes to muffle the sound of them clanking together, but I couldn't take the risk of being seen by one of my sisters. By the time I got all the plates loaded into the duffel bag, it was full and nearly too heavy to lift. The rest of the china would have to stay.

I strained to carry the bag, especially without making a noise, and as I crept past my parents' wing and down the stairs, I acknowledged to myself that taking the china was unlikely to stop the wedding, but it was all I could think to do. I'd chip away at the wedding in any way I could. Maybe it would all add up to something meaningful.

There was no smell of coffee to greet me at the bottom of the stairs as there usually was. Dovey wasn't up and Mrs. O'Connor hadn't arrived, so the kitchen was empty and only dimly lit by the hint of the sun through the windows. I slipped out the kitchen door and shut it quietly behind me.

It was already warm outside; whatever chill there'd been in the night had been unable to overtake the residual heat of the previous day. Once I got to the edge of the forest, I set down the bag and dragged it behind me by one of its straps, pulling it along over the fallen branches and tree roots, the bag making an awful clatter that echoed and scared the birds. All the time I was walking, I could hear my mother's voice: *They're coming for us, Iris. Run!*

What did she mean? I didn't know who was coming for us, but I pulled the bag along, hoping to arrive soon at the clearing where we'd buried the other things. I was suddenly annoyed that my sisters were luxuriating in their beds while I was working all by myself to stop whatever calamity awaited Aster and therefore awaited us all. Even my mother was asleep or else in her room, lost to her hauntings.

I can't help but think now, all these many decades later, that if I'd had any foresight back then I would have dropped the bag and kept trudging through the forest up through Massachusetts and Vermont to the Canadian border and beyond, far away from the wedding cake and Bellflower Village. I could have lived in a cave and saved myself the trauma that lay just ahead. But hindsight is twenty-twenty, as the cliché goes, and who could have imagined what was in fact to come. Not even Edgar Allan Poe, I'd say.

. . .

When I arrived in the clearing, my arms aching and burning, I decided not to dig another hole. I sat on a log at the edge of the clearing, the duffel bag at my feet, and looked at the previous hole, or at least the top of it that was covered with earth, the grave of Aster's wedding dreams. The two shovels Zelie and I had left behind were crisscrossed on top of it.

After resting for a bit, I took the plates from the bag and dropped them one by one onto the ground around the previous hole. Some landed faceup, others facedown, but none of them broke. They looked like fragile things, but they were sturdy and would have lasted many decades in Aster's kitchen. I felt a twinge of nostalgia for an imagined future (is there a word for that?), but it wasn't enough to stop me.

I finished scattering the plates, the white circles resting on the dark ground of the clearing like some sort of offering to the gods or an alien landing pattern. I took the blade of my shovel and stabbed one of the dinner plates in the center, finding its tender place and cracking it in half. I stabbed it again and again, breaking it into wedges as if it were some dainty pale citrus fruit.

I moved on to the rest of the plates, letting out a whoop, a little war cry, with every attack. It felt good to destroy the dishes. I had that rush I'd had the day before during the digging, a feeling of exhilaration. I could smell the earth and the blood between my legs, and I kept whooping as I cracked the china, then I cried, and then it was over. The ground was covered in places by white shards, a fine white powder that looked like summer snow. I hoped, somehow, it might be enough.

6.

I fell asleep in the forest on top of the empty duffel bag. I woke to the sound of Belinda's voice: *Run!*

It was too hot to run. I didn't know what time it was, but I knew that I was in the thick of the day, one of those days from June 1950 that felt as if the earth had moved closer to the sun.

Standing up, I noticed a trail of blood running down my inner right leg into my sandal. I tried to wipe it away with my hand but only managed to smear it all over my calf. The sight of it reminded me of the scrapes of childhood when I'd limp back to the house after some minor injury and Dovey would wipe it off with a cotton pad and dab it with antiseptic.

I left the clearing and walked back to the house, leaving the filthy duffel bag behind but taking one of the shovels with me. They'd both have to be put back in the shed before anyone noticed they were missing, but I left one behind in case I found a time to return.

Mr. Warner, the groundskeeper, laughed when he saw me limping toward the shed, overheated and thirsty and carrying his shovel. "Still digging for buried treasure, I see." Several summers before, inspired by a series of children's novels about pirates, Zelie and I had borrowed trowels from Mr. Warner and spent our days digging for treasure all over the property, leaving upturned patches of earth that looked like they were made by some wandering rodent.

I handed Mr. Warner his shovel and smiled without saying anything, praying he didn't notice the blood on my leg. As I left him and turned toward the house, I saw Aster standing in the open kitchen doorway, waiting for me. The sight of her brought dread.

"Iris?" she said.

By the tone of her voice — bland inquisitiveness — I couldn't tell if she knew what I'd done. I didn't answer but headed through Mrs. O'Connor's vegetable patch, the rows of carrots and lettuce and basil, careful not to trample any of it, no longer free to destroy what I wanted. Aster looked me up and down, an expression of bafflement on her face. She didn't seem ready to pounce. Maybe she didn't know.

"What have you been doing?" she said. Zelie appeared behind her, and when she saw me, she turned away, knowing very well what I'd been doing.

"I went for a walk," I said, slinking past Aster through the doorway, not making eye contact.

"You missed breakfast *and* lunch," she said to my back, as I made my way out of the kitchen and began to walk upstairs to the girls' wing.

"Get cleaned up," Aster called after me. "We're going out."

I rinsed myself off in the tub, the dirt and blood going down the drain. Freshly bathed and dressed, I headed to find my sisters, assuming they hadn't given up waiting for me. The doors in my parents' wing were closed, the corridor dark, and I thought of my mother stewing in the poisoned air of her sitting room. I paused for a moment, considering whether to tell her what I was up to; it might have put her at ease.

"Iris?" Aster shouted from downstairs. "Where are you?"

I moved on; I didn't have time to deal with Belinda. I walked down the central staircase and saw my sisters in a gaggle in the entryway. They looked up at me en masse as I descended, as if I were a debutante at a ball. I was uncomfortable in their attention, a discomfort born of guilt. I hadn't realized I felt guilty until I walked down those steps. I tugged at the bottom of my dress in case they could see the belt and the pad. They all looked mildly annoyed. Maybe Zelie had tattled and they knew what I'd done. I forged ahead bravely, down the last few steps, wading into their midst, into the swish of sherbet cotton dresses, the cloud of lilac and honeysuckle perfumes. They shuffled their feet to make room for me, a quiet scuffing on the entry tiles, their eyes fixed on me all the while, the deep blues and rich greens.

"Finally," Aster said, packing so much into that single word that I knew she would make an excellent mother. She had been mothering me my whole life after all.

Aster opened the front door and a wall of heat slammed into us. My sisters followed her out to the car; I brought up the rear and closed the door behind us. Rosalind and Calla sat in the front next to Aster, with Daphne, Zelie, and me in the back seat. Zelie and I were next to each other, the hems of our dresses touching, but we didn't look at each other or speak.

Aster was taking us into the village. We relied on her for all our outings, and I wasn't sure what we'd do when she was gone. I supposed Rosalind would take her place; she'd failed her driving test but was getting ready to take it again. Aster had full use of the car our father had bought for our mother, a wood-paneled Hudson Commodore that Belinda never drove. I don't even know if she had a license.

I enjoyed the ride into the village despite being the outcast. They were all upset with me, though none of them besides Zelie knew the real reason they should be upset. For now, it was just irritation — I'd strayed without explanation, and without Zelie, and had returned sulky. I rolled down the window and leaned my head partially out, letting the breeze have its way with me and studying the countryside, the canyons of emerald and peridot I adored. I was learning about color in art class. A shade I call Connecticut green still makes its way onto my palette now, and oh how I would love to see the real thing again.

"Iris," Rosalind said, having turned around to look at me. "If you run face-first into a telephone pole, you'll ruin the wedding photos with your bloody bandages."

I pulled my head in. There were already storm clouds swirling through the car; I didn't need to make it worse by being needlessly defiant.

In the village, Main Street was nearly empty. Most of the children and their mothers were off swimming: pool, ocean, lake, it didn't matter. Any body of water would do. Aster parked the car in front of the ice cream parlor and we trooped out in our bright sundresses. We sat in a corner booth near the window. Aster and Rosalind ordered cherry Cokes, Zelie and I our usual clown sundaes. Daphne chose the largest banana split on the menu and devoured it within minutes while Calla ordered nothing, then the two of them asked to be excused, Daphne to spend the afternoon with her friend Veronica Cream and Calla to the library.

Aster was clearly annoyed at their wanting to leave. "We won't have many more of these outings together," she said with a tone of sentimentality.

"Then don't marry Matthew and stay with us," Daphne said. It was meant as a joke, but it didn't land that way. I'm sure it just reminded Aster once more of Belinda's warning.

"Go on, then," Aster said. When they'd left, she glanced at me. I knew I didn't have the option of going anywhere.

The sundae was my first food of the day, and the strawberry ice cream sat uneasily in my stomach. Aster and Rosalind spread out wedding magazines on the table, and a couple of their friends joined us, local girls from the village. I can't remember exactly who, but I believe Pauline Popplewell was there. (Yes, *that* Pauline Popplewell. I've now taken a retroactive dislike to her although at the time I didn't mind her.) Aster and Rosalind had planned every aspect of the wedding, and almost everything was finished, but still they pawed through the magazines, searching for even more ways to make this one day perfect no matter that the wedding was on Saturday. I couldn't understand how they weren't tired of thinking about it. It had plagued us for so many months, like the chicken pox I'd had a few years earlier, though that had blessedly resolved itself much faster.

The girls talked about the honeymoon for a while, marveling that by this time next week Aster and Matthew would have set sail for Europe on the Cunard Line. They would visit London, Paris, Rome, Athens, and finally the Holy Land, a whole month of travel as newlywed husband and wife. Aster had already packed for the trip, her cases full of dresses and handbags and matching shoes all having been taken to the home she and Matthew would share after the wedding. Zelie and I had been promised postcards from each stop on the tour.

Aster's hairstyle for the wedding was the next topic since she had changed her mind about it so many times. Up or down? That was the burning question, and they discussed it as if they were at a United Nations summit. Zelie participated eagerly, suggesting they hold a vote to see which hairstyle from the magazines was best. I looked outside at the empty street, nibbling the sugar-cone clown hat. The bellflowers in the flower boxes were wilted and shriveled. The only people on the village green were lying on the grass, appearing overtaken by some spreading contagion. A man in a suit napped, his hat over his face to block the sun. A baby crawled on the grass and over its lethargic mother. As bad as it was in the village, it was worse in the cities. Dovey had gone to New York on her day off and said the city was baked in, with boiling asphalt and concrete, and sweaty, flush-faced hordes that looked as if every one of them worked in a laundry.

"Which hairstyle do you like, Iris?" Aster pushed two magazines toward me, each of them open at the desired place. While I'd been staring out the window, they'd voted, and the two images Aster had pushed in my direction were the finalists. One of the brides was an apple-cheeked brunette with her hair in soft curls draped over her bare shoulders while the other bride was an icy-looking blonde with her hair in a French twist.

"Who cares?" I said, and pushed the magazines back to Aster.

"What's wrong with you today?" she said.

"Ignore the little devil, she's hormonal," Rosalind said. She closed the magazines and the half circle of female faces around the booth frowned at me in unison.

I hated to see Aster hurt. Of all my sisters, even Zelie, it pained me the most when I did something to hurt Aster. But this was for her own good. I was trying to save her.

7.

"Back to the manse?" Rosalind asked after we'd climbed into the car minus Daphne and Calla. Zelie, alone with me in the back seat, refused to look in my direction.

Aster considered Rosalind's question, gripping the steering wheel, the car's engine gently purring. "No," she said, putting it into gear. "Let's go to the house. *My* house."

Rosalind and Zelie jumped to agree, and Aster glanced at me through the rearview mirror; I stared back blankly. She pulled away from the curb onto Main Street and we were off, headed to the home of the future Mr. and Mrs. Matthew Maybrick of Rye, New York. None of us had seen the house, not even Rosalind to her dismay. Matthew had finalized the purchase only a week before, and Aster had wanted us to visit after they'd set things up. But apparently she'd changed her mind.

We left Bellflower Village through the green canyons again until we arrived in Greenwich, then turned onto the highway to Rye. We passed billboards and neon signs, dull in the daytime, and filling stations and hamburger stands, all with their saturated artificial colors — a short drive but a long way from the gem tones of Bellflower Village and the grandeur of the wedding cake.

I had my window rolled down again, but I didn't stick my head out. Aster and Rosalind and Zelie were chattering on about the wedding, having moved on from hairstyles to flowers, and how disappointed Aster was that she couldn't use any flowers from our mother's garden in her bouquet, given how they were sagging in the heat, so all the flowers were being brought in from a florist in New York City.

It was the first time Belinda had been mentioned all day. Since that dinner, life had gone on without our mother as it always had, and my sisters didn't seem to notice or care. Though I supposed the reverse was also true; Belinda likely didn't even know we'd left the house.

Off the highway and onto the Boston Post Road, we were enveloped by trees again. Aster drove us by the station so we could see where Matthew would catch the train to the city every day.

"He's enjoying his last few days of city life," Aster said, as she stopped to let a young woman pushing a baby carriage cross the road. Aster and Matthew hadn't seen each other for more than a week. Matthew was working long hours before the wedding and honeymoon, and after work he'd enjoyed not one but two bachelor parties.

"Last few days of freedom, more like it," Rosalind said. I watched for Aster's reaction, but she only joined in the laughing. Whenever anyone talked about the wedding, they spoke about it as the start of something exciting for Aster but as an end for Matthew. I didn't understand why, since it was Matthew who'd courted Aster and Matthew who had proposed. Matthew did all the asking, and Aster only had to say yes.

Rosalind leaned over and elbowed Aster. "I kid, sister dear. Although I think I'd rather live in the city than here," she said, as we idled outside a dry cleaner's and a bank. "Come to *Rye* and *die* of boredom. New town motto."

"Rozzy," Aster said. "I think it's charming. And you know I'm not one for city life. Every time we go into New York, I get a terrible headache."

"Then at least keep a little pied-à-terre near Central Park. You might need it."

"Need it for what?"

"To keep yourself from going stark raving mad, that's what. Just look at Mother. It's in our blood, you know."

"*Rozzy*," Aster said again. She looked through the rearview mirror to see if Zelie and I had been paying attention.

"What's in our blood?" Zelie asked.

"Nothing," Aster said. "There's nothing in our blood."

When the woman with the baby carriage was safely on the sidewalk, Aster proceeded, driving us to the end of the main road then turning into the residential streets. She took several wrong turns, only having been to the house twice before. Matthew had taken care of everything to do with the place up to this point, but when they moved in, Aster would take over.

"He said I can pick out the rest of the furniture myself," she said excitedly, as we drove along. "And I can choose the wallpaper too. I'll have a budget, but knowing Matthew, it'll be generous."

"He knows he's marrying a woman of great taste," Rosalind said. "Maybe once you finish with your house, you'll become a professional decorator."

"You know he'd never allow that."

"I was only kidding. I know Matthew has *rules*."

"Nothing I didn't happily agree to. I never wanted a career."

We eventually passed a sign that said APPLESEED ESTATES, the housing development where Aster and Matthew would live, where every house was new; not long after, we arrived at Grouse Court, a small cul-de-sac with the colonial Matthew had bought in the very center.

Before we turned into Grouse Court, Aster wanted us to take a moment to admire the house from across the street. "Matthew says it's called a four-over-four," she said. "Four rooms downstairs and four rooms up. Completely symmetrical." It was a boxy white house with a steep pitched roof and red-brick chimney. There were four windows on the bottom floor and four on the top, and they were perfectly aligned, with black decorative shutters on either side. The entire house would have fit on the front lawn of the wedding cake with plenty of room to spare.

"Do you like it?" Aster asked us.

"Oh yes!" said Rosalind.

"It's dreamy!" Zelie said. She scooted over next to me to get a better look.

"Forget what I said earlier, I need one of these for myself, it's simply darling," Rosalind said.

"It's not a pocketbook, Roz."

"I know, but I want one *and* I want the man who comes with it. A matching set."

There were two other houses in Grouse Court, one on either side of Aster and Matthew's, another colonial, that one yellow, and a brownish house shaped like a barn. Outside the yellow colonial, a little girl who couldn't have been more than a year old stood on the sidewalk, naked except for a diaper, her bottle dangling from her mouth. She had a little gut that extended over the top of her diaper, which looked to be pinned too tightly around her waist.

"Look at that horrid little creature," Rosalind said, and we all strained for a better look. "She's like a gargoyle on Notre Dame Cathedral. Where's her mother?"

Just then, a harried young woman stomped out of the house, a high school student by the looks of her. She picked up the little girl and carried her inside.

"Babysitter," Aster said.

"Don't ask for her telephone number," Rosalind replied.

8.

I can recall every inch of Aster's house as if I were there only yesterday. It is, as they say, burned into my memory. It rests there in the underworld of my mind where that June day was nestled into the soft tissue, stitched up and cauterized (hence the burning). The white colonial at 64 Grouse Court (see, I remember the address) and perhaps all of Appleseed Estates is there, with its tidy flower beds and hedgerows, and its porch lights to guide me when I go wandering in my dreams and don't know where I am.

The inside of the house smelled like fresh paint and pine, unlike the musty nineteenth-century breath of the wedding cake. The walls were white and bare, and there wasn't a lot of furniture yet. Just inside the front door was a staircase. To the left was a living room, sunken by two steps, with a sofa, a wingback chair, and a coffee table, all of them wrapped in plastic. In the dining room to the right, there was a long mahogany table and six chairs as well as a china hutch, likewise wrapped in plastic.

I'd never been inside a new house before. It was startlingly blank and empty with possibility. Zelie had run outside to the backyard, which was fenced in with grass and a ring of saplings. I stayed inside while Aster showed Rosalind around. They moved from room to room, and I trailed behind as Aster pointed out various things and Rosalind predictably gushed over them. Aster mentioned certain wedding presents, pointing to where a particular vase or the pair of crystal candlesticks would go, things that I knew were dead in their forest grave. She hoped that while they were in Europe for their honeymoon they would find the perfect painting to hang above the fireplace.

"Maybe if you ask nicely, Daddy will let you take the Annie Oakley portrait," Rosalind said in jest.

"No guns in this house, please."

"Not even a pistol to stash in a nightstand? Could be useful in case you need to shoot a burglar."

"There's no crime here," Aster assured her. "This is an exclusive area."

The two of them went upstairs and I stayed in the living room, taking a seat on the plastic-wrapped sofa, which was white with some sort of blue flowers peeking through. Always flowers. I heard their footsteps above me as they explored the bedrooms, moving through each one quickly. They were empty; there wasn't much to see. They talked about setting up a nursery, and Rosalind said she was willing to bet they'd need it by next summer, and I thought of the gargoyle baby with the bottle dangling from her mouth.

"Are you sure you want to spend your wedding night here?" Rosalind said in hushed tones, but her voice echoed and trailed down the stairs — Rosalind never realized how loud she was. Even at a remove, I heard the exaggerated scandal in her voice as she said "wedding night."

I had a vague idea what a wedding night was. Daphne had told Zelie and me about the basics of sex. She said that after a woman has sex for the first time there's blood on the sheets, and every man wants to see the blood so he knows his wife was a virgin before him. When Zelie asked Daphne where the blood came from, she had no explanation. She described everything in the most superficial way, likely not understanding most of it herself.

As I waited for Aster and Rosalind to come back downstairs, I wondered what Daphne would have made of the new house. Maybe Aster had brought us to see it precisely because Daphne wasn't with us to sully the place. Daphne was the only one of us to use bad language, read pulpy novels, and bring home smut, like the photo of a naked lady she'd cut out of a magazine and an old photo from Victorian times of a naked man on top of a naked woman. We never knew where she got any of it; I suspected these things came from her friend Veronica, the friend she was spending the afternoon with while I had to endure this tour of Grouse Court.

"Don't you think it's romantic?" Aster said from upstairs. "To spend our first night together in our own home?"

"I think the Plaza is *more* romantic."

"Oh Roz," Aster said. She must have said "Roz" or "Rozzy" a hundred times a day in the same tone of playful chastisement. I imagined her alone in the house all day when Matthew was at work. "Oh Roz!" she would say, but no one would be there to hear it.

"We'll only be here two nights before the honeymoon. He told me the house is off-limits on Friday, so I think he has something planned, you know, to set up for after the wedding."

Rosalind sighed loudly, dramatically. "Spare a thought for me at home in the flower shop, will you? When you're on your honeymoon, maybe I'll have Daphne break in here and paint all the walls just like at home. Picture it: a desert landscape with tumbleweeds in the living room, a Venus flytrap in your bedroom —"

"Stop!"

"Seaweed in the bathroom, a haunted oak tree in the baby's nursery."

"Don't you dare."

They came back down the stairs and I got up from the sofa, following them into the kitchen, the next stop on the tour. The kitchen was blinding in its infinite yellow, with lemon-colored cabinets and appliances, and Formica countertops speckled with gold. In front of the French doors that led to the backyard, there was an empty space where a kitchen table would go, where Aster's children would eat cereal and toast before school, and Matthew would read the newspaper and drink coffee, all of it served up by Aster since she wouldn't have a cook. Aster pulled various things from the kitchen cupboards to show Rosalind — a bag of flour, a bottle of cooking oil, boxes of cake mix, canned peas. "When I came out last time, I made Matthew take me to the supermarket to buy a few things just to make the house more homey."

"Please tell me you're not going to cook again," Rosalind said.

"I'm going to be a married woman soon. And it's what Matthew wants." As she said Matthew's name, she held her bejeweled left hand out in front of her and admired it, doing so instinctually like a pregnant woman rubs her belly.

"What's the point of marrying a rich man if you don't get the perks? Even our frugal father shells out for a cook. You might as well move into a cave and wear burlap."

"It's a new era," Aster said. "It's 1950."

"*Pft,*" Rosalind said, then she turned to me. "You're awfully quiet, you nasty creature. Aren't you impressed by Casa Maybrick?"

I shrugged, standing in front of the French doors and looking out to where Zelie was in the backyard. She chased after a white cat that must have climbed over the fence. The small yard exemplified how I felt about the house — penned in. I envied Aster for getting to leave the wedding cake, but this house didn't feel like freedom to me, with its low ceilings and thin walls, its perfect symmetry, its tiny patch of grass out back crammed together with the rest of the neighborhood. There was barely anywhere to move or breathe, to be alone, to keep secrets. The wedding cake was full of secrets.

"Iris, are you upset by what Mother said at dinner the other night?" Aster said. "I can't think of any other explanation for your attitude."

I turned from the window to her; she was standing in front of the oven. "I don't want something terrible to happen to you." In the cramped house, I felt panicky, suffocated. I fanned myself with my hand. "Why do you have to move here?" I asked. "Why can't you stay in college and get married later?"

Aster looked down at her ring finger, distress on her face. I was hurting her again and I didn't want to do that.

Rosalind walked over to me, her heels gently tapping on the linoleum. She grasped my shoulders and demanded that I make eye contact. "Mother tries to scare us with all sorts of dark ideas, but none of them are true." She paused, clearly wanting to say something but holding back. "How can I put this delicately?" She bit her bottom lip, her standard move when thinking. "You know that when our mother was born, *her* mother died?" I nodded. I didn't know much about my mother's past then, but I did know that her mother was named Rose, that Rose had died giving birth to her, and that Belinda hated roses.

"It was a horrible trauma for our poor mother, to have killed her *own* mother, and that's what's caused all her problems." (See, we were all always trying to find the root of the problem.) "To make matters worse, she doesn't know what it means to be a mother because she was never mothered herself. Do you see? She's made a mess of everything, but it's not her fault. Imagine a wolf from the forest being captured and brought in to raise six human babies."

"Rozzy," Aster said.

"It's not far off. All that howling. Good grief."

I had a thought just then, something that hadn't occurred to me before. I wanted to think for a minute, to bite my lip like Rosalind did, but they were waiting for my response. "Maybe what happened to Grandma Rose is going to happen to you," I said to Aster. "You're going to have a baby and die." Aster flinched. Like a muddy footprint, the word *die* didn't belong in her neat new house.

"Is that what you're worried about?" she asked. "That I'm going to die in childbirth?"

"There's no death here," Rosalind said. "This is an exclusive area."

Aster frowned at Rosalind, then turned to me. "I can assure you nothing like that is going to happen to me. Women don't die in childbirth anymore."

"Iris has a point, though," Rosalind said. "In our mother's distorted mind, marriage equals sex —"

"Rosalind!" First death, now sex. Aster was horrified.

"Darling, be quiet," Rosalind said. "Iris is a big girl now. As I was saying, in our mother's mind, marriage equals sex, sex equals babies, babies equal death. That's how it was for her mother and her mother's mother and so on."

"But our mother didn't die," Aster said, growing exasperated. "She had six babies and survived. This is all nonsense."

"She carries the horrors of the past with her. She's a product of her past, and though I hate to think of it, so are we." Rosalind shuddered. "And to make matters worse, she hates our father and never wanted to be married. She never wanted *us* either."

"That's an awful thing to say," Aster said.

"Of course it's awful. It also happens to be true. The life she's had since meeting our father — well, it's been like a kind of death for her, hasn't it? Maybe that's the *something terrible* she wants you to avoid."

Aster walked over to where we were standing, likely afraid of what Rosalind would say next. They seemed to have planned this little talk, which had veered off course. "The point of this discussion is just to say that nothing terrible is going to happen, we promise. This is supposed to be a happy time and I wish you could enjoy it."

I nodded in agreement but only to appease her. I knew there was no use in arguing with them. But while I couldn't be certain that Belinda was right, I also couldn't be certain that she wasn't. I'd seen the headless bride in the hole in the forest, had even heard Aster's voice calling for me.

"Can I look around upstairs before we leave?" I asked, anxious to get away.

Aster appeared relieved and told me to explore the bedrooms while she showed Rosalind the laundry room. "Oh goody," Rosalind said.

At the top of the stairs, I stood on the landing. The entire second floor of Aster's house was smaller than the girls' wing at home. There were two bedrooms on either side of the landing and a bathroom in seashell pink straight ahead. Down a hallway, the master suite already had an ornate four-poster bed, its mattress and box spring wrapped in plastic.

I sat on the edge of the bed, then scooted back and lay down. The endless white of the walls was blinding compared to our bedrooms at home. From downstairs, I could hear Aster and Rosalind talking to each other, their voices, the occasional phrase.

"Poached eggs would be lovely," Rosalind said.

I splayed my arms out and moved them back and forth on the plastic. I thought about the wedding night. Aster would be in this bed with Matthew on top of her, both of them naked like the couple in the photo. "Oh Roz," I heard Aster say from downstairs, and I wondered why there would be blood.

9.

At home there was a pile of wedding presents in the entry hall that had been delivered that afternoon, all of them wrapped in shades of ivory and silver and gold with elaborate bows and ribbons. We each grabbed a couple and followed Aster upstairs to the girls' library, where I feared my crimes were about to be discovered. Zelie glanced back at me nervously as Aster and Rosalind led us down the long hallway. I let them go ahead, waiting for the inevitable shouts and screams.

But no, Aster remained unaware of what I'd done, directing us to set the packages down just inside the doorway and barely glancing into the library before heading to her bedroom, deep in conversation with Rosalind the entire time. I set down my packages and looked at the tables where the unwrapped gifts were displayed and saw the gaps where the china and crystal should have been.

Then I heard a squeal of delight coming from Aster and Rosalind's bedroom, then another and another; they seemed to be spreading. When I arrived, I saw that Dovey had brought up the flower-girl dresses for Zelie and me, which had been delivered that afternoon. They were smaller versions of the bridesmaids' dresses for Rosalind, Calla, and Daphne that had been delivered weeks ago. All the dresses were in a light shade of seafoam green, perfect, I thought, for Aster's wedding to the sea creature. She didn't know I called him that in my mind, and she would never know, but she said Cape Cod inspired the color choice, the place she and Matthew had met, where our family had always been happiest.

"The dresses couldn't be more darling," Dovey said with her standard look of happiness, an ever so slight smile, one that would make the Mona Lisa appear ecstatic with joy by comparison.

Aster held up the dresses by their wooden hangers so we could see them, and every time Zelie tried to grab hers, Aster pulled it away, explaining that we couldn't try on the dresses until tomorrow after a bath. We knew they fit, having tried them on at the bridal shop on Meadow Street before Aster had sent them away to have colorful beads shaped like tiny seashells sewn along the necklines.

"What's so exciting?" Daphne said, as she came into the room wearing shorts (we weren't allowed to wear shorts), her knees scuffed, her legs unshaved. Calla wasn't far behind, blinking as if she were just up from a nap.

"The flower-girl dresses are here," Zelie said, causing Daphne to grunt and flop onto Rosalind's bed.

The dresses disappeared into Aster's wardrobe, but that wasn't the end of the surprises. "Your father went to Boston for the day and won't return home until late tonight," Dovey said. "There'll be a cold supper this evening whenever you want it."

Dovey left, and Rosalind spoke with a thrill unfurling in her voice. "Do you know what I'm thinking?" she said, clapping her hands. "How about girls' night?"

"Oh I would love that!" Aster placed her hands over her heart. She was already missing us.

The plan excited us all, even the least excitable among us — Calla and

Daphne perennially, though I had joined them as of late. "Girls' night" meant a picnic dinner outdoors when it was warm or in the girls' sitting room in colder weather. Our father insisted on a hot meal every night, even on the hottest of days, and we were giddy to be liberated from the formality and stuffiness of the dining room where our mother's place would be empty yet again and everything would be awkward.

We relaxed in the girls' sitting room until dinnertime, lazing on the viridescent fabrics, the whole room the shade of tree buds bursting into spring. Aster had brought in a tray of lipsticks, the ones she was considering for the wedding, and Rosalind tried them on so Aster could see how they looked on someone else. Rosalind would apply one of the lipsticks, smile, pucker, and give air kisses before wiping it off with a tissue and trying on another. They were all in shades of pink and red. After Rosalind modeled seven different shades from fuchsia and amaranth to ballet slipper and carnation, Aster decided on her favorite: Cherry Blossom, a light springy pink. This had been her favorite all along, and Rosalind — who'd advocated for Blushing Coral — felt her modeling had been for naught. Calla then read to us from Tennyson; no one listened but me. Zelie took the discarded lipsticks and sat in a corner with them, trying on each of them without wiping any off, a cocktail of pink on her lips. Aster and Rosalind filed their nails and chatted while Daphne sketched.

Calla continued to read even as she was interrupted by jokes and shrieks of laughter until finally the noise in the room became too much for Rosalind, who said: "I'm hungry, let's go!"

We collected the food from the kitchen and headed out to the meadow with blankets and picnic baskets and candles in lanterns for later. We passed the back of the house and Belinda's smaller garden, her "moon garden," as she called it, which contained only night-blooming flowers, those that release their fragrance after the sun goes down — white heliotrope, tuberose, evening primrose, four-o'clocks, and a twisty vine of glow-in-the-dark moonflowers. The air was perfumed with orange, lemon, and vanilla; I inhaled it happily, then looked up and was startled to see Belinda standing at her bedroom window. Dressed in her white nightgown, her long white hair down, she held one of her candles in a jar.

I stopped and called up to her. "Mother!"

My sisters, startled by my voice, paused and stumbled into one another. Belinda was staring out at the grounds, not down at us. Perhaps she'd heard us talking. Even from a distance, I thought she looked frightened, as if she were bracing herself for the night. She must have dreaded the sight of the setting sun, the hour the ghosts were set free in our house.

Rosalind mumbled something, and she and the rest of my sisters walked on, leaving me alone.

"Mother, I'm right here!" I shouted, hoping she'd look down and see me. I wanted to make her smile, to break the night's hold on her. But she just blew out the candle, and in a puff of smoke, disappeared.

10.

In summertime, the meadow practically sparkled with wildflowers — red poppies and lemon bee balm, blue bachelor's buttons and lupine, oxeye daisies and black-eyed Susans. Some of the tall grasses were waist-high. It was a secluded place. We couldn't see the house from the meadow; it was surrounded by trees the way Central Park is surrounded by skyscrapers.

We took off our shoes and spread out our blankets, two sisters to each one. Ravished with hunger, we opened the picnic baskets and pulled out the plates of food Mrs. O'Connor had made for us. We hadn't brought napkins or cutlery; we simply spread out the plates in the center where our blankets intersected and ate with our fingers, picking up bright pieces of cold salmon filet and stuffing them into our mouths, eating hard-boiled eggs in two bites, stripping the meat off chicken legs with our front teeth and tossing the bones aside. We could be like a pack of animals sometimes. We ate all the meat first, then tore the round loaf of brown bread into pieces and wiped the plates clean with it. We ate the wheat crackers and chunks of cheddar, and emptied the jar of green olives, spitting the pits into the grass. Then we moved on to the vegetables, the blanched green beans and radishes with butter. For dessert, cinnamon stars and lemonade; and when we were finally finished, we lay back on our blankets to catch our breath.

It was quiet for a bit as the sky streaked rose, then orange. No one said what we were all thinking: It was our last true night together. Aster was attending a barbecue with Matthew's family the following night, and the next day was wedding eve and the rehearsal; she'd be far too busy and nervous to lounge around with us. There was a heaviness in the air for all of us, and for me, there was something more, a sense of urgency. I hadn't done enough.

Calla enlisted Zelie in the task of making daisy chains, and they sat quietly at the edge of our blankets as they braided the stems together. Daphne pulled a book of matches and a pack of cigarettes from her pocket.

"Do you have to do that?" Aster asked, sitting up and fluffing her ponytail.

"Yes, as a matter of fact."

"Ooh, I want one," said Rosalind, scooting over next to Daphne, the two of them cross-legged and hovering around the lit match between them like two insects.

Daphne lit the candles inside the two lanterns, and I joined Calla and Zelie in making daisy chains.

"Let's go somewhere," Rosalind said, blowing out a cloud of smoke and coughing. "We could go to New York and go dancing."

"And how do you propose we get there?" Aster said, playing along.

"You'll drive us to the station in Greenwich and we'll take the train," Daphne said.

"You, *Daph?*" Aster said. "*You* want to go dancing with boys in New York?"

"There's more to New York than *boys*," Daphne said, smoking much more effortlessly than Rosalind.

"Who cares about boys?" Rosalind said. "I need a man."

"*Rozzy,*" Aster said.

"I want to be engaged by Christmas and married next June. This June it's your turn, Aster dear. Next June it's me. Wait a couple of years and it'll be Calla's turn, then —"

"Stop right there," Daphne said.

"Oh that's right, you're going to *art school* in *Europe*," Rosalind said, putting on airs.

"You and your dull husband can come visit me," Daphne said to Rosalind. "Paris, I'm thinking, or Amsterdam."

Rosalind frowned at this. "Why do you assume my husband will be *dull?*"

"A few days ago, you told us you don't care who he is as long as you're out of here by next summer. That time frame doesn't suggest a careful search for the perfect man."

"*Pft,*" Rosalind replied. "Maybe we won't visit you in Europe *at all*. Now, where was I?" Rosalind looked around at her sisters scattered on the blankets, as if she'd lost track of what she was saying. "Right. Calla goes after me, then we skip Daphne and move on to Iris, but that'll have to wait a few years."

"Yes it certainly will," Aster said.

"And then finally Zelie," Rosalind continued.

"Why am I always last?" Zelie said.

"Because you *are* last, Zelie my darling. Now listen, next June it's my turn," Rosalind explained. "I need to find a man and they don't grow on trees, you know. Tonight could be the most important night of my life."

"Come off it," Daphne said.

"Think of all of them down there, the glittering parties, the nightlife," Rosalind said, moving her shoulders to a silent beat. She usually spoke about New York as being "down there," as if the whole city were kept in our cellar. "They're all down there and we're *here,* practically in a forest, like feral creatures, dirty and uncivil —"

"That's enough of that," Aster said. "We are not dirty, thank you."

We were all insulted by Rosalind at the time, but in a way, she was right, which I can only see now, looking back on things. We weren't dirty or feral, but we weren't very cultured either, considering our family's money and social status. And despite our proximity to New York City, there was something slightly *rural* about us, we six pieces of rose quartz freshly dug from the earth but not yet polished. It was just as well that Aster had wanted to live in the suburbs, since she would have been a lamb surrounded by wolves in New York society. We'd never even been to Europe, although the war had complicated the opportunity for that. But we'd never traveled outside the Northeast at all. We may have lived like princesses compared to the average American girl, but unlike other girls of our class, we had seen and experienced very little.

"We have to go to New York *tonight,* that's the event that sets everything else in motion," Rosalind said. "And for you, Aster dear, it'll be one last *splash* before married life."

"When have we ever experienced any kind of *splash*?" Calla said, not looking up from her daisies.

"Precisely! When have we ever done anything fun at all?" Rosalind said.

"You'll have fun on Saturday at my wedding, remember that?"

"We heard something about it," Daphne said. "Every minute of every day, in fact."

"When you're married, it'll be too late to go dancing," Rosalind said, sinking into disappointment.

"Too late to go dancing?" Aster said. "Heavens, I'm not being sent to a prison camp."

"You know what I mean," Rosalind said. "You can't go out with me to meet *men* when you're married."

"I can't do that *now,*" Aster said, becoming exasperated by Rosalind but trying to suppress it. "Don't fret. I won't be far away, and we'll still have all kinds of fun."

"Fine," Rosalind said, giving up easily; she'd known it was a lark. There was no chance we'd take off to New York City without our father's permission, which he would never have given. We had always been good girls. Even Daphne, the naughtiest among us, was mostly well-behaved. We'd had little supervision as we'd grown collectively older, but we didn't stray. It was as if there were one of those electric fences around our house, the kind that gives a dog a zap of electricity if it wanders off the property. Eventually, the owner can turn the electricity off because the dog doesn't dare go too far. That was us. In our silence, we listened to the woodland melody, the crickets and katydids and frogs. The candles glimmered inside the lanterns and reflected off the glass, creating chandeliers of light on the blankets.

The moon, which had been hiding behind the blue, had at last revealed itself in the blackened sky and that was Calla's cue to stand up. "The black bat, night," she said.

She stood behind Aster with a crown of daisies in her hands. She directed Aster to remove her ponytail and let her hair down. Aster did as she was directed, fluffing the dark curls around her shoulders. The crown was made of three winding chains of daisies, and Calla continued to hold it above Aster's head. "And the soul of the rose went into my blood," she recited in her booming poet's voice.

"That's lovely," Aster said. "Who wrote that?"

"Tennyson!" we all said at once.

"Do you know that Matthew hates poetry?" Aster said.

"Then you shall not marry him," Calla said.

"I have to marry him, the wedding's on Saturday." Aster began to laugh, a nervous laugh, a release.

"By this time next week, you'll have been deflowered," Daphne said.

"Daph!" Aster said, looking to Zelie and me, and on cue, Zelie asked: "What's deflowered?"

Aster held her hand over her mouth to stifle her giggling and looked to Rosalind for help. "It's the opposite of *flowered*," Rosalind explained.

With a great deal of solemnity, which didn't seem to be feigned, Calla set the crown of daisies on top of Aster's head. "I crown you the queen rose of the rosebud garden of girls," she said. "Shine out, little head, sunning over with curls, to the flowers, and be their sun."

Rosalind moved one of the lanterns and set it in front of Aster, a makeshift sun. Aster sat primly on the blanket, her legs tucked beneath her, posing like a queen. The lantern's glow illuminated her pink sundress and her rosy smiling face; the white daisy petals in the tumble of her chestnut curls caught the light and shimmered on top of her head. She sat there soaking in our adoration, a scene so heartbreakingly beautiful that it didn't seem like real life. We clasped hands, a circle of six sisters. We inhaled the flowery air, with the insects singing and the twinkling fireflies wrapping themselves around us like a necklace.

This fleeting moment is a forever image. I see it sometimes, as quick as the pop of a flash from a camera: Aster our queen in the rosebud garden of girls in that moment of glowing skin and sparkly daisies. I've seen this flash of Aster sometimes as I'm driving down the road or shopping at the supermarket, the most mundane times. It's not as neatly buried as my other memories, and it reveals itself from time to time before quickly disappearing again, this single moment. The last happy moment of my childhood.

11.

Aster had done her best to keep Matthew and his family away from us during their courtship and the months since their engagement. Whenever Matthew would pick up Aster for a date, she'd wait for him outside, even in the winter, not wanting him to come inside our imposing home, where he might bump into Belinda, or encounter the oddness of Calla and Daphne, or be subjected to endless questions from chatty Zelie. Not that any of these things would have sent Matthew running for his life down the driveway (except, perhaps, for Belinda), but I suspect — and of course I'll never know exactly what went on in my sister's mind — that she was afraid she might lose him to someone more worldly and glamorous, perhaps someone with fewer complications, a young woman from a family with a bit of adultery here and there or unscrupulous financial dealings, those kinds of simple run-of-the-mill scandals that plagued the rich but were miles away from the state of the Chapel family, with our supernatural visitations and reclusiveness, our many floral-scented daughters, a seemingly endless string of us and not a male heir in sight.

Aster and Matthew spent their time together with Matthew's family and friends at gatherings at estates along the Connecticut coastline and on Long

Island, at dinner parties and concerts in New York, and at the Maybrick summer home in the Hudson River Valley. Sometimes Rosalind would tag along, hunting for a man of her own. They'd make a threesome, and when Matthew drove the girls home, Aster would never invite him inside for a drink. Perhaps that added to her allure.

But with just two days left until the wedding, Aster couldn't put them off anymore. Matthew, his parents, and his younger sister were driving from New York up to New Haven, where Mrs. Maybrick's brother and his family lived; he was a dean at Yale, and they were having a backyard barbecue to celebrate something or other. Mrs. Maybrick had suggested they stop along the way to have a drink with all of us, then take Aster and Rosalind along with them. Aster had said she thought this was part of a plot by Mrs. Maybrick to get herself inside our house (not her first attempt). She wanted to see us in our natural habitat. Aster said she would have wondered if there even was a barbecue in New Haven if she hadn't been invited to it.

We had spent the entire day preparing for the four o'clock arrival of the Maybricks, helping Aster rearrange the furniture in the front parlor then rearrange it again and again. This room had more of a museum quality than the other rooms, and the décor was prewar — pre–World War One, that is. Like most of the house, it had been decorated by our grandmother, our father's mother. Belinda hadn't changed much of anything when she moved in as a young bride; she didn't care about dead objects like furniture and paintings.

We tried many different arrangements for the Eastlake chairs and the two sofas, a champagne-colored silk sofa with floral stitching and a velvet sofa in emerald green with a serpentine back. We moved around the side tables with the glass lamps and delicate china ornaments. A few severe portraits of our Chapel ancestors, pinch-faced and disapproving, hung on the walls along with several antique Chapel rifles, but there was nothing we could do about those. The rifles upset Aster, who said they made our house look like a hunting lodge. She said Matthew's family home, a townhouse on the Upper East Side, was elegantly decorated in shades of butter and cream, with tasteful paintings of sailboats and ocean scenes on the walls.

"All that matters is how you decorate your *own* home at Goose Court," Rosalind said, attempting to reassure Aster.

"*Grouse* Court."

"The point is that Matthew's mother won't hold this heaping relic against *you*. Our mother and father, perhaps, but not you."

This calmed Aster as much as it was possible to calm her, her nerves likely tangled inside like a cord from an old lamp. She went to the kitchen to check on the food and drinks before heading upstairs to get dressed, demanding that we follow her and be ready by 3:45 in case the Maybricks arrived early. We headed upstairs, following Aster like a string of ducklings. She paused in front of our parents' wing, where our mother's sitting room door was closed. "Iris, get dressed quickly, will you? Then go check on Mother. Dovey reminded her about the Maybricks' visit, but I want to make sure she's ready."

"Are you sure you want her there?" Daphne said.

Aster sighed. "I don't, but Mrs. Maybrick will insist on seeing her."

I wasn't sure why I'd been selected for this job, but I agreed to do it. After putting on my party dress, surely some bright ensemble Aster had selected for me, I went to Belinda's sitting room and knocked on the door.

"Dovey?" she said.

"No, Mother, it's me," I said, my hand on the doorknob, waiting to be invited in. She didn't respond.

"It's Iris," I clarified.

She opened the door and startled me, the doorknob I'd been gripping pulled from my hand. She stood before me wearing a white blouse, a lavender skirt that fell just below her knees, and low black heels. It was surprising to see any color on her. The lavender skirt meant she was making an effort or at least wanted to appear to be doing so.

I stepped into her sitting room, which was unbearably stuffy like the last time I'd visited. The curtains were partly open, and the vase of lilies and her spirit journal were still on the table next to the sofa. She'd been in this room all week, breathing in the poisoned air from the flowers, which I was sure had only made her fears about the wedding worse.

After letting me in and closing the door, she had gone to the mirror, where she was fastening a brooch to her blouse. "Do I look all right?" she asked, turning toward me. Her hands were trembling and she balled them into fists.

I thought her clothes were fine, but her hair was pinned too tightly, revealing her missing earlobes. She sat down on the sofa so I could fix her. I loosened some of the strands at the sides so they'd fall a bit lower to hide her deformity. "Perfect," I said, and she seemed relieved but not entirely well. She pulled a white handkerchief from her pocket and breathed into it. I didn't know she was smelling the roses again, but it was obvious she was sick.

"Should I tell them you're feeling ill?"

"No, no," she said, her voice slightly muffled by the handkerchief. "That'll only create a fuss."

I took a seat next to her since she didn't seem to be intending to leave the room right away even though we'd heard the doorbell. She continued to breathe into the handkerchief, staring ahead at nothing in particular, and I didn't know what to say. I so often craved my mother's attention, but when I had it, I couldn't handle it. She made me nervous.

She lowered the handkerchief and spread it out on her lap, taking several deep breaths, then retching. When I tried to hand her a glass of water from the coffee table, she waved it away. "I failed," she said, smoothing the handkerchief over her knees. The white handkerchief was embroidered with tiny bees. That's what her father had called her when she was a little girl: Bee.

"Why doesn't anyone ever listen to me?"

"I listened," I said, and hesitated to confess what I'd been doing, unsure how she'd react. But she seemed so upset, I was desperate to make it better. "I'm trying to stop the wedding," I told her. "I know it's not enough, but I've already broken Aster's wedding china and some other things. I buried them in the forest. I was going to do more tonight while she's out."

She looked at me, confused.

"I thought if enough of the wedding supplies were gone, maybe she'd have to postpone. I wasn't sure what else to do."

Belinda patted me gently on the knee, and in that pat, I knew she appreciated me. "I know what the terrible feeling is," I said, taking her hand in mine as it rested on my knee. "You think Aster is going to have a baby and die like Grandmother Rose."

At the mention of Rose, her eyes grew more alert; she seemed surprised. She pursed her lips into a kind of faint smile, an acknowledgment of my efforts to understand her. Then her face became serious, and she squeezed my hand tightly, and said, "Aster will never have a child."

She picked up her handkerchief and pressed it to her mouth again, closing her eyes. I thought of the colonial house and the empty bedrooms waiting to be filled with babies. I felt sick at my mother's words. I didn't understand how she could know such things, but I'd felt something was wrong at Grouse Court. Rosalind had warned me about Mother's dark ideas, but I no longer knew which were mine and which were hers.

"I think you should go downstairs and tell them I'll be down in a moment," she said. "I need to collect myself."

I felt she should stay in her sitting room, that in her present state being unleashed into the front parlor with the Maybricks would be like tossing a lit match into a gas tank. But I didn't know how to tell her this, and I knew that if she didn't go downstairs Aster would be cross with both of us.

"All right," I said, and left her.

12.

I sat unnoticed on the central staircase and looked down at the gathering in the front parlor. Matthew's father stood in front of the fireplace with Rosalind, who told a story, moving her hands wildly and laughing, charming Mr. Maybrick as she charmed everyone. My father stood in a corner with Matthew's mother and sister, a much quieter conversation. Calla and Daphne sat next to each other in a pair of Eastlake chairs and emanated boredom while Zelie flitted about the room, eavesdropping on the different conversations and not being included in any of them.

I wondered why Matthew and Aster weren't there, but then I heard the door to the courtyard open and soon they were passing through the entry hall, taking no notice of me above them on the stairs.

"You're being awfully cruel," Aster whispered to Matthew as they walked toward the front parlor, the two of them in the middle of a conversation. "I don't like it when you're cruel."

As he walked behind her, he pinched her side, squeezing a roll of fat. "You know I love your extra flesh," he said, and laughed. "All I meant was that I don't want you to grow any fleshier. You're big enough. What's wrong with that?"

Aster stopped, turning to face him. I could see that she was about to cry.

"Come on, don't get so upset," he said, pulling her close to him, placing his arms around her waist. "You're the one I chose. I don't regret it."

"You mean it?" she asked. He didn't answer and leaned over to kiss her.

They walked together into the parlor, one of his arms still tucked around her waist. For a moment, I wondered if Belinda and I didn't need to worry, that Aster might call off the wedding herself. She'd never mentioned that Matthew could be cruel. But once the two of them joined the others, they gave no hint of the tension I'd just witnessed, and soon the room filled with gaiety, with laughter and smiles, with drinks in hands. I could feel the gaiety edge out toward me like the warmth of a fire.

I stayed on the stairs and watched. In a room of dark heads, my eyes were drawn to golden-haired Matthew. He was dressed casually, his slacks a shade of grassy green, with a striped madras shirt. In my mind, I saw the original version of him, the sea creature splashing out of the water, which would always be the original version. He looked funny fully clothed, unnatural in a way, like a slender blond ape dressed for a party.

The rest of his family appeared drab by comparison, his big bear of a father in muted gray, with a fluffy mustache to match, and his mother in a sleeveless off-white dress the shade of an icicle, with a dainty gold belt around her waist. Her hair, in a tight French twist, was jet-black, enhanced no doubt by dye, and the sharp contrast between her pale skin and dark hair brought to mind a skunk. Matthew's sister, who must have been around Aster's age, was entirely forgettable.

A cold hand on my shoulder made me start. "Are you coming to join us?" my mother asked, as she passed me on the stairs. I said I would in a minute. She continued on, the match about to enter the room, which I feared was already swirling with invisible fumes. All the heads turned to her as she entered, and the room reconfigured as if a dignitary had arrived. My father went to stand next to his wife. She shook hands with Matthew's mother, then his father, then Matthew, who leaned over and gave her a kiss on the cheek.

My father guided my mother onto one of the sofas. Better to get her seated; she'd be more dangerous moving about. Matthew's mother sat on the sofa across from her, and the men sat next to their wives. Matthew and Aster remained standing, each with an arm around the other's waist, their bodies pressed together as they stood side by side.

Matthew had been discussed endlessly but not seen for months by anyone in our family except Aster and Rosalind. My parents and sisters couldn't turn away from him now that he was in our midst and neither could I, with his boyish face and vibrant, beating heart. Aster changed in his presence, and with everyone watching her, it was as if she were putting on a performance — transforming effortlessly from the girl she was with us into the other half of this steel executive, this war hero.

Matthew was talking now, and Belinda reached into her pocket for her handkerchief and placed it over her mouth. I gripped the banister, knowing this was a bad sign. She didn't like Matthew, and I think everyone in the room knew that but didn't know why. I couldn't read my mother's mind, but I knew how she thought, and while I couldn't have articulated it then, it's clear looking back. Where everyone else saw a war hero, my mother saw something different, another version of her husband — a man who'd been engaged in the business of death. She didn't think in terms of heroes and villains, only of violence. Her husband hadn't killed anyone directly — he didn't have the courage for that — but to her, he was only at a slight remove from every pull of a Chapel trigger. Matthew, on the other hand, had killed many people himself, women and children included, as part of a firebombing air raid over Tokyo that had left as many as 100,000 dead. I knew what my mother was thinking as she looked up at him: Soon the hands that had dropped those bombs would be caressing her daughter's naked body.

Matthew stopped talking and Belinda said something, I don't know what — her voice was too quiet and I was too far away to hear — but there was a disturbance in the parlor, I could see it, as mouths opened and heads turned as whatever she said rippled across the room like a wave on the sea.

"Mother, how could you!" Aster shrieked.

Dovey came running from the kitchen, her ears highly attuned to any such disturbance, and she and my father helped Belinda up from the sofa. Dovey hustled her out of the room and outside to her flower garden. Dovey's cure for everything was fresh air.

In the commotion, Mother had dropped her handkerchief on the entry hall tiles, and I walked down the final few steps to pick it up. I didn't look into the parlor, recoiling from the tension that the drama had created, and returned upstairs to my bedroom holding the embroidered bees over my mouth. I didn't want to watch what happened next. This was bad, but it wasn't the explosion. That was still to come.

13.

I sat at the desk in my room for a while, sketching a single calla lily in the middle of the page. Zelie came in eventually, carrying both our flower-girl dresses on their hangers. "Iris, you'll never believe what happened," she said. "Aster is so upset. Mother told the Maybricks we need to cancel the wedding. She said the same thing she did before, that something terrible would happen if we don't."

I wasn't surprised. Belinda's behavior hadn't exactly been unpredictable. "Why do you have our dresses?" I asked.

Zelie said we needed to try them on, that Aster was bringing Mrs. Maybrick and Matthew's sister upstairs to see her wedding gown and that Aster wanted us to model our dresses for them. I grew nervous, not having expected them to come upstairs. I thought they wanted to get to the barbecue in New Haven.

I reluctantly changed, throwing off my party dress and sliding the seafoam fabric over my head. Zelie had dashed from the room in her dress, excited to wear it finally. I didn't follow her but returned to my desk and my drawing, waiting to be called. Aster was certain to discover what I'd done now; it was only a matter of time — minutes, really. No need to rush into it before I had to.

I sketched a little more, then heard echoes of my sisters and the Maybrick women coming upstairs together. I continued drawing, working on one of the delicate curls of the tubular lily, listening to the lively conversation through the open doorway of my bedroom. Aster had recovered from what Belinda had done or was at least pretending to for the sake of the Maybricks. I assumed they had arrived in the girls' library when I heard Matthew's mother and sister gasp, and say, "It's beautiful. It's lovely, like a dream," at the sight of the headless bride.

"I'm so glad you like it," Aster said. Her voice wasn't her usual sweet, milky tone but something slightly soured. Matthew's family probably didn't know her well enough to notice.

More chatter, then came what I'd been waiting for: "Where's my wedding china? Where's the vase and the crystal?" A few minutes passed while they must have been searching the library, then I heard Rosalind's voice: "These boxes are empty. Where are the place settings, the gifts? Zelie, run and get Dovey."

I set down my pencil. Zelie knew who the culprit was, but she must not have said anything, afraid that I'd implicate her too. I heard her running down the hallway and down the stairs. She returned with Dovey soon after, who was as baffled as everyone else. "The maids aren't allowed in this room," she said. "I dust and vacuum in here myself."

"These things didn't just walk off," Aster said, sounding frantic. "I wonder if . . ." She sounded ready to share some theory or other, but then her voice changed, and she spoke in a deeper, more certain tone. "Mother. She did this."

"I can't imagine that Mother would . . . ," Rosalind said, certain at first, then growing less so and finally abandoning her thought.

"I don't think Mrs. Chapel would do something like this," Dovey said, proving that she was the only one in the library who really knew Belinda. Our mother operated in the realm of the psychological — dreams, hauntings, strange ideas — not physical mayhem.

"We'll soon find out," Aster said.

Matthew's mother and sister hadn't spoken since their earlier admiration of the dress, and I wondered if they were still in the room, and if so, what they made of this afternoon matinee at the Chapel residence. If Mrs. Maybrick had in fact invited herself to the wedding cake to gawk at us, she certainly was getting more of a spectacle than she ever could have hoped for, and a behind-the-scenes tour to boot.

I heard loud footsteps down the hallway toward my parents' wing. "Mother!" Aster shouted. There was a hush of other voices as everyone else followed behind. "Come out here, please."

As much as I wanted to stay in my bedroom and pretend none of this was happening, I couldn't let Belinda be blamed for what I'd done. I raced out of my bedroom and ran down the hallway of the girls' wing, then turned right into the hallway that led to my parents' wing, where all the women were gathered.

"Wait!" I called, and they all turned to look at me. Mrs. Maybrick and her daughter were still there, and even at my young age, I knew that good manners should have compelled them to go downstairs and let this family drama unfold in private. But instead they stood on the outer edge of my sisters and Dovey, nearest to the top of the stairs, watching me along with everyone else.

"I did it," I said. "I'm the one to blame."

"What did you do?" Aster asked. She was trying to stay measured in front of her future in-laws, and I was unexpectedly grateful for their bad manners.

"I ruined your china and crystal. I ruined all of it."

"*Ruined* it? What do you mean?"

"I destroyed it."

The group struggled to absorb this news.

"But why?" Aster asked.

I glanced at the Maybricks, trying to think of a way to finesse this, but it wasn't possible. "I wanted to stop the wedding."

As had happened earlier in the parlor, a wave spread across the group as they turned to look at one another in disbelief. Then Mrs. Maybrick strode boldly forward into the center of things.

"Is there some reason you and your mother don't want Aster to marry my Matthew? Do you think Matthew isn't good enough for *this* family?" As she spoke, she jabbed her finger in my direction, three gold bangles clattering on her arm. "Because I can assure you that —" She paused for a burst of bitter laughter, her face contorted in barely suppressed rage. I braced myself for whatever cruelty would come next, but Aster stepped in before she could finish.

"Delyth," Aster said, putting her arm around her future mother-in-law. "This is a difficult situation to explain, but it has nothing to do with Matthew."

"I should hope not."

Dovey made an attempt to usher Mrs. Maybrick and her daughter down the stairs, but they weren't as easy to hustle away as my mother. Neither of them budged. For all Belinda's challenges, she was easy to keep stashed in a room out of sight.

"Iris," Aster said, her head held high with whatever pride she had left. "Go to your room and we'll talk about this later."

The others seemed to disappear for a moment as Aster and I locked eyes. Hers, usually so light and friendly, were weary, her lids heavy. The Aster from the night before, the beautiful queen rose of the rosebud garden of girls, was fading away even then, a watercolor painting drenched with rain.

"Aster," I said, hating that I had added to her hurt on this most difficult day. "I was trying to help you. It's not just Mother who has a bad feeling. I think I do too."

"Enough," she said, covering her face with her hands for a moment, trying not to scream. "Just go to your room." I knew there was nothing more I could say. I turned and walked away.

I'd only taken a few steps, however, when Aster shouted: "Iris, look what you've done!" She came up behind me and pulled up the back of my dress. I turned to see bright-red blood saturating the seafoam fabric. The stain was a coral reef, jagged and enormous.

"Oh no," I said at the shock of red.

Calla, in her poet's voice, began to speak: "'The curse is come upon me,' cried the Lady of Shalott." Aster told her to shush.

I'd been keeping my emotions contained, but now tears filled my eyes, hot salty humiliation. I'd bled on and off for months, and I'd kept it private until now, when it was revealed to all: my scarlet shame. I tugged the back of my dress from Aster's hands, wanting desperately to hide. Eight sets of eyes were on me and there was no sympathy to be found, no commiserating glance, not even the kindness of looking away. There was a sense, I could feel it, that I'd gotten what I deserved. But karma rarely works so swiftly.

Aster grabbed my upper arm, her fingernails cutting into me. "Ow," I said, as she pulled me down the hallway and around the corner to the girls' wing. Dovey and Rosalind were right behind us. Dovey tried to calm Aster, but she wouldn't let go of my arm, the day's rage finally finding an outlet. We arrived at my bedroom and she pushed me inside and I went stumbling forward into the bed. She came up behind me and attempted to wrestle the dress off of me.

"You ruined it," she shouted. "And I wouldn't doubt you did it on purpose." She was trying to hike the dress up over my head, but I wouldn't cooperate, keeping my arms pinned straight at my sides, crying heavily now. My lack of cooperation inflamed her temper, and she kept tugging at the dress until I heard the fabric tear.

Dovey and Rosalind tried to pull her off me, but she elbowed them away. "We have to wash it," she said through gritted teeth.

"Aster dear," Dovey said, finally wrenching the fabric from her hands. "The dress is ruined. Washing it won't help."

There was a moment of silence, a catching of breath. I turned around to face Aster, pulling down my dress and brushing the hair away from my wet face. "Take the dress and burn it for all I care," Aster said. "You're not going to be a flower girl. Zelie will do it herself. In fact," she went on, determined, "I don't want you to come to the wedding at all."

"This wasn't her fault," Rosalind said.

"Oh? And what about everything else she's done?"

"Why don't we talk about this later?" Rosalind, who was normally so confident, seemed cowed by Aster's outburst.

"I don't want Mother at the wedding either. Dovey, will you tell her? Not that she'll care. She'll probably be relieved."

"Aster," Dovey said, reaching out. "Your own mother?" Aster pulled away and left the room. Rosalind and Dovey followed quickly behind.

Alone again, I placed my hand on the edge of the bed to steady myself, the rest of my body as rigid as a clothespin. I heard consoling coos and footsteps going down the hallway to the stairs. And then everything went quiet.

After a few moments, during which I was unable to find the will to move, I wanted to know if the Maybricks had left. I went to the girls' library, which had a window with a view out the front. Matthew's father had opened the door of his silver sedan for his wife and daughter, both of whom got into the front seat, then he went around to the driver's side and got in himself. While that was happening, Matthew, Aster, and Rosalind went outside, Rosalind walking slightly ahead to give the couple privacy. As he had in the parlor, Matthew had his arm around Aster's waist but now was gently rubbing her side.

I should have felt sorry for Aster; the day had been disastrous, exceeding even her worst fears. But I didn't. As the Maybricks' car drove away, my tears flared up again and so did my anger. I'd acted out of love, a desire to protect my sister, and she'd embarrassed me in front of everyone.

I wanted to take a bath and wash off the blood and the tears. I turned to leave the library and faced the headless bride. I'd seen her so many times over the past few months, I didn't always pay attention. But now her beauty stopped me, the creamy silk and feminine lines, the curves of Aster's body the dress had been fitted around.

My anger swelled again and a bit of madness with it, my mother's madness running through my blood. I pulled up my seafoam flower-girl dress and stuck my right hand into my underpants, then my left, until both were sticky with traces of blood, then I rubbed them together.

The creamy silk of the gown was as luscious as I had imagined. I pressed my hands onto the bodice, moving down the front of it, marking it with blood. My anger melted away, replaced by waves of pleasure.

14.

That night there was a thunderstorm, with ferocious gusts of rain and veins of white lightning spreading across the sky. From time to time, I'd crack open my eyes and see flashes of light through the window. I was vaguely aware that the heat wave had broken, that the lightning had zapped it, shattered it like glass.

The storm seemed to continue for hours before moving on. In the morning, I was sleeping deeply after a night of interruptions, but I awoke to a clamor in the distance, a faraway cacophony that started moving closer. I pulled the sheet tighter around me, burrowing into my little crevice in the center of the bed. The clamor continued, soon accompanied by a screeching wind, the wail of a banshee. I'd never known the wind to scream like that, and I was grateful to be safe in bed, my cheek nestled into my pillow.

A thunderous boom jolted me up again. There was more wind now, louder, inside my bedroom. I picked up my head in confusion and felt warm hands pulling at my shoulders and sides. The room went spinning as I fell out of bed and landed on the floor with a thud as the back of my head hit the hardwood. I was startled and dazed, but through the blur, I saw Aster bending over me, pummeling me with her fists.

15.

I spent the rest of the day with my mother in her sitting room, lying on the sofa with a compress to my head. Dovey administered occasional doses of aspirin and hot broth. She tended to me, but she couldn't hide her disappointment in my behavior. The pain in my body and the lingering shock from Aster's attack prevented my guilt from consuming me. I couldn't believe what I'd done to Aster's dress. I hadn't been myself. Or was I becoming a different self? But if this was the new me, it wasn't a me that I liked. Lying on the sofa, all I felt was an aching head and a heavy heart; I was a collection of random parts, not even a person.

Dovey had forced my mother to open the window in her sitting room to let in the fresh air, and I agreed that this was what we needed — airing out. Belinda knew what I'd done, but she didn't chastise me, having barely acknowledged me at all. The wedding had pushed her farther inside herself, since acting out hadn't worked. She was like one of her ghosts, a spectral figure, present but not really there. I listened to the sound of her pencil as she sketched, the soft scuffing across the textured paper the only sound she made.

Later that day, I would learn from Dovey that my sisters had spent this last day before the wedding in rainy Manhattan, racing between department stores and bridal boutiques. They were all soggy to the bone but desperate to find a new gown that would fit Aster's short-waisted, curvy frame without any alterations. The June bridal rush had left stocks low, but Aster found something at the last minute: a frilly confection of a dress in a synthetic satin called Moondream, a dress that no one else had wanted. She hated it.

I would see the dress briefly the next afternoon as Aster and my sisters left for the wedding. I'd spent the night on the sofa in my mother's sitting room, knowing I wasn't welcome in the girls' wing; not even Zelie had come to see me. When I heard the rustle of dresses and the footsteps in the hallway, I peeked my head out and whispered for my mother to join me, but she was staring out at her flower garden, gripping the sides of her desk so hard that I could see the strain in her fingers.

Aster stood at the top of the stairs, facing away from me. The new dress was enormous, its construction as vast and intricate as a cathedral's, with layers of ruffles that poofed out all over, completely different from the streamlined elegance of the dress I'd destroyed. She still had her original veil of imported French lace with orange blossoms sewn into it. I couldn't see her head or her hair or any part of her body — she was entirely enveloped, a pillar of white. I could see her, but at that same time, like my mother, she wasn't really there.

My sisters stood around her in their seafoam dresses, sprigs of baby's breath in their hair. Rosalind, at Aster's side, saw me. She leaned over and pulled back the veil to whisper in Aster's ear, but whatever she said brought no visible reaction.

Rosalind told the girls to go ahead down the stairs to help guide Aster on her way. After they dispersed, Aster stood at the top of the stairs by herself for a moment, and I hoped she would turn around, but she refused to give me that, and I knew I didn't deserve it. I watched as she began her descent; the bottom half of her disappeared, then her middle, until all that was visible was the top of her head. I wanted to reach out to her, a sob stuck in my throat, but she disappeared quickly, wading into deep water and slipping beneath the surface.

16.

I returned to my bedroom once everyone had gone. I couldn't stand to be in my mother's sitting room any longer. She and I were alone in the house since the staff had been invited to the wedding.

Mrs. O'Connor had left sandwiches in the icebox, tuna salad and the usual ham and mustard. I ate two at my desk while sketching, then took a long nap, then returned to sketching, finishing the calla lily I'd started two days before. I tucked some baby's breath, foxglove, delphinium, morning glories, and wolfsbane around it — all toxic, a poisonous bridal bouquet.

It was dark by the time I'd finished, and as I added more detail, I thought of the reception that was happening without me, the dancing and the cake and the clink of glasses. I wondered if the terrible thing was about to happen, but at that point, I knew that it either would or it wouldn't, and there was nothing more I could do.

Around midnight, still drawing at my desk, I heard my sisters rolling in, their heels clicking against the floorboards, their cheery voices speaking en masse. Zelie came into our room. She had a little white bundle in each of her hands; she set them on top of her vanity without explaining what they were. "Oh Iris," she whispered, too excited to continue shunning me. "What a night!" She spoke so quickly that she could barely keep up with herself, details fizzing from her mouth as if from a bottle of seltzer that was about to explode. She started at the beginning with the church ceremony, then moved on to Wentworth Hall and the reception, but her account was tangled and difficult to follow. I managed to catch only snippets.

Aster was the most beautiful bride, she said, even in the tacky Moondream dress — when Zelie mentioned the dress, she didn't even pause to chastise me — there was too much to tell.

"I scattered the flower petals down the church aisle," she said. "Rose petals since Mother wasn't there." Rosalind looked "like a princess" standing near Aster at the altar; Daphne and Calla didn't smile enough but were still lovely. Zelie described the moment our father gave Aster away — *he gave her away;* she was so matter-of-fact, I imagined a bag of old clothes being handed over to a charity drive.

The church was bursting with guests, and there were people lined up outside to catch a glimpse of the bride, the first of the Chapel sisters to walk down the aisle; the attention made Zelie feel like a film star. After the ceremony, they had portraits taken, including one of Aster surrounded by her sisters — "except for you." Our father posed for a portrait with Aster, a bride missing a mother on her big day. Although maybe that wasn't so different than usual; Belinda had always been mostly absent. They rode to the reception in a Rolls-Royce. The reception hall looked like an "enchanted forest," Zelie said, drawing on the fairy tales that shaped her mental landscape. (I thought there needed to be witches, but perhaps they were my mother and me.) She explained that the inside of the hall was draped in garlands of cream-colored roses, a last-minute change once Mother was disinvited. "Aster said you can't have a wedding without roses," Zelie explained, so I supposed it was convenient Mother wasn't there. Each table featured a vase of asters and jasmine, with vines of ivy wrapped around the backs of chairs and burning candles everywhere. White paper lanterns hung from the ceiling like tiny moons.

Matthew was dreamy, of course. Dashing. Suave. Every adjective from the Cinderella thesaurus. She even got to dance with him to Doris Day's "It's Magic"; Zelie did a little pirouette as she said this. She danced with our father to an old-fashioned waltz, and with Daphne and Calla. Daphne ate more steak and potatoes than any of the men.

At the end of the night, Matthew drove Aster away in his convertible with the top down. The guests threw confetti and rose petals, clapping and cheering until the newlyweds were out of sight. I pictured the convertible pulling into Grouse Court, the gargoyle baby waiting to welcome them.

"The cake was *lemon cream,*" Zelie said, rubbing her belly. "I had two pieces." She walked to her vanity and picked up one of the white bundles. "Look," she said, setting it on the edge of my desk and peeling back the linen to reveal a tiny sliver of the cake no larger than one of Rosalind's tortoise-shell combs.

"I'm not hungry," I said, the first words I'd spoken since she'd come home. The cake was squished, the frosting melted; it had been in Zelie's hot hands the whole ride home.

"It's not to eat, silly. It's to place under your pillow so you'll dream of your future husband."

I must have scowled because she finally went away and resumed shunning me. I turned back to my drawing, adding a few blooms of mountain laurel, my head ringing with the details of the ceremony and reception. I'd never felt more left out of anything even if I hadn't cared about it the way Zelie had. Even if I'd tried to ruin it.

Zelie returned from the bathroom in her nightgown. She picked up her bundle of cake from the vanity and placed it under her pillow. "The grandest night of our lives," she said, as she climbed into bed, the baby's breath still in her hair, the spite in her voice.

I stayed at my desk until the sound of her breathing let me know she was asleep. I'd finished the bouquet and pinned it to my bulletin board, then I took off my robe and sat on the edge of my bed, ready to turn off the lamp and lie down, ready for this day to become memory — the grandest day of their lives was the worst of mine so far. But then I noticed the bundle of wedding cake still on my desk. It was a silly notion, and a messy one, to place a slice of cake under a pillow, but I couldn't resist. I'd never given my future husband much thought. All I knew was that I'd have one whether I wanted one or not. Maybe if I caught a glimpse of him in a dream, I'd know which man to look for later.

I rested the back of my head gingerly on my pillow and waited for the cake to send me its message. I couldn't sleep right away; we were five girls in our wing that night, our first without Aster, and everything felt lopsided.

17.

A howl in the night.

I was dreaming, but I didn't know it. I thought what was happening was real, and who's to say it wasn't.

At first, I thought the howl came from Belinda, but this sounded different, like the wail of a wounded animal. Then came footsteps, loud and booming, that shook the floor and rattled the glass in the windowpanes the closer they came.

Was this my future husband?

I gripped the sides of my bed, terrified. The footsteps grew louder and louder until they were right outside the door, then there was banging. I wanted to run away, to hide, but my limbs felt too heavy to lift. All I could do was close my eyes, the only defense I had, the power to choose not to see.

When the door swung open, creaking on its hinges, I knew it wasn't my future husband who had come to me. Something feminine had arrived, the room filling with the scent of roses. I inhaled in short, quick gasps. It was unbearable, filling up my lungs, the air so humid with perfume that it became difficult to breathe. Whatever was standing at the door came in, its footsteps normal now, almost delicate. There was a *swish, swish* against the foot of my bed, and finally I opened my eyes and saw the headless bride.

She was as beautiful as she'd always been, with her long sleeves and basque bodice and yards of train that spilled out into the hallway like a trail of starlight. It was dark in the bedroom, but she was illuminated by the moon, her silk a luminescent lunar cream. The dress was only marred by blood. My blood. But aside from that, she glowed as every bride should glow on her wedding day.

The headless bride came to stand at my bedside, then leaned over me as I shook with fear. She positioned the empty space where her head and mouth should have been right next to my ear, and she whispered ever so softly.

Why didn't you save me?

THE BLUE DIARY

Volume Two

Aster

1950

I.

The morning after Aster's wedding, I ate breakfast alone in the kitchen, knowing my sisters wouldn't want to see me. Mrs. O'Connor served me a plate of scrambled eggs, and as she was pouring me a glass of apple juice, she said: "I've a mind not to feed you at all."

I could hear my father and sisters in the dining room next door, speaking quietly, all of them tired from the night before. Mrs. O'Connor took eggs to my father, but my sisters, even Daphne, had requested only toast and tea, their stomachs having not yet recovered from the decadence of the wedding reception. Once she'd finished serving, Mrs. O'Connor came back to the kitchen and sat at the table across from me, eating what was left of the eggs straight out of the cast-iron skillet.

Dovey soon joined us, carrying Belinda's breakfast tray, which hadn't been touched. "She says she isn't hungry," Dovey said, and I knew that if I hadn't been there she would have said much more. They scavenged the rejected tray, Mrs. O'Connor taking the plate of toast and the little pot of raspberry jam, and Dovey taking the egg in the cup and the mug of milky tea.

I ate in silence, wanting to finish my breakfast quickly so I could go back upstairs before my sisters were done eating. I didn't know how long I'd have to stay sequestered in my bedroom. This was to be my fate, I thought at the time, taking my meals in the kitchen with the servants, living like a mouse that scurried along the floorboards, hoping to remain unseen.

Then the telephone rang, and fate took a different turn.

Rosalind picked up the telephone in the entry hall — "Chapel residence" — her voice cutting through the silence. A second later, with obvious concern, she asked, "Matthew, what's the matter?"

Mrs. O'Connor, Dovey, and I looked up at one another. We set down our forks, cups, and napkins, then turned our attention to the open kitchen doorway.

"Sick?" Rosalind said. "Oh dear. Can I speak to her?" Rosalind listened to whatever Matthew was saying in response, and all we could hear were a few "uh-huhs" until she said, "All right then. Drive carefully."

As soon as she set down the phone, my sisters all called out variations of "What's wrong?" at the same time. I went into the entry hall and moved closer to the dining room, out of view but near enough to better hear what was happening.

"Aster's sick with a low fever," Rosalind explained to my father and sisters. "She asked Matthew to bring her home."

"Why would he do that?" our father said. "This isn't her home anymore." His words bordered on cruelty, but I confess I also found it odd that Aster wanted Matthew to bring her back to the wedding cake. She wasn't a little girl who needed her mother to make everything better. We'd never had that kind of mother anyway.

Rosalind was clearly worried and didn't chastise our father for his clumsy words as she normally would have. Instead, she replied: "I don't know."

"She's scared," Calla said.

"What do you mean?" Daphne said.

"Aster's scared because of what Mother said. That something terrible will happen. Remember?"

"We all remember," our father said. "No need to relive the moment."

"But maybe Calla's right," Rosalind said. "Aster woke up this morning feeling a bit unwell, which *is* understandable after the week she's had. The stress of a wedding is more than enough for *any* woman, but then on top of that, she had to deal with so much more thanks to" — Rosalind paused to clear her throat, then continued more quietly — "thanks to that *awful* business with Mother and Iris. Poor thing is probably worried this mild cold is some fatal illness."

"Perhaps you're right," our father said.

"Of course I'm right. Matthew will bring her here and we'll give her some sisterly love and she'll be tickety-boo by dinnertime. She and Matthew will go back to that darling little house and Aster will coo —" Rosalind stopped herself. "Well, maybe they can go to a restaurant."

It sounded as if Rosalind had diffused the alarm that Matthew's call had brought, but since I couldn't see anyone's faces, I didn't know if they truly believed her or even if she believed herself. I didn't return to my unfinished breakfast and went upstairs before they could disperse, the mouse dashing past my parents' darkened wing. Belinda was shut in her sitting room, utterly unaware of what was going on, but I certainly wasn't going to tell her.

2.

When Aster arrived half an hour later, she moved slowly down the hallway of the girls' wing. The glowing pillar of white that had left us not even twenty-four hours earlier had returned, and though we lined the hallway and smiled at her encouragingly, we all could see that something was seriously wrong.

Matthew held her up on one side, my father on the other. She didn't look as if she had a mild cold. She wore her bathrobe, with slippers on her feet, and shuffled down the hall. Her eyes were only half open, and she stared ahead as if she couldn't see us. Her hair was still pinned in places and stiff with spray. She clearly hadn't bathed. There was a dull hint of Cherry Blossom still on her lips, and a grayish shadow of liner and mascara stained the skin around her eyes. This was how she returned to us, in a liminal state between bride and wife.

Matthew and my father got her into bed and took off her robe, revealing a gauzy lilac nightgown with no back and bell sleeves; it was lacy and alluring, the half-moons of her dark areolas visible, something our father shouldn't have seen. As soon as Aster was tucked into her old bed, he took his leave. He rarely visited the girls' wing, and this episode only confirmed why. On his way out, he told Dovey to call the doctor.

We were all gathered around Aster's bed, my sisters and I back in our usual formation. Our shared fear had brought me back into the fold. Rosalind sat in a chair next to the bed, dabbing Aster's forehead and neck with a cloth. She wet the cloth every few minutes in a bowl of cold water that Calla held in her hands. At the end of the bed, Daphne placed a reassuring hand on one of Aster's feet, caressing her toes through the crocheted blanket. Zelie took my hand as we stood to the side, motionless.

Matthew, out in the hallway, was dressed in a beige summer suit. He nervously jangled the keys and coins in his pockets. "We sail tomorrow," he said. "Is she going to be all right?"

We didn't acknowledge him. Whatever was wrong with Aster was his fault; I knew it, we all knew it. She'd been with us all our lives, and after just one night with him, look at the state of her. He strained to see her from where he was standing near the doorway, but he didn't move any closer. We'd encircled her single bed — there was no room left for him.

Aster hadn't said anything since she'd arrived; it wasn't clear if she was even capable of speaking. She was dimmed, like a lamp that had just been switched off, still warm but not illuminated. I watched her closely, waiting for her to light up again. Despite everything that had happened, Belinda's premonition and my encounter with the headless bride, it seemed impossible that she wouldn't.

I reached over and touched her arm. "Say something," I whispered, pleading with her. I would have welcomed a flush of pink in her cheeks at the sight of me, a rush of anger at how I'd betrayed her. Anything to snap her back to reality. I would have been pleased if she'd opened her mouth and banished me from the room if it meant she'd come back to us.

Rosalind gently cupped her hands around Aster's face. "Aster?" she said quietly. "Can you hear me, darling?"

I wanted Aster to open her eyes and say in a playful scold: "Rozzy, get that wet cloth off me," but there was nothing. No acknowledgment, no movement, no glimmer of recognition. If anything, she seemed to be slipping deeper into whatever had her in its grip.

"Aster, wake up," I said loudly, taking hold of her shoulder and shaking her. She didn't flinch or blink.

"What's wrong with her?" Zelie said, swallowing a cry. She looked up at me as if I'd have the answer, then around at the rest of our sisters. Rosalind, Calla, and Daphne were holding themselves together, staring at Aster almost as blankly as she stared ahead, and I knew what they were thinking; it was what I was thinking too — this was the *something terrible*.

There were voices in the distance, a man somewhere.

"Is that the doctor finally?" Matthew asked. I'd forgotten he was there.

Dr. Green, likely fresh from church in his brown corduroy suit, arrived with Dovey by his side. He was roughly the same age as our father — short, portly, with a gray beard and wire-rimmed glasses. He had been our family doctor since before I was born.

He and Matthew spoke for a few moments. ("She was fine last night," I heard Matthew say. "This morning she seemed a bit unwell, and then . . . and then it just got worse.") Dr. Green, having received his briefing, came into the bedroom carrying his black medical bag. "It's surely just exhaustion," he said, nudging Rosalind and Calla aside so he could stand next to the bed.

He gazed down at Aster in her lilac negligee, the stains of bridal makeup on her face, her chestnut curls as stiff as straw. She looked like an old mannequin discarded from a department store and tossed in the dumpster. *No one should see her this way,* I thought, growing upset for her dignity. I wanted to pull the covers up to her chin, to take the wet cloth and wipe her face.

Her eyes were still open but just barely. Dr. Green looked her over and briefly pinched his brow in concern, but when he noticed me staring at him, he let a smile unfold across his broad, jowly face. "Yes, it's just what I thought: exhaustion." He lifted Aster's arm and felt the underside of her wrist for a pulse.

"We sail tomorrow," Matthew called from the hallway.

"Shouldn't be a problem, Mr. Maybrick," Dr. Green said. He set Aster's arm down and felt her forehead. "Pulse is a bit weak, and she's warm. Let her rest today and she should be fine by tomorrow." He looked around at us. "Better give her some air, ladies," but none of us moved.

He shrugged, as if to say, *Suit yourselves,* backed away, and picked up his black bag, which he hadn't even opened.

"That's all you're going to do?" Rosalind said.

"She's exhausted," the doctor said. "It's the excitement of the wedding, that's all. Nothing to worry about."

"But you haven't even examined her."

"My dear —"

"Maybe we should take her to the hospital?" Calla said.

"*The hospital?*" Dr. Green said. "You're crowding her, that's certainly not helping matters. I suggest you ladies go outside for some air and let her rest for a while. Come back in an hour and she'll be herself again."

"You don't know what you're talking about," Daphne said.

Dr. Green laughed in surprise at her assertiveness. "My dear, I know it's hard to see your sister in this state, but I hardly think I need to remind you which one of us went to Yale medical school." His tone was one of forced lightheartedness. That we were Henry Chapel's daughters likely afforded us some degree of insubordination. "Put yourself at ease. She's fine. Really."

"But she can't move," Rosalind said. "She can't speak. She doesn't even know we're here."

"Maybe the sea air will do her some good," Matthew said from the doorway. "We sail tomorrow," he repeated. Daphne groaned.

"That's just the ticket," Dr. Green said with a frown, looking at Daphne disapprovingly. "New York to Southampton, is it?" he asked Matthew.

"That's right," Matthew said. "London, then Paris and so on."

"Fantastic. Some shipboard relaxation is just what this young woman needs. Doctor's orders."

I couldn't imagine Aster boarding a ship. She'd have to be carried up the gangway on a stretcher, but Dr. Green didn't seem concerned. He left her bedside and joined Matthew and Dovey in the hallway, squeezing Matthew's shoulder with his free hand. "I've got three daughters. They can be fragile."

"Yes," Matthew said. "So I'm learning."

"It's best to ease them into married life." He slapped Matthew on the back, and the two men exchanged a look and a chuckle that I didn't quite understand. I thought maybe it had to do with the wedding night when the man made the woman bleed. I wondered why Matthew and Dr. Green would laugh at such a thing. Where there was blood, there was pain, or so I had always thought.

"Phone me if anything changes with Mrs. Maybrick," Dr. Green said, and Dovey escorted him away. Matthew said that he needed to make a telephone call downstairs and left as well. Dr. Green's pronouncement of "exhaustion" seemed to be enough for him.

"What do we do now?" Rosalind said, when we were alone again. Her helplessness frightened me. Aster and Rosalind had always taken charge of any situation; I worried we were lost in a way we'd never been before. I wanted to place a daisy crown on Aster's head again, make her the queen rose of the rosebud garden of girls once more so she'd glow like she did that night in the meadow. Instead, I looked up at the wall of aster stars behind her bed. *I wish, I wish.*

3.

"Any news?"

Rosalind had turned to Zelie as she entered the girls' sitting room, anxious for the latest report.

"She's still sitting there," Zelie said. "Not saying anything."

Belinda had been at Aster's bedside for hours. She'd entered the room gently, wearing her usual linen dress, her hair pinned up as always, as white as a moth from head to toe; her eyes were fixed on Aster, as if the rest of us weren't there. She asked us to leave them alone so we did, and she'd sat quietly at her daughter's bedside ever since, holding her hand, occasionally dabbing her brow with the wet cloth.

Dovey delivered a tray of sandwiches to us in the sitting room, ham and mustard in triangular halves, and a pitcher of lemonade with shriveled mint leaves bobbing along the surface, the ice having already melted.

Zelie, taking a sandwich half, perched on the windowsill. "Matthew's in the garden," she said, looking outside, nibbling a corner of bread half-heartedly.

"What's he doing?" Rosalind asked.

"Smoking a cigarette and pacing."

Rosalind had pleaded with our father and Matthew to ignore Dr. Green and take Aster to the hospital, but the men had clung to his diagnosis of exhaustion and wouldn't budge.

"I don't understand why no one is doing anything," Rosalind said. "Our sister is lying in her bed, a shell of her former self, and there's no sense of urgency to be found anywhere in this house. Matthew is outside smoking, our father is God knows where, and our mother — our crazy mother! — who has predicted the end of the world all week is now just sitting at Aster's bedside, completely silent." Rosalind finally broke, if only for a moment; she quickly wiped away her tears with a few brusque movements, clearly annoyed that they'd dared interfere with her righteous rage. Calla, who was sitting next to her, reached over to pat her shoulder, but Rosalind sprung up at her touch.

"No," she said. "This won't do. We know Aster better than anyone. She's not well." She took a breath to steel herself. This was the Rosalind I had been waiting to see all morning.

"We could take Aster to the hospital ourselves," Daphne said.

"Yes," Rosalind agreed before Daphne had even finished speaking. "Matthew's outside and Daddy's probably hidden away in his den. They won't be any the wiser until we've already left."

"Why don't we call an ambulance?" Calla said.

"Daddy would probably send them away," Rosalind said. "We can't afford to waste any more time, don't you see?"

"But how do we get Aster to the car?" Calla said.

"Easy," Daphne said. "Two of us take her arms, two of us her legs, the other leads the way."

"I don't think we can manage that," Calla said.

"Sure we can," Rosalind said. "And I can drive us."

"But won't the doctors at the hospital be like Dr. Green? They'll send us away," Calla said.

"We won't let them." I hadn't spoken since we'd left Aster's bedroom. I knew I wasn't entirely welcome even if no one was focused on me at the moment, but I couldn't stay quiet any longer. I knew Rosalind was right, that something terrible was going to happen to Aster if we didn't act soon. Belinda had known something terrible was going to happen all week long, and at last someone besides me agreed. "We'll refuse to leave the hospital until they treat her," I said. "If they try to make us leave, we'll make a scene. They'll have to call the police to remove us."

"Right," Rosalind said in agreement. "We'll have to be quick. Zelie, you'll go ahead of us. Get the keys to the car and wait for us at the front door."

We all stood up, falling in line behind Rosalind, who stood in the doorway of the sitting room. She looked down the empty hallway. There was no sound coming from anywhere, no one in sight. She nodded at us.

We flooded into the hallway, walking quickly toward Aster and Rosalind's bedroom, ready to pick up our sister and carry her away. We were briefly exhilarated. We were unstoppable. *We* were going to save her.

And then —

A scream. It wasn't one of Belinda's; we were familiar with hers. This was something different, more like a howl. My sisters raced ahead to the bedroom, but I stopped in the middle of the hallway, unable to move. I'd heard that howl the night before.

We were too late.

4.

I couldn't see Aster — my sisters, in their panic, were crowded around her — but I could see my mother backed up against the wall near the window, hand over her mouth, eyes wide and terrified. She glanced over at me and our eyes briefly locked. We both knew.

Aster, still in her bed, continued to howl. When I reached her bedside, I saw her hands clasped at the base of her neck; her eyes were open but still vacant, deadened. Her howling was endless, without a single pause for air. Our father rushed into the bedroom, followed by Matthew and Dovey. "What's happening?" Matthew said. "What's going on?" No longer lingering outside or in the hallway, he was now pushing his way to Aster's bedside, the warrior springing into action.

"I've called the doctor," Dovey said. She was breathless from running and gripped the dresser for support.

Our father tried to pull Aster's hands from her neck, but she was grasping her flesh so tightly that he couldn't wrench her hands away. Matthew joined in until they'd pulled her hands free, leaving her neck bright pink with claw marks. She didn't fight them. She stopped howling and went limp.

She lay in bed the same as before, eyes open, blank stare. My sisters were trembling and tearful. No one knew what to do.

But the silence was only a brief reprieve. Aster sat up in bed, something she hadn't seemed able to do before, opened her mouth, and howled again. Instead of holding her hands to her throat, she extended her arms straight out in front of her, as rigid as boards.

"Oh my God," Rosalind said, backing away from the bed. Dovey rushed forward and pulled Zelie into the hallway.

"Aster, sweetheart," Matthew said. "Please tell us what's wrong." He gulped down a cry. I had never seen a man cry; he tried hard to rein it in but kept choking on it. "I love you," he managed to say.

At this profession of love, Aster stopped her howling and began to laugh, a loud and deranged cackle. She put her arms down and used them to steady herself as she swung her legs out of bed, laughing all the while.

We could see her nipples through the lilac gown. If she'd been in her right mind, she would have been mortified. She picked up the Tiffany lamp from the bedside table, the green glass matching the forest painted on the wall, and she stood up, ripping the lamp's cord from the socket. Matthew approached, attempting to take the lamp from her, and she stopped laughing and stared at him.

"Sweetheart," he said, trying to maneuver her back into bed. She swung the lamp in his direction, hitting him hard on the side of the face and sending him to the floor crying out in pain. Once Matthew was down, she dropped the lamp beside him and rushed to the window. She punched her fist through the glass and pulled it back dripping with blood. She was seriously injured but hadn't cried out or winced from the pain; she just looked at her bloodied hand dispassionately.

None of us said anything, none of us moved, as she slowly pulled down the lilac nightgown, revealing one of her bare breasts and rubbing the blood from her injured hand all over it in soft, gentle caresses. She pulled down the other side and the nightgown slipped to the floor. She rubbed blood all over her neck and breasts, her torso and stomach and hips. Then she held her arms up above her head, almost joyously, and howled louder than before. Her body vibrated and hummed with each scream, twisted and writhed. She looked

like a woman gripped by ecstasy, her head held high like a wolf's, releasing a
pure animal sound.

When it was over, she collapsed to the floor and died.

5.

Dr. Green arrived to a scene of horror. I don't know how my father explained
it to him. The doctor suggested an autopsy, but my father said no, he didn't
want his daughter carved up. Matthew, who had been taken to the hospital
for stitches, wasn't consulted. Aster was back in her father's house and he had
assumed responsibility for her once again. He'd given Aster away at the altar,
and in her death, he'd taken her back.

Belinda was stunned, as we all were. She stood like a ceramic figurine
near the edge of a table, about to fall to the floor at any moment and break
into pieces, never to be repaired. Dr. Green forced her to take Veronal, then
he doled more pills out to my older sisters, but he said Zelie and I were too
young. Within an hour of the tragedy, Belinda was asleep in her bedroom,
my older sisters on the sofas in the girls' sitting room, all of them content in
the milky warmth of amnesia.

Dovey consoled Zelie in our bedroom, and Mrs. O'Connor brought me
downstairs. She sat me at the kitchen table and gave me a mug of Ovaltine.
I was back where I'd started that morning, with no idea what time it was or
how long it had been since breakfast.

My father and Dr. Green were in the dining room next door, each with
glasses of whiskey. Dr. Green had settled on influenza as a cause of death.

"She had a fever when I examined her this morning," Dr. Green said to
my father. "That's a sure sign of a virus. I suspected flu but didn't want to
alarm anyone. I know Mr. Maybrick was concerned about traveling tomorrow." He explained that in rare cases the flu can cause hallucinations.

"I see," my father said quietly, accepting this explanation as he had accepted the diagnosis of exhaustion earlier. Dr. Green could have said malaria

or kidney disease and I was sure, despite what he had just witnessed, that my father would still have replied, "I see."

There was a knock at the front door. I peeked into the entry hall and saw my father and Dr. Green greet two men in black suits, one of them carrying a gurney. The four of them went upstairs.

The front parlor had a clear view of the entry hall, so I went there to wait to see what was going to happen. They looked like they could have been doctors, but why would Aster need a doctor now?

When the men in suits came back downstairs a little while later, they were carrying the gurney; there was a long black bag lying on top of it, zippered shut. They wheeled it outside, my father and Dr. Green trailing behind, leaving in their wake an empty silence that threatened to engulf me.

I ran to the kitchen and out the side door through the vegetable garden toward the back of the house. I kept running—I didn't know what else to do—past my mother's flower garden and the frog pond into the meadow. My bare feet slammed into sharp branches and stones, but the pain didn't stop me. I ran across the meadow, Aster's hypnotic howl coursing through my ears; and for a brief moment, I thought I could outrun what was chasing me. But eventually my legs gave out and I collapsed. After a minute or so facedown in the grass and flowers, I felt sick and rose to all fours, gagging and choking, trying to vomit, but nothing came up. It wasn't nausea, I soon realized, but sobs. They were filling my chest and throat, building up an almost unbearable pressure. The grief had caught me. No matter how hard I tried to swallow my sobs, they burst through.

6.

Two days passed between Aster's death and her funeral. Rather than coming together, my sisters and I fractured in our grief, each of us caught in the maw of it, left to fight our own way out.

I drifted in and out of rooms, in and out of conversations, unable to focus clearly on anything that was happening. Living in the wedding cake had always felt like living in a fishbowl but never more so than during that time. We were all swimming through the cloudy water, unable to see outside the glass. What I remember most about those two days, besides my own grief, was the dizzying mix of the morbid and the mundane. One morning I'd see the maids scrubbing blood out of the floorboards in Aster and Rosalind's bedroom while downstairs Mrs. O'Connor made dainty éclairs for the postfuneral reception. Blood splatter and pastry, these are the things I remember.

I kept hearing the word *buried*. It was a word I'd only seen in storybooks before — *buried treasure, buried secrets,* pharaohs' tombs and pirates' plunder. But this was different. It began with an overheard argument between Rosalind and Delyth, Matthew's mother, who wanted Aster to wear her wedding dress, that tacky Moondream gown. Everything had been taken away from the Maybricks, not just Aster but the funeral arrangements too, which our father had organized without consulting them, and on this, Delyth was taking a stand.

"My sister will not be *buried* in that awful dress," Rosalind said, her voice hoarse, a handkerchief clenched in her hand. There it was, said aloud for the first time: buried.

"Your sister died as Matthew's bride. She will remain his bride forever."

"She spent one night as Matthew's bride and it didn't end very well for her," Rosalind said. "I should think that being Matthew's bride isn't the thing we'd want to memorialize."

"How dare you say something so cruel," Mrs. Maybrick said.

"Rosalind, that's enough," our father said. He was clearly losing patience with the entire conversation.

"Daddy, you're not going to allow Aster to be buried in that *thing,* are you?" There it was again: buried.

"It's not up to him," Mrs. Maybrick said. "Aster was my son's wife."

"Only briefly," Rosalind said.

"Matthew wants her to be buried in the dress," Mrs. Maybrick said. "And that is the end of the discussion." Once I noticed it, I couldn't stop: *bur-*

ied. Just twenty-four hours after Aster's death, words that had once been un-imaginable were now part of our vocabulary.

Matthew, who'd been waiting in the car while his mother argued with Rosalind, opened the front door and stumbled into the house, grasping the doorknob so he didn't fall over. "I told you to wait for me outside," Delyth said, and I could see why. Matthew was a wreck, his face bandaged from where Aster had hit him. He wore his clothes from the previous day, the beige suit wrinkled and damp, smelling of booze and sweat. His tie dangled around his neck like a noose, as if he'd escaped the hangman and had been on a bender ever since.

"The last thing I want is to come back to this fucking prison, but I've gotta take a piss." It was a terrible sight, the splendid sea creature from the previous summer now nothing more than jetsam washed ashore. The war hero's story had taken a tragic turn; he was blindsided.

Dovey led him to the bathroom, Matthew grasping her arm for support. While he was gone, Delyth and Rosalind continued to argue, this time over jewelry, from earrings to necklaces and finally to rings. Delyth said Aster couldn't be buried with her diamond engagement ring. "Matthew would like to keep it as a memento."

"Keep what as a memento?" Matthew asked, when he returned, still zipping up his pants.

Delyth stiffened at her son's reappearance and raised a pale hand to pat her skunk-black hair. "Wait for me in the car."

"I want to talk to Mrs. Chapel," he said, resting against the entry-hall table for support.

"She's asleep," my father said. He glanced at Delyth, waiting for her to do something about her son. He had a keen sense of approaching trouble, could smell it like a dog smells rain.

"Well go and wake her up," Matthew said belligerently.

"She's unwell."

"No, you see," Matthew said, slamming his fist down on the table. "I don't think she is unwell. I think she's the only one around here who really knows what's going on, and I want to talk to her."

Delyth walked to his side, attempting to take his arm, but he pushed her away. "Are we all going to pretend that Mrs. Chapel didn't predict this whole thing?"

"Come along, dear," Delyth said, reaching again for his arm.

"Mrs. Chapel!" Matthew screamed, his voice vibrating through the entry hall. He made a move for the stairs but wasn't steady enough to bound up them. He collapsed partway up and lay there, his forehead resting on the edge of a step. He was still. I thought he may have fallen asleep, but then I realized he was crying.

Overwhelmed, I went to my mother's flower garden, pulling up whatever was nearby, a fistful of salvia and a hydrangea bloom. Belinda had no idea what was happening; my father had hired a nurse to keep her sedated.

Are we all going to pretend that Mrs. Chapel didn't predict this whole thing?

Yes, Matthew. We are.

That evening, Dovey sent Zelie and me upstairs to choose our dresses for the funeral. Zelie pulled most of her dresses out of the wardrobe and piled them on her bed. "Zelie, you're supposed to choose *one* dress. We're not packing for vacation."

"I want to look at everything," she said, eyes downcast, her plump little mouth turned into a grimace. I'd lost track of her that day, seeking a solitude in my grief that didn't include her. I wondered who had been looking after her, but given her stained dress and scraggly hair, I imagined no one had.

"Where do you think Aster is right now?" she asked, as she put the last of her dresses onto the bed.

This was another reason I'd avoided Zelie: her endless questions that I couldn't answer.

"She's in heaven," I said matter-of-factly, no different than I would have said, "She's at the drugstore." I'd already picked out my own dress for the funeral, a dark brown one I often wore to church.

"What's heaven like?"

"*Zelie*," I said in exasperation. "How should I know? Do you think I've been there?" I started looking through her pile of dresses, hanging up the bright summery ones that were clearly inappropriate. That left a couple of dresses in navy blue and nothing in black. Neither of us had ever had a need for black.

"Do you think Aster will become an angel and watch over us?" Zelie had walked to the window and was looking out.

"Maybe," I said. We went to church every Sunday, my father and sisters and me, but what was discussed there — God and angels and so on — was never mentioned at home. We weren't a religious family despite our church attendance. Our father made his living by creating and selling weapons, so perhaps he didn't want to spend too much time thinking about where people went when they were blasted from this life to the next and his role in that. Belinda had her visions of the afterlife, but she didn't share the details with us, and her screams certainly didn't offer much comfort. Where she stood on the issue of angels and whether her eldest daughter might have become one, I didn't know.

"Maybe Mother will tell us when she wakes up," I said, selecting a dress for Zelie that matched mine in style if not in color. I put the rest away and slipped out, heading to the girls' library, a room I hadn't been in since before the wedding. The headless bride was still there, the white satin fabric stained with my blood. I moved closer, wondering if maybe the blood had faded, if it might be possible for Aster to wear the dress in her casket rather than the replacement. I couldn't bear the thought of her wearing for eternity that awful dress she hated. But the stain hadn't faded; it had settled into a dark maroon.

"Iris, where are you?" Zelie called.

I walked back down the hall, passing by Aster and Rosalind's room on my way; the door was closed. Zelie waved me over to the window in our room and pointed outside. "Look."

Our father, a shovel in his hands, was digging a hole in our family plot. He wore dark trousers with suspenders, his white shirt rolled up at the sleeves. I suspected he didn't own any casual clothes; I'd never seen him garden or exercise. He belonged at a desk.

I made a sound — not a word, just something guttural in my horror. I turned to Zelie, her face contorted, no tears coming out. She seemed too stunned to cry.

I put my arm instinctively around her and pulled her close. We stood like that for what must have been several minutes, watching our father jump into the deepening hole and hurl shovelfuls of dirt up to the surface.

Rosalind came in at some point. "What are you two staring at? You're completely mesmerized."

We didn't answer her. There was no way to say it.

She came up to the window and looked out. "What's he doing?" she asked, catching sight of our father's silhouette against the darkening sky. I couldn't answer.

She placed her hand to the glass as she peered out, the gold band of her coral cameo ring clinking against the windowpane. She strained to get a better look. It took a moment for it to hit her, and when it did, she parted her lips wide. She froze like that for just a second, then moved her hand to her mouth to stifle her cries.

7.

On the morning of Aster's funeral, we went to the meadow and set about gathering flowers, each of us bent over like a worker in a field, pulling up stems, the sound of our quiet weeping caught in the breeze around us like the saddest birdsong.

We rode in a chauffeured car to the church in Bellflower Village where Aster was waiting for us. My sisters and I were alone in the back seat; our parents were driving separately with Dovey and the nurse. The five of us sat quietly on the short ride, piles of flowers in our laps; Calla braided a daisy crown. We'd become five, but not in the way we'd anticipated. We didn't know then that five would become four, then three, and so on. At that moment, riding to the church with our flowers, we thought this was the worst thing that would ever happen to us.

We appeared muted, dressed in the dull colors of winter, the colors of grief. Rosalind and Calla had made half-hearted attempts to curl their hair, but the curls hung limply at their shoulders. Their faces were bare — wearing makeup seemed in bad taste.

As the car turned onto Main Street, we saw it was lined with workers from the Chapel factory. They had walked over in their uniforms, the men in overalls, the women in dresses with denim aprons. "These dear people," Rosalind said. There must have been hundreds of factory workers bowing their heads as we drove by.

The car pulled up at the Bellflower church, which looked like a small cathedral, and we went through the side entrance into one of the rooms off the chapel where Aster would be waiting for us. We hadn't seen her since she'd collapsed on her bedroom floor. No one but our family and Matthew's family would see Aster in her casket; my father didn't want her on display for everyone else. She'd been in the same church for her wedding only days before, and that's how they would have to remember her. Forever a bride, as Delyth had said.

The antechamber was made of the same gray stone as the rest of the church, with thick stone slabs on the floor and walls, and there was a stained-glass window, which cast flecks of red and yellow and blue light across the floor that looked like a scattering of petals. We could see the casket, made of glossy pine, but our view of Aster was blocked by our parents, who'd arrived before us. They were standing together, taking one last look at their first-born. My father had his arm around my mother's shoulder in what looked to be an act of tenderness, but I supposed he was only trying to hold her up. The drugs had made her weak; she was barely able to walk.

My sisters and I clustered in the doorway, grateful for a moment to brace ourselves. As my parents left the room, Belinda's face was blank, her eyes as cloudy as stones in a river. She had seen Aster but not really; I wondered if she'd even remember this day later. For her sake, I hoped that she wouldn't.

It was our turn, and at first none of us moved. "We can do it," Daphne finally said with conviction. She went first, and Rosalind and Calla followed, and Zelie and I did too.

Aster appeared as she had on the morning Matthew returned her to us drained of life. The Moondream dress barely fit into the casket, its yards and yards of bright white fabric stuffed in and around her body. She seemed stuck in it, a wick trapped by melted candle wax. From the neck down, her body was lost to the fabric, the lace, and the cheap satin and sequins. Only her hands were visible, neatly folded at the waist, the left hand on top of her right to display her gold wedding band.

Whoever had done Aster's makeup had a heavier hand than Aster had ever had, her lips in dramatic red, her cheeks rosy like a doll's. But her hair was a glorious mane, a cascade of brown curls that framed her face and extended well below her shoulders. Rosalind snapped off a red poppy and set the bloom in Aster's hair just above her ear, then gradually added the rest, the marigolds and daisies, arranging them inside her curls until Aster was lit with color.

The rest of us joined in. We worked silently, snapping off the flower heads and gently placing them in her hair, on her chest, nestling them at her sides. I placed a single iris near her shoulder; their season was passing and the bloom had wilted slightly, but it was still a vibrant-enough purple. "I'm sorry," I whispered, and I hoped she was near enough to hear me.

Rosalind set a red rose next to my iris, and we finished with vanilla-scented heliotrope and a knot of blue violets that we placed in her hands. All that was left was for Calla to place the daisies on Aster's head, a half crown left tenderly atop her as Calla spoke: "Shine out, little head, sunning over with curls, to the flowers, and be their sun."

Soon after, the undertaker closed the lid, sealing Aster, *our* sun, alone in the black.

alabaster aster
a vision in moondream —
starry sequins and —
satin cream.

then
a bridal fever,

and a mother,
up in the night —
dead daughter
moonscreaming

now we are five

— calla chapel

The Haunted Mother

1950

I.

When Belinda was a baby, she screamed. She screamed so loudly that her wails filled the whole house and could be heard out on the street. She paused her screaming only to eat and sleep, and she would only sleep after she had completely exhausted herself, her throat red and raw.

She was haunted, the governess said before she quit, her nerves in tatters. A baby haunted by the ghost of her mother.

Belinda's father, Levi Holland, was a professor of botany at Harvard College, a prodigy who had achieved a full professorship by age twenty-four. His first wife, with whom he had a son, had died of pneumonia, and several years after her death, he'd married again, to a spinster of twenty-seven named Rose Harrison. Within months of the marriage, Rose became pregnant, only to die in childbirth in January of 1900.

. . .

Every governess Levi hired to take care of his children quit, none of them able to bear the screaming baby. The housekeeper quit, the cook quit, even the reverend of the local church asked Levi and his family to stay away. Desperate for help, he went to the Deaf school and hired a young Dutch immigrant named Johanna to look after his daughter. She'd hold Belinda against her chest and rock her, feeling her tiny body vibrate but unable to hear the sound. Two of Johanna's friends from the school also joined the household, a jovial pair of sisters who served as the housekeeper and the cook. It made Johanna happy to have her friends working in the same house, and Levi would do anything to keep her happy since she was the only woman able to care for his daughter. The three women pampered the baby and did what they could to make her comfortable if not content.

Belinda's half brother, James, who was seven years older, was sent away to live with relatives and then to boarding school, and as a result, he never cared for the sister he felt had pushed him out of his house and family. But Levi saw no other option. Even he could barely endure life with Belinda. He spent long hours at work, and at home he put cotton in his ears, but there was no way to block out the sound entirely. The house was only ever quiet when Belinda was asleep, but even in the night she would occasionally awaken and let out a scream. He took Belinda to doctors all over Boston and Cambridge and New York, but they couldn't figure out what was wrong with her.

Despite the screaming, Belinda somehow developed normally. She learned to crawl, then walk, and she could talk as well, but the few words she said were screamed. "Papa!" she'd howl. "Hungry!" she'd shout. "Mother!" she'd wail, whenever she saw the framed photograph of Rose on the table next to the sofa.

As she grew older, she began to knock her head against the walls and pull at her ears and shout, "Out! Out!" No one knew why; so much about Belinda was a mystery. She had to be supervised at all times since she'd taken to hitting her head against any hard surface, the table legs and floors. One day while Levi was at work, Johanna, suffering from a cold, had fallen asleep; Belinda went out the back door into the greenhouse where her father kept his specimens for work. When he came home from teaching his classes, he discovered the women in the house frantically searching for Belinda, who had disappeared; since they couldn't hear her screams, they had no way of finding her.

When Levi found her in the greenhouse, it was a horrible scene. Belinda, with a pair of gardening shears, was trying to cut off her ears. At four years old, she wasn't strong enough or coordinated enough to succeed, but she had used the razor-sharp blades to gnaw at her earlobes, screaming in pain all the while. Her white dress was covered in blood and she was rushed to the hospital. The doctors weren't able to repair the damage, but they made clean incisions so the earlobes looked more presentable. Belinda sat in a crib at the hospital with her head bandaged, quiet for once in the stupor of the sedatives. The doctors said she was disturbed and would need to be sent to an institution.

Levi didn't want that to happen. His wife had died giving birth to Belinda; she was her mother's legacy. He sat with his daughter in the hospital and asked her questions that he hoped she might finally understand. "Belinda, why do you scream?"

"Scream," Belinda said, pointing to her ears. "Mother."

"You can hear your mother screaming?"

Belinda nodded.

He knew the screaming that Belinda was talking about. His wife's screams as she gave birth and simultaneously died had filled the house, the wretched sound burrowing in his own ears for days after. He had never before connected his dying wife's screams to his daughter's.

"When do you hear your mother screaming?" Levi asked.

"Always," Belinda said, placing her hands over her bandaged ears.

Through hours of conversation over many days, the doctors learned that Belinda had heard her mother's dying screams echoing in her ears since birth. In response, she had screamed out of fear, and when she grew older, she had tried to hit her head to make the screaming stop. And then she'd tried to cut off her ears.

After the sedative wore off, Belinda said she could still hear the screaming but that it was farther away. Belinda's violent attempt to silence her mother had somehow worked, at least to an extent — when she was older, she would compare her mother's screams to the sound of the ocean in a seashell, a distant roar.

When Belinda left the hospital, she didn't scream anymore. Levi took a year's sabbatical from his job to tend to Belinda full-time. Each day they worked in the greenhouse. He gave her a little corner of her own, where she played with soil and seeds, and began to grow her own plants. She was too young to understand the science of botany, but she liked watching the plants grow and putting her hands in the soil. Most of all, she loved the flowers. Whenever Belinda told us the story of her missing earlobes, the story of her mother and the screaming, she ended it all the same way: The flowers, she said, had healed her.

She spent the next twenty-five years living in harmony with her father. She was schooled at home, with an interest in the sciences, particularly botany. As she grew older, she ran the household, even helping her father grade papers, and in the evenings, they worked together companionably in the greenhouse. She was like a wife in many ways, as many spinster daughters were to their widower fathers, and in the summers, they traveled to different places, Japan and Portugal and the Galápagos Islands, collecting and examining specimens. Belinda expected her father to live to old age; she had no interest in marriage or children and wanted her life to continue the way it was for as long as possible. When her father did eventually die, a day she envisioned happening far in the future, she imagined herself staying in their home and living out her remaining years in solitude with her greenhouse.

Her father, however, would never see old age. One evening, as he walked home from Harvard, he collapsed in the middle of Brattle Street, clutching his chest, dead from a heart attack at fifty-eight. Belinda's half brother, with his wife and two young children in tow, came to sort out Levi's affairs and soon discovered he was deeply in debt. There was nothing to do but sell the house and its contents to pay off the bank. There'd be nowhere left for Belinda to live and nothing for her to live on.

Belinda, only two months on from her father's death, was still in the deepest grief when she went to stay with James and his family in Boston. Her half brother was a surgeon, and the family lived in a townhouse in Back Bay, but despite the size of his house and his plentiful income, he told Belinda she could stay for only a short time, that she'd have to make her own way in the world. She'd need a man to care for her, and that was a husband's job, not a half brother's.

Belinda didn't want to marry; she had no interest in men. For her foremothers, marriage had always been a death sentence — marriage, pregnancy, then the grave. She wasn't going to let that happen to her, so James said she'd have to find employment instead.

For a while, she served as a companion to an elderly lady who lived in Brookline. The woman wanted someone to read to her, to sit and knit with her, to make the odd cup of tea. But after only a month, she tired of Belinda's grief, her constant crying over her father and the life she had lost. The elderly woman sent Belinda back to James's house, and he sent her to be a governess in the home of a wealthy family, his wife's cousins. The family had three young children and Belinda was overwhelmed by them; she was so inattentive that their older boy ran out of the house one afternoon and was nearly hit by a streetcar.

Since Belinda wasn't fit for domestic service, James rented her a room in a boardinghouse in Lowell and arranged for a job at a newly opened button factory across the street. She couldn't keep up with the other women, who were nice enough but hard-edged, mostly immigrants from southern Europe. They tried to help Belinda with her work, but each day she'd fall far behind and eventually she was fired.

James made her stay in the boardinghouse and kept a tally of the rent he was paying so she could reimburse him later. She spent her days going on interviews, but she had no references and no experience. Belinda applied to work in a department store, but she wasn't fashionable enough. She applied to work in a bakery, but she couldn't bake and they weren't willing to teach her. She inquired about working in a flower shop and as a secretary, but no one was interested.

Once a week she went to James's house for dinner. She didn't like him and knew he was taking a sick sort of revenge against her for having pushed him out all those years ago, for having robbed him of his father. She went to the weekly dinners anyway, willing to do anything to get away from the dingy boardinghouse, where she shared a room with two women and a bathroom with six others. Hers had become a shabby life, and she luxuriated in that hour or two at James's home, eating off china plates and drinking wine from crystal glasses.

One night there was a man at dinner, Henry Chapel, who'd been at Harvard with James. He was thirty-six, like James, and he was the vice president of the Chapel Firearms Company in Connecticut. His father was mostly retired so he ran the company, and he came to Boston quite often on business. At the end of the evening, he asked Belinda if she'd like to attend a concert the following week, but she said no. She could see what was happening, that James had arranged for her to meet Mr. Chapel. She had no idea what a successful man like him would want with her, nearly thirty years old and reduced to living in poverty. The shabby boardinghouse had made her shabby as well, and she couldn't bear to see herself in the hallway mirror in James's house.

At the end of the evening, after she had rejected Mr. Chapel, James told her that he would pay the rent for only two more months.

"And then what?" Belinda asked.

"And then you'll have to survive on your own."

Belinda didn't know what that meant. Survive how, exactly? If she couldn't find a job to pay for the boardinghouse, would she have to live on the streets? She asked if she could enroll in a ladies college to study to be a science teacher, but James said he wouldn't pay for that since he had his children's futures to worry about. Besides, he said, she was too old for college.

Eventually, she agreed to go out with Henry Chapel. If she appeared to be making an effort, then maybe James would agree to keep paying the rent past the deadline he had set. Henry Chapel was a boring man who never said much, but he got her out of her room to concerts and dinners in restaurants.

On their third date, he explained that he had only ever focused on work, but that his parents were pressing him to marry, to have a son who could take over the business one day. She realized only later that he was proposing to her in a roundabout way, that he needed to marry but didn't want to bother looking for a wife. She was in front of him, the sister of his friend, from a respectable family, and he thought she would suffice. He seemed to know nothing of her past and didn't bother asking.

The weeks passed, and James said he wouldn't extend the deadline. Belinda wondered whether he would really let her live on the streets. She doubted it, but she couldn't be sure. He seemed cruel enough to do such a thing, but still she had trouble imagining it. In the worst-case scenario, if he did leave her on her own without a cent, she worried she might starve or else freeze to death beneath a bridge. Would that be worse than marrying Henry Chapel and likely dying while giving birth to his child? She decided that it would be.

And so they were married.

These were the stories our mother told us when we were growing up. We knew she'd spent her earliest years screaming and that she'd never wanted to marry our father. But the stories of her life always ended at her wedding day, as fairy tales so often do. Most children can't imagine their mothers having a life before them, but for my sisters and me, it was the opposite. The wedding day was always the end of her story. We were the epilogue.

2.

Belinda spent the first four years of her life screaming, but then she stopped and didn't scream again until she married my father and moved into his house.

She'd always felt a connection to the spirit world because of the circumstances of her birth. As Belinda entered the world, her mother had left it; they were two spirits intertwined, one on the way out, one on the way in. But she had never actually seen a spirit until she moved into the wedding cake. The house was paid for in blood money, and she could see the spirits that haunted it night after night.

But in the weeks after Aster died, Belinda, for once, went quiet. The nurse remained with us, and Belinda remained sedated. It was as if she'd sipped from the River Lethe and forgotten about Aster. She stayed in her bedroom and sitting room day and night, tended to by the nurse, who administered her drugs and brought her meals up on a tray from the kitchen.

Belinda was more removed from the family than she'd ever been. She'd always remained at the edges of our lives, but now her chair in the dining room was empty every day, and the nights were silent, no shrieking to wake us up, no screams at the procession of spirits, the cowboys and Indians, the pioneer women and runaway slaves and soldiers.

I hadn't thought it was possible for drugs to work on her in such a way, to clear out the haunted corridors of her troubled mind, to turn on the lights and sweep up the cobwebs and prop open a door to let in a bit of fresh air.

The medication worked like magic, but after only a couple of weeks, the nurse said Belinda would need to be weaned off it, otherwise she'd risk becoming addicted. Our father already had his hands full with Belinda, whether one thought of her as haunted or mentally ill. He certainly didn't want her to become a drug addict on top of it, but Belinda without drugs in the wake of Aster's death was a frightening thought. I imagined her out of control, shrieking throughout the house like a rabid dog, even though there was no precedent for this. Belinda's outbursts were largely confined to her bedroom screams. But we all expected her mental state to have deteriorated more after everything that had happened. When our father arranged with Dr. Green to send Belinda to Fern Hollow, a private psychiatric clinic near Greenwich, so she could quit sedatives and rest for a couple of months, none of us tried to stop him.

"This should have been done *long ago*," Dr. Green said to Dovey on the day Belinda was taken away; I'd overheard them talking in the kitchen.

"Years ago," Dr. Green added, as Belinda was escorted out the door with no idea where she was going. "Poor woman."

My sisters and I, while not drugged as our mother had been, were immobilized by a profound sadness that had settled over us during what Calla, quoting Tennyson, had labeled our "joyless June." We went from room to room, ate our meals, and passed the hours of the day at a much slower speed than usual, our senses numb. Our rambling old house had always been an island, but in the wake of Aster's death, it seemed as if our parcel of land had finally detached itself from the rest of Connecticut and was floating out to sea.

We soon fell into a dreary routine. After breakfast, we took our places in the front parlor, Calla in a chair near the window with a book (she'd taken up Victorian novels that summer); Daphne silently sketching in a corner; and Rosalind on one of the sofas with her fashion magazines, though often she did nothing more than sit and stare at the floor. Zelie and I would play cards or other games, or put together puzzles. If we made too much noise, Rosalind would tell us to be quiet, that we were giving her a headache, and on really bad days, she'd shout: "Why don't you two *go outside?*" making a show of massaging her temples. One time she picked up our board game and flung the pieces into the fireplace, prompting Daphne — who rarely came to anyone's defense — to scold her.

If Aster had been alive, we would have been counting down the days until she returned from her honeymoon, then we would have spent the rest of the summer at Grouse Court helping her set up house. That had been the plan. I wondered what would happen to Grouse Court, if Matthew would live there alone or sell it. I imagined Aster and Matthew's empty cabin on the ship and all the hotel rooms they'd booked in Europe, all the beds not slept in on the Left Bank in Paris, on the canals in Venice, in the Alps. There was a trail of empty rooms where Aster should have been.

Belinda's rooms were also empty, and I went into them sometimes to sit on her bed, to peek behind the wardrobe at the secret snake painted on the wall, to run my fingers along the soft feathers of her stuffed wren. ("It's bad luck to kill a wren," she had told me once, which caused me to wonder who had killed her wren and what had happened to them.) I'd go into her sitting room and look at the mementos in her display case and sit at her desk, with its view of her flower garden. Mr. Warner tended to her garden, which was abundant with summer flowers, and I wished that we could take her a bouquet, but we weren't allowed to visit her. Our father asked us to write her letters, but she didn't write back.

I wanted to ask her if she felt guilty for what we'd done to Aster. Scenes from the week before the wedding kept playing out in vivid detail in my mind: Aster trying to rip my flower-girl's dress off me; the ruined wedding gifts; the headless bride smeared with my blood; and Aster, descending the stairs in the Moondream dress. All physical evidence of that week was blessedly gone. Dovey and the maids had cleared out the girls' library in the days after Aster's funeral, and the wedding gifts were donated to the poor since Matthew didn't want them; Mr. Warner had incinerated the wedding dress and my flower-girl's dress. I was left with only my guilt, and I wondered if Belinda felt the same. It didn't matter that we'd been right about the terrible thing; Aster hadn't listened, and she was gone, and all we had achieved was ruining the last week of her life.

3.

July passed, then August. At the beginning of September, with only a few days until school was due to start, the topic of Belinda came up again. It was a Saturday evening, and Mrs. O'Connor had set up an end-of-summer barbecue on the terrace behind the house. She'd made things look festive, covering our table in a red-and-white-checked tablecloth, tying balloons to the backs of our chairs, and arranging a bouquet of sunflowers as a centerpiece. She'd tried that summer to give us a bit of joy. We didn't take our vacation to Cape Cod, not that anyone was in the mood for it, so Mrs. O'Connor sent us on various trips in her own culinary way. I can only assume she didn't ask our father's permission when she deviated from our usual menu, designing a Polynesian night (avocado halves filled with seafood salad, drinks served inside carved-out pineapples with paper umbrellas) and a French night (duck à l'orange, crêpes suzette). Sometimes she gave us donuts for breakfast, and root beer with lunch, and bowls of buttered popcorn to take to our sitting room as an after-dinner snack. Dovey did her part too. Whenever she went on errands in the village, she'd bring home piles of magazines, bottles of nail polish, or comic books.

On barbecue night, Mrs. O'Connor grilled hamburgers and franks for us on a portable charcoal grill. Colorful Pyrex serving dishes spanned the length of our table, filled with corn cobbettes, potato salad, bowls of Fritos and dill pickles. We were each given a bottle of 7UP. My sisters and I, with the exception of Calla, were grabbing food and filling our plates, wearing our sundresses one last time before they were packed away. For once, we were anxious for summer to be over. Our father, who sat at the head of the table, his rolled-up sleeves the only concession to summer, seemed overwhelmed by the chaos of a serve-yourself dinner with so many components; he held a hamburger bun in one hand and a cobbette in the other, utterly lost. He finally decided on a hamburger sans bun, which he ate with a knife and fork. Once we'd settled into our dinner, he made an announcement, speaking loudly enough so he could be heard over multiple conversations. "I want to talk about your mother," he said.

"I don't want her to come home," Rosalind said, sensing where the conversation was going. We'd gone for weeks without any mention of when Belinda might be returning to us.

"Rosalind, don't be heartless," Calla said. She picked up her naked frank and nibbled the end of it; there was nothing on her plate, no chips or pickles. Calla, who preferred green salads, looked all wrong eating this kind of food, like a figure from a Botticelli painting dropped into a child's birthday party.

"Don't tell me you feel *sorry* for her?" Rosalind said. She was the only one of us wearing sunglasses. Her gold bangles slid down her arms as she rested her elbows on the table, and despite her obvious anxiety, she still possessed the glamour of a film star.

"Our mother is locked away in an asylum. Can't you spare a little sympathy?"

"It's a clinic," our father said. "She's not in an asylum."

"What's the difference?" Zelie asked.

"Money," Calla said, setting down her frank and scowling as she wiped away the grease on her fingers.

"She's not a character in one of your *novels*," Rosalind said.

"Joan Eyre, the unhappy housewife of suburban Connecticut," Daphne joked.

Rosalind ignored her. "I know it's tempting to romanticize our mother. Then we don't have to think about how utterly insane she is."

She sunk back in her chair, a sullen look on her face. We had always paired off—Aster and Rosalind, Calla and Daphne, Zelie and I—and it seemed that without her other half Rosalind was lost. Her spark and wit required another person to play off of. Without Aster, without "Oh Roz," she was only half a person, and her barbs turned cruel.

"I'll tell you what I think," she said, moving her sunglasses to the top of her head, her eyes narrowing. "Mother didn't just predict what happened to Aster. She caused it to happen. And if we let her back here, who knows what will happen next."

"How could she have caused it?" asked Zelie, her hands messy with ketchup.

"Rosalind," said our father, who was no doubt prompted to intercede by the distressed face of his youngest daughter.

"She's poison, that's how," said Rosalind. She couldn't be so easily reined in. "She's been infecting us with her poison our whole lives, and it finally killed Aster."

"You know that Aster died of the flu," our father said.

"*The flu.*" Rosalind laughed in a wicked sort of way. "She went mad. We all saw it and we know who caused it."

"Your mother had nothing to do with it," he responded, not especially convincingly. "Now, what I wanted to tell you"—he desperately tried to pull back the intended conversation from the edge of the cliff where it dangled

— "what I wanted to say is that your mother is coming home on Monday. It's already been arranged."

Rosalind put her sunglasses back on, but she couldn't hide her anger behind them. "I thought you said she couldn't come home until she's better?"

"The doctors say she's doing better. We decided she can come home on trial."

"What does that mean: *on trial?*" Rosalind asked.

"It means," Calla said, "that Goody Proctor has to prove she's not a witch."

"Calla," our father said sternly, stroking his auburn beard. "A trial simply means we'll see how she copes with life at home."

"And if she can't *cope?*" Rosalind asked. "Because, of course, she can't."

"She'll be sedated again," our father said. "And if that doesn't work —"

"*The gallows,*" Daphne said.

Our father let out a deep sigh. He appeared overwhelmed by the onslaught of his daughters, like a man set upon by bees. "She'll be sent back to the clinic. But I expect that you'll all help her adjust when she gets home."

"Not me," Rosalind said, standing up, her chair screeching across the slate tiles, the orange balloon tied to its back bopping her on the back of the head. "I'm eighteen now, and I'll be out of this house as soon as I have somewhere to go."

"Relax, kid," Daphne said. "You're not going anywhere."

"Just you wait," Rosalind said. She left the table and walked across the grass toward the meadow, finally vanishing into the thick beams of sunlight filtering through the trees.

4.

When Belinda returned home from the sanitarium a couple of days later, she behaved like her usual self — remaining sequestered in her sitting room for most of the day, keeping quiet through the occasional meals she shared with us, screaming in the night. For any other woman, this would have been a sign that she had succumbed to the deepest despair, that she was not, in fact, *coping*, as the terms of her trial dictated. But to our surprise, it turned out that Belinda as her usual self and Belinda in mourning were exactly the same person.

My sisters, rather than being relieved that Belinda was behaving normally, at least by her standards, seemed upset by the relative calm, and it soon became offensive to them. "I can't understand it," Rosalind said, as we chatted one night in our sitting room. "She hasn't cried for Aster once that I've seen. She sits stony-faced at dinner. When I pass by her rooms, she's quiet. She has the lungs to scream for those wretched Chapel victims who come calling every night but no tears for her daughter."

"Maybe she cries for Aster in private?" Calla said.

"Silently, *to herself*?" Rosalind asked, incredulous.

"Mother loves to put on a show," Daphne said. "If she was sobbing for Aster, we'd know it."

As far as my sisters were concerned, Belinda couldn't win. No matter how she behaved, they'd find fault. But I couldn't deny that my relief over our mother's subdued behavior had perhaps blinded me to her lack of any visible emotion over Aster. One would have thought that returning to the wedding cake, where Aster was born and so recently had died, would elicit some sort of noticeable response. I thought, though, that we should have been glad she was quiet regardless of the reason. I didn't know that the reason would become clear soon enough.

Around the middle of September, when Belinda had been back for nearly two weeks, Calla, Daphne, Zelie, and I came home from school one afternoon, and as always, my sisters raced inside, eager to remove their uniforms, blue-and-green-plaid skirts and white blouses. But I walked around the side of the house to visit the family plot. I stayed at the gate, not brave enough to step inside. There was still no headstone on Aster's grave, just a mound of earth, on top of which someone had placed a bouquet of autumn flowers, some purple crocuses and golden dahlias.

I remained there for a few minutes, then went inside the house. Zelie was sitting at the kitchen table eating her after-school snack, a toasted peanut butter sandwich and a glass of milk. She looked up from her sandwich as I entered the kitchen, knowing where I'd been.

"You took your time getting here," Mrs. O'Connor said, setting my sandwich and milk on the table. Zelie and I ate in silence as Mrs. O'Connor continued on with her dinner preparations, rolling out dough for what looked to be potpie. The lingering tightness in my throat made the peanut butter difficult to swallow, and I gave up.

After our snack, we went upstairs to start our homework. On our way to the girls' wing, I wanted to stop at our mother's sitting room and waved for Zelie to follow. Every day after school, I checked to make sure Belinda was still there, and Zelie, being nosy, couldn't resist finding out for herself. Our father said that if she failed the trial she'd be sedated before she was taken away, but I had no way of knowing if he'd change his mind.

I approached the sitting-room doorway, Zelie close behind, and peeked inside. Belinda sat on the sofa, holding a cup of tea in her hands. She wasn't drinking the tea; she wasn't doing anything, really; but I turned to Zelie and nodded so she'd know Belinda was there.

But before Zelie and I could leave, Belinda stopped us. "You can come in, blossoms."

Zelie and I returned reluctantly to the sitting room. We were both afraid that Belinda's restrained manner wasn't going to last. Zelie sat cautiously on the opposite end of the sofa from our mother while I sat in an overstuffed chair across the coffee table from them.

Belinda, looking down at my book bag on the table, asked: "How was school?" Motherly small talk never sounded natural coming from her.

"I hate school," Zelie said, eyeing Belinda with curiosity. She looked the same as she always did — white dress, her hair pulled back into a bun, a few strands left down at the sides to cover her missing earlobes. "And I hate being at home too."

"You must have something you enjoy?"

"I like playing the piano."

"I'd love for you to play for me sometime," Belinda said, setting her teacup on the side table. "And you, Iris?"

I told her what I had studied at school that day — French, *Romeo and Juliet,* astronomy. Belinda listened with what seemed to be interest, but she didn't pepper me with questions. She just nodded along as I spoke.

I wanted to ask her about the sanitarium, but I didn't dare. Zelie, as always, was bolder, or at least more tactless: "Why are you behaving yourself? Is it because you don't want to be sent away again?"

"I don't know what you mean, dear," Belinda said.

"We thought you'd be crying all day. It doesn't seem like you're very sad about Aster."

"Of course I am," Belinda said. "What a thing to say."

The right side of Zelie's mouth dipped into a frown. "Then why are you so calm?"

"You mistake my patience for calm," Belinda said. "Aster will come to me when she's ready. In the meantime, I'm happy to wait."

And there it was. She thought Aster would visit her, joining the spirits who came to her bedroom every night.

"You're waiting for Aster's *ghost?*" Zelie asked, clearly spooked.

"*Spirit,*" Belinda said. "And yes, I've been waiting for her to come to me since I came home. Your sister may have passed over, but she's still with us. I'm waiting for her to tell me she's all right."

"Why wouldn't she be all right?" I asked.

"We don't know where she is," Belinda said quietly. "I hate not knowing."

The thought of Aster haunting our hallways with Belinda's other spirits gave me a fright. I stood up and bent over the coffee table to pick up my book bag. "We better go, Mother. We both have to study for our spelling tests."

As soon as I'd stood up, Zelie made for the door and was gone without a word of goodbye. I lifted my books and Belinda leaned over, grabbing hold of my arm. "She might come to you too."

"What do you mean?" Her hand was hot, almost feverishly so. I thought she might have known about my encounter with the headless bride, but that was impossible.

"You tried to save her. We both did. She'll understand that now even if she didn't then." Belinda stared up at me, her eyes a dazzling hydrangea blue.

"Do you really think she'll visit us?"

"I hope so."

Zelie walked ahead of me down the hallway, both of us rattled by the conversation with our mother. Then we heard our sisters' voices coming from the girls' sitting room.

"We spent *all afternoon* on it," Rosalind said. "Why do I have to learn to make an *apple brown Betty*? I've never cared for apples. I wouldn't *deign* to marry a man who even *liked* apples."

As Zelie approached the doorway, I whispered to her: "Don't tell them what Mother said. She might get into trouble," but Zelie didn't turn around or respond as she entered the room.

Rosalind and Daphne were sitting on the windowsill in front of an open window, smoking cigarettes. Calla, reclining on one of the sofas, had her eyes closed, a cloth on her forehead. Their bright summer sundresses had been replaced by skirts with blouses and cardigans in dark jewel tones — sapphire, garnet, emerald.

I sat on the sofa across from Calla, where Rosalind's pillow and bed linens were piled on one of the cushions. Rosalind slept here now, refusing to sleep in the room she'd shared with Aster. She only went in there to get clothes and whatever she needed to complete her toilette; the rest of the time, the door stayed closed.

"Where've you two miscreants been?" she asked.

"We were visiting Mother," Zelie said, settling onto the floor at Rosalind's and Daphne's feet.

"Oh." Rosalind groaned. "How is she?"

Zelie hesitated for a moment, glancing over at me before forging ahead.

"She said she's waiting for Aster's ghost to visit her. That's why she hasn't been crying."

"*Zelie,*" I said.

Rosalind and Daphne looked at each other with their mouths open wide; Calla removed the washcloth from her forehead and sat up. I huffed my annoyance at Zelie, but she was too busy soaking up the attention to notice.

"I knew it!" Rosalind said. She stubbed out her cigarette and tossed it through the open window.

"She had to be up to something," Daphne said.

"She's not *up to something,*" I said. "She hopes Aster will visit her, that's all." I couldn't be seen to leap to Belinda's defense, but she had been right before — something terrible had happened to Aster. I didn't understand why they continued to disregard her. "We don't have to tell anyone about it," I said, hoping my father wouldn't find out what she'd said. "It was nothing. Zelie's exaggerating."

"I am not!"

"Of course you're not, petal," Rosalind said, leaning over to pat her head. "That's Mother through and through."

Zelie turned to me, smugly satisfied. She was perched at Rosalind's feet; she needed a queen bee, and without Aster, that was Rosalind.

"I thought all the ghosts who visited Mother were killed by Chapel rifles," Zelie said. "So why is she expecting Aster to visit her?"

"Zelie darling," Rosalind said. "Don't look for logic in the ravings of a madwoman."

"She's not mad," I said.

"She's as mad as a hatter," Rosalind said. "But the two of you share a kinship, so you don't see it." She stared at me, a look that dared me to disagree. "You both certainly worked as a team in June, or have you forgotten about that? I can assure you none of us have." Rosalind took another cigarette from Daphne's pack of Lucky Strikes and lit up.

"It wasn't like that."

"Wasn't it?"

"She was right about Aster before."

"Well then, I suppose she's right about this too. You can both welcome Aster's ghost tonight and reminisce about old times."

Calla put her head in her hands and began rocking back and forth on the edge of the sofa, seemingly on the verge of some kind of fit. She made guttural sounds, which eventually took on the shape of words: *"No,"* she said quietly, then more loudly: *"No, no. Stop!"*

"Calla, what on earth is the matter?" Rosalind asked, as she gripped the windowsill she was sitting on with both hands, bracing herself for some new horror.

"Our sister is not a ghost," Calla said with a cry.

"Of course she's not," Rosalind said, as Calla rushed from the room.

"That could be a poem," Daphne said. "Our sister is not a ghost / Our mother is crazier than most. See, anyone can be a poet." Daphne took Rosalind's cigarette from her. "Luckily, there's no shortage of inspiration around here. If Keats lived with us, he'd have a field day."

"Good thing Keats is dead, then," I said, and followed Calla out.

5.

That night, after our dinner of potpie — Calla was absent, and no one told our father about Belinda's revelation — I waited until Zelie was asleep before positioning my desk chair in front of the window in our bedroom. I stuffed my pillow behind me and draped a blanket over my lap. It wasn't comfortable, but it would do.

It was completely dark outside, no light coming through from anywhere. I looked toward the family plot but couldn't see anything. Belinda hoped Aster would visit, and my sisters thought the idea was laughable — I was stuck somewhere in the middle as always. But if Aster did come, I didn't want to be asleep. The headless bride had terrified me, and I didn't want an encounter with Aster to be like that, her sneaking up on me in the night.

I sat in the chair until morning, the hard wood not offering a bit of comfort, and watched outside for any sign of activity. Despite my best efforts to stay awake, I dozed off from time to time, the side of my head resting against the glass. But nothing happened.

On the second night, daunted at the thought of facing endless hours in the chair again, I took a pocket flashlight from the kitchen and used it to read a book under my blanket, one of Zelie's Nancy Drew novels.

I stayed up two nights in a row, and both nights ended the same way, with dawn lighting up the sky through the yellowing leaves of the trees, with the mist of an autumn morning descending. There was no visit from Aster, and I didn't know if I should be disappointed or relieved.

I dressed for school before Zelie was awake; she was a sound sleeper, and I didn't think she had any idea I hadn't been sleeping in my bed. On my way down to breakfast, I'd stop to see my mother, who was usually sitting up in bed, running a finger down the back of her wren, the softness of its feathers soothing her.

"Did she visit you?" I'd ask, envious that she got to stay in bed while I, carrying my heavy book bag, had to leave for school on very little sleep.

"No," Belinda said, her white hair down below her shoulders. "You?" she'd ask, and I'd shake my head and go downstairs to eat my cornflakes, bleary-eyed.

I stayed up every night for one week, then two, having fallen under Belinda's spell again. That's truly how it felt, like going under, as if my mother had placed a rag with chloroform over my face, sending me not to sleep but into another world, *her world,* where I began to see things as she saw them.

Night after night, and Aster didn't come. But I didn't want to give up; somehow I only became more convinced of her imminent arrival. There were encouraging signs. Once I fell asleep and woke up with a startle, convinced something had brushed past me, leaving a shiver on my skin; another night I heard the rustle of a skirt in the hallway. There were nights I awoke suddenly, not to any physical or aural sensation but to a smell in my nose, the scent of

Yardley's English lavender, Aster's perfume. In the morning, I would sometimes feel as if I'd been with her, enjoyed the warmth of her company even if I hadn't actually seen her.

At night I was living in Belinda's world, the world of the dead, but during the day, thanks to lack of sleep, everything around me was a blur. The brightness of the sun and the lights at school hurt my eyes; I followed very little of what my teachers said during class, and they were easy with me, the grief-stricken girl. As they wrote math equations and vocabulary words and important dates from history on the blackboard, I ached for sleep. Sleep was like the sound a mouse makes as it scratches behind the walls, only the walls were inside my brain. *Scratch, scratch.* I heard it all day long, but I couldn't reach it.

One day in geography class, I heard my teacher calling my name: "Iris Chapel?" Her voice was coming from the end of a dark tunnel. "Miss Chapel, are you all right?" There was the sound of girls laughing. Only when I opened my eyes did I realize I'd fallen asleep at my desk. My teacher sent me to the principal's office, not as a punishment but out of concern.

The principal, Miss Hawkins, had been a history teacher before being recently promoted. "Your teachers tell me you've been falling asleep in class," she said. She couldn't have been more than forty, with blond hair curled under at the shoulders, wearing a rust-colored figure-hugging dress with a leopard-skin belt around her waist. I wondered if she was married and looked to her ring finger, which was bare. She was like Millie Stevens, my piano teacher, who had chosen to do something else with her life besides have a family, the type of woman my mother had wanted Aster to be. If Aster had chosen that path, maybe she wouldn't be dead.

"Iris?" Miss Hawkins said.

"Yes?" I replied, forgetting for a moment where I was.

"They say you don't pay attention in class and seem distracted. Is this true?"

"I suppose so," I said, wanting to crawl into the dark space beneath her desk and fall asleep.

"I knew your sister when she was a student here. Such a lovely girl, so kind and smart. I'm incredibly sorry for your loss. Are you coping all right?"

I shrugged.

Miss Hawkins held a brown file folder in her hands and thumbed through its scant papers. It must have been my file, but I had done very little of note as a student at the Seward School for Girls, either good or bad. "Would you like to see the school counselor?"

"I'm having trouble sleeping, that's all," I said, trying to dispel her worry. "I've had insomnia all my life. Ask anyone." I wasn't usually much of a liar, but she had me cornered.

"I see," she said, closing the file. "Iris, I want to be understanding, but if this behavior continues, I'm going to have to call your mother."

I laughed at the idea. *Go ahead,* I thought, trying not to laugh again. It'd probably be easier to get President Truman on the phone.

Miss Hawkins stared at me across the desk, ready to render her judgment. "Why don't I take you to the nurse's room to lie down for a while?" she said, and I felt a swell of happiness.

She walked me to the small windowless room down the hall. There was a white examining table pushed up against one of the walls, and on the opposite wall were shelves stuffed with bandages and bottles of aspirin and boxes of sanitary napkins. The nurse directed me to lie down on the table, then draped a blanket over me and told me to go to sleep. She shut the door, and I heard her talking to Miss Hawkins out in the hallway.

"She's one of the Chapel girls," Miss Hawkins said.

"Poor little lamb," the nurse said in reply.

"Did you ever hear what killed the older sister?"

"A friend of a friend works in Dr. Green's office over in Bellflower Village. Apparently, they don't know what it was. Bit of a mystery there."

The women's heels clicked away down the corridor. *Bit of a mystery there,* I repeated in my mind, realizing that's how other people talked about us behind our backs. It seemed everyone knew Aster hadn't really died of the flu.

I closed my eyes and fell quickly into a deep sleep — no dreams, no ghosts. I swam in the black, feeling comforted by it, until a voice called my name: "Iris?"

In response, I screamed. Not a startle, not a flinch, but a full-throated scream, like a child on Halloween. I had thought I was in my bedroom and that Aster was calling me. But it was only the nurse letting me know the school day was finished and it was time to go home.

There was a line of cars outside the front gates, and I was sure all of them had mothers in the drivers' seats except for ours.

"Hurry up," Dovey said to me, as I was the last one to get in the car. "I've got groceries in the back."

"So we can't go for ice cream?" Zelie asked, as if that might have been an option. Aster was the only person who ever took us on outings; without her, we'd stopped going for ice cream or to the cinema. Zelie was desperate for the old days, but it wasn't Dovey's job to take Aster's place and entertain us. Losing Aster was like losing a mother, and it was clear Rosalind was incapable of taking her place.

Since I didn't share any classes with my sisters, they didn't know about my nap in the nurse's office. On the ride home from school, they chatted excitedly about a girl who had apparently brought a boy into the lunchroom and had been suspended. That girl was the scandal of the day; my being sent to the principal's office hadn't even made it into the grapevine.

We turned onto the road that led to our house, driving beneath a marquee of tree branches; Dovey had to run the windshield wipers to clear off the leaves so she could see. We rounded the bend at the top of the drive, and I felt my throat tighten at the sight of the house, the heap of the wedding cake in its decaying splendor.

When the car stopped, my sisters raced into the house as always, and once they were inside, I went around to the family plot and opened the gate. I set my book bag on the ground, lowered myself onto the mound of earth that covered Aster, and sat cross-legged. There was a slip of paper under a rock, a quote from a poem in Calla's handwriting.

> *pressed in my heart, like flowers within a book*
> *— henry wadsworth longfellow*

I returned the paper to its place under the rock, pleased I wasn't the only one who visited. The crocuses and dahlias on the mound were gone, replaced by a posy of dark pink autumn asters.

"I wish you would visit Mother," I said to Aster, running a stick in circles through the dirt. "She's worried you're not all right." In my heart I knew that if Aster didn't come soon Belinda was going to unravel again. It had already started; the first loops of thread were off the spool.

I reclined on the dirt, using my book bag as a pillow, and stared up at the trees, listening to the soft drop of the leaves. I clasped my hands at my waist so I was in the same position as Aster, who was six feet below.

"What *on earth* are you doing?" Rosalind's voice awakened me from my sleep. When I opened my eyes, I was surprised to see it was nearly dark.

She took my hand, pulling me up from the dirt and escorting me into the house, then into the dining room where the rest of the family, including Belinda, was gathered for dinner. "I found her outside. She was *sleeping* on top of *Aster's grave.*"

"You're all dirty," Zelie said, her nose scrunched.

"Iris," my father said. "What were you thinking?"

I spread my napkin on my lap, avoiding his question since I didn't have an answer. I glanced at Belinda as I stabbed my pork chop with a fork. She reached over and pulled a twig from my tangled hair.

"You know she's not out there," Belinda said to me, and though she'd said it quietly, Rosalind, at the other end of the table, had heard.

"Enlighten us, Mother," Rosalind said. "If Aster isn't in her grave, then where is she?"

"Her body is in the ground," Belinda said. "But she is not."

Talk of Aster in the ground had stopped everyone else from eating. They looked forlornly at their dinner plates or at Belinda and me in our corner of the table. Belinda hadn't done her hair; it was down and unbrushed, as it had been that morning, the skin under her eyes ashen.

"You know, Mother," Rosalind said. "You should set up a stall on the side of the road. You could call yourself *Madame Belinda, the spiritualist.* I'm sure people would pay good money for your insights into the afterlife." She laughed, and so did Daphne.

"And don't forget her assistant," Daphne said, looking at me. My father and the rest of my sisters looked at me too, and I turned away, embarrassed.

I passed an interminable evening in the girls' sitting room, keeping quiet and playing a game with Zelie so as not to draw attention to myself. Rosalind, painting her nails with Revlon's Touch of Pink, then reading the latest issue of *Mademoiselle,* kept an eye on me the whole time until finally she started to yawn, which meant we had to leave the sitting room so she could sleep.

No matter my trouble at school, I continued my nightly vigil: blanket, pillow, flashlight, Nancy Drew. Zelie woke up unexpectedly early the next morning; I'd fallen asleep and she shook me awake in my chair, staring down at me. I startled at the sight of her in her blue nightgown with her long chestnut hair. "Did you sleep there all night?" she asked, looking out the window in the direction that my chair faced to see what was in view.

"Mother said she's not out there," Zelie said, and crawled back into bed.

On the night of the full moon, I finished the last novel on Zelie's shelf — *The Mystery at the Moss-Covered Mansion* — and turned off my flashlight. I couldn't remember half of what I'd read, but turning the pages gave me something to do. I closed my eyes for a few moments to let them adjust to the darkness, and when I opened them, I saw something outside.

A white figure, illuminated by the moonlight, was walking through the family plot. Gooseflesh spread over me like a rash. I stood up, sending the flashlight and the book tumbling to the floor.

"What happened?" Zelie mumbled, before rolling over and going back to sleep.

My instinct was to hide in bed, but I couldn't do that. I wasn't sure what was outside, but it might have been Aster. I opened the bedroom door as quietly as I could. I heard Rosalind's soft snores coming from the sitting room as I tiptoed down the hallway, making my way to the stairs.

My parents' wing was completely dark, and while I was tempted to wake my mother, I didn't want to raise her hopes until I was sure. I stood at the top of the stairs, waiting to hear if the front door would open. If it did, I would run into Belinda's bedroom and take cover.

After many minutes of listening to the tick of the hall clock, with no sound coming from the front door, I decided to descend, gripping the banister tightly, afraid I might trip on the way down. I couldn't see a thing, but eventually I felt my way to the front door, finding it unlocked and slightly ajar. I pulled the door open, letting in the cold autumn air, and realized I didn't have a sweater or a coat or even a bathrobe over my pale-pink nightgown nor was I wearing shoes. I didn't want to waste time going back upstairs, so I ran down the front steps and around the side of the house, my feet squishing into the damp cold of the grass.

The figure was still in the family plot, more of a blur in the moonlight than anything else. I moved one foot forward, then another, until I reached the gate. As it creaked open, the figure turned, and said: "Aster?" I could see now it was my mother. She was the ghost.

"*Mother*," I said in a hiss, looking back toward the house. "What are you doing out here? You're going to get into trouble."

"Aster?" she said again in her hopeful, frail voice.

"No, it's Iris."

She came closer to me, grabbing both my upper arms. Her eyes were wild with terror. I'd seen this look the week before the wedding: *They're coming for us, Iris. Run!* It was the same terror I'd seen in Aster's eyes during her dying moments.

"It's Iris," I said, wanting to bring her back to reality, the look in her eyes unbearable. "It's Iris," I said again. "It's Iris!" Slowly she focused on me, a daughter but not the daughter she wanted to see.

"I know she's not here," Belinda said at last, her voice heavy. "But I needed to make sure. I used to catch the scent of her in the house at night, but that's gone now."

"Her perfume?" I asked, and Belinda nodded. She'd smelled it too. I couldn't have imagined it. Aster *had* been in our house.

She let go of my arms, almost going limp. I reached out and grabbed ahold of her. "It's all right, Mother."

"It's not all right. I've been home nearly a month and still no sign of her. I need to know," Belinda said, her voice cracking. All these weeks she hadn't cried, and here it was finally. I turned away, knowing this was a bad sign.

"I need to know she's all right," she cried.

I persuaded Belinda to return to the house with me; neither of us were wearing shoes or a coat. I turned the light on inside the entry hall, and we left a trail of dirt from the front door up the stairs. I guided her down the hallway to her bedroom. "Let me get a towel," I whispered, but she climbed into bed, dirty feet and all, and pulled the blanket up to her chin.

She didn't invite me, but I slid in next to her. I nestled next to her body, trying to get warm. I'd never been in her room in the middle of the night, and I wondered if the spirits of the Chapel dead were encircling us. If so, she gave no sign that she saw them. Her eyes wide open, she stared up at the ceiling.

"Mother?" I said, but she didn't respond. I pushed my head into the crook of her arm and fell asleep.

In the morning, luxuriating in the feel of a bed with pillows and sheets rather than my hard wooden chair, I pulled the blankets around me, inhaling their warmth. I was vaguely aware of my mother's body next to mine, but

I was still in the daze of half sleep, the events of the night before far from my mind.

With my eyes still closed, I attempted to drift away again, but the bed started to vibrate gently. I opened one eye to see Belinda, hands covering her face. She was quietly weeping.

"My darling girl," she said.

I found my way through the tangle of blankets into a sitting position. "Was Aster here?" I asked, placing a hand on Belinda's arm and glancing around the room. The room was empty except for us, but I was filled with hope; all I could think was that Aster had come to Belinda during the night and at last our ordeal would be over.

"She wasn't here," Belinda said. "She's not coming."

"She'll come," I added, wanting it to be true.

Belinda removed her hands from her face and wiped her eyes with the back of her hand, having ceased her crying. "She's far away now. I can't feel her anymore."

"Maybe she was angry at us for what we did?"

"No, blossom. I know that when she passed over she understood why we did what we did. She loved us more for it."

"How do you know?"

"I have a gift, I suppose you could call it. I always have. My mother passed it on to me when she died. I don't know if she had it herself, but thanks to her, I've always known things, *felt* things that other people aren't aware of. In this house, for instance, I see spirits every night that no one else sees."

"The Chapel victims."

"They're attracted to this house, to the darkness within it. But I've come to think they don't mean us any harm. I think what they want is to be seen. I should be happy that Aster isn't here, that she's gone on to a place of light, and yet —"

Something inside her cracked open, I could see it. The terror flashed in her eyes and I knew this was the moment. She was about to turn rabid.

"It's all right, Mother," I said in my most soothing voice, trying to pull her back.

"I can't bear the pain of not seeing her again," she said, and then a great knot of pain escaped from her. She began to scream more loudly than I'd ever heard anyone scream. She held her hands to the sides of her head, the veins in her neck and forehead enlarged, her face as red as could be, mouth opened so wide that a flock of birds could have flown right out of it; it was an ungodly sound she made, and on she went, her body convulsing from the force of it, a great Edvard Munchian scream, the most terrifying thing I had ever heard.

I tumbled out of bed and stood in the corner of the room with my hands covering my ears. "Stop!" I shouted at her, but she wouldn't. "Mother, *be quiet!*" Her screaming would have penetrated every corner of the house and I was sure the door was about to open. My instinct was to rush and lock it, to protect her, but before I could, the door swung open and my father walked in, dressed for the day in his brown suit. He grabbed my wrist and guided me to the door, where Rosalind stood just outside. She was also dressed for the day, coiffed and neat, and she took my arm from my father as if it were a baton being passed on. Once I was outside the bedroom, he shut the door, muffling the screams, and Rosalind said: "Come along, Iris, this is the end."

6.

A new nurse came to live with us. She worked under the supervision of Dr. Green and seemed more amenable to keeping Belinda on Veronal for an indefinite period of time. Belinda was sedated at night and slept peacefully until morning. No more waiting for Aster, no more visits from Chapel victims, no more screaming. Our father didn't want her to have any more bad dreams, as he called them. He wanted her knocked out, lost to a place where dreams were impossible.

She wasn't sedated during the day unless it was necessary to keep her calm, but there was a hangover effect, and as a result, she was usually lucid for only a small window of time, and even then, she wasn't her normal self. She became like a ghost, there but not there, haunting us.

The nurse, who had a room on the third floor next to Dovey's, watched Belinda whenever she was awake, and Rosalind watched me. I wasn't allowed to visit Aster's grave anymore, and at night, I had to keep my bedroom door open so Rosalind could check to make sure I was asleep in my bed. Somehow the adults in my family knew what I'd been doing, staying up all night, falling asleep in class, conspiring with Belinda.

Rosalind passed her driving test (the number of times she'd taken it not inspiring much confidence in her driving ability) and she began to take us on outings. We visited a pumpkin patch, went apple picking, and attended a football game at Yale. We slowly drifted away from the fever dream of those few weeks I'd spent under Belinda's spell, but though no one mentioned what had happened, I knew they hadn't forgotten it.

One day after school, Rosalind took us for ice cream in the village despite the chill in the air, much to Zelie's delight. Before I was allowed to join my sisters, Rosalind walked me a few doors down to Dr. Green's office.

"I'm not sick," I said.

Rosalind opened the door and held it open for me. "This'll only take a few minutes," she said, and when I didn't budge, she added: "Daddy made the appointment, and I don't think he's going to be very happy if you refuse to go inside."

She waited for me in the reception area as Dr. Green's secretary directed me into his office and closed the door, leaving me alone with him. It was a dark office, wood paneled, with only a small window, and a lamp was on in the middle of the day. From behind his desk, Dr. Green stood up as I entered and pointed to a chair across from him. His desk was covered in books and papers, and next to his telephone, on a square of wax paper, there was a half-eaten corned-beef sandwich.

"How are you feeling?" he asked, and as I looked at him, I couldn't help but remember the day that Aster died and his squeezing Matthew's shoulder. *I've got three daughters. They can be fragile.*

"Fine," I said in a surly way.

"Good," he said, pushing back slightly in his chair and tenting his fingers in front of him.

"Why am I here?"

"Your father asked me to speak with you. He's worried that your mother is exerting her influence over you. I gather from him that your sisters tend to ignore her, but you don't. He thinks you may be starting to believe in ghosts as well."

"I'm not sure," I said, refusing to commit either way. "She was right about something happening to Aster. I don't understand why no one ever listens to her."

He stared at me across the desk with an expression that said, *So this is how it's going to be.* He looked down at his corned-beef sandwich, realizing he wouldn't get to finish it as soon as he'd hoped.

"So you think your mother is a reliable source of information?"

"Aster is dead. She predicted it."

He leaned forward, resting his elbows on the desk, a grimace on his face. "She did no such thing. I want you to understand that your mother is a sick woman. She's sick in the head."

"But she warned everyone—"

"Miss Chapel, what do we do when people are sick?"

I hated the way he was speaking to me, as if I were a child. "Give them medicine."

"Correct. If someone has an infection, I prescribe penicillin. Now there's no cure for what's wrong with her, but I can make her more comfortable. I can take away her suffering. I became a doctor to stop people suffering, do you see? She isn't scared anymore. She doesn't have to worry that your sister is roaming the hallways looking for her."

"She wasn't worried about that. She wanted Aster to visit. She—"

"Stop right there. Ghosts aren't real. I'm a doctor and I've been with many people when they've passed on. When I was in the army, I did autopsies. Do you know what they are?"

"Yes."

"When someone is dead, they're dead. They're in heaven doing the Lord's work. They're not down here in Bellflower Village wandering around in the middle of the night and scaring us out of our wits. They're in another place, a much better place, where we will all go eventually. Do you understand? Because if you don't —"

"I understand," I said, not wanting him to finish his sentence. I didn't want to know what fate would befall me if I continued down the path I was on.

He sat up straighter, examining me with his doctor's gaze, unsure if he should believe me. I'd acquiesced awfully quickly, for which I was ashamed, but I didn't want to be drugged or sent to Fern Hollow like Belinda had been. Arguing with him, no matter how wrong he was, no matter how much I hated him, was only going to make my situation worse.

"I understand," I said again, to make sure he had heard me.

"Good." He eyed his sandwich. "If you ever have disturbing thoughts, you can come talk to me. Do you understand?"

"Yes."

He stood up and came around to my side of the desk. "Good girl," he said, patting me lightly on the back. He released me into the waiting room and shut his office door; he was probably eating his sandwich and calling my father to debrief; the sanity of the Chapel women was like a weather report, ever changing.

"Everything all right?" Rosalind said to me over the top of that month's *Glamour*. I nodded and smiled, knowing that this was expected. Rosalind couldn't be trusted, she'd proven that.

"Good," she said, and we went outside. As we were walking to meet our sisters, she said: "I hope you've learned your lesson."

"What lesson?"

"That our mother is crazy, and if you're not careful, you're going to end up like her."

Rosalind went ahead of me into the ice cream parlor, leaving me alone on the sidewalk with the sting of her words. Through the glass, I saw Zelie at a table with Daphne and Calla, an enormous hot fudge sundae in front of her. She was spooning ice cream into her mouth and laughing at something Daphne had said. For the first time in a long while, she looked happy.

Rosalind

1951

I.

In late October 1950, Paramount Pictures released *Chapel '70: The Gun That Won the West*. It starred Jimmy Stewart and Janet Leigh, and told the story of the legendary Chapel repeating rifle, first produced in 1870 and used in the genocide of the American Indians in the later years of the so-called settling of the American West.

A couple of the other Connecticut gun manufacturers insisted *their* guns were the ones that actually won the West, the Winchester Model 1873 and the Colt Peacemaker specifically, but the Chapel '70 had come first. My father took great pride in being singled out by Hollywood, and to mark the film's release, he rented out the Bellflower Cinema for an entire week. The workers at the Chapel factory were allowed to leave one afternoon during that week to see the film, and residents of the village and company executives were invited to see it in the evenings. Admission was free, as were the concessions, a significant extravagance for my frugal father, a man who typically didn't like to call attention to himself or his family.

Slightly more than four months after Aster's death, my sisters and I weren't as exuberant as we normally would have been about a Hollywood film celebrating our family name, but the prospect of the film was still exciting, there was no denying that. On opening night, our father brought us to the cinema with him so we could greet Chapel executives and their families as they arrived. Belinda wasn't there, thankfully—a film glorifying Chapel rifles would surely have sent her into cardiac arrest.

Without his wife at the premiere, it was important for our father to have his daughters by his side so as to appear the consummate family man with a loving home life. At Calla's insistence, we wore black dresses, which we'd purchased at a boutique in Greenwich the day before. Ever the Victorian, Calla insisted it would be in poor taste for us to appear in color at a public event so soon after Aster's death. The result of Calla's fashion advice was not that the five of us looked united in mourning but that we looked chic in our black dresses and matching shoes.

It was the way Rosalind looked in her knee-length black dress, a string of pearls around her neck, a touch of rose on her lips, that surely caught the eye of the man she would end up marrying five months later.

Peter Tollman was a senior vice president of something or other at the Chapel Firearms Company, having worked for my father for more than twenty years. He brought his wife, Adele, to the opening night of the film, and Adele brought her cousin. I saw him before we were ever introduced since he was taller than every other man in the lobby of the Bellflower Cinema. He would have been taller than everyone else even with a bare head and feet, but as it was, he wore cowboy boots and a ten-gallon hat so he towered above everyone there.

The lobby was crowded with executives and their wives and children, everyone chatting before the film, the adults enjoying wine, the children Coca-Cola. The man with the cowboy hat moved around the lobby; it took a while for him to reach my father and sisters and me since we were standing on the opposite side of the room from the entrance, with Zelie and I perched on the steps that led to the balcony. From my slightly elevated position, I could see the man's hat moving through the crowd like a shark's fin until finally he, along with Peter and Adele, stood before us.

"I'd like to introduce my cousin, Roderick Whiteley," Adele said, her hair a sleek blond bob, her face a map of the most exquisite fine lines. "He's here from Texas."

"But I'm a Connecticut native, Adele. You always forget that," Roderick said warmly, shaking my father's hand. Roderick wasn't necessarily a handsome man, but he was striking, with full lips that stayed parted and revealed two large front teeth that, while not sticking out, made me think of Bugs Bunny. And he was bulging, his khaki trousers hugging his rounded thighs and calves, his dark brown blazer snug around his shoulders and biceps. He wore what I would later learn was a bolo tie, which looked more like a necklace than a tie, a silver medallion in the shape of a buffalo fastened to a dark brown cord. At the time, I wasn't sure if he always dressed this way or if his clothes were meant to match the theme of the night. People in the lobby looked at him as if he were a character that had come to promote the film.

"It's such an honor to meet you, sir," Roderick said to our father, and Zelie and I glanced at each other, knowing what would happen next, the same thing that happened whenever a young man who'd been in the war met our father. We were used to hearing battle stories from the beaches of Europe to the islands of the Pacific. For Zelie and me, they always seemed like fairy tales, the Chapel rifle a dragon sent to slay the enemy in distant lands. These young men talked about how they held the rifle in their calloused hands, day after day, month after month, year after year, the rifle the only thing between them and death, and now to meet the man behind the gun — it was like meeting your guardian angel or even God. Roderick was no exception. "I was in the 82nd Airborne," Roderick said to my father, unprompted, as if bearing testimony. "I clung to my Chapel rifle like a rosary, prayed with it in my hands, ate with it in my lap, killed a few Italians with it."

He turned to my sisters and me. "My apologies, ladies, but such is war."

My father, taking this break in the story as an opportunity, turned to introduce us, starting with Rosalind. "This is my eldest —" Then he caught himself. "This is my daughter Rosalind."

Roderick took off his hat, revealing himself to be a brunette with thick, wavy hair. "Miss Rosalind Chapel," Roderick said, taking her hand in his and shaking his head in what seemed to be astonishment. "I just can't get over it. Another real-life Chapel, and this one such a beauty too." He smiled at her, revealing the rest of his mammoth-size teeth.

Rosalind plumped her hair with her free hand. The men who approached our father tended to blend into one another like toy soldiers on a shelf; Roderick's story was more of the same, and it was likely that Rosalind hadn't been paying attention to him at all until he took her hand in his so intimately.

"Your cousin is certainly charming," she said to Adele.

"Isn't he?" Adele said. "Too charming for his own good sometimes," she added, nudging Roderick along through the rest of the introductions, to Calla and Daphne, who received perfunctory handshakes, and finally to Zelie and me.

"Howdy, girls," he said, as the two of us gave little waves from the steps. *Was that a serious howdy,* I wondered, *and did anyone actually speak that way?*

"If you don't mind my saying so, Miss Chapel," Roderick said, returning to Rosalind. "Your father does a grave disservice to the country using GIs and sportsmen and cowboys in his ad campaigns when he has a group of such lovely ladies here. I guarantee, you gals would send those rifles flying off the shelves."

Rosalind's face opened up like a rose; she so loved to be adored. "You're too kind," she said, and turned to smile at Calla and Daphne, both of whom looked bored. Roderick's charms, whatever they might have been, didn't faze them. Rosalind put her hand to her neck and twisted her strand of pearls, wrapping them around her ruby fingernails. She and Roderick looked each other over for an embarrassingly long time, particularly given that our father was standing right next to them. Our father, for his part, was trying to move along the line of people waiting to greet him; Adele and Peter, taking notice, steered Roderick toward the bar to get a glass of wine.

That was the night the clock began to tick. Rosalind had said she'd be next — the next to be married, which meant the next to die. For the Chapel sisters, it would soon become clear there was little difference.

2.

It was a dreadful film, I thought, nowhere near as good as *Annie Get Your Gun,* which at least had Annie Oakley and singing and dancing. *Chapel '70* was just a bunch of men with guns, men who looked like they hadn't bathed in months, riding through the Technicolor Western landscape on horseback. The setting was the only thing that held my interest, all that saffron and amber we didn't have at home, the mesas and deep canyons and Shiprock, the endless sky. But the splendor of it was marred by the fighting scenes and the destruction caused by the Chapel '70, with the bodies piled up in the red dirt.

The Chapel repeating rifle was the real star of *Chapel '70,* as the name of the film implied. Before the invention of the repeating rifle, guns were loaded with a single shot, but the repeating rifle made it possible to load many cartridges into the rifle's magazine and fire uninterrupted. Before firearms like the Chapel '70, the kind of slaughter shown in the film had been impossible. This was the achievement of the Chapel family: mass death. I was glad Belinda wasn't there to see it.

After the film, the sound of gunfire still echoing in my head, we bundled in our coats and scarves to walk two blocks to Meadow & Main, the chophouse in Bellflower Village. My father and the Tollmans joined other Chapel executives at a round table in the center of the dining room. Calla and Daphne claimed a table for two in the corner near the bar while our father forced Zelie and me to sit with Roderick and Rosalind, much to their dismay. They sat across from each other with a candle in a red jar flickering between them; the table, thanks to Roderick's enormous appetite, was covered in white plates of steak and lobster and crab, platters of potatoes of every sort — baked, mashed, lyonnaise.

He was an oilman, he said, born in Connecticut; his parents both had deep roots in the state. When he was ten, his father moved the family, Roderick and his two younger brothers and their mother, to Texas so he could work for Gulf Oil. His father was wildly successful and soon started his own company, Whiteley Petroleum, and from the way Roderick talked, it seemed the family had made loads of money. They'd kept a home in Darien, on Contentment Island Road, right on the Sound, which they visited every chance they got — summer holidays, Christmas, and Easter. They were desperate for any chance to leave Midland, Texas, which Roderick said was completely lacking in civilized culture.

Roderick was living full-time in Connecticut, albeit temporarily, having enrolled in the graduate program in engineering at Yale. He lived on campus during the week and spent the weekends at his family's vacation home. He'd been at Yale for a year and a half by the time we met him, his June graduation date and a return to Texas not far away before he resumed his job in the family business, where he was primed to take over for his father within the next several years.

"D'you know I have a dream of ditching Midland all together?" Roderick said, his spoon cracking the surface of a crème brûlée. "I'd live in Connecticut and work in New York and do something else with my life besides oil." He pronounced *oil* like *awl*.

"Then why don't you stay here?" Rosalind said, rather shamelessly. She'd dipped her spoon into his brûlée despite having said she didn't want dessert. Zelie and I, meanwhile, were each tucking into a towering wedge of chocolate fudge cake with vanilla ice cream and raspberry sauce, eating quickly before anyone noticed just how much we had.

"I'd be a fool to walk away from what my father built, that's the truth. I can make a life for myself out there. Lemons into lemonade and all that jazz. I bought a house, do you want to see it?"

He reached for his wallet and took out a folded photograph. He passed it to Rosalind first, then to me and Zelie. It was a ranch house with a massive oak tree in front of it, surrounded by what looked to be many acres of barren land. I could see the horizon line on either side of the house, flat land touching the sky far in the distance.

"Is that where you live when you're back home?" Rosalind said.

"Not yet. I bought it before I came to school out here. See there," Roderick said, pointing to the empty space around the house. "There's plenty of room to build stables."

"For horses?" Zelie said, her mouth full of cake. She seemed delighted by the idea.

"Yes, ma'am, for horses."

"I've never ridden on a horse," Zelie said.

"Then you've never truly lived," Roderick said. "You can come visit me anytime. Consider this an open invitation to Palomino Road."

"*Palomino Road,*" Rosalind said dreamily. "It seems a world away from here."

"Oh it is," Roderick said. "It's another planet from here."

He put the photo back in his wallet, and as the dishes were being cleared away, he asked Rosalind if she wanted to accompany him to a classical music concert the following afternoon. She enthusiastically accepted, even going so far as to claim she loved classical music.

"No you *don't,*" Zelie said. "You told us classical music is for old folks who are hard of hearing."

Rosalind gave her a look. "That must have been Daphne."

"So we have a date," Roderick said, smiling brightly at Rosalind, then leaning over to Zelie and whispering conspiratorially: "Next time it'll be jazz. Does she like jazz?" He winked and put on his cowboy hat.

3.

The classical music concert was the first of many dates over the following weeks. Roderick took Rosalind to parties and potlucks at his cousins' houses —he had cousins all over Connecticut, their homes dotting the landscape with the frequency of filling stations. Personally, I was glad Rosalind was out of the house more often. When she wasn't around, there was no one to spy on me, to remind me with a never-ending string of displeased looks that she thought I was crazy and only getting worse.

After her dates, she'd swan into the girls' sitting room, bringing with her a trail of winter chill, crunchy flakes of snow caught in her hair and collar, the smell of pine and smoke (fireplace and cigarette), the leftovers of wine caught on her breath. She'd talk about what they'd eaten, Italian food in Watertown or Chinese dumplings in New Haven, and what they did after, a jazz club or hot chocolate in a cozy café. Her evenings out with Roderick made our lives seem ever more dreary: our long days at school, our brown dinners — beef stew, meat loaf, shepherd's pie — and evenings stuck at home with the darkness of winter wrapped as tightly around us as a scarf around the neck; unlike Rosalind's, our winter didn't sparkle with snow and twinkling lights; it didn't smell like roaring fires and hot drinks; it smelled of grief, a stale, moldy smell that lingered in the floorboards and carpets and made it difficult to breathe.

We endured our first Christmas without Aster, and when the new year arrived, we were relieved to see 1950 pass into history. We toasted the arrival of 1951 with champagne in the girls' sitting room; Roderick had bought us a bottle of Moët & Chandon, and even Zelie and I were allowed a few sips.

In the new year, Roderick and Rosalind saw each other practically every day. Roderick had offered Rosalind a ticket out, and by the end of January, they were engaged. The wedding would be another kind of a ticket, a more permanent one, and even if the ticket was to Midland, Texas, Rosalind was desperate for it. She was determined to hitch herself to Roderick's wagon — though this is perhaps too obvious a metaphor for a man who looked like he'd stepped off a wagon train, that's my abiding impression of him.

They planned to marry on March 31 while Roderick's family was still in Connecticut for their Easter vacation. A March wedding didn't scream romance, but June was out of the question — that month would forever be Aster's. Most of April and May would be filled with Roderick's final exams, so the last day of March it was. Rosalind and Roderick would live in the Whiteleys' vacation home in Darien until Roderick graduated from Yale with his master's degree, and for their delayed honeymoon, they'd drive from Connecticut to Texas in Roderick's Cadillac, stay in roadside motels with shimmery turquoise pools, and eat hamburgers at drive-ins. When they would eventually arrive in the barren plains of Midland, they'd move to Palomino Road, where they'd fill the stables with horses and have the daughter Rosalind wanted (just the one). The little girl's name, Rosalind informed us, would be Aster Rose.

It had all happened so quickly — the courtship, the engagement, the plans for a wedding, and the future laid out before them like a banquet on a table, a table assumed by all to be so long that no one could see where it ended. It seemed too soon for this to be happening, Aster's wedding and death not even a year behind us, but none of us dared mention it. Rosalind, like one of Roderick's horses, galloped confidently ahead, and we knew what would happen if we dared step in her path.

"Me and my Yankee child bride," Roderick sang on the night of their engagement to a honky-tonk tune; he was twenty-eight, Rosalind was nineteen. We were gathered in the parlor on the bleakest of January nights, with snow whipping against the windows and the fire struggling to keep us warm. Belinda made a brief appearance, then excused herself, claiming to have a headache.

"Oh Roddy," Rosalind said, perched daintily on his lap. She kissed him on the cheek and removed his hat from his head. "You've made me so happy, just when I thought I could never be happy again." She lowered the hat onto her own head and it slid so far down that half her face disappeared.

4.

The two months leading up to the wedding passed relatively uneventfully, which was itself noteworthy. What had happened to Aster was unimaginable, and it was unimaginable that it would happen again. Even Belinda had accepted her second daughter's engagement without fuss, though that didn't necessarily count for much — her ability to actually cause a fuss had been dulled by the Veronal the nurse administered. Nurse Marsh continued to live with us to sedate Belinda at night and keep watch over her during the day.

Rosalind had planned a simpler wedding than Aster's: no flower girls, no bridesmaids, no groomsmen. Only family and a few close friends had been invited. There would be a ceremony at the church in Bellflower Village followed by a reception at Hotel Cream. Rosalind had bought an understated dress and kept it, and everything else for the wedding, stored at the Whiteleys' vacation home, far away from our house. Though Belinda was perennially sedated and I'd been behaving myself, I supposed she didn't want to take any chances. There were no signs of the wedding in the house except for the trunk she'd packed, which was sitting in the hallway of the girls' wing. Rosalind had dropped out of Darlow's Ladies College and was so busy in the lead-up to the wedding that we rarely saw her. It felt like she'd already left.

We were about a week away from the wedding when spring break began. The end of March was balmy that year, heading out like the gentlest of lambs and leading us into the most intoxicating time of the year, with the days growing longer, and pale blossoms overtaking the trees, the torment of the winter months melting away like the Wicked Witch of the West. Surviving a New England winter was always an accomplishment; that year it felt even more so than most.

When the weather turned, Aster's tombstone was planted in the family plot. The stone had only her first name on it, and beneath that, a starlike aster flower had been chiseled into the granite. Our father had refused to surrender her completely to the Maybrick family, but he couldn't very well call her Aster Chapel either. In death, she apparently belonged to no one.

The break from school almost made it seem like summer. Rosalind was always gone, Calla had set herself up in the girls' library to write a book of poetry, and Daphne spent most of her days with her friend Veronica Cream, whose family owned the hotel where Rosalind's wedding reception was to be held. Daphne flitted between the hotel and home, Veronica's mother chauffeuring them around. That left Zelie and me on our own. We trudged around the property, surveying our kingdom as it came out of hibernation; I carried my sketchbook and pencils, and Zelie always had one of her mystery novels.

One day early that week, I headed out alone while Zelie had her piano lesson. I'd given up the piano by that point and had decided to focus on art. I sketched for a while near Belinda's flower garden, all tulips and daffodils, then I moved on to the frog pond, where the trees, with their newly green buds, reflected on the surface of the water. I tried to capture the sparkle of sunlight atop the murky gray.

As I sketched, I heard laughter through the trees, a high-pitched girly giggle. "Zelie?" I called out. She should still have been having her lesson, but there was no one else it could have been. Calla was the only one of our sisters at home, and she was in the house writing. Besides, she rarely laughed.

A squirrel raced by, and I started adding it to my drawing. But then I heard more laughter. "Zelie? Stop being silly."

No answer. I set my sketchbook aside and stood up, walking around the pond toward the sound. I was heading in the direction of the meadow through the trees that encircled it, and suddenly I was awash in pink as I stepped into a thicket of cherry trees in full bloom, a blushing forest.

The laughter was coming from my right. I walked softly in that direction, not wanting to make a noise, unsure of who was laughing. After a few moments, I saw Daphne and Veronica. I hadn't known Daphne was at home, but she and Veronica had spread out a blanket between two cherry trees. Daphne, with her back to me, was sitting on a tree stump while Veronica, who I couldn't quite see, was sitting on the blanket in front of her.

I didn't want them to spot me so I moved to stand behind the trunk of a nearby maple, and from there, I could see Veronica. From the waist down, she was wearing a simple linen skirt that matched the shade of the cherry blossoms. From the waist up, she wasn't wearing anything at all, her blouse and bra discarded on the blanket beside her. She was kneeling, sitting on the backs of her legs. Her arms extended behind her, hands resting on the blanket, propping her up like an easel. She had her back arched, her head thrown back, eyes closed, soaking up the sun that filtered through the pink canopy of blossoms above her, her torso all creamy skin, her long black hair pinned messily up, her lips a shade of coral.

Daphne had her sketch pad in her lap and was drawing Veronica's nearly naked form. Occasionally, she'd say something to Veronica that I couldn't hear, and the two of them would laugh. Then Daphne mumbled something, and Veronica sat up straight, clasping her hands in front of her. Her breasts were heavy and large, with wide areolas that matched the color of her skirt and the blossoms in the trees, light pink on a palette, a splash of white mixed in. When she sat up, I could see her delicate, bony shoulders.

My hands on the bark of the tree, my face peeking around the trunk, I was afraid that one of them might see me, but I couldn't look away. Daphne turned to a new page of her sketch pad and worked silently. Veronica, eyes closed again, head tilted back, bathed in the pink light. She was basking in Daphne's attention, not knowing she had mine too, that there were two sets of eyes running over her body.

We three stayed in our positions for quite a while; I could have stayed there all day watching Veronica.

Finally, Daphne stood up, and I moved back, fearing I'd be caught. But she didn't turn in my direction. She set down her sketch pad and went to Veronica, the two of them kneeling before each other. Daphne reached over and moved aside the strands of hair that had fallen over Veronica's face, then she leaned in and kissed her on the mouth. She kissed her neck, then down to her breasts; I couldn't watch and turned away, feeling an unexpected stab of jealousy. My face was burning hot, my heart pumping so fast that I felt like I might faint. I gripped the tree tighter, the rough bark a welcome contrast to my wooziness. I had seen Daphne's pulpy novels in the sitting room for years — *Vixen, Sin on Wheels, Women at War* — but I thought they were just trashy romance novels. And they were, I supposed, but of an entirely different sort than I could have imagined.

When I looked back in their direction, Veronica was lying down on her back. Daphne pulled off Veronica's skirt and tossed it aside, then she, still dressed in her shorts and blouse, crawled on top of Veronica, and the two of them began to laugh again. I didn't know what they were doing, but I couldn't watch any longer. I retraced my steps out of the thicket of cherry trees, the sound of their laughter replaced by Veronica's soft moans.

5.

I walked around for quite a while after that, deep in the forest where no one would see me, my face burning hot for so long that I worried it would stay that way, forever aflame.

Inside the house, I heard Zelie playing the piano, which she usually did for a couple of hours after her lesson. I could always tell what kind of mood she was in by what she chose to play. Before Aster had died, she was fond of songs from Broadway shows and movies — "The Surrey with the Fringe on Top," "When You Wish Upon a Star" — but she'd taken a melancholy turn through the winter, practicing (or at least attempting to) Beethoven's *Moonlight Sonata* and Liszt's *Consolations* endlessly.

As I made my way up to the girls' wing, she was playing Wagner's "Bridal Chorus." She was angry at Rosalind for not having any flower girls or brides-maids at the wedding, and perhaps her choice of music was meant to guilt Rosalind, who wasn't home to hear it. I passed my mother's wing, worried what the music might conjure in her, but I was thankful that her door was closed for her afternoon nap.

I poked my head into the girls' library where Calla, at a desk in front of the window, was hunched over, scribbling away. A candle flickered on top of a pewter dish even though the room was full of sunshine. "Who's there?" she said, without looking up.

"It's Iris."

"Please tell Zelie to stop playing that *wretched* music," she said, but I had no plans to do so. If Calla wanted Zelie to stop, she could tell her herself.

I walked down the hallway of the girls' wing past the closed door of As-ter and Rosalind's bedroom. Behind me, someone came bounding down the corridor. I turned to see Daphne rushing around the corner, sketch pad and pencils clutched in her hand. The unexpected sight of her burned my skin again. Had she seen me spying on her and Veronica? I didn't think she had, but faced with her now, I panicked.

"What's wrong with you?" she said, going into her bedroom and setting her things down on her desk. I watched from the doorway as she took off her shorts and pulled on a black skirt.

"Nothing," I said, gradually coming to terms with the fact that she had a whole secret life I'd known nothing about. I thought she and Veronica had spent their afternoons smoking cigarettes and listening to records. It would have been impossible for me to guess the truth.

Daphne stood before the mirror and combed her hair, what was left of it. At the first sign of spring, she'd gone to the hairdresser's and exchanged her bland pageboy for a dramatic pixie cut. If her hair had been red instead of brown, she would have looked like a matchstick. Our father had been far less imaginative in his assessment — "You look like a boy," he'd said, disgust audible in his voice. I recalled her on top of Veronica and closed my eyes as if that would make the image go away. No matter how hard I tried, all I could see was their bare limbs entwined, their midsections pressed together.

I opened my eyes to see Daphne before me, a smirk on her face. "You're an odd one, kid," she said, and slipped past me through the doorway. "I'm going to the hotel with Veronica," she said over her shoulder. "If anyone asks" — no one would — "I'll be back for dinner."

When Daphne was out of sight, I considered making a move for the sketch pad she'd left behind, but Zelie appeared then, claiming her fingers were numb from too much piano. She begged me to play a game with her, and so I did, reluctantly.

On our way to dinner that evening, we stopped by Belinda's sitting room. During the winter, our father had assigned Zelie and me this job — visiting with Belinda in the half hour leading up to dinner, then accompanying her to the dining room. "Your mother needs company," he'd said when he gave us this task, likely knowing that Zelie and I would be the only two of his daughters amenable to it.

When we arrived, the nurse, sitting in her usual chair near the window, set down her needlework; eager to take her leave, she went down to the kitchen to eat with Dovey and Mrs. O'Connor.

"Blossoms," Belinda said when the nurse was gone, inviting Zelie and me inside. She closed the book she was reading and asked us to sit down. I took the chair across from the sofa where she sat, but Zelie set about exploring the items displayed on the various shelves, which held for her an endless allure, these souvenirs from our mother's past.

Belinda wore her usual white dress. She had grown thinner and frailer since Aster had died, her skin an unhealthy hue from lack of sun. She rarely went outside anymore.

"How was your day?" she asked us, as she always did.

"We played Clue," Zelie said, picking up a tiny porcelain box and removing the lid.

"You're fond of that game. I'll have to play it with you sometime."

"You wouldn't like it," Zelie said. "It's about murder."

Since spring had arrived, it was still light outside at the dinner hour. We sat in silence for a bit, conversation never flowing easily between mother and daughters even at the best of times.

"Are you all right, Iris?"

Looking out the window, I thought of the cherry blossoms but didn't say so. "I was thinking about Rosalind," I said, which wasn't true. "It's hard to believe she's getting married in a week." I was stating the obvious, but I wanted to see her reaction when I mentioned the wedding. Thus far, she'd had none unless disinterest counted.

"Yes, she'll be moving to Texas, won't she?" Belinda said blandly, not portraying any emotion. I wanted to know how she truly felt, but the mother I had known was gone, drugged into submission. Years later, I read a book of Emily Dickinson's letters and found a line that made me think of my mother in these later years of her life: "I am out with lanterns, looking for myself." Even as a young girl, I suspected that once the nurse had come to live with us the real Belinda was trapped inside herself, wandering, lost in the darkness.

"Shall we have dinner?" she said at last, having put in the necessary time.

Zelie set down a Limoges candlestick. "Are you actually hungry tonight?"

"No, not really," Belinda said, standing up with a sigh. She knew dinner with the family wasn't optional; she was still, in a sense, on trial.

• • •

"Sugar, we gotta see Mount Vernon," Roderick said, as Zelie, Belinda, and I entered the dining room and sat down. Everyone else was already seated. "We can't drive right by and not see it."

"Roddy," Rosalind said, with a playful glint in her eyes. "You promised me *fun* on our honeymoon. George Washington *does not* fit into that category."

"Washington was the father of our country," our father said with mild horror, not understanding that Rosalind, as she was fond of doing, was just engaging in banter, not a serious conversation. "I certainly think his home is worth seeing."

"All right, Daddy," Rosalind said, as Mrs. O'Connor came in to serve. "If you and Roddy insist."

We were having meat loaf for dinner; it was slathered in some kind of barbecue sauce, a nod, perhaps, to Roderick's home state. Belinda, to my right, picked at the corn bread on her plate, following the conversation with the vacant smile of an airline hostess. She was used to Roderick and he to her. While Aster had been careful to keep Matthew away from us, Rosalind took a different approach, believing that familiarity would make Roderick's presence in our lives seem less threatening.

"What do you think, Mrs. C?" Roderick asked Belinda, his informality like a needle scratching across a record. He often tried to involve her in conversation.

Belinda, never comfortable when the attention turned to her, pushed her plate aside. "About what?" Her eyelids were heavy now.

"Mount Vernon," Rosalind said impatiently, speaking loudly as if Belinda were elderly.

"The home of George Washington," Daphne added, cutting herself a second slice of meat loaf, seemingly famished. Listening to her made me think of Veronica again, and I feared I might turn red, but no one was looking at me.

"I suppose you could stop there if you're interested in American history,"

Belinda said, attempting to rouse herself. "I doubt there's much that's interesting in Texas. You might find yourself quite bored there."

Daphne and Calla laughed; Rosalind turned to Roderick and rolled her eyes.

"We'll get you out to Texas soon, Mrs. C," Roderick said. "Then you can see how boring it is for yourself."

"*Roddy,*" Rosalind whispered, clearly dismayed at the thought of Belinda venturing west.

"Mother can't go to *Texas,*" Zelie said, and laughed. She was right, it was a funny thought; Belinda could be imagined only in situ, at the wedding cake or on Cape Cod. It seemed impossible that she could exist anywhere else.

"I'm afraid my traveling days are behind me," she said, standing up and holding on to the table for support. She came to dinner every night but rarely stayed long.

"Nurse Marsh," my father called out. He demanded Belinda's presence at meals but always seemed relieved when she departed early. The nurse came and took Belinda by the arm. She said goodnight and left the room, leaning on the nurse to steady herself.

"Only one more week of this," Rosalind said to Roddy once Belinda was gone.

"One more week for *you*. The rest of us will still be here," Calla said. It was hard for me to believe that Calla would soon become the oldest Chapel girl; Rosalind had done a poor-enough job, but with Calla at the helm, everything was bound to fall apart — the total breakdown of order, our wolfpack returning to its ancestral form. I could see it all before us: chaos.

"God, I pity you," Rosalind said, as if she could see it as well. "When I escape this awful place, I will miss you all desperately, except for our mother. She's always been the specter at the feast."

"That's enough, Roz." I thought at first it was our father's scolding voice, but I looked up from my plate to see that it was Roderick who'd spoken, his jokey demeanor having slipped away. "I warned you. Be nice."

"Sorry," Rosalind said quietly, not arguing back as I knew she would have with anyone else.

"I'll have my hands full with her," Roderick said. He elbowed Rosalind gently, then turned to our father. "She never listens, does she?"

"Not normally, no."

"That nasty temper gets the best of her."

"I said I'm sorry, Roddy." Rosalind seemed chastened, as she rarely was, and next to Roderick's hulking figure, she appeared smaller, the difference in their age and experience suddenly so visible.

I turned away from them to the empty doorway. Rosalind was escaping but to what? If Belinda had been herself, I felt certain she would have tried to stop Rosalind from marrying Roderick. She might have warned of *something terrible* happening, which I realized then didn't have to mean death. There were many kinds of terrible.

After dinner, Roderick drove my sisters into the village to see *The Redhead and the Cowboy,* but I made my excuses and stayed home. I had other plans.

When I had the girls' wing to myself, I went to Calla and Daphne's bedroom and picked up the sketch pad Daphne had with her that afternoon. I flipped through it; most of the pages had been filled. Veronica flitted by, the whole book devoted to her.

I went back to the beginning and studied the work more closely. In the first drawing, Veronica was sitting at a table, a teacup in front of her. She had a finger looped through the ear-shaped handle, some of the links in her bracelet touching the table. The detail in the drawing was incredible. Veronica looked to be in a café or perhaps at the restaurant in her parents' hotel. Her body faced forward, a light sweater buttoned snugly against her chest, a little scarf tied around her neck like a kerchief. Her head was turned to the side, and she was presumably staring out a window, watching the world go by. Her gaze was pensive, which is how I'd always wanted Zelie to look when she posed for me.

There were dozens more drawings of Veronica fully clothed, in a sundress on the beach, standing in a meadow, reclining on a bed. I'd never really seen her until that day. She lived in the village; her family had moved in perhaps two years earlier, but she didn't attend our school or church. The Creams were Catholic and attended Our Lady of Sorrows in Greenwich; Veronica, an only child, was enrolled as a student at the attached school. I didn't know how Daphne had met her. I'd seen the two of them walking side by side down the street in the village a couple of times, Veronica nothing more than a dark-haired blur, but she'd never come inside our house to my knowledge. That wasn't unusual. We never brought friends to our house, and in general, none of us really had many friends to begin with, preferring instead the company of our sisters.

I kept turning the pages of the sketch pad, listening to make sure my sisters hadn't come home early. Daphne was an exceptional artist. The more erotic sketches (I say "more" erotic because they all, regardless of dress, showed the tension between Veronica and the person with the pencil) came slowly, a tease unfolding page by page. They started with Veronica on the beach pulling down her bathing suit with one finger to reveal part of her left breast, an inscrutable smile on her face with an undertone of sass, that Mona Lisa smile that Nat King Cole sang about.

In the next drawing, the bathing suit had been pulled all the way down, enticing the artist as well as the viewer, and from there, they grew more explicit: Veronica with her skirt pulled up; Veronica fully naked from behind; Veronica in a bathtub; Veronica on a chaise lounge straddling the sides. I arrived eventually at the cherry blossoms, but they weren't what I'd expected. The other drawings were realistic, but here the blossoms weren't just a background to Veronica; she had become one with them. As she knelt on the blanket, cherry blossoms fell from the sky around her, a lush floral rainstorm, leaving blooms in her hair, on her shoulders and knees. Veronica appeared to have been grown in a garden — a garden nymph.

I expected that to be the end, but I turned the page to find one more. It shocked me more than any of the others. It was another scene on the blanket, which Daphne must have drawn after I left. Veronica was lying on the blanket, her legs spread wide apart, and Daphne had sketched what she saw there.

I had never seen that part of a woman's body, not even my own. I'd seen naked Greek statues in textbooks at school, the women with the puffy V between their legs hiding whatever was inside. It was the way I looked on the rare occasions I observed my body fully naked in the bathroom mirror. But Daphne's drawing charted the whole area in great detail; it was almost floral, the layers and folds of a rose or an iris. I closed the book. I didn't know what was wrong with me that I enjoyed looking at such a thing.

6.

That night, I drifted between full sleep and wakefulness as a series of memories from the day played through my mind, a blurry, flickering filmstrip of forests and cherry trees, of pencil drawings and coral lips and delicate shoulders and pink areolas. I writhed in bed as if I had a fever, kicking my blanket to the floor, my nightgown twisting tighter around me as I rolled from side to side. Then I felt a hand on my arm.

It felt good after a day of longing to be touched. I moaned a little purr of delight. I could feel myself smiling and opened my eyes, piercing the thin glaze of sleep and expecting to see no one and nothing but the dark bedroom. I'd been dreaming, after all, but no — there was an actual hand gripping my arm, and I snatched it away as if from a snake. A person stood next to my bed bent over at the waist and staring down at me.

"Mother?" I said with a start. "Why aren't you in your room?"

"I slipped out," she whispered.

She sat down on the edge of my bed and leaned toward me. "The nurse fell asleep. She forgot to give me my pills. Listen." She placed her hands on either side of my face. "I don't have much time."

It was startling to hear her speak with such intensity. She kept me waiting for a few seconds before saying what she needed to say, as if giving me time to brace myself. I grew nervous, then I knew.

"Don't say it," I pleaded with her, pulling away. "Mother, no."

"Something terrible is going to happen if Rosalind marries that man," she said, taking me by the upper arms and grasping me tightly. "I've been smelling the roses again."

"What does that mean?"

"Roses warn of trouble ahead."

I wriggled free of her grasp. "Please go away," I begged her. She was panicked, and I couldn't be drawn back into that. "We'll both get in trouble again."

"Iris!" my mother shouted in a loud whisper. I looked over at Zelie, who hadn't stirred.

"Rosalind is asleep in the sitting room," I said. "Talk to her yourself."

"No one ever listens to me," she said. "You're the only one who can save her."

"No one listens to me either." I cried at the thought of Rosalind in the ground next to her Aster. "You have to be wrong this time."

"I wish I was." She stood up and kissed me on top of the head, then rushed out.

I listened to the sound of her footsteps fade away, and as I did, I recalled the feeling I'd had in the dining room. I'd known somehow that this was going to happen.

7.

The next day was Easter Sunday. My sisters were excited about their new dresses, which came in the pastel shades of Easter eggs: Rosalind's in rose pink, Calla's in lavender, Daphne's in pistachio, mine in yellow, and Zelie's in baby blue. By the time I opened my eyes, they were rushing around the girls' wing getting ready — Rosalind and Calla with curlers in their hair, powder compacts and tubes of lipstick in their hands; Zelie calling out for someone to help her; and Daphne pacing up and down the hallway in her bra and underpants, looking for the comb she'd lost.

While they dressed, I stayed in bed. I was still trying to shake off the night before and convince myself that Belinda was just afraid, not clairvoyant like she'd been with Aster. Lightning didn't strike in the same place twice, or at least that's what I'd always been told.

Finally, I got up and headed to the bathroom. The door to Aster and Rosalind's bedroom was open, Rosalind was in front of the mirror putting rouge on her cheeks. Her pink dress hugged her torso, but the skirt flared out; her hair was perfectly curled, her lips burgundy, the black heels on her feet elevating her calves. She looked so vibrant and alive that I couldn't imagine how anything bad would ever happen to her.

"Rough night?" she asked, and I shrugged.

"Can someone help me?" Zelie shouted from somewhere in the girls' wing, and Rosalind answered the call, brushing past me with a pat on the shoulder. I went into her bedroom, walking to the window that had had to be repaired after Aster had shattered it. I bent over and saw the blood between the floorboards, a dark black now, like mold. The maids had tried to scrub it out, but it was in every crevice.

"You better get dressed," Rosalind said quietly. I hadn't heard her return, and I stood up quickly and blushed, a little girl caught.

I plodded down the hallway to the bathroom, then back to my bedroom. I pulled on my dress, which was as yellow and soft as a chick. *I'm not going to say anything,* I thought to myself as I put on the little bolero jacket that came with the dress. A bird squawked outside and I turned to the window. The bird had vanished; my eyes landed instead on Aster's grave.

No, I said to myself. *That's not a sign.*

We were too old for Easter baskets, but waiting for us on the dining-room table were chocolate bunnies wrapped in colorful foil, packets of jelly beans, and plastic eggs filled with trinkets. They were the centerpiece of the table, tucked among tufts of green plastic grass and twin vases of daffodils, all artfully arranged, presumably, by Dovey and Mrs. O'Connor.

We ate a late breakfast of poached eggs on toast and freshly squeezed orange juice. Belinda hadn't made an appearance, and I was glad of that. After breakfast, my father, my sisters, and I filed out of the house to go to church. My sisters and I put on our hats and gloves as we walked outside, checking our reflections in the car windows.

At the Easter service, I took off my gloves and nibbled my nails during the morbid hymns and readings about death and resurrection. Eventually, I just had to get out. I whispered to Rosalind that I had to go to the ladies' room and slid out of our pew. Outside, there were fathers who'd escaped for a cigarette break. I saw Dr. Green's office, which is where I knew I'd end up if I dared disrupt Rosalind's wedding.

I felt a flare of anger at Belinda and what she'd done to me. *You're the only one who can save her.* What a terrible thing to say! It was a mother's job to save her child, and Belinda had dumped it on me, though I knew that if she intervened my father would send her away. I didn't have any special power to stop Rosalind; the only reason our mother singled me out was because I listened to her when no one else would.

I walked around to the side of the church into a courtyard of tall shrubbery and a cherry tree in full bloom, its pink petals scattered on the stone slabs. The sight of the tree brought to mind Veronica, and I wondered if the two would forever be intertwined in my mind; like Pavlov's dog, I would be filled with longing and a scarlet blush of shame at the sight of a cherry tree. But the day before seemed like a lifetime ago by then; all I'd had to worry about was my inappropriate lust. Belinda couldn't just let me be, let me have the normal anxieties of a girl my age; she had to twist my life as if we were in a Nancy Drew book — one written by Mary Shelley.

I entered the side door of the church and walked into the stone room where Aster's casket had been on display. Now there were just some folding chairs and a table stacked with Bibles and hymnals. I unfolded one of the chairs and sat down.

Though I was wearing my bolero jacket, I shivered in the chill of the room and the memories so thick inside. It wasn't only Aster's body that had been in this place, but all of Bellflower Village's dead dating back more than a century. It was a room of spirits; perhaps that's what made me shiver most of all.

I sat in the chill and wondered what I was going to do. After what had happened with Aster, I'd tried to move on; I couldn't make sense of any of it, but Belinda had been constrained, and without her prodding me, I was able, for the most part, to push what had happened out of my mind. Now Belinda's warning had plunged me into an impossible situation once again, one that I feared wouldn't have a good outcome for anyone. I knew it would be a mistake to ignore my mother given that she'd been right before. But Dr. Green had told me that Belinda was sick, and Rosalind had said I was becoming just like her. Was Belinda actually sick? I didn't think so; it was more that she couldn't be tamed — that's what they didn't like, and since they couldn't tame her, they sedated her. But maybe I was wrong about that. I really wasn't sure what to believe anymore. That's what my family and the doctor had taught me the previous autumn — that I couldn't trust myself.

8.

Roderick was waiting for us at home; he'd been invited to Easter dinner. His parents and siblings had been invited as well, but they had obligations with family elsewhere.

We were scheduled to have dinner early — holiday dinners were always in the afternoon, one of Mrs. O'Connor's unwritten rules — and my sisters and Roderick and I played Monopoly on the terrace while we waited. Mrs. O'Connor had set out pitchers of lemonade and a platter of crustless cucumber-and-cream-cheese sandwiches to hold us over, but everyone seemed more interested in the chocolate bunnies and jelly beans.

It should have been a carefree day, a beautiful spring holiday in the sun, and I supposed for everyone else, even Calla, it was — they certainly looked merry sitting around the table in their Easter finery, Roderick anchoring the group. He wore his cowboy hat and a blue-and-white-checked button-down with short sleeves, the buffalo bolo tie around his neck.

My sisters passed his hat around the table and took turns trying it on. They giggled at his jokes, as they always did, though it seemed that the novelty of having a man around was more amusing than the man himself. Our house was full of feminine energy, and our father wasn't home enough to dilute it; Roderick was like a monkey visiting from the zoo. A curiosity at best, fun for a while, but all of us (except for Rosalind) were happy to see him go at the end of the day.

They were all talking and laughing, so my silence blended into the background. I wondered if I should tell them about Belinda's warning. Maybe I could play it off as lighthearted: *Rosalind,* I could say. *You'll never guess what happened last night. Mother was back to her old tricks!*

Our mother, Rosalind would say with a playful sigh. *Always* such *a kidder!*

But I knew there was no way to make it funny; it *wasn't* funny.

"Somebody's a million miles away," Roderick said with a chuckle, holding out the dice to me. They were all staring at me, Daphne biting the head off a chocolate bunny, Calla daintily eating jelly beans one by one, and Zelie, her mouth stained from all the artificially colored candy. Rosalind, meanwhile, smirked with annoyance. She didn't want her fiancé to see that I was odd. He already knew about our mother.

I reached out, and as my hand touched Roderick's across the table, I looked closely at his hand and arm, the dark hair, the contours of his muscles, and I could feel the heat of him. It was different from my arms or my sisters', we with our pale hairless appendages, our muscles and bones wrapped in an invisible layer of fat, as thin and delicate as the cream skimmed off milk. Roderick's arm was beastly, his hand so enormous compared to mine that he could have crushed it and turned my bones into powder.

He gave me the dice, then I dropped them onto the game board, and Zelie immediately began to move my piece around since I seemed incapable of doing it.

"You play for me, Zelie," I said.

I needed to clear my head, so I got up and walked toward the forest, with Rosalind calling after me, "Iris, where are you going?"

I took off my hat and fanned myself with it as I walked deeper into the forest north of the house. I still didn't know what to do about my mother's warning. Could I even be sure I'd talked to her the night before? Maybe the whole thing had been a nightmare. I continued on, enjoying the greening of the early spring forest with its dark columns of trees, a Parthenon of nature. The birds sang overhead, and the sun filtered through the lace of the branches, pulling me in still deeper. I worried I had gotten lost until I stepped into a clearing and saw the graveyard of Aster's wedding dreams.

No, I thought. *This isn't a sign.*

The mounds of earth covering Aster's wedding china and gifts, which would have been buried in snow all winter, no longer looked freshly dug, and the shards of china I'd left on top were half-buried, sharp points of white sticking up through the dirt. I tugged at one and pulled it free. The apple-blossom design poked my guilt and my grief, neither ever very far from the surface.

Hot from my walk, I took off my bolero jacket and sat down, leaning against a tree trunk, my legs splayed out in front of me. I was tired and closed my eyes and soon fell asleep. I dreamt of Veronica kneeling on top of the mound where I'd buried Aster's things. She looked the same as she had the day before, in her pink linen skirt and nothing else, but now she was posing for me; it was my hand moving across the page.

In my dreams, I was a better artist. I'd started at the knees and moved up to the stomach and breasts and shoulders; when I began to draw Veronica's face, I noticed that her mouth was moving, but from across the expanse of the clearing, I couldn't hear what she was saying. I kept drawing and her mouth kept moving, straining as if she were pleading with me.

"Veronica," I called out — I'd never said her name before.

I set down my sketch pad and tried to go to her, but the dream was fading, something had punctured it, a sound coming from the forest, twigs cracking under the weight of footsteps. Someone was in the clearing with me.

I opened my eyes and looked around. "Hello?" I said timidly. I heard the twigs crack again but I couldn't tell from which direction.

"Who's there?" I'd wanted to shout, but my words only creaked out. I scrambled to my feet and hid behind the tree trunk, still holding the cracked piece of china in my hand, sharp enough to hurt someone if I needed to. I heard the sound again and peeked around the trunk, my eyes scanning the clearing, hoping no one was there. I didn't see anything, but I felt as if I weren't alone.

I wanted desperately to cry out for help, but no one would hear me. To my right, I saw the path that led back to the house. I braced myself, then sprinted in that direction

As I ran, I heard the footsteps behind me, as quick as mine, moving closer and closer. I glanced over my shoulder in the hopes I could see who was chasing me, but I couldn't make out anything distinct through the blur of trees and sunshine. I kept running, pushing myself to go faster, glancing back every few seconds; then I came to an abrupt halt, my body slamming into a tree. Not face-first, but my shoulder had hit the trunk hard and knocked me to the ground. I screamed and writhed around, eventually curling into a ball in the dirt. I heard footsteps over my heavy breathing. Someone was still there, circling me. I didn't know how far I was from the house or whether anyone would hear me shout if I tried. All I had to protect me was a scrap of china.

I cried a little, a tiny meow of fear; then I heard a voice speaking with urgency. "They're coming for us, Iris."

I knew that voice. I hadn't heard it in nine months. I sat up and looked around, but no one was there.

"Aster?"

It was her. I knew it was her.

9.

I limped back to the house, still clutching the china. I had no idea what time it was, but I assumed everyone else had gathered for dinner and were wondering where I was. A confrontation loomed.

In the kitchen, Mrs. O'Connor widened her eyes when she saw me. I'd left my hat and jacket in the forest, and without the jacket, I couldn't hide that my arm was scraped up and bruising. I was filthy from lying on the ground, and my hand was bloodied from the china. "I'm fine," I said, although she hadn't asked. As I approached the dining room, I heard Rosalind say, "Rosalind Whiteley has a nice ring to it, don't you think? And Roddy and I will have the same initials."

"But you can't borrow my cuff links," Roderick said to laughter.

When I walked into the dining room, Rosalind was holding her hand out in front of her, admiring her diamond. They all turned to me as I entered, including Belinda, who was seated at one end of the table opposite my father. For Easter, the nurse had put her in a yellow dress that was similar in color to mine, and she had pinned her hair just right and fastened her carnelian and diamond brooch above her breast. She'd been spiffed up to celebrate the resurrection of a man she didn't believe in.

"Iris, are you all right?" my father asked, then Zelie said in a worried tone: "What happened? We couldn't find you."

"You're *bleeding*," Calla added.

"That's how I looked when I got thrown off my horse last summer," Roderick said with a chuckle.

"Just ignore her," Rosalind said, her smirk of annoyance reappearing. "She's a queer little thing."

I took my seat, Zelie to my left and my mother to my right. I set the bloodied piece of china on the table next to my plate, then picked up the white linen napkin to wipe more of the blood from my hand. When I was finished, I spread the napkin on my lap. "I got lost in the forest," I said. "And ran into a tree."

A laugh sputtered from Daphne's lips. She turned to Rosalind, and they shared a knowing glance. "You've outdone yourself this time," Daphne said, pointing to the shard of china. "Is that some totem you found in the forest?"

Mrs. O'Connor chose that moment to bring in the platter of ham, and the attention shifted away from me. Belinda looked at me, and behind her deadened eyes, I thought I saw a flicker of who she'd been the night before. Her eyes were asking me a question. I nodded.

Mrs. O'Connor made her way around the table, triumphant with her Easter ham, and placed a slice on each of our plates, then loaded them up with everything else she'd made for Easter dinner, peas, green salad, and new potatoes with parsley butter sauce. She set a coconut cake in the middle of the table, as white and fluffy as a bunny with colorful jelly beans around the rim, which everyone admired.

Everyone except Belinda and me began to eat. I was working up my nerve to speak when my father cleared his throat. We turned to him, awaiting whatever dull news he was about to share, but for once, he had something of note. "I've had a letter from Matthew," he said.

"Have you?" Rosalind said with surprise.

"Who's Matthew?" Roderick asked, taking another slice of ham from the platter.

"You know," Rosalind said. *"Matthew."*

"Aster's widow," Zelie said.

"Widower," Calla corrected her.

"Yes, well," our father said, trying to grab hold of the conversation before it slipped away from him. "He apparently sold the house on Grouse Court and all the furnishings several months ago. He's going to resign his position at his father's company this summer and move to Charlottesville to attend law school at the University of Virginia."

"He's going to become a lawyer?" Rosalind asked, though the answer was self-evident.

"It would seem so," our father said. "He wants to go into politics eventually. He called this his fresh start."

Rosalind set down her knife and fork. I knew she was dying to say something snide about Matthew and his *fresh start,* but she knew she couldn't, given that she was less than a week away from her own fresh start. Luckily for her, Daphne jumped in.

"I wish Aster had the chance to start over again."

"Indeed," Rosalind replied, unable to resist. Then she went further. "Would it have hurt him to drop by and visit his in-laws? We haven't seen him since the funeral, and now he's off to Virginia."

"I assume this house holds painful memories for him that he doesn't wish to revisit," our father said.

"It holds painful memories for all of us, and yet here we are," Calla said, picking up her glass of water and taking a drink.

The talk of Aster only reminded me of what had happened in the forest. When the table fell silent, I heard Aster's voice again. *They're coming for us, Iris.* I knew I had to act.

I stood up and they all turned to me except for Belinda, who stared down at her plate. I picked up my glass.

"A toast?" Rosalind asked warily.

"Not a toast," I said, gulping down the rest of my water as if it were whiskey. "I just wanted to say . . ." I paused, gripped by fear.

"Out with it, kid," Daphne said.

"I think you should cancel the wedding," I said to Rosalind.

"Iris!" She popped up out of her chair, with Roderick stumbling up to stand beside her.

All of them except for Belinda took a turn at saying my name, a long string of Irises that sounded like the hiss of a snake.

"Explain yourself," Rosalind demanded.

"I'm worried that" — my foot was dangling off the edge of the cliff; I should have backed up, but I knew I couldn't — "if you marry Roderick you're going to die."

"You horrid little creature!" Rosalind screamed. Roderick held her around her midsection to keep her from coming at me. "You're wicked, that's what you are!"

Our father stood up to help Roderick try to contain Rosalind, but she defied both of them by continuing to kick and shout. "I know this came from *you*," she said, pointing at Belinda. I had avoided looking at my mother, not wanting to signal any collusion between us, but now I quickly glanced in her direction. She was staring at Rosalind, her face placid. I imagined the real Belinda, buried beneath her tranquilizers, wasn't feeling so calm.

"You put this idea into Iris's head," Rosalind said. "Like some wicked old witch."

"That's enough," Roderick said, taking her arm. "Let's go outside."

"You don't know the half of it, Roddy," Rosalind said, pulling away from him. "She's poisonous."

"I know you feel that way," Roderick said, reaching for Rosalind's arm again. "But there's no need to make a scene. We're getting married, and that's that."

Rosalind smiled at him tenderly and they embraced. Roderick had calmed her for a moment, but her defiance soon returned. When they parted, she stared down the table, looking at each of us. "What happened to Aster isn't going to happen to me," she said with confidence.

"But what if it does happen to you?" Zelie said, erupting into tears and tugging on my hand, as if I could stop it from happening. I'd expected everyone else at the table to turn on me as Rosalind had, but Calla began to rock back and forth in her chair, holding her head in her hands. "Not again," she cried. "Not again." Daphne, meanwhile, sat quietly in her chair, no snide comments or jokes. She stared straight ahead, eyes open wide, as if she were about to be hit by an oncoming truck.

I'd thought we'd recovered from Aster's death as much as we ever would, but I could see now how fragile we all still were. Crying intensified around the table. We were coming unhinged.

"No one is going to die," our father said, and he shouted for Nurse Marsh, who quickly appeared. No doubt she'd been listening around the corner with Dovey and Mrs. O'Connor.

"Please take Mrs. Chapel up to her bedroom," he said, and the nurse took Belinda's arm and guided her up from her chair. Our mother hadn't said a thing, but they all knew who was behind my outburst.

I tried to follow Belinda from the room, but my father stopped me. "Iris, sit down at once." I obeyed. I'd done the deed; there was nothing to do but await my punishment.

Rosalind sat in her chair as well, with Roderick behind her, his hands on her shoulders, a gesture of comfort, perhaps, or restraint. He seemed stunned at the events that had just unfolded. Whiteley gatherings were probably lighthearted, boisterous affairs, with platters of spareribs and talk of horses and oil.

"My dears, please stop," our father said to Calla and Zelie, both still in tears. "No one is going to die."

"That's what everyone said last time," Calla said. "We all just thought it was Mother acting crazy, but then she was right. We didn't listen and Aster died."

Our father had no good response to that; he suggested she go upstairs and lie down, an invitation she eagerly accepted.

Once she was gone, he turned in my direction. "Iris, did your mother put these ideas in your head?"

Rosalind glared at me. I knew lying was useless — they already knew the truth — but I couldn't admit to it. I couldn't let them send Belinda away to the clinic.

"Iris, answer me."

I was cornered, exhausted, and I broke into sobs. "Don't send her away," I said. "It's not her fault."

Roderick bent over and rubbed his cheek against Rosalind's. "Get me out of here, Roddy," she said. "If I have to stay in this house for one more minute, I'll scream."

10.

Roderick and Rosalind left, and our father sent the rest of us upstairs. I followed Daphne and Zelie and joined Calla in the girls' sitting room. I didn't know if my father was plotting to send Belinda away — maybe even me as well. But I didn't care anymore. I was numb.

The mood in the sitting room was one of mourning. I had expected the rest of my sisters to turn on me as Rosalind had, but no, they seemed to believe me — or at least they believed Belinda, with me as her messenger. I wasn't even sure if I fully believed it myself, but they were spooked, and I was grateful to be able to lie down on the sofa and rest my head on a pillow without feeling like I was in an enemy combat zone.

They must have talked for at least an hour, trying to make sense of what had happened at dinner.

"Did Mother really poison us?" Zelie asked.

"Of course not," Daphne said. "Rosalind didn't mean that literally."

"Then what did she mean?"

"It's just a way to explain what our mother passed on to us," Calla said, sitting on the floor and hugging her knees to her chest. "Our maternal lineage is a necklace wrapped so tightly around our necks that we can't breathe."

"Huh?" Zelie mumbled in confusion.

I didn't participate in the conversation except to confirm that my warning had come from our mother; I had nothing else to say. At one point, I left to take a bath, washing the blood and dirt off of me, and returned snug in my robe, curling up on the sofa again as the discussion of Rosalind's fate continued.

They would have gone on discussing it all night — "None of us can escape," Calla said — but the conversation stopped abruptly when Rosalind opened the sitting-room door, her fury hot. "I hope you're pleased with yourselves," she said. "Especially *you*." She glanced at me, then turned away in disgust.

"I'm glad you came home," Calla said with relief.

"I haven't, not really," Rosalind replied. "I've taken a room at the Hotel Cream and I'll stay there until my wedding day. Roddy is outside waiting for me."

"You don't want to live with us anymore?" Zelie asked, clearly hurt.

"No I do not."

"Why the hotel?" Daphne asked. "Why not just stay with Roddy?"

"I am many things, but I am not *that kind of girl*," Rosalind said. "If I even suggested such a thing, he would lose all respect for me, and quite right too."

"You can't marry him," Calla pleaded. "Why can't you see what's going to happen?"

Rosalind placed her hand on the back of the sofa; I knew she was trying

to stay calm, that Roderick had probably given her one of his warnings —
even without him physically there, she obeyed. "Daphne, will you talk some
sense into her, please? I'm drained."

"Listen," Daphne said to Rosalind. "Maybe it wouldn't hurt to slow
things down a bit."

"Daph!" Rosalind said. "You're not telling me that you believe *our
mother?*"

"Maybe just think about it," Daphne said, shrugging in an attempt to
seem casual.

"She's insane!" Rosalind said. There was that word again. She loved using it.

"She was right last time, old sport. What's the rush anyway? He's just a
man in a funny hat. Wouldn't you rather stay here with us?"

"I would rather *die* than spend another night in this house." Rosalind
flounced through the doorway and down the hall, and we thought she was
gone for good. But she returned to the girls' wing a few minutes later with a
suitcase and a train case. She went into her bedroom and began to pack.

"One of Roddy's cousins will come pick up my trunk this week," she said,
as we gathered around her in the bedroom. She was dumping the contents
of her vanity into her train case, leaving behind the unwanted perfumes and
compacts. Then she opened her suitcase on the bed, stuffing nightgowns and
dresses into it seemingly at random. The important items had already been
packed in the trunk.

"Roz," Daphne said, trying to get her attention, but Rosalind stomped
around the room, grabbing what else she thought she might need. She pulled
the only pair of slacks she owned from the bureau drawer and held them
up to consider. "Roddy doesn't like me in slacks," she said, and tossed them
aside.

"We just want to help," Daphne said.

"Oh yes, you're all a *great help,*" Rosalind said. "I have a mind to disin-
vite you rotten things from the wedding, but I can't very well do that, can I?
I can't have Roddy with his family on one side and only a father on my side.
How would that look? It's bad enough that I don't really have a mother."

She threw some jewelry into the train case, a tangle of chains and costume beads. "I'm warning all of you now that if you do *anything* to embarrass me at my wedding I will *never* speak to you again. Do you understand? Surely you can pretend to be normal for a single day?"

"We're scared for you," Calla said, tugging on the suitcase, but Rosalind swatted her hand away. She fastened the suitcase shut, her hands trembling.

"Roddy has helped me understand just how much everyone in this house has a distorted way of thinking," Rosalind said. "And as for our mother — she isn't clairvoyant. The truth of the matter is that she hates men. She thinks every married woman is as miserable as she is, but it's simply not true, and she's not going to prevent me from having the life I want to have."

She picked up the suitcase and the train case from the bed and glanced back at us, the bedroom, and the rose and aster walls with the forest in the corner. "Right," she said, bracing herself, and pushed past us out the door.

"Oh no," Calla said. She followed Rosalind out into the hall, then we all ran after her. "Don't leave," Calla called. "Please don't go."

But Rosalind didn't listen. Bags in each hand, her heels clicking against the floorboards, she walked briskly away like a woman rushing to catch a train.

11.

When we went down to breakfast the next morning, our father was seated at the head of the table wearing his brown suit for work. He normally didn't have breakfast with us on workdays, so it was clear something was wrong. We entered reticently, taking our usual seats, with Calla and Zelie and me on one side of the table, and Daphne now alone on the other. We didn't speak.

"Calla, move to the other side," our father directed. The asymmetry apparently bothered him.

Once Calla was in Rosalind's chair, Mrs. O'Connor came into the dining room and brought us all plates with wedges of quiche and orange slices. Her face, never warm, was obviously tense. She moved around the table mechanically, clearly in a hurry to get back to the kitchen.

"Where's Mother?" I asked, nervous.

"Iris, eat your breakfast," our father replied, and we all picked up our forks, not wanting to anger him anymore.

We ate in silence for several minutes, then there was a knock at the front door. We had a partial view of the entry hall from where we sat, and we watched as Dovey moved rapidly to the door as if she'd been expecting someone.

A moment later, Dovey passed by with two men in suits on their way to the stairs. I turned to my father and saw that he was watching me, poised to prevent an outburst. But I knew there was nothing I could do to stop this, nothing I could do for Belinda. Like Rosalind, she was at the mercy of her fate.

I went back to my half-eaten quiche, pretending that nothing was happening, that none of it was real. That was the day I began to develop what would become a lifelong habit, pressing my pain deep into a dark place inside me. I'd been doing this since I was a little girl but never as consciously and deliberately. With each bite of quiche, I swallowed the reality of what was happening to my mother deeper and deeper down. I told myself that it wasn't my fault she was being sent away; I'd done what she'd asked me to do even if I'd done it poorly.

Several minutes later, Dovey and the men, along with the nurse, returned to the entry hall, the nurse gripping Belinda's arm and guiding her to the door. Our mother didn't see us watching.

"Where are we going?" I heard her ask, her voice faint through a fog of drugs, but no one responded.

The front door closed and that was that. We were quiet, each of us waiting for our father to say something, to make a speech about why our mother had to be sent away again. But he didn't speak. He just finished his quiche and coffee, then picked up his napkin and wiped his mouth.

"Is Mother going back to Fern Hollow?" Zelie asked in her highest pitch, her words barely squeaking out.

"No," our father said. "She's going to the St. Aubert Sanitarium up the coast. She'll like it there."

"When's she coming back?" Zelie asked.

"She's never coming back," he said.

And with that, we were finally, actually motherless.

12.

The rest of the week — well, what is there to say? Our mother was gone. Rosalind was gone too, and whatever her ultimate fate would be, she certainly wouldn't be coming back to our house. It was our second week of spring break, still unseasonably sunny and warm, but we mostly moped around the house, lying on the sofas in the sitting room half-heartedly reading magazines or books. Only Daphne ventured out, spending a couple of afternoons with Veronica. We lived in a weird sort of limbo that week, characters at the end of a chapter whose next sentences were being written at a torturously slow pace on an old typewriter that was running out of ribbon.

On the day of the wedding, our father warned us at breakfast that he didn't want any "nonsense." We got dressed that afternoon, having pushed the dreaded task to as late as possible. We wore identical dresses, which had been picked out by Rosalind in a happier time. They were long, in rosy pink, the same shade as Rosalind's Easter dress, and made of satin with a gauzy overlay. Tiny crystals were sewn into the scooped necks, and we wore pink gloves that stretched to our elbows.

Daphne dressed quickly and went to the sitting room with her sketch pad, her short hair only requiring the most cursory brushing; she never bothered with makeup. Calla, Zelie, and I took turns pinning up one another's hair. None of us spoke except for the simplest of styling directions.

A chauffeured car came to take the four of us to the church; our father had left in another car to pick up Rosalind at the hotel. I assumed she must have dressed in her wedding gown alone unless one of Roderick's female relatives had stepped in to take the place of the absent mother and sisters. Had

Rosalind abandoned us, or had we abandoned her? Either way, I felt badly that she was alone that day.

Most of the guests had arrived at the church before us. It was a modest crowd, with only some of Roderick's family and a few friends; most of the pews were empty, but that's how Rosalind had wanted it. Nothing showy. I'd feared that Roderick's family would come dressed for a rodeo, but they really were New Englanders: demure, boring even, in their bland tweeds and matronly hats adorned with artificial flowers. I spotted Adele and Peter Tollman, whose inadvertent matchmaking at the premiere had set us on this potentially disastrous path, but I turned away before they could wave.

A young woman, presumably one of Roderick's cousins, led us to the pew that had been set aside for us, and we sat down without acknowledging anyone. Roderick, in a baby-blue tuxedo and wearing his usual cowboy hat, bolo tie, and boots, was standing at the front of the church, waiting for his bride. He walked over to where we were sitting, and said: "You ladies look like you're about to walk the plank." He stood at the end of our pew and waited for a chuckle, which he did not receive.

"Come on, can't y'all be happy for your sister on her big day?" He thought he could jolly us out of our funereal demeanor as if it were nothing more than a bad mood. I surmised that Rosalind had given him the sanitized version of what had happened to Aster — a sudden flu — and had left out the howling, the broken glass, the nakedness, and the smeared blood. She had likely given him Dr. Green's version, which even he didn't believe.

As Roderick spoke, Zelie gripped my hand and stared up at the stained-glass window behind the pulpit, a colorful kaleidoscope of apostles. Roderick lingered at the end of the pew like a gnat until Daphne finally said: "We'll fake it when she gets here, okay, Rod?" But, of course, when the moment came, we couldn't.

There was a flutter in the church as if a flock of birds were taking flight, and we turned to see Rosalind standing at the entrance, arm linked with our father's. We stood up along with the other guests — except for Calla, who remained seated, bent over, her head in her hands. Zelie squeezed my hand tighter. Daphne was stoic.

The church organist began to play the bridal march, and our father and Rosalind moved forward. This was the first time we had seen her dress. It looked like a lily that had closed up and been turned upside down. Rosalind had a veil over her face, and as she approached, I could see only a hint of her. She sailed by without turning our way, her eyes fixed on Roderick, her ticket out.

Our father handed her off to Roderick, then sat down in the front pew alone. The ceremony proceeded, but I wasn't aware of much besides Zelie's squeezing my hand and Calla's soft weeping. Daphne nudged Calla, and whispered, "Cut it out," but she couldn't, and soon Roderick's relatives on the other side of the aisle were straining to see where the crying was coming from. There was no way to mistake her sobs for tears of joy, and soon even the reverend was looking in our direction, attention that only made Calla weep harder. Our father glanced over his shoulder, prompting Daphne to stand up and take Calla's arm, tugging her until she stood up. They went outside and the ceremony continued. Rosalind didn't turn around even once to acknowledge what was happening.

With Calla gone, Zelie took over the crying but did so silently. Tears pooled beneath her eyes as we watched the ceremony, the vows, the exchange of rings. Daphne and Calla tiptoed back in and sat down right as the reverend asked if there were any objections to the union. Some of Roderick's family members turned in our direction, but we were silent. We'd already voiced our objections and they'd been ignored.

"I now present to you Mr. and Mrs. Roderick Whiteley," the reverend said, and Roderick leaned down to kiss his bride. The rest of the crowd was exuberant, standing and breaking into applause.

"*No!*" Calla cried, but only my sisters and I could hear her.

13.

The same driver who'd taken us to the church took us to the Hotel Cream for the reception. Calla was inconsolable on the ride, and the driver had to pull over not far outside Bellflower Village so she could throw up on the side of the road, Daphne dutifully holding back her hair. The rest of us sat quietly, Calla the vessel for our unexpressed emotions.

I'd never been to the Hotel Cream, where Daphne spent so much of her time doing heaven knows what with Veronica. It was a converted turn-of-the-century mansion, bright yellow with dormered windows and white columns flanking the entrance. It gave an air of grandness but was still quaint, and it sat on the shore right next to the sea. The weather was still warm, with ample sunshine, the sky a cerulean blue, and I realized that despite everything I was happy for Rosalind that she had this gorgeous day.

There was a queue at the entrance, and I inhaled the sea air happily, wishing I could stay outside until the reception was over, though I knew I couldn't — one wrong move and I'd be in trouble.

Just inside the hotel entrance, Veronica stood with her parents as they greeted the wedding guests. Her mother was also tall and brunette, and both of them wore purple dresses, dark shades of amethyst that seemed out of place among the guests' spring colors. Improbably, Veronica's mother was named Cerise — Cerise Cream, which sounded like a dessert at a French restaurant. Veronica's father, meanwhile, was plain old Sidney, a small, beaky man with thick glasses and hideously crooked teeth who must have had a lot of money and a lot of heart to attract someone like Cerise. He stood sandwiched between his wife and daughter as the guests arrived; they towered over him like purple flamingos.

When Veronica spotted Daphne, she waved excitedly, more immature than she'd seemed among the cherry blossoms. Standing next to her parents, she was playing the role of daughter; I could see how practiced she was at wearing masks, something I'd observed in Daphne's drawings as well. Being near her after what I had seen of her, after what I'd felt toward her, was unbearable; I was relieved when Mrs. Cream directed my sisters and me to the elevator. We were supposed to go upstairs for photographs. The other guests were sent to the dining room for a cocktail hour.

On the top floor of the hotel, we found the room with BRIDAL SUITE painted delicately above the door and went inside. Roderick and Rosalind were already being photographed in front of a charcoal backdrop, Rosalind sitting in a chair with Roderick standing behind her. She grasped a dainty bouquet of red roses in her hands, her namesake, the forbidden flower.

The suite was sprawling, with a balcony that overlooked the ocean. My sisters went out there to wait for our turn, but I explored the suite, walking down a long hallway to the bedroom. The door was open, revealing a four-poster bed with a dark chestnut frame and a white lacy bedspread that looked as if it were made from a discarded wedding gown, something left behind by a former bride. There were rose petals scattered all over the bed.

"Come along now," a woman said from behind me, and she reached around to close the door, as if the bed with the petals wasn't fit for me to see. The woman, who turned out to be Roderick's mother, wore an elegant skirt and jacket in a fabric that was pewter in color with a bit of shimmer. She led me back to the main room where my sisters had replaced Roderick behind Rosalind. I took my place beside them, and the photographer rearranged us a few times until he was satisfied, our father watching from the side.

"Bright smiles," the photographer said, and somehow, for those few minutes, we managed it.

After we were photographed, my sisters and I were escorted from the bridal suite. Rosalind had not spoken to us or acknowledged us in any way all while maintaining the appearance of a blissful bride — quite the feat.

Downstairs, the dining room opened up, with windows all around looking out at Long Island Sound glistening and twinkling in its early evening glory. The tables were positioned around the edges of the room, leaving space in the middle for dancing. A four-man band played music as the guests mingled with their drinks and wandered between the dining room and the terrace. Each white-skirted table had an arrangement of red roses in the middle.

Zelie found our table and waved us over. I was thankful that there was room for only the four of us, each of our names written in calligraphy on little cards. Our table had a lovely view to the outside, but Calla parked herself in the chair with its back to the window and didn't move for the rest of the night.

Rosalind and Roderick arrived to applause just as the sun was starting to set, the newlywed couple basking in the glow of a citrus and apricot sky. They worked the room hand in hand, accepting congratulations from the relatively small number of guests while managing to miss our table entirely, and when they were done greeting everyone else, they took their places at the head table with our father and Roderick's parents.

"She hates us," Daphne said, peeling off her pink gloves and tossing them onto the table. Zelie and I followed her lead, but Calla remained gloved and glowering. The waitstaff began to bring out the food, and as the first course of shrimp cocktail was set before us, Daphne said: "We might as well enjoy ourselves," and dug in.

Dish after dish was brought out, the food reflecting Rosalind's refined tastes; the menu included white asparagus soup, fettuccine with lemon cream sauce, and lamb chops with mashed potatoes. Calla ate nothing, Daphne ate everything, and Zelie and I nibbled.

After dinner, the dancing began. My sisters and I watched, none of us in the mood to join in. Rosalind spun around the dance floor — with Roderick, with our father, with Roderick's father, then with his brothers. Whenever I scanned the room to find her, Rosalind was inevitably in the arms of some man or other and being whisked across the pine floor. She was plunging ahead into married life with unbridled glee. She had always said our mother was insane, and it was clear she truly believed it.

That night I tried to live in the moment, not thinking about what might come later. I refused to let my mind wander there, neither having the energy for it nor the adrenaline I'd need to panic over it. Numbness — it was working surprisingly well for me; I should have tried it long ago.

I went to get cake for my sisters and me at one point and brushed right by Rosalind as she trotted past with the other dancers; the band had taken a break, and a record player was blasting some kind of Texas tune that Roderick and his family liked. The guests grew a bit rowdier, and there were a few *yee-haws!* As I passed Rosalind, she didn't acknowledge me, her sister, the Ghost of Ruined Weddings Past.

As we ate the elderflower-and-lemon sponge, Adele Tollman stopped by our table. I can only imagine what we looked like to the other guests, the sisters of the bride huddled around a table, not a single smile to be found. Even for the Chapels, this was odd behavior.

"How are you, ladies?" she asked, slightly wobbly, a glass of champagne in her hand — likely just one in a string of many.

"We've been better, Adele," Daphne said, gulping down her own glass of champagne, which she wasn't allowed to have.

"Weddings are hard for you, I understand," Adele said. "But maybe you could try to see things from Rosalind's point of view. It's the happiest day of her life. Couldn't you at least pretend to celebrate with her?"

"She knows us too well to fall for that," Daphne said. Adele smiled, a faint closed-lip smile, and nodded before heading back to the bar for more champagne.

But soon we had more visitors.

Roderick and a friend came over, both men with amber bottles of beer in their hands. "These are my sisters-in-law," Roderick said, as he slapped his friend on the back. "They look like they're going to be shot at dawn, don't they?" The man with Roderick laughed hesitantly, unsure if he should.

"This is Teddy Vandiver," Roderick said. "He's a buddy of mine from Yale. Ever heard of him?"

"Should we have heard of him?" Daphne asked, sliding Calla's untouched slice of cake onto her own plate.

"Captain of the Yale football team? The man's a local legend," Roderick said, and Daphne shrugged in response. "They don't get out much, Ted," Roderick whispered in his friend's ear, loudly enough for us to hear.

Teddy was nearly as tall as Roderick and wore a gray suit with a yellow tie that had a little brass football as a clip. He was husky, as if his football padding were tucked beneath his suit. His short hair, a dark auburn, was greased into place; his face was puglike, with a sprinkling of freckles over his nose and cheeks. A hulking man, like Roderick, and as polished as a penny.

Roderick told us a story about the night before; he and his cousins and Teddy and a few other friends had gone to a shooting range with their Chapel rifles. "In honor of the bride and her family," Roderick said, describing the outing as an impromptu bachelor party. Roderick laughed about how Teddy had missed the target over and over again. "These young fellas are spoiled," Roderick said. "They've never had to fight for their lives."

Teddy turned pink, and Roderick scrambled to make things right. "He sure can throw a football, though!" Roderick said, then chugged down the last of his beer and set the bottle on our table. "Cheer up, gals," he said in a tone bordering on snide, and made his exit. Teddy didn't follow. Instead, he took Zelie's seat when she went to the ladies' room.

"Say, would you like to dance?" Teddy said to Calla, and Daphne laughed. Nothing about Calla's demeanor that night welcomed an invitation.

"No thank you," Calla said, her first words since we'd entered the dining room.

"What's your name?"

"Her name is Calla," Daphne said.

Teddy looked confused for a moment. "You mean like calla lily?"

"You got it," Daphne said. "Captain of the football team and smart too."

"Rosalind, Calla ...," Teddy mused. "You're all named after flowers, huh?"

"Righto," Daphne said.

"So, Calla Lily, why don't you want to dance? I'm not a bad dancer, I promise."

"I just don't care to dance."

"Why not?" Teddy seemed genuinely surprised, apparently unaccustomed to being rejected.

Calla stared at Rosalind as she whirled past. "Because the world is coming to an end," she said, not specifying that she meant *our* world, not *the* world.

Teddy sipped his beer. "You're gloomy, huh? I don't mind that. I like gloomy girls. The cheerleading type isn't for me."

"Can't you tell she's not interested?" Daphne said, licking the last of the icing off her fork. "Beat it."

Teddy flinched as if she'd splashed him with cold water and stumbled out of the chair and away from our table. Daphne soon left us as well, grabbing another glass of champagne from a waiter and walking out of the dining room, likely in search of Veronica. Calla and I were left alone at the table.

Another man stopped by our table to ask Calla to dance and I was surprised. She'd always been in Aster's and Rosalind's shadows; men went for them, never for her. But then I realized she was one of the only women at the wedding who wasn't related to the Whiteleys, and with Rosalind married, Calla had moved to the front of the pack, a position I didn't think she'd enjoy — nowhere there to hide.

"She's not feeling well," I said to the man, one of Roderick's tweedy cousins, far too old for Calla.

"Sorry to hear it," he said, then a flicker of recognition crossed his face. "Hey, she was the one crying during the ceremony!" He spoke as if he'd just spotted a celebrity. "I'd cry too if my sister was marrying Roderick," he said, laughing as he walked away.

Teddy Vandiver, dancing with another of Roderick's cousins, a curvy woman in a tight green dress, glanced over at Calla every chance he got, seemingly taken with her for reasons unknown. When the music ended, he returned to our table, assuming it was safe, I suppose, since Daphne wasn't there.

"I forgot to ask," Teddy said, taking a glass from a passing waiter. "The Spring Fling is next Saturday. Do you know what that is?"

Calla didn't respond, and I felt badly for Teddy, standing there like an idiot, waiting for an answer he wouldn't receive.

"No," I said, throwing him a rope. "We've never heard of it."

"It's a dance, next Saturday at Yale," he said, then added: "A week from today," in case we didn't know what the current day was, as if our own sister's wedding hadn't been marked on the calendar. "My girlfriend and I broke up, and, well, if you'd like to go," Teddy said to Calla, "I'd love to take you."

I wasn't wise to the ways of men, but it seemed to me Teddy enjoyed a challenge. Calla had been nothing but indifferent to his advances, yet here he was, making another pass. Football was a rough sport; maybe Teddy enjoyed pain.

"I know you're only in high school," Teddy said, and shrugged. "But I'm only twenty-one myself, and you seem more interesting than the girls I know."

I wasn't sure if Calla had even heard him; she had a way of staring right through people, and once again, she was focused on Rosalind, now in the arms of her father-in-law.

"She'll let you know," I said, wanting the agony of the conversation to end.

"Okay," Teddy said, smiling at me. "I live in Roberts House. She can call there and ask for me."

"Sure," I said, mystified by his hopefulness.

Zelie returned from the bathroom and sat down. "Teddy again?" she said, rolling her eyes. I'd assumed she'd be swept up in the reception, that she'd forget about the looming sense of doom when presented with dancing and music and fancy food, the princess dresses and dashing men, but she was deep in her fear.

"Can we go home?" she asked.

"Yes, please," Calla said. "Is our driver here?"

I offered to go outside and look; I was also anxious to leave — I hadn't wanted to come in the first place. I weaved through the dancers, spotting my father deep in conversation with Roderick's mother at their table across the room. We could sneak out without his even noticing.

I didn't realize how stuffy it was in the dining room until I stepped away from the body heat and battling scents of perfume and roasted meat and sweat. It was perfectly dark and cool outside, quiet except for the sound of the waves.

"Everything all right, dear?" Mrs. Cream asked. She'd come out of the hotel behind me.

"My sisters and I would like to go home. Is our car here?" The circular drive in front of the hotel was lined with cars, silent and still, their drivers nowhere around.

Mrs. Cream went back into the hotel to arrange for our ride, and I took the opportunity to walk over to the beach, the water as black as oil in the darkness. I left my shoes where the pavement turned to sand and headed toward the water. We lived fairly close to the ocean, yet we rarely visited it; I was determined to change that once I was old enough to drive.

My feet, covered by my tights, sunk into the soft sand as I walked. The lights from the dining room illuminated the area around me just enough so I could see where I was going. To my left, I saw two figures in shadow underneath the terrace. I paused, and as my eyes adjusted, I saw a purple dress and a pink dress, and I knew it was Veronica and Daphne. Veronica was backed up against the wall, facing Daphne, the two of them wrapped in an embrace, bodies pressed tightly together. I couldn't hear anything because of the sound of the waves, but I could see them kissing, their mouths pressed together as wide as they would open, insatiable for each other. I watched for a moment, a flutter in my stomach, then walked on, not wanting to risk being seen.

I stood at the edge of the water to catch my breath, then headed up the stairs to the terrace, knowing Veronica and Daphne were beneath me. Through the window, I could look in on the reception. The music and laughter and conversation were all muted, swirling together with the roar of the sea. Rosalind and Roderick were on the dance floor, just the two of them; everyone else had stepped aside.

The band was playing a jazzy number at a dizzying speed. Roderick spun Rosalind around so quickly that she nearly disappeared, her wedding dress a column of whirling white, like one of those dirt devils I was sure they had on the Texas prairie.

At the end of her twirl, she collapsed into Roderick's arms, sweaty but glowing. She rested her head against his chest and he kissed the top of her head, his face lost in her hair. The guests applauded and whistled as he held his bride on the dance floor. Rosalind had a look on her face I would never forget — eyes closed, soaking it in, the love that she felt, the love that filled her from head to toe with light. She was caught in a daydream that Saturday night, happier than she'd ever been.

By Tuesday, she was in the ground.

Calla & Daphne

1951

I.

Calla had begged me to go to New York with her. She'd wanted all of us to go — "all of us" meaning Daphne and Zelie and me, all of us who were left — but Daphne was sick, and Zelie was weepy and fragile, and was spending most of her time in bed or in the kitchen, where Mrs. O'Connor and Dovey fluttered around her with cocoa and cookies. Zelie needed that, hot drinks, hugs, fuss. There weren't any grown women left in our family, so she found mothering where she could.

That left me to go to New York with Calla. She needed to buy a dress for the Spring Fling, having accepted Teddy Vandiver's invitation to the dance at the last minute. I couldn't understand why she'd accepted Teddy. Calla never went on dates in the first place, and agreeing to go to a dance with Teddy just days after Rosalind's funeral was beyond comprehension.

But Calla insisted, and she insisted on going to New York to buy a dress. "I want to feel New York vibrate through my bones," she said, as we waited on the train platform; the weather had taken a turn and we both shivered. "I want the thrum of the city on my skin. To be in New York is to be *alive*."

Calla spoke nonsense at the best of times, and I had no idea what she was talking about now. I was still in shock over Rosalind's death, and running off to New York just to feel *alive* seemed coldhearted. It felt wrong to be waiting for a train into Manhattan. After Aster had died, we'd cocooned ourselves at home for months, and that's what we should have been doing now; Rosalind deserved that much.

I wanted to tell Calla no, that I wouldn't go with her, but I could see that she needed me and that she was clearly going to the city no matter what. She wasn't herself—none of us were ourselves, maybe we never would be again—and I imagined her getting lost in the maze of streets, stepping off the sidewalk into the path of a taxi or falling through a subway grate. So I put on my stockings, buttoned my raincoat, and went with Calla as she took the car keys and drove us to the train station in Greenwich even though she didn't have her license. When the train stopped at our station, the morning commuters, most of them men, jostled to board, and Calla and I were briefly separated. Eventually, we found seats together, and as the train pulled away, we watched the rain lash the windows.

I had expected we'd hail a taxi at Grand Central, but Calla insisted we walk the seventeen blocks uptown through the drizzle. The rush of traffic and pedestrians outside the station invigorated her, and she seemed as full of life as a character in a musical, like Judy Garland in *Easter Parade,* which we'd seen at the Bellflower Cinema.

She walked ahead of me, the hem of her lavender dress peeking out beneath her raincoat. Above her head, she held the parasol Belinda had used for gardening, the pink one that always reminded me of a dahlia. I followed the parasol, the only color on the gray sidewalk. We continued on, block after exhausting block, splashed and jostled, my ears assaulted with more noise than I could handle in my delicate state. I longed to be in my bedroom at home or in the kitchen drinking cocoa with Zelie.

When the art deco facade of Bloomingdale's came into view, I was relieved. In the vestibule, we tried to shake off the rain, but it had seeped into us. We checked our raincoats and Calla's parasol, then, unencumbered by everything but our grief, we set about getting what Calla needed for the dance.

She spent what seemed like ages wandering around the cosmetics on the ground floor, the islands of lipstick and perfume and powder. I trailed behind her like a bored child might her mother. Eager salesgirls spritzed us as we walked by, and Calla tried on several shades of lipstick from light pink to coral to bright red, each time wiping it off with a tissue, and saying, "Not for me." She browsed at Helena Rubinstein, Estée Lauder, and Lancôme before visiting the Elizabeth Arden counter, and there she was immediately drawn to a box set called Moonlit Kisses. As was I. The small box was covered in silver velveteen and fastened with a snap closure; nestled inside under pearly tissue paper was a star-shaped powder compact, a miniature bottle of Evening Eclipse perfume, a glittery tube of lipstick in Arden Pink, a glass pot of pale lustrous eye shadow called Milky Way, and a barrette decorated with a moonstone.

"We'll take two," Calla said, pulling a checkbook out of her handbag. It looked like the checkbook Dovey kept in a drawer in the kitchen, which she used for grocery shopping.

We hadn't eaten breakfast, so we went to the café on the top floor and ordered Earl Grey tea and coffee cake. We sat by a window with a view of two skyscrapers shrouded in clouds; at the other tables, women chatted and smoked over coffee and pastry. Calla ate quickly, then stared out the window, mesmerized by the clouds. The view from the café must have been similar to the view from an airplane, I supposed, though I had never been on one.

"Do you think this is what heaven looks like?" Calla asked, still not taking her eyes off the window. I saw the cuts she'd made on her wrists and arms in the days since Rosalind's funeral. She hadn't bothered to hide them with long sleeves or bandages.

"I don't know," I said, pretending I hadn't noticed Calla using her napkin to wipe her eyes. I didn't know what I would do if she had a fit like she'd been having at home, but I was glad I'd come with her.

"I think heaven probably looks very different from how we imagine it," she said, setting down her cup. She opened her handbag and pulled out a gold compact in the shape of a seashell.

"Shelley wrote a poem from the perspective of a cloud," she continued, as she began to powder her nose. "I am the daughter of Earth and Water, and the nursling of the Sky, I pass through the pores of the ocean and shores; I change, but I cannot die." She snapped the compact shut. "Isn't that lovely?" she said, a smile on her face.

"Sure." I was relieved her melancholia seemed to have subsided for a moment.

"Are you ready to go?" she said. "I'd like to look at dresses next."

In the Juniors section on the third floor, there was a sign that said EN-CHANTING FORMALS. A whole corner of the store was dedicated to girls' formals, and we waded into a sea of sequins and beads and rhinestones, taffeta and tulle and velvet, colors from pale pink to turquoise to scarlet. Calla led me to the dressing rooms and directed me to a chair, gave me her handbag, and told me to relax. For more than an hour, she tried on dresses with the help of a salesgirl while I sat outside her dressing room stall, watching her feet, seeing her slip the outfits on and off, all the while fighting off tears over Rosalind. Some of the dresses were rejected outright; some she showed me for my opinion. Did I like a cream-colored dress with a garland of flowers sewn into the neckline? I didn't. What about a sapphire dress with a sequined bodice and a skirt that would make a ballerina jealous? Not that one either. It was a beautiful dress, but it was too flashy for Calla, who had never stood out among my quartet of older sisters. She was taller than all of them, and the slenderest, but despite those physical distinctions, she usually disappeared. Her face was pretty enough, but it bordered on plain; her movements lacked grace; her personality was too weird to be engaging. Many years later I would see a portrait of the Brontë siblings, Charlotte, Emily, and Anne; their brother, Branwell, had been in the painting originally, but he'd erased himself, leaving nothing behind but a faded blur. The dark-haired, pale-skinned trio of Brontë sisters reminded me of Aster, Rosalind, and Daphne, each singularly bold, striking, commanding. The blur was Calla, there but not there, disappearing herself in her sisters' shadows.

I watched her go in and out of the dressing room, nervously tucking her pageboy behind her ears. "What do you think, Iris?" she asked, as she stepped out of her stall wearing a sleeveless knee-length rayon taffeta dress in two tones of kelly green, dark and light. From the waist down, layers of light-colored netting descended over the darker taffeta. The dress was a vision of seasonal green, and Calla a fairy out of *A Midsummer Night's Dream*.

"You look beautiful," I said, and I meant it.

The salesgirl placed the dress in a box and tied it up with string. I carried the box and our bag as Calla explored the other floors, buying nylons and a strapless Peter Pan bra with "Magicups," which would give her small bust the bullet look that was so fashionable then. She bought an evening bag in shimmery silver. We stopped at the jewelry counter, where she tried on a moonstone ring with a silver band to match the barrette.

"That ring looks terrif on you," the salesgirl said, admiring my sister's long dainty fingers. Calla bought the moonstone ring and a pair of silver hoop earrings.

In the shoe department, she parked me in a chair again, then tried on most of the ladies' footwear on offer, eventually settling on a pair of silver backless heels. After she paid for them, she sat next to me, seemingly exhausted; she'd never been one for shopping, and I couldn't understand why Teddy Vandiver deserved all this, why she'd accepted his invitation in the first place. Everything felt wrong.

We took a taxi back to Grand Central, but Calla wasn't ready to catch the train home yet. As the taxi neared the station, she spotted something out the window and told the driver to stop. The rain had paused, and Calla guided me down the sidewalk, each of us weighed down with boxes and bags. "Let's have lunch," she said, entering a restaurant called Llewellyn's on Park.

Inside, everything was chestnut wood — the paneled walls, the booths and tables, the ornate bar with its shelves of colorful bottles that I could picture on a luxury liner sailing to Europe. Instead of regular windows, there was stained glass, and despite the chandeliers hanging from the ceiling, it was incredibly dark, almost like a cave. Every table was surrounded by men in suits who smoked and ate steak and drank whiskey, the kind of men who'd been on the train platform that morning. This is what they were doing while their wives were home ironing and changing diapers; I felt like we'd barged in on their private club. As we followed the waiter to the back corner of the restaurant, the men stared at us, the young women who should have been in school. "Maybe we should go home?" I whispered to Calla, as we slid into our booth that was tucked away in the back.

"Nonsense," Calla said, as the waiter left us to settle in. "Let's enjoy ourselves for once. Besides, we never spend any time together." The waiter returned with our menus, and he asked Calla if she wanted the drinks menu. He couldn't have thought she was old enough to drink, but he — a handsome young man who I imagined to be an aspiring Broadway actor — seemed amused by Calla as she played the role of a much older woman.

She glanced over the menu as if she were a pro, and when he returned, she was ready. "I'll have a cocktail," she said, giving the menu one last skim. "An American Beauty."

A few minutes later, he brought her an American Beauty and me a Shirley Temple, both our drinks vibrantly red from grenadine syrup. My drink had a maraschino cherry bobbing on top, but Calla's cocktail was far more elegant, with a red rose petal as a garnish. She didn't remove the petal, allowing it to brush against her upper lip as she sipped her cocktail.

Along with our drinks, the waiter had brought a small baguette on a board with a silver dish of whipped butter on the side. Calla tore off a hunk of bread and spread butter all over it, then stuffed it in her mouth. She had always eaten like a bird at home, much like Belinda. But then she wasn't herself right now; she was a woman of the city. If we hadn't been in mourning, it would have been a fun game.

The waiter came back to take our order and Calla went all in, choosing a salad with Roquefort, prime rib with horseradish sauce, a baked Idaho potato with extra butter, and fresh asparagus. "Is that for the two of you to share?" the waiter asked; one look at Calla and it wasn't clear where she'd put all that food.

"No," Calla said, pulling a pack of Lucky Strikes from her handbag. "She can order what she wants."

I'd subsisted on very little food all week, and what I had eaten was bland. I couldn't handle a feast like Calla's, so from the Ladies Prefer section of the menu, I chose the tomato stuffed with chicken salad. The waiter lit Calla's cigarette for her before leaving.

"Daphne will be furious when she realizes I took these," she said, blowing a puff of smoke my way. The car, the checkbook, the cigarettes — I didn't know how Calla would explain all this when we got home. I had a sudden thought that maybe she wasn't planning on going home, that she'd excuse herself to go to the ladies' room, then sneak out to catch a taxi to LaGuardia. If so, I wouldn't have blamed her. It was growing more and more impossible to live in our house — two dead sisters and a mother at St. Aubert's.

When the food came, Calla ate with gusto, eating as I had never seen her eat before, running forkfuls of the rare meat through the horseradish sauce and devouring them. She cleaned her plate of meat, potato, and asparagus, then washed it down with the rest of her cocktail and lit another cigarette. I assumed it was her grief that was causing her to act so differently, it must have knocked her off her axis. Unlike her, I could barely finish even half my tomato; my stomach was clenched.

As I ate, Calla observed me and smoked. We didn't speak for a bit — she was never a big talker, preferring instead to watch and listen, to read and write, and I didn't know how to make conversation with her.

"What do you want to be when you grow up?" she finally asked.

I didn't know how to answer that question, having never been asked it before. I didn't know it could be a question.

"Would you choose to have a family or a career?" she prodded. "You can't have both."

"A career," I said, and Calla smiled her approval. Marriage had become taboo in our family very quickly.

"Good. Having a family isn't safe."

"I want to be an artist," I said, unexpectedly enjoying this conversation. This was the first time I had ever acknowledged my ambition. Calla's question pushed me to imagine a different future from the one I always expected to have, and if I could be anything, I would choose to be an artist. I had never seen a painting by a woman artist, not once in my art or Western Civ classes, but I was sure they existed.

"You and Daphne have that in common," Calla said. I wondered if she'd seen inside Daphne's sketch pad.

The waiter cleared our plates and brought out the slices of rhubarb pie that Calla had ordered for us. He set a pitcher of warm, creamy custard in the middle of the table. I poured a dollop onto my pie, and Calla drenched her slice with the rest of it.

"You have to promise me you'll become an artist," she said, scooping up some pie and custard with her spoon; she briefly closed her eyes to luxuriate in the taste. "You'll have to fight for it. It won't be easy, but maybe things will have changed a little bit by the time you're older."

I couldn't imagine what the life of an artist was like — I pictured Michelangelo on a scaffold, painting the Sistine Chapel — but the possibility of it took hold of me.

"Do you promise me?" she asked. "I want to imagine you in that life."

I should have realized what a strange question it was, how strange that it seemed so urgent. But it didn't occur to me until it was too late.

"I promise," I said.

2.

The days leading up to this one had been days of horror. I'm not going to dwell on the details of how we lost Rosalind, but suffice it to say, her last day unfolded almost exactly as Aster's had. Rosalind had vowed never to return to us, but everyone wants their mother at the end, and the house was the closest thing she had to one, the womb of the wedding cake.

When Roderick brought her back to us the morning after the wedding, he helped her out of the car, and she stared at us as they walked up the front steps. These were her last lucid moments, and it was obvious she knew what was happening to her. We had been right, and she had been wrong not to listen to us, and now it was too late to do anything about it. All that was left was to surrender.

The end came far more quickly for Rosalind than it did for Aster. We had barely got her upstairs and into her bed before it happened: the screaming, the laughing, the howling. In her final moments, Rosalind picked up a chair and shattered the same window Aster had broken with her fist, then she leaned out of it, slashing her stomach with the jagged glass. There was blood everywhere, buckets of blood, much more than Aster had left behind —Rosalind always had been the one for drama.

Roderick fainted in the face of it all. When Dr. Green arrived, he had to focus on Roderick before turning to Rosalind, who was beyond help anyway. Dr. Green was as useless as he'd been before. Our father again refused an autopsy, so the cause of death was officially "influenza." I would have thought that two young women in good health dying from the flu within nine months of each other, and with such bizarre symptoms, would have been a statistical oddity, but we had always been an odd family, and this seemed to be a factor in Dr. Green's reasoning. We knew he didn't really believe that's how either of them had died, but he didn't press the matter, perhaps assuming the cause was unknowable. Our mother was "sick in the head," so it wasn't a leap to think there was something wrong with her offspring too, something unknown to medical science.

"This is the second time this has happened," I heard Dr. Green whisper to the nurse who had accompanied him. She was new and didn't know our family. "These Chapel girls get married, then they crack up. It's remarkable." That's as close as I would ever get to a medical explanation for the deaths of my two older sisters: a crack-up.

Belinda hadn't been informed of Rosalind's death. When my father called to tell her doctors, they said her adjustment to life at St. Aubert's had been a difficult one and they didn't think she could handle the news until she was more stable. But I knew Belinda didn't have to be told; she had predicted Rosalind's death, just as she had predicted Aster's, and once again, it had come to pass.

At the funeral, besides being objects of pity, we were now objects of disbelief. In less than a year, two Chapel girls had gotten married, and both had died the next day. I knew the whole village was talking about us. Outside the church, we heard a group of children sing a rhyme while playing jump rope.

> The Chapel sisters:
> first they get married
> then they get buried

My father chastised them and chased them away, but the rhyme would linger for years to come, echoing in my ears.

At Rosalind's graveside, after she'd been lowered into the ground, Roderick screamed at us, at Calla, Daphne, Zelie, and me: "What have you done to her? You poisoned her, you *witchy girls* and your mother. She always said you were poisonous." That was the day I started to become aware of a stigma that had attached itself to us, but what that would mean for our lives was as yet unknown. So we retreated into the house as we always had.

Roderick flew back to Texas the day after the funeral, away from New England, away from the Chapel women. His cousin Adele told us that he had left his Cadillac behind, as well as his classes at Yale. He didn't finish his degree, no matter how close he was to the end of it, and we never saw him again.

We locked ourselves in the girls' sitting room for two whole days after we buried Rosalind. We didn't change out of our funeral dresses — this time we'd worn black, the same dresses we'd worn to the film premiere. We only left the room to use the toilet, and we didn't bathe, and though the room started to smell, we didn't mind. Dovey would set a tray of food outside the door from time to time, bland mourning food Mrs. O'Connor had made, the kind of food that wouldn't upset the stomach. When we were hungry, we'd drag the tray into the room and pick at the contents, eating only to survive. Before we locked ourselves away, Dovey had brought up several vases of lush red roses that the Whiteleys had sent to us — *roses* for *Rosalind* must have been their thinking — which proved they didn't know our family at all. Since Belinda was gone, Dovey probably hadn't seen any harm in filling our sitting room with something pretty and fragrant, but after we locked ourselves into the darkness, the roses looked blacker than red — and ominous.

We'd turned off the lights and lit a bunch of candles, and for several hours, we sat sunk in the swamp of our grief. There was nothing to say, nothing that hadn't already been said in the wake of Aster's passing. Rosalind's death was like a twin that had appeared nine months after its sibling — it seemed impossible, an identical one falling into our laps, and yet here it was.

There was no way to deal with any of it, so we didn't. We just watched the hours tick by, taking us farther away from the last moment Rosalind had been alive. With every minute that passed, she was being pushed further into memory, the sound of her voice, the way she smelled, her laughter — over time it would fade, so we sat quietly while what parts of her that remained still resonated. She was still so fresh, we would have bottled that if we could — the essence of her.

We slept and cried, and Daphne drank a string of miniature bottles of booze she'd stolen from the Hotel Cream. At some point, Calla pulled a rose from one of the vases and pricked her right index finger with it, squeezing the droplet of blood onto her tongue. Zelie and I both exclaimed in horror, asking in unison: "What are you doing?"

"It feels good," Calla replied with a shrug. "Pain and more pain. That's a woman's fate."

"What is?" I asked.

"*Blood. Pain.* And it's even worse for us Chapel girls." She pricked her finger again.

"Behold our sister, Briar Rose," Daphne said, her words slurred. She'd opened a bottle of what smelled like rum, the miniature empties lined up next to her on the floor.

"Briar Rose pricked her finger and fell asleep for a hundred years," Zelie said.

Calla pricked her other fingers with the rose's thorn, then licked the blood. "For us Chapel girls, it's different," she said. "The embrace of a man doesn't wake us up, it sends us to sleep, an eternal slumber from which we will never wake."

"That's not true," Zelie said. Romance was the only thing she really wanted in the future; she wouldn't give it up easily despite the mounting evidence against it.

"Isn't it? Look what happened to Aster and Rosalind."

"They died of the flu," Zelie said.

Calla began stabbing her wrist, then her arm, with the thorn. "*The flu,*" she said, and smiled.

"You better listen to Sister Grimm, girls," Daphne said. "A prick from a rose won't send you to sleep, but a man's prick will." Daphne laughed darkly and fell over into her nest of blankets. She rolled over and her leg hit the row of empty bottles, sending them crashing into the wall. "Not that I'll have to worry about that," she said, laughing again before descending into hiccups.

I didn't understand what was funny, nor had I understood much of what Calla had said. She spoke in codes, in riddles and poetry, Arthurian legend and fairy tales. It was too much for me even on a normal day, but she'd managed to scare Zelie, who was crying, her face buried in a pillow.

"It's all right, Zelie," I said, trying to summon even an ounce of the nurturance that being an older sister required.

"See what you've done, Sister Grimm," Daphne said through her hiccups.

"I didn't write the story," Calla said, gently licking the blood from her arm. "It was written before we were born. It's our fate; it's in our blood. Excuse me for being the only one who can see it."

Daphne sat up and dug into her bag. "Here, you need one of these," she said, tossing a bottle at Calla, who yelped in pain as it hit her elbow. She threw the bottle at the wall in a rage; it cracked apart and filled the room with the smell of whiskey.

The two of them began to argue. I dragged myself off the couch and opened the door, bending over and pulling one of Dovey's trays inside, shutting the door quickly behind me to block out the light from the hall. As I turned back to the dark room, light spotted my vision, and I saw Rosalind's silhouette, luggage in her hands as she rushed down the hall away from us. There were certain images that would stay forever.

I picked up a pitcher of ice water and two glasses from the tray, filling them and handing one to Zelie, keeping the other for myself. Calla and Daphne could get their own. Zelie sat up and wiped her eyes, then drank the water, clearly grateful for it. I placed the plate of cheese sandwiches on the table and handed her half of one, insisting that she eat it and she did. When she was done with that, I gave her a peanut butter cookie and a handful of grapes. She took whatever I gave her and ate it obediently, like a child, which she was, of course.

When we were finished eating, Daphne, by that time completely drunk, threw up into one of the potted ferns. No one bothered to clean it out or open the door or a window. Calla removed another rose from the vase and continued cutting herself with the thorns. She'd started smearing her blood onto one of the pillows. When she was done with the roses, her arms covered in tiny wounds, she pulled up her dress and dripped candle wax onto her thigh, wincing as it dripped onto her skin. When she was finished, she said: "I'm next. That's how it goes. One, two, three."

We went on like this for two days. In a perverse way, it felt good to sink into our own grime, the blood and vomit and despair. When Calla read us Rimbaud, it all made sense: *a season in hell.*

Rosalind had been buried on Tuesday, and sometime on Thursday afternoon, I woke up from a nap and saw that the door to the sitting room was open. Calla, fresh from a bath in her fluffy white robe, was picking up trash.

Zelie woke up soon after me while Daphne stayed passed out on the floor, mouth agape, drool running into her hair.

Calla seemed to be back to her normal self, the madness of the past few days having subsided. She picked up the discarded roses and the empty booze bottles, and tossed them into the trash can.

"What's going on?" Zelie said quietly, her mouth gummy from sleep.

"I know what I have to do," Calla said, determined, though we weren't sure to what end.

She opened the curtains, flooding the room with light, then she opened the windows to let in the breeze of a spring day. She stood staring out the window, her back to us, like a queen on a balcony.

"What do you have to do?" I said, but she kept staring out the window in silence. After days in the dark, the light hurt my eyes.

"I must go in," she said. "The fog is rising."

She left the room, and Zelie and I stared at each other in confusion. There was no fog, and she was already inside, but I knew her words weren't meant to make sense to me. They were intended for an audience of one, herself, the mistress of riddles.

We stood up and followed after her. She wasn't in her bedroom or the bathroom, so we walked down the corridor to the stairway. There, over the banister, we could see her picking up the telephone from the entry-hall table. She asked the operator to connect her to Yale University.

"I'd like to speak to Roberts House," she said, then to the next person who answered: "Teddy Vandiver, please."

"Who's Teddy Vandiver?" Zelie whispered to me, and at first I didn't know, but then it came to me: Roderick's friend, the Yale football player from the wedding.

Calla waited for a minute or two. "Teddy? This is Calla Chapel. If your invitation to the Spring Fling still stands, I'd like to accept." She listened for a moment. "Yes, thank you, it's been a tragic week for the Chapel family." Zelie and I looked at each other, baffled by her casual tone. "No, no, I'll be all right. I think it would do me some good to get out and have fun." She spoke with a faux cheeriness. Anyone who knew her would know she was never genuinely cheerful.

She waited for another moment while Teddy spoke, then said: "Saturday at six o'clock is perfect. See you then."

3.

The next day Calla and I went to New York. When we arrived home in the midafternoon carrying our packages from Bloomingdale's, we discovered that no one had even noticed we were gone.

"Bloomingdale's?" Dovey said with amusement before turning back to her coffee. Dovey and Zelie were in the kitchen with Mrs. O'Connor as she baked. Zelie had a slice of lemon poppy seed cake and some kind of fritter, the scent of which had filled the kitchen with cinnamon.

Calla slipped the checkbook back in the drawer, then she and I went upstairs and divided up the packages, a Moonlit Kisses box set for me and everything else for her. As I sat on my bed opening up the box of treasures, Calla poked her head into my room. "I'm going to write in the library," she said. "Tell them no dinner for me tonight, I'm stuffed."

"Uh-huh," I replied, fastening the moonstone barrette in my hair.

In the morning, Zelie and I ate breakfast with our father while Calla had her hair waved at the beauty parlor in the village. Daphne was ill in bed, saying she'd "scorched" her stomach by drinking so much hard liquor; she slept and moaned in pain for most of the day.

We assumed we'd reached our apex of tragedy for the week, for the year, for the decade, and beyond, so we didn't know to treat the ordinary events of that day as momentous, the "last of this" and the "last of that." Zelie and I couldn't stand to be in the girls' sitting room after what had happened that week, and we didn't want to be in our bedroom with its view of the freshly turned earth in the family plot, so we set ourselves up in the front parlor. This was the start of our moving away from the girls' wing completely although we didn't know it at the time.

We played games — Sorry! and Clue and old maid. My sisters and I had always loved old maid, our deck well-worn. Whoever got stuck with the old maid card at the end of the game would always shriek dramatically in horror. But on that Saturday, when Zelie and I played alone and I ended up with the old maid, I studied what was supposed to be her hideous face, her double chin and splotchy skin, her bulging eyes behind thick glasses, her protruding teeth. She was supposed to be scary; she was meant to frighten little girls. But given what had happened to Aster and Rosalind, maybe the old maid was the lucky one.

That afternoon, we played several hands of the game, and when we grew bored, we went upstairs to see if Calla was getting ready for the dance. It was early evening, and Teddy would soon arrive to pick her up. We found Calla sitting at her vanity, wearing her Peter Pan bra with the Magicups, her girdle, garter belt, and stockings. She had the silver hoops in her ears; she was wearing the moonstone ring and had fastened the moonstone barrette in her hair. She examined her face closely in the mirror, applying the lipstick from the Moonlit Kisses set.

Daphne was asleep in her bed on the other side of the room; if she'd been awake, she surely would have teased Calla about her date with Teddy, but instead the room was quiet. Zelie and I watched silently as Calla finished her lips, brushed the Milky Way shadow across her eyelids, and powdered her nose. Her hands trembled as if she were an actress preparing to perform in a play. She slipped on her green formal and her silver backless heels, then stood in front of the mirror, turning this way and that.

"*Dreamy,*" Zelie said.

"Lovely," Dovey added, having just arrived in the doorway. "There's a young man downstairs waiting for you."

Calla placed a hand to her chest and glanced at me; I saw a quick flicker of terror, but she blinked it away. She picked up her handbag, and on the way out the bedroom door, she called to Daphne. "Wake up. Come see me off." Daphne grumbled something from beneath the covers. Calla paused in the doorway to take in the room, the calla lilies and the laurel tree on the walls. She inhaled slowly, as if she could smell them.

Teddy was in the front parlor with our father, excitedly pointing to the Chapel rifle on the wall like a boy on a trip to a museum. "My older brother has one of these hanging on a wall in his house," Teddy said. "He brought it home from the war."

Zelie and I, watching from the entry hall, glanced at each other; some kind of secondhand war story was inevitably coming next.

"He lives in New Rochelle with his wife and kids," Teddy said. "He's an architect."

"Such an interesting profession," our father said, looking up at the gun along with Teddy. "Architecture." I knew my father well enough to know that it pained him to have to make small talk.

"His wife didn't want a gun hanging in the living room, but my brother said that without his Chapel rifle he wouldn't have survived the war. He owes everything he has to that gun."

"I'm heartened to hear that," our father said with as much conviction as a politician on a rope line. Then he had an out finally; he gestured toward the entry hall and Teddy turned to see Calla.

"Gosh, you look beautiful," Teddy said.

Calla walked up to him and smiled shyly. Zelie and I hovered near the stairs as burly Teddy, shaped like a barrel, chatted away while Calla and our father nodded along half-heartedly. Calla was breathing quickly, her hands fidgeting with her purse. I wondered if she was having second thoughts about the date; I half expected her to go running upstairs to her bedroom. It seemed so much more in character than her leaving the house on Teddy's arm to go to the Spring Fling.

Teddy, meanwhile, was buoyant, complimenting Calla's appearance again and describing the Chinese restaurant where they'd have dinner with some of Teddy's Yale friends before the dance. "Have you ever had an egg roll?" he asked, and Calla shrugged with one shoulder.

"I just love Chinese fo —" Teddy paused as Daphne came stumbling down the stairs in her denim dungarees, wrinkled gingham shirt, and bare feet.

"Oh," Daphne said, when she spotted Teddy. "It's you."

"Yes, hello again," Teddy said tersely. "We were just leaving." He placed a hand on Calla's waist and prodded her lightly. The two of them began to walk toward the door with our father following behind.

"Wait a moment," Calla said. Teddy pulled his hand away from her waist and she turned to look at Daphne, Zelie, and me. "The three of you stand together," she said, motioning with her hands like a photographer setting up a shot. And that's what she seemed to be doing, taking a mental snapshot of us.

"My beautiful sisters," she said at last, her eyes damp, and I thought: *Oh dear.* "The love I've felt for you is the most exquisite kind of love there is," she said, as she brushed the tears from her cheeks.

I didn't know why she was crying. Teddy looked to our father, bewildered, but our father gave nothing away. He was accustomed to odd scenes; and it would take a lot more than that to rattle him. But I was rattled. Calla's words, the terror I'd seen flash in her eyes, her unusual behavior the past two days — it had begun to sound an alarm in my head, but at that point, the siren was still too far away.

Our father opened the front door to usher Calla and her date outside. "Be back by eleven," he said.

Calla and Teddy stepped onto the porch, but Calla extended her arm to keep our father from shutting the door behind them. She peeked around him to my sisters and me, and I'll never forget how she looked in that green dress, the forest princess, her silver slippers glowing like moonlight.

"Parting is such sweet sorrow," she said, and blew us a kiss goodbye.

When she and Teddy had gone, our father led the way to the dining room for dinner. Mrs. O'Connor ladled beef stew into our bowls and we ate quietly. I knew we were all thinking about Calla, trying to make sense of her behavior. Finally, Daphne said: "If you ask me, the kid's lost her marbles."

Later that night, after Zelie and I had played games for hours in the front parlor, we went upstairs to find Daphne sitting at her desk, sketching and drinking from one of her miniature bottles, of which she seemed to have an endless supply.

"I thought your stomach was scorched," I said, but she went on sketching as if I weren't there.

Zelie and I brushed our teeth and changed for bed. I planned to read until Calla came home; after her peculiar behavior, I knew that I wouldn't be able to sleep until she was back. I fluffed my pillow before crawling into bed and heard a crackle beneath. I picked up the pillow and found a folded slip of paper.

night-blooming iris

silver iridescence in
lunar dust
shimmering on a riverbank
at the edge of elysium

we'll wait for you

> *— calla chapel*

I didn't understand the poem. I'd never excelled at poetry, and the things Calla wrote and said confused me. "Elysium," I said aloud.

"The Elysian Fields," Daphne said from the hallway. She'd been on her way to the sitting room but had stopped at our doorway.

"What's that?" I asked.

"It's from Greek mythology. Elysium is kind of like . . . *heaven*. Why?"

I held out the slip of paper, and Daphne came and took it. She read it, then looked at me as if to say, *So?*

"Calla left that for me under my pillow."

"That's Calla," Daphne said. "She's always leaving poems around."

"I know, but this feels different."

"Why?"

"It feels like she's sending me a message." I told her what happened in New York, how Calla had behaved, how she'd asked me to promise I'd pursue a career, her sense of urgency. Then there was the scene at the door earlier.

"You think she's run away from home?" Daphne laughed. "If Calla was going to run away, she would have told me."

"No," I said, unable to articulate the thought that had popped into my head: Calla dying like one of her heroines, like the Lady of Shalott or, more likely, Ophelia.

"What?" Daphne said, growing nervous at my silence, at how obviously I was holding back what I really wanted to say. "Wait, do you think she's going to *kill herself?*"

"Calla?" Zelie said with panic. "But *why?*"

"No," Daphne scoffed. She waved a dismissive hand at Zelie to calm her down. "Calla wouldn't — she just . . . she *couldn't.* You don't know the kid like I do." I wondered how much Daphne had had to drink. "If that's what she's planning, why go out with Ricky?"

"Teddy," I said.

"Is she going to ask Teddy to strangle her with her stockings? Nah, Calla is fine."

Daphne handed me back the poem and left the room. In her wake, I didn't move or say anything, and neither did Zelie. A moment later, Daphne returned with two mini bottles in each hand.

"It *was* odd how she said goodbye at the door." She tapped the bottles lightly together, apprehensive. "Let's go downstairs and wait for her."

· · ·

We waited in the front parlor. Zelie sat in a chair near the window, watching for any sign of Teddy's car. Our father hadn't checked to see if Calla had arrived home, and it's likely she could have stayed out all night and he wouldn't have known.

While Zelie kept watch, Daphne sat on the sofa across from me in her dungarees, legs spread wide apart, hair unbrushed. "She'll be fine," she said, and repeated it to herself every so often like an incantation, as if the repetition would make it so. The more she drank, the more she began to drift in and out of sleep, but I was too tense even to close my eyes. My reserves of anxiety were running low after the weeks we'd had, the lead-up to the wedding and the aftermath, but there was enough left in me to feel sick at Calla's tardiness.

The clock chimed one, then two, then three. No Calla. The four o'clock chime woke Daphne and she sat up, setting her empty bottle on the coffee table. She turned to Zelie, who, like me, was awake; Zelie continued to watch out the front window, and said, "No sign of her."

"I hope that kid isn't out there doing anything stupid," Daphne said, opening her last bottle and drinking from it.

"What do you think she's doing?" I asked. My own thoughts were dark. I thought of Ophelia as painted by Millais. Calla floating faceup in a river, her dark green dress with the pale green netting, the moon-kissed pallor. But no, that was too romantic. Painters imagined the deaths of young women as beautiful, but I knew otherwise.

"*Briar Rose,*" Daphne said. "The sleeping beauty. Or the opposite of that. Calla told us herself, remember? The embrace of a man, the eternal slumber."

Zelie left her post near the window and came over to sit on the sofa next to Daphne. She offered Zelie the bottle, but Zelie shook her head. "What do you mean?" she asked.

"I mean she might be shacked up somewhere with Teddy, and if so, we all know what happens next."

"Calla isn't loose," I said. "She doesn't even care about boys. She wouldn't do that."

"Under normal circumstances, no. But you said it yourself earlier. She wants to die." Daphne began to tremble and took another drink. She walked to the front entry hall and picked up the car keys from the table. "We have to go find her."

It seemed like a bad idea from the start — Daphne was clearly drunk — but at the same time, it seemed like our only hope. Our father wouldn't have understood, and I recalled his inaction on the day Aster died. He was upstairs asleep, unaware that Calla had missed her curfew.

Zelie and I were in our pajamas, but Daphne said there wasn't time to change. We took our coats from the closet, and since our shoes were upstairs, we put on galoshes. We followed Daphne to the Hudson, the two of us climbing into the back seat. Daphne struggled to get the key in the ignition, but eventually the car roared to life.

Before we set off, she handed me the road map of Connecticut from the glove box and a small flashlight kept there for emergencies. "Be my Fred Noonan," she said, which seemed to doom the journey from the start.

Zelie held the flashlight while I opened the map. "Where are we going?" I asked, the vastness of Connecticut spread across my lap. "We don't even know where she is." *Needles and haystacks,* that's what I was thinking.

"We'll start at Yale," Daphne said confidently, as if she had a plan. I knew that New Haven was more than an hour away. I hadn't even found Bellflower Village on the map before Daphne was heading into the night without any real clue where she was going.

Out on the road in front of our house, the car jerked and swerved; Zelie dropped the flashlight on the floor. I worried that the odds of our crashing into a ditch were higher than the odds of reaching Yale as Daphne drifted over the centerline and back again. There were very few streetlights in Bellflower Village, which didn't help matters. We breezed right through the intersection that was down the road from our house; Daphne didn't notice the stop sign even though Zelie and I shouted at her to stop. I knew we needed to turn left there to head into the village and reach the way to the highway.

When I pointed this out to Daphne, she stopped the car in the middle of the road so quickly that Zelie and I hit the front seat. She jerked the car backward and forward, trying to get it facing the right direction. The head-lights lit the forest around us, the trees so black they were indistinguishable from the night sky.

She finally got the car facing the right way, but instead of going forward to the intersection, she let her head fall back on the seat. The car started to roll backward, and I didn't know what was happening until I heard her snore. Zelie, who was sitting directly behind Daphne, flicked her on the back of her head. "Wake up, Daphne! We have to hurry!"

"Huh?" Daphne said, jerking awake and stepping on the gas. We made it to the intersection and turned right and soon arrived at the bottom of Main Street.

"Turn right," I said. I still hadn't located Bellflower Village on the map, but I was certain that we needed to turn right to get to the highway. But Daphne turned left, heading into the heart of the village.

"You're going the wrong way," Zelie said.

"No I'm not," Daphne replied.

Main Street was lit up with lamps; through the front windshield, I could see them snaking ahead of us down the road like a line of enormous glow-ing insects. We practically crawled down the road, passing the cinema, the ice cream parlor, Dr. Green's office, and the church. As we rounded the town green, Daphne swerved suddenly, and the right side of the car, where I was sitting, jumped the curb. The whole car jolted, and Zelie and I bounced up in our seats, then I fell over into her. The car went on like that for a few min-utes, the right side still up on the curb, Zelie and I screaming at Daphne to get back on the road. A streetlight scraped into the car doors, and then an-other one did, then we thudded back down onto the pavement. Daphne kept going as if nothing had happened.

"We better go home," I said with urgency. I didn't want to involve our father, but it was clear we'd never find Calla without him. "Turn around," I said to Daphne, but she was ignoring me, so I shouted, "We're wasting time!" Finally, she pulled to the side of the road.

"I need a nap," she said, putting the car into park. "Then I'll be all right.

Just give me a minute." Before I could yell at her again, she slumped over sideways onto the bench seat and started snoring.

We sat in the car at the north end of the village with the engine running, the headlights blazing, as Daphne slept. We'd never been away from home at that time of night and certainly not alone on Main Street, our drunken sister at the wheel. Worst of all, Calla was out there somewhere, and wherever she was, we weren't getting any closer. "What should we do?" Zelie asked with fright. It was obvious Daphne wasn't anywhere close to waking up. I thought of Aster and Rosalind, and of Calla's words, which began to play in my mind like a kind of poetry: *Do you think this is what heaven looks like?* she'd said. And *You have to promise me you'll become an artist.* How could I have been so stupid not to notice what she was telling me? Then there was her poem, its last line: *we'll wait for you.* She was joining Aster and Rosalind.

I didn't want to scare Zelie, so I held in my fear. I opened my door and went around to the driver's side of the car, opening Daphne's door and attempting to push her to the passenger's side of the bench seat.

"What are you doing?" Zelie cried.

"We have to get home," I said. I pushed as hard as I could but Daphne hadn't moved an inch. "Get up!" I screamed, punching her on the hip with my fists as hard as I could.

She mumbled something and crawled across the bench seat toward the passenger door, leaving just enough room for me to sit in the driver's seat. I'd never driven a car, and I couldn't figure out how to switch gears, but I eventually realized that I had to put my foot on the brake to do so. We lurched forward and I drove us down Main Street, the car more difficult to operate than I'd anticipated. We were heading in the wrong direction, but I didn't think I could manage to turn the car around in the middle of the road. I turned left onto a residential street and hoped I could weave my way back to that intersection Daphne had driven us through earlier, which I knew was close to our house. It was difficult to orient myself without the lights of Main Street though, and I made a series of turns, taking us in what seemed to be circles, but it was hard to tell.

As I drove, I imagined Calla with Teddy, who was taking off her green dress, the Peter Pan bra with the Magicups, the girdle and garter, and the nylons. I pressed harder on the accelerator, frantic to get home. "Slow down!" Zelie shouted.

We arrived at an intersection, but it wasn't the one I was looking for. I stopped to steady myself. I saw Teddy's mouth on Calla's mouth; I saw his lips on her breast, his hands exploring her body, spreading her legs apart. I started to cry again but not quietly enough to keep it hidden from Zelie.

"You're scaring me," she said.

"I know, I'm sorry." I wiped my eyes and looked around for any point of reference.

The street sign, which I could barely make out, said St. Ronan Street. "Isn't St. Ronan the street that runs behind the meadow?" I asked Zelie. Behind the meadow on the other side of a short stretch of forest was the dead end of a residential road that led into the village. We had walked that route in the days before Aster had learned to drive when we wanted to go into the village and had no one to take us.

Zelie leaned over my shoulder. "This is the street," she said. "Turn right."

"I think it's left," I said. "Turning right takes us to the dead end. We want to get back to the main road."

"I'm sure it's right," Zelie said, so I went that way. St. Ronan was one of the wider streets, more rural than the streets closer to Main Street. The houses were set farther apart, on larger pieces of land. The street was nearly black, like all the other streets, and I accelerated, relieved to be almost home.

Then something dashed in front of the car, a dog or a fox or a raccoon. I saw its dark silhouette crossing the road just at the edge of my headlights, and I panicked, turning sharply to the right. We bumped off the road, the car lurching as the pavement met the grass. Zelie screamed as our headlights illuminated a looming tree. I hit the brakes hard but not hard enough. We smashed into the trunk.

As we collided with the tree, Daphne rolled onto the floor, and Zelie slammed into the back of my seat just as my head hit the steering wheel. The maple tree was in front of a house, and I could see lights turning on. The house was painted robin's-egg blue. The Popplewells' house.

The front door opened and some dark figures stepped onto the porch. Daphne, who'd crawled back up onto the seat, opened the door and ran away from the car, then fell to her knees and vomited.

"That's Daphne Chapel," one of the Popplewells said.

Zelie opened my door and peered down at me. "Are you all right?" she said, as she rubbed her arm. I grabbed on to her for support as I climbed out of the car, its hood partially accordioned against the tree.

"I think so. Are you?"

She nodded.

As the Popplewells gathered around Daphne, I crawled into the back seat to look for the flashlight on the floor. I took it in one hand and grabbed Zelie's arm with the other, pulling her along. The end of St. Ronan Street, the dead end at the edge of our property, was only yards away. I was startled and dazed but needed to get home.

"What about Daphne?" Zelie asked, as we ran.

"Who cares?" Let her take the blame for the crash. Let her get arrested for drunk driving. It's what she deserved.

As we entered the forest, I turned on the small flashlight. There was a dirt path that led from the end of the road to the meadow, and the flashlight lit up the path just enough so we could see where we were going.

We made it to the meadow and stopped for a moment to catch our breath. I thought of Calla's poem, of the night-blooming iris at the edge of Elysium, the field of the dead. I hoped there was still time to find her down here in the world of the living.

By the time we got nearer to the house, Zelie and I were exhausted from our trek and numb from the cold. I could see that some of the lights in the house were on, both upstairs and down. I wasn't sure what time it was, but it seemed too early for anyone to be up; I wondered if Calla had come home.

When we finally got to the side door off the kitchen, I saw Dovey in her housecoat, making coffee. I banged on the glass pane in the door, giving her a fright. "Where have you girls been? Is Calla with you?"

"She's not here?"

"No, and Daphne's been in an accident. Your father went to pick her up."

I hadn't expected that my father wouldn't be home and wondered if I should run back to the scene of the accident to find him. But Dovey had hold of my arm and was guiding me into a chair at the kitchen table. "You girls sit down and tell me what happened."

My head hurt from the accident, and I needed a chance to rest, to think. While Dovey made us mugs of hot cocoa, I explained that Calla hadn't come home from her date, that Daphne took us out in the car to find her, that we'd wanted to go to Yale but never made it out of the village, then we crashed into the tree. I didn't mention that I'd been driving.

"Why didn't you wake up your father?" Dovey said, setting mugs in front of us and sitting down with her coffee.

"We didn't think he'd understand."

"You girls," Dovey said in dismay. "Sometimes you lack common sense completely. Now drink up. You could have caught your death out there."

"But Calla's in trouble," I said, my panic returning. "We have to find her."

"She's going to be in a lot of trouble when she gets home. Imagine staying out all these hours past her curfew. But that's not your concern."

"I think we should call the police," I said, and ran to the entry-hall telephone. Dovey came up behind me and took the receiver, setting it back in its cradle.

"The police?" she said, at the edge of exasperation. "There's no need for that."

As I tried to explain the urgency of the situation, Zelie went into the front parlor to resume her vigil. Not long after, she shouted: "I see headlights!"

I ran into the parlor as Zelie peered out the window, trying to get a better look. "It's Teddy's car!"

I had never felt such relief. I chastised myself for panicking. I hadn't considered any innocent explanations for Calla's delay in coming home. Perhaps

Teddy had car trouble; maybe he'd run out of fuel. There were all sorts of understandable reasons for why his car was just now pulling up in front of our house when the dawn was beginning to crack the black sky.

Dovey, Zelie, and I walked down the front steps to meet the car. Teddy, his suit jacket off, his tie undone, raced from the driver's side to the passenger's door, which was nearest to us. He looked harried and frantic, the jittery white rabbit from Wonderland.

When Teddy opened Calla's door, she practically fell out of the car, her body limp.

"Sweet Mary, mother of God," Dovey said, crossing herself.

Dovey knew. Zelie knew. And so did I.

I opened my mouth wide, my throat vibrating; it took several seconds for me to realize I was screaming. Dovey grabbed me. She put her face in front of mine, and I saw that she was saying my name over and over: "I-*ris!*" I didn't hear anything, neither her nor myself, but she kept at it until I shut my mouth.

"Stay with your sister," she said, and I assumed she was talking to me, but she was actually talking to Zelie, who took hold of my hand.

Dovey ran to the car. "What have you done to this girl?" she shouted at Teddy.

"I didn't do anything, honest!" Teddy said. "I don't know what's wrong with her. I wanted to take her to the hospital, but she insisted on coming here."

"How did she get this way?" Dovey said, cupping Calla's face in her hands. From where I stood, I couldn't tell if Calla was breathing.

"After the dance, we went to a motel. It was her idea, honest," Teddy said, and I could tell he had rehearsed this, what he would say. Teddy had never seen anything like this before; he didn't know what it meant. He didn't think anyone would believe him.

"I told her I needed to bring her home by eleven, that there was no time for a motel, but she begged me. She kept saying stuff that didn't make sense. 'You have to seduce me,' she said. 'It's my destiny.' When I refused, she demanded that I let her out of the car on the side of the highway. She tried to open the door and jump out! She was hysterical. What could I do?"

"So you went to a motel?" Dovey asked. "You seduced her?"

Teddy looked down at the pavement. "Ma'am, I didn't hurt her, I promise," he said, his voice cracking. "I don't know why she's like this."

"Answer my question," Dovey said. "What did you do at the motel?"

"Only what she wanted."

Dovey leaned over and put an arm around Calla, whose head fell forward sharply, her chin coming to rest on her chest. "Zelie, call Dr. Green," Dovey said, and Zelie ran into the house as if there was still something that could be done. Another set of headlights came up the drive, white pinpricks in the bluish light, and as the car grew closer, I saw that it was my father's car. It came to a stop behind Teddy's car and the passenger's door flew open. Daphne, who had apparently sobered up, rushed to Calla's side. When she saw the state of her, she fell to her knees and cried.

It was hard to follow what happened after that — Daphne in a heap on the ground; Zelie in tears, pulling at my arm to get my attention, which I wasn't able to give; my father arguing with Teddy and lifting Calla out of the car; Teddy driving away. Dovey and my father walked Calla inside sandwiched between them, her silver heels dragging on the floor.

Upstairs in the girls' wing, they got her into bed. She tumbled onto the mattress, then sprawled out, one leg dangling off the end, the other over the side, her arms spread out beside her like angel wings. Her nylons were missing, but the silver heels hadn't fallen off. She was already screaming, rolling her head from side to side.

"Larded all with sweet flowers," she called out, "which bewept to the ground did not go with true-love showers." She started to laugh, then came the last words she ever spoke: "Good night, ladies; good night, sweet ladies; good night, good night."

I couldn't watch it happen; I couldn't stay with her to the end. I ran to my bedroom and jumped into bed, pulling the covers up over my head. "Calla, please forgive me," I cried into my pillow. Then came the sound of shattering glass. The curtain dropped.

4.

Calla's body was taken from our house to the medical examiner's office. "I have to insist this time, Henry," Dr. Green said. "I'm terribly sorry."

She was returned to us a couple of days later via the Hewson Funeral Home in Greenwich, the examiner having found no obvious cause of death. On Calla's death certificate, the cause was tentatively listed as "unknown," which they said they would amend once they received the results of various tests they had run. But the certificate would never be amended.

Given the seedy nature of his encounter with Calla — a cheap motel, the two of them unmarried — Teddy was questioned by the police. "Yale Quarterback Questioned by Police in Mysterious Death" a headline in the *New Haven Echo* read. In the end, however, Teddy was found to have done nothing wrong.

We didn't have a proper funeral for Calla. Our days of being on display at the church in Bellflower Village were finished, our father said. Over the previous year, we'd had two weddings followed by two funerals, and he refused to make it three. We wouldn't become a spectacle, he said, although I knew it was too late for that.

5.

Calla's death had come exactly one week after Rosalind's. Zelie and I were caught anew in the peaks and valleys of grief, a dizzying ride through exhaustion, violent jags of tears, and numbness. By the time the funeral came, we had settled into the valley, dead inside.

Daphne behaved differently. Calla and Daphne had been an odd pair,

but they were a pair nonetheless, and Daphne carried on in the days after
Calla's passing as she hadn't done for Aster and Rosalind. Her wailing carried through the girls' wing and beyond, and when I look back, it didn't seem
so much from mourning as pain, the brutal pain of being cleaved from her
beloved.

On the way to the funeral home, Daphne cried and banged her head
against the car window. At the sight of Calla in her casket, she picked up a
chair and threw it against the wall. She calmed down long enough for the
reverend to say a prayer and for Zelie and me to place two calla lilies in Calla's
hands, one from each of us; then Daphne placed a crown of daisies on top of
Calla's head. Aster and Rosalind had been buried in their wedding dresses.
Calla, never a bride, wore a simple white dress, delicate and accented with
lacy embroidery, that someone — I didn't know who — had pulled from her
wardrobe.

Before the lid was closed, Daphne partially lifted Calla up out of her casket high enough to hug her. She held her tightly and wouldn't let go, sobbing
into Calla's shoulder, her face nestled in her hair. Calla's head flopped over,
her arms hanging at her sides. It was heartbreaking and horrifying; I turned
away, unable to take it all in. It took my father and the reverend and one of
the undertakers to pull Daphne away, and Calla was quickly fixed up — her
dress adjusted, wayward strands of her hair patted down, the daisy crown
straightened. Before the lid was closed, I removed the moonstone ring from
her finger, wanting to keep it as a memento of her and our day together in
the city.

Once we were home, Daphne ran inside and wouldn't come out for the
graveside service. She couldn't bear to watch Calla lowered into the ground,
taking her place next to Aster and Rosalind, the three of them lined up like
piano keys. Zelie and I held hands for comfort but also for protection; it was
difficult not to think, looking at those three plots in a row, that there was
still plenty of room for us.

It was an April morning, the sky the color of a gray pearl. We pulled our
coats around us tightly as the reverend spoke. "Ashes to ashes," he said, and I
knew Calla would have been appalled at such overused verse.

• • •

In the house, Mrs. O'Connor set out a spread for us in the front parlor using the Chapel family's heirloom silver service. It was a routine by now, the
cucumber and egg-salad sandwiches cut into triangles, the shortbread cookies, the cups of tea — dainty food and drink for unsettled stomachs. If Mrs.
O'Connor ever decided to leave our employ, she could set up her own cater-
ing business: Food for the Bereaved. She excelled at it so.

Zelie and I sat in the parlor with our father, sipping tea from white china
cups. Belinda hadn't been told about Calla's death, but I wondered if she already knew. She'd entered the St. Aubert Sanitarium almost three weeks earlier as the mother of five living daughters; now she had just three. I didn't
know when the doctors were going to tell her; my father said he'd left it up
to them.

Daphne was upstairs; we could hear her cries from the parlor though none
of us acknowledged them. From the parlor, her crying sounded far away, as if
Zelie and my father and I had locked our own grief in a room upstairs and it
was banging on the walls, trying to get out.

Eventually, our father set down his cup and said he had a headache, that
if we didn't need him he was going to take a nap. "Please go look in on your
sister," he said, as he left, and I wondered why he couldn't do it himself.

But Zelie and I lingered in the front parlor a while longer. I wasn't ready
to face Daphne yet, so I drank a second cup of tea, and Zelie nibbled at a
sandwich and a cookie. It was a relief to be numb. It was a comfort, numbness; a blanket.

Daphne's wailing stopped, and I assumed she'd gone to bed and passed
out drunk; she'd run out of her mini bottles, but she had stolen a large bottle of scotch from our father's den that she'd been sipping on for days. We
knew, in her silence, that it was finally safe to go upstairs, so we stood up and
walked to the girls' wing. When we arrived, to my surprise, Daphne wasn't in
bed or knocked out; she was packing, filling a knapsack with clothes.

"I'm leaving," she said, her face so red and puffy that it looked as if she'd
suffered an allergic reaction.

"I'm next, right? That's how it goes," Daphne said. "Aster, Roz, Calla, and now me." She paused to gulp down some of the scotch. "We don't know what's going on, how any of this works. You know what Calla said" — at the mention of Calla, Daphne swallowed a sob — "Briar Rose, *the sleeping beauty,* remember? It's in our blood, our legacy."

She picked up her sketch pad and stuffed it into her bag. "But you're not interested in men," I said, no longer caring if she knew that I'd snooped.

"How do you know that will protect me?" Daphne finished packing. "I have to go. I can't die here." She wiped her nose with her arm and picked up the knapsack. Then she looked around the room just as Rosalind and Calla had done before her.

"Goodbye, girls," Daphne said, as she approached the doorway. I should have reached out to her, begged her to stay — but I couldn't. There was nothing left in me.

"I'll miss you," she added, most uncharacteristically, patting each of us gently on the tops of our heads as she left.

When she was gone, I shrugged at Zelie, who seemed unsure how she should react. "She'll be back," I said. "She's just upset."

"It sure doesn't seem like she's coming back."

"She's sixteen. She doesn't have any money. Where's she going to go?"

Zelie shrugged this time. She said she was going to change and take a nap. I was about to follow her but paused. I saw on top of Daphne's bureau an overturned canvas as small as a paperback book. On the back, written in pencil, it said: THE WHITE IRIS, MARCH 1951. I flipped the canvas around to see the painting: a creamy white flower with pink and blue shading set against a pale-green background. I blushed, but I wasn't sure why. And then I realized what the subject of the painting actually was. It was an iris, yes, but it was also Veronica. Daphne had transformed her sketch of the space between Veronica's legs, the delicate curves and folds, into a flower.

I turned the canvas back around. At that point, I was certain Daphne would return home, but since she wasn't there, I took the painting to my bedroom and hid it in the back of my wardrobe.

6.

The call came in during dinner.

Mrs. O'Connor had made chicken noodle soup and fresh bread, and our father had insisted that we join him and eat something. We'd taken our usual seats in the dining room, Zelie and I on one side of the table, our father at the end. All the other seats were empty.

My father started on his soup. He was still wearing his clothes from the funeral — funerals were the only time he deviated from his normal brown suit to black — but he wasn't wearing his jacket or a tie; his eyes were glassy and the skin beneath them puffy. I had never seen him cry, but he certainly didn't look like his normal self now, slumping in his chair, his voice strained and difficult to hear.

"Where's Daphne?" he asked.

I'd been dreading that question. I didn't answer, hoping Zelie might, and spooned up some of the broth, which was comforting.

"Well?" he asked, as Zelie remained silent.

"I don't know where she is," I said, and didn't elaborate. I assumed she'd gone to see Veronica.

Then the telephone rang. Dovey answered it, and moments later, she told my father he needed to take the call. It was urgent.

We drove to the Hotel Cream. Zelie and I had insisted on going with our father and he'd agreed without any resistance; Sidney Cream had said on the phone that there was something wrong with Daphne, and our father probably wanted us with him since he'd never been able to deal with her on his own.

When we arrived at the hotel, there were several police cars parked out front and men in rain slickers running back and forth from the beach, shouting commands at one another. "What did Daphne do?" Zelie said with alarm. "Is she in the water?" She pressed her face up against the rainy window as a truck towing a boat pulled up beside us. I waited for my father to do something, to take charge of the situation, but he just sat there behind the wheel, engine idling, the blurry red of the police lights surrounding us.

At last someone noticed that we'd arrived. Sidney Cream ran from the hotel entrance to our car holding a folded newspaper over his head. He didn't wait for our father to shut off the engine before he opened the driver's door. "I'm sorry to do this to you, Henry. I know it's been an awful day, but Daphne's gone missing."

"*Missing?*" our father said, his voice still quiet and strained as it had been at dinner. It was then that Sidney glanced into the back seat and saw Zelie and me. "Hello, girls," he said, trying to assure us with a smile.

"I didn't say anything on the telephone since I assumed we'd have found her by the time you got here. Please come inside," he said, then he ran back to the hotel.

Sidney led us into the dining room, with its familiar arched windows looking out on Long Island Sound, which at this time of night was nothing but a dark formless mass. It was the last place I wanted to be, the scene of Rosalind's reception.

At a large round table in the center of the room, Veronica, damp from the rain and wrapped in a blanket, sat next to her mother. Mrs. Cream comforted her daughter, rubbing a hand up and down her back, removing wet strands of hair from her forehead. "There, there, sweet one," she said, sounding the way I imagined a cat would sound if it could talk.

There were a couple of policemen at another table studying a map and drinking coffee from thermoses. From the looks of them, they'd been outside for a while. I wondered how long Veronica's father had waited before telephoning us.

My father followed Sidney to the table where Veronica sat with her mother. Sidney motioned for all of us to sit down, and a waitress brought over a tray with mugs of coffee. My father immediately took a mug and began to drink.

"Veronica, tell Mr. Chapel what happened," Sidney said.

Mrs. Cream, left arm wrapped tightly around her daughter's shoulders, squeezed her in a gesture of support. Veronica sniffled into a tissue, her face a mess from crying, black eye makeup staining her cheeks.

"She went swimming," she whispered.

"Before that," her father said. "Start at the beginning."

Veronica turned to her mother, who nodded reassuringly. "She arrived at the hotel somehow. I don't know how she got here," Veronica said, and I realized I had never heard her speak before. Her voice sounded like her mother's, low and smooth. "She was awful sad over Calla. She said she couldn't live at home anymore."

"We checked her into a room," Mrs. Cream said. "We said she could stay for a few days."

"We were going to call you," Mr. Cream added. Our father couldn't very well complain that the Creams had taken possession of his daughter; he hadn't even noticed she'd left the house.

Veronica explained that Daphne had slept for a few hours in her room, that she and her mother had taken turns looking in on her. When Daphne woke up, she and Veronica had shared a roast chicken dinner in the room and Veronica supplied them with alcohol. At this part of the story, Veronica clearly couldn't face her parents' looks of disappointment, so she stared through the window at the policemen on the terrace off the dining room that led to the beach.

According to Veronica, Daphne quickly became drunk and told Veronica she couldn't live without Calla, without Aster and Rosalind. "She kept saying: 'I'm next.'" Zelie and I glanced at each other, but neither of us dared tell our father that this was how Daphne had behaved at home too. He'd told us to check on her, and we'd done a poor job of it.

"She began to cry. She became hysterical," Veronica said. "She ran out of the room and onto the beach. It was so dark and cold." She shivered, as if from the memory. "She waded into the water and I shouted at her to stop, but she kept going. Knee-deep, then waist-deep. I was screaming at her to come back, but she swam out. She went so far out that I couldn't see her anymore, and then" — Veronica was about to crack but eked out the rest of her story — "she screamed for help. She said she was being pulled under. I didn't know what to do, so I ran for my mother —" That was it for Veronica, who doubled over in anguish.

"We rushed out to the beach," Mrs. Cream said, as she ran her hand down her daughter's back. "We screamed for Daphne but she didn't answer."

More policemen filtered in and out of the dining room, using the terrace to reach the beach. My father, Zelie, and I sat quietly for a moment, trying to absorb the story. "It's not possible," my father said finally, finishing the last of his coffee. "Not today. It's simply not possible. I'd like to search the hotel and the grounds. She's probably just hiding somewhere."

Mrs. Cream looked offended. "Veronica saw her go under."

"She didn't say that," my father said. "She said she swam too far out to be seen."

"Earlier, after Calla's funeral," I said, glancing at Zelie, "Daphne said she wanted to run away. She packed some of her things."

"There you have it," my father said with irritation.

Mrs. Cream began to defend her daughter's version of events once again, but her husband stepped in. "I'll organize a search," Sidney said, and set off with my father to round up some of the hotel staff.

Zelie and I were left at the table with Veronica and her mother. A waitress refreshed the table with coffee and cocoa and a plate of shortbread — clearly the refreshment of choice for the bereaved. Mrs. Cream left the table and came back with a small bottle of brandy. She poured some into her mug of coffee, than added some to Veronica's. "There's no chance Daphne is in the hotel," she said, though it wasn't clear to whom she was speaking. "She would never put us through all this."

"You don't know her like we do," I said, and Mrs. Cream turned to me in surprise. She had apparently been speaking to Veronica, not to Zelie and me.

"I'd love nothing more than to find Daphne hiding in a closet somewhere, sweetheart," she said in a genuinely kind voice. *This was what it was like to have a mother,* I thought. It meant having someone to call you sweetheart.

"The problem," Mrs. Cream continued, "is that Daphne swam far out into the Sound and the water is very cold. Hypothermia sets in within minutes. I don't mean to be cruel by saying this, but I also don't want your father to get your hopes up unnecessarily."

I stood up, wanting to get out of the dining room and away from Veronica, who made me uncomfortable. Zelie, as always, followed me, and I told her we could make ourselves useful by searching for Daphne.

"Do you really think she's hiding?" Zelie asked.

"I don't know. Maybe," I said. We walked along the first floor, the floorboards noisy and lumpy and slanted to one side. We tried all the doors but they were locked. The hotel was quiet in the off-season, and we didn't see any guests except for an elderly couple that hurried quickly into their room when they saw us. They were surely aware of what was going on; it would be a story they could tell their grandkids, how a girl at the hotel went missing on their trip to Connecticut. For them, it was only background.

We climbed the stairs to the second floor and tried the doors. One of them was unlocked. I knocked to make sure no one was there, then opened the door. A lamp was on in the room, which contained two single beds, one of them unmade. On the desk near the window were the remains of a chicken dinner on a tray. This must have been Daphne's room. I wondered what had happened to the knapsack.

Zelie helped me look for it; it wasn't sitting out in any obvious place. We looked in the bathroom, under the bed, in the dark corners of the room. "Why do we need the knapsack?" Zelie asked.

"If the knapsack is gone, then maybe she *is* hiding somewhere. She'd need her knapsack if she was going to run away." I felt hopeful suddenly. We looked around, and it seemed for a few minutes like a matter of life and death. Then Zelie exclaimed that she'd found it; it was stuffed behind the bureau.

We began to pick through it, pulling out a pair of denim dungarees wad-

ded into a ball, a yellow blouse, and a pair of white socks. The sketch pad
wasn't there. "Does this mean she didn't run away?" Zelie asked me.

"I don't know," I said, but I knew it was a bad sign.

We stayed in the room for the rest of the night, mostly sleeping or lying quietly and listening to the waves outside. No one came looking for us — they
rarely ever did. In the morning, we walked to the dining room. Mrs. Cream
and Veronica had apparently stayed there all night, sitting at the round table in the middle of the room, Mrs. Cream somberly caressing her devastated
daughter.

I led Zelie to another table and we sat down. The sun was already up, the
sky a mix of gray and bright white, the rain a light spatter. My father stood
out on the terrace, a mug of coffee in his hands, talking to the police captain
and Sidney Cream as they looked out over Long Island Sound. They hadn't
found Daphne hiding in the hotel, that much was clear. A waitress appeared,
the same one who'd been working the night before. She gave us glasses of
orange juice, and a few minutes later, she brought out toast and tea. The
view outside was a scene of chaos, with boats and scores of policemen on the
beach. Zelie and I watched everything as we spread our toast with butter and
raspberry jam, drank tea, and stuffed our mouths. It didn't seem appropriate to be eating, and yet we were hungry. The scene continued to thrum with
activity for quite a while, but then it stopped rather suddenly. The rain grew
heavy, the boats returned to shore, and some of the policemen went back to
their cars.

"Oh God," I said, and set down my tea.

"What?" Zelie asked.

"They've stopped looking for her, can't you see?"

"You mean they *found* her?"

My father came inside and I gripped the table. "Are you girls all right?" he
asked, coming over to us. He looked even worse than he had the night before
— unshaven, wet hair and clothes, his voice hovering just above a whisper.

Sidney Cream and the police captain also came inside. "Any news?" Mrs.

Cream asked, when she saw her husband. A groggy Veronica sat up straight in her chair and sipped some coffee.

"I'm afraid not," Mr. Cream said, and he nodded to my father, who took his cue.

"The police have decided to call off the search," he announced.

I was confused. "What do you mean? Did you find her?"

"We haven't found her," he said.

"She's been out there since last night, through the rain and cold," the police captain said. "There's no sign of her anywhere. It's impossible for anyone to survive those conditions. I'm sorry."

My father turned to Zelie and me, waiting for our reaction, waiting to see how we'd have to be managed. I thought I heard the captain say: "Her body will probably wash up on shore in a few days." But he couldn't have said that, could he?

Zelie appeared to be in shock. She was pale, trembling. Before either of us could do anything, we heard the most violent cry. Veronica had broken free from her mother; she was standing in the center of the room, shrieking to the heavens. Her mother and father tried to control her, but it was impossible to stop her from bellowing her agony.

This was a spectacle I didn't want to hear or see. I stood up, pushing past my father, and left the hotel. Daphne was gone. I felt for Veronica, but I couldn't watch her carrying on. I was finished with tears and screaming — my own or anyone else's.

From the door of the hotel, I ran to the beach, breathing in the rain as it fell around me, as it soaked through me and washed me clean. *Run!* I heard my mother say. That's what Daphne had done; she'd run into the water and swum until she was exhausted and frozen; she'd swum into oblivion. But that couldn't have been what my mother meant.

I looked at the gray waves. Daphne was out there, and Calla, Rosalind, and Aster were in the ground, all four swallowed up by the earth. But not me, not yet. Maybe I would be the next sister to die, but there, in that moment at least, I was alive. That had to count for something.

I glanced back at the hotel and saw Zelie come outside, squinting at the sky. I watched as she wandered around, searching for me. "Iris?" she called. "Where are you?"

"I'm here," I said, too quietly for her to hear, knowing she'd find me anyway. When she spotted me on the beach, she walked over and took my hand.

And then there were two.

We stood together at the edge of the sea — *IrisandZelie* — with what seemed like all the world spread out before us. I vowed that what had happened to our sisters wouldn't happen to us.

We would figure out what it meant to run, and we would run together.

THE BLUE DIARY

Volume Three

Corpse Flower

1957

It was the last day of the semester; the summer stretched out before me like a lazy cat on a sun-drenched rug. The girls in my art class invited me to have lunch with them to celebrate the start of summer vacation, so I followed them, the Joans and the Bettys, across the street to a delicatessen. They'd invited me only because I was in earshot when they made their plans during class, but I didn't mind. I was hungry.

In the packed deli, they scouted a table next to a window overlooking the busy main street. I made sure to get a seat by the glass. My classmates ordered daintily: chef's salads, cups of tomato soup with oyster crackers. I ordered pastrami on rye with extra mustard.

"Half?" the harried waiter asked, already writing it on his pad.

"Whole," I said, and he raised one of his woolly eyebrows in surprise. The eyebrow annoyed me.

"*And* I'll have matzo ball soup." I hadn't wanted the soup, but I wanted to shock him. I was only twenty years old, but I'd known for years how little it took for a woman to shock a man.

"Cup?"

"*Bowl.*" I folded the menu and handed it back to him. "Cream soda too." He took the menu, raising his eyebrow again as he walked away.

As we waited for our food, the conversation turned to summer plans. The other girls had their adventures mapped out: camping in the Adirondacks, a road trip to visit grandparents in Wisconsin, staying in a resort in the Catskills, seeing Niagara Falls. I listened to them talk, looking at the red-brick facade of the college across the street. I'd completed my second year at Grace Street Teacher's College; I was officially halfway through my degree. Even after two years, I marveled that my father had allowed me to attend, that he had agreed that pursuing a professional life — a modest professional life, something appropriate for a woman — was a good idea for me. Neither of us ever said marriage wasn't an option but only because it didn't need to be said. We both knew.

"Iris won't be having much fun this summer," one of the Joans said, and when I turned to her, she winked at me kindly, the tagalong invited to lunch out of charity. I'd enrolled in the Summer Art Intensive at the college, which would meet Monday through Friday for all of June and July, blessedly filling up two-thirds of my summer. This was preferable to spending that time at home with Zelie.

"And after the art intensive, Iris?" a Betty asked. "I hope you're going to do something *fun* for the rest of the summer," she said, as she stirred sugar into her ice tea. They all thought I was a dud. I'm sure I came across as aloof, but I couldn't make real friends. I couldn't open up to anyone, couldn't be one of the girls. I had too many secrets.

"No, nothing," I said, not bothering to dispel their assumptions about me. "I'm not doing anything at all."

We'd stopped going to Cape Cod every July. Those trips ended after Aster had died and never resumed. For a couple of years after Belinda was sent away, after Rosalind, Calla, and Daphne had left us, we didn't do anything in the summertime. ("Left us" — I sometimes used euphemisms for my sisters' deaths that made it seem as if they'd gone on an extended holiday — and maybe they had; maybe that's what heaven is.) After those dreary summers, our father, for whatever reason, decided Zelie and I should see the world so he took us to Europe in the summer of 1953, and after Zelie had begged him, we went again in 1955. After those glorious visits, we returned to doing nothing during summer vacation. When Zelie had asked if we could go again this summer, he said he had a lot on his mind with the business. After the boom years of the war, Chapel Firearms had steadily fallen into a slump. Peacetime was good for most Americans, but not for us.

The waiter brought our lunches. My sandwich was enormous, as was the bowl of soup, which I pushed aside. "My, you must be hungry," said one of the Bettys, her fork perched over a chunk of iceberg lettuce. The other girls spoke often of "slimming," of staying trim for fiancés or boyfriends or the mere anticipation of a man, but I would never have to worry about that. I dug in. The Bettys watched as I tried to fit the sandwich into my mouth. It wasn't ladylike to open one's mouth so wide in public. Maybe not anywhere.

They continued their chatter about summer vacation, which allowed me to focus on my sandwich and its rich layers of salty meat and tangy mustard. I had a way of sinking into myself that blotted out what was happening around me, and soon all I could hear was my own chewing and the occasional muffled shout of a gruff waiter from across the dining room. I couldn't hear the three Bettys sitting across from me, but I could see their mouths moving. I was more familiar with the backs of their heads, since the three of them had sat in front of me all year in art class. For my final project of the class, I had drawn them from behind as three birds perched on a branch, each bird with a swingy blond ponytail. I titled the painting *The Betty Birds*. They thought I'd been mocking them with my project but I hadn't been. In a way, I was envious of them. Everyone knew what it meant to be a Betty. No one knew what it meant to be an Iris, not even me.

When afternoon classes ended, a frisson of excitement filled the hallways. I played along, smiling brightly as I passed my classmates on my way out, wishing them a happy summer though I was anything but happy.

I walked the few blocks to where I'd parked my car, a 1955 Citroën DS in a deep shade of polished jade. My father bought it for me when I graduated from high school. We'd visited a used-car lot together since he'd ruled out a new car, saying it would be too extravagant for someone my age. I'd wanted the Citroën as soon as I saw it and even more so when the salesman told us that *DS* in French is pronounced like *déesse,* the word for "goddess." They showed me Fords and Chevrolets, but I wasn't interested. "I want this one," I said to my father, running my hand along the Citroën's glossy green hood. He replied that the car was unsuitable for me, but I didn't think so. Iris was the goddess of the rainbow, something Belinda had told me many times when I was growing up, before she was sent away. I'd never asked for much. I deserved to have this goddess car.

The salesman told us the car had been abandoned by a professor at Yale who'd had to move home to Lyon in haste, so we'd be getting a good deal. I made the argument to my father that it was more efficient than the hulking American cars that were so popular then; it was a car of the future and I'd keep it for a long time. Eventually, he gave in.

I always parked the car several blocks from college. Most of my classmates took the bus or train to school, and I worried my car revealed too much about me. Not a single classmate or professor had ever asked me about my last name, never said: "The *firearm* Chapels?" Maybe because it was mostly women at the school. Though the college was only half an hour's drive from home, my classmates came from all over — New York City, New Jersey, and Westchester — and while they were mostly white, there were students of all ethnicities. I was anonymous among this cosmopolitan crowd, which I liked. I wasn't one of the survivors like I was in Bellflower Village. When anyone asked if I had siblings, I'd say: "Yes, I have a sister." Perhaps even then I'd begun to reinvent myself.

When I got into my car, it was only three o'clock, too early to go home. I normally picked Zelie up from high school. My father liked me to collect her and take her home; he didn't want her to be left unsupervised. He worried she might get into trouble on her own, and by "trouble," he meant boys. But Zelie had graduated from high school the week before, so she didn't need me to pick her up. She was already at home, and I wasn't in a hurry to join her.

I decided to take a drive. I loved to drive around in my car, treasuring the freedom it gave me. The Citroën was the only thing I owned that mattered. Yes, I had dresses and shoes and jewelry, but they could all be stuffed into a trash can; they were ephemeral things. My car could — and it would someday — take me anywhere, all the way to San Francisco or Mexico City or the Yukon, to countless points in between. Sometimes I lay awake at night thinking about the possibilities.

Driving through the commercial streets of Rye, I passed bakeries and dress shops, women pushing strollers and old ladies walking tiny dogs. I was headed toward Appleseed Estates. I didn't go there often, but I'd driven through often enough to know the way and where to turn. I passed the colonials, Tudors, Cape Cods, and ranch houses; the children on bicycles, the mail trucks; and mothers driving station wagons — then I arrived at Grouse Court.

I didn't pull into the cul-de-sac but parked on the road just outside it where Aster had stopped the day she took Rosalind and Zelie and me to admire her white colonial four-over-four. I turned off the car and rolled down my window for a better view. The house had had two previous owners that I had seen — a family with a little boy who liked to read on the front porch had cleared out in the early spring and another family had moved in. I'd seen only a glimpse of the man of the house arriving home and picking up a discarded tricycle or football on his way to the front door. I knew a wife and children were inside, but I had never seen them. I never lingered there long. The sight of the place was unbearable, and yet I couldn't help but visit from time to time.

It had been seven years since Aster's wedding day. If she had lived, her oldest child would be in school already. I often thought of the unlived lives of my four older sisters. Aster would have had three children, I'd decided.

Three daughters, since she was used to that — taking charge of a gaggle of girls. She'd be active in the garden club, a dedicated volunteer at her children's school; and she'd plan fun weekend outings to the zoo and the botanical gardens. Her beloved Matthew would have had an affair with some large-chested secretary he met at an office party and taken up coming home late with flimsy excuses and gin on his breath. Eventually, he'd die coming home from a business trip to Chicago, his plane crashing into a cornfield.

Rosalind, despite her plans for a daughter, would have had rough-and-tumble twin boys and that would have been enough for her. ("I am simply *done* with childbearing, Roddy!") She'd be the doyenne of horse ranching in Midland, Texas, and she'd shine on Roddy's arm as they entertained the oil A-list. Roddy would also, at some point, die in a plane crash when he was coming back from speculating in Venezuela.

With Calla and Daphne, I used more of my imagination: their paths in life hadn't been clear. They would have made it to Europe somehow, sharing a garret in Paris while Daphne painted and Calla wrote poetry. Daphne would earn money by drawing funny portraits for tourists along the Seine while Calla waitressed in a café, a tiny book of poems stuffed into her apron pocket. After a few years abroad, they would have moved home. Daphne would have lived in New York City — I could see her in black turtlenecks and trousers, a pixie cut and a slash of red lipstick — while sharing an apartment with a "friend" called Marjorie or Suzanne. Calla, meanwhile, would move into an abandoned cloister in the Hudson River Valley and live by candlelight. She'd eat only bread and water, and would feed the birds her crusts and continue her writing. She wouldn't be published until after her death at a very old age from a lung infection caused by an ancient strain of bacteria lurking in the cold, wet stones of her home.

And what about the future lives of Iris and Zelie? I was working on that.

On the highway, I enjoyed my last bit of freedom before turning off near Greenwich and heading northeast toward home down country lanes thick with trees, their branches heavy with the green of late spring. The air was perfumed, as it always was around Bellflower Village, and I rolled up my window to block out the scent. Home was intrusive like that — it wafted its way into every part of you.

Before going to the house, I stopped at the bakery in the village. I avoided the village as much as possible and hated every second I spent there, but I wanted to pick up a treat for Zelie and me to enjoy over tea, hoping this might make her happy. Parking on Main Street outside the ice cream parlor, I gathered my things and stepped out of the car. As I shut my door, I saw Dr. Green and his wife seated at a table near the window with a little boy and girl who must have been their grandchildren. Dr. Green had retired a couple of years ago, and I hadn't been to see his replacement; I tended to avoid doctors.

Dr. Green and his wife were watching me, he with that examining doctor's stare. I met their stares, matching the coldness of their looks, and didn't acknowledge them with a smile or wave, as would have been expected. Then I turned away abruptly and dashed across the street to the bakery.

Inside, there was a line and I was annoyed at having to wait. As I took my place, the women ahead of me turned to stare. Some of them smiled and nodded, others stole glances. I shifted under their collective gaze, smiling blandly, handbag stashed under my arm as if it were a baguette, and looked down at my shoes.

"Miss Chapel, we don't see you in here often," Mr. Tuttle said, when I stepped forward to the counter.

I studied the bakery cases, the pastries and sandwiches and breads. "I don't come into the village that much anymore," I said to him, as everyone around me strained to listen. I selected meringue shells filled with lemon curd and fresh blackberries, something sophisticated that I hoped Zelie would like. Mr. Tuttle packed my order and handed me a pink bakery box with a smile, saying, "Come again," and I thought, *Not very likely.*

At home, I stopped the car partially up the driveway just as the wedding cake came into view. I gripped the steering wheel at the sight of it, that enormous white confection. My goddess car could have taken me anywhere I wanted to go and yet, day after day, I came home.

Zelie. It was her fault.

I drove the rest of the way and parked at the top of the drive, leaving my bag and bakery box in the car so I could take a walk before going inside as I often did. (Anything to delay the inevitable.) As I walked around the right side of the house, I avoided looking at the family plot, which held the bodies of my four older sisters. (Daphne's body had been recovered by fishermen a week after her disappearance.) For several years, I'd compulsively tended the graves, planting flowers around the tombstones, becoming obsessed with the idea of roots penetrating the earth where my sisters lay in repose and using them as the soil for their growth. But over time, I stopped; it only made me feel farther from them. I couldn't walk the line between the living and the dead like my mother did. I'd left all that ghostly nonsense behind.

Around the back of the house I went, passing Belinda's garden, still tended by our groundskeeper, Mr. Warner. I continued on across the terrace, past the frog pond to the meadow. In the meadow, I took off my heels and set them on the ground, delighting in the cool ground against my stockinged feet. I walked through a swath of oxeye daisies, listening to the birds singing, running my hands along the tops of the tall grass; I delighted in the constellations of yellow starlight spread out before me, an endless array of golden poppies.

In the middle of the meadow, I stopped and knelt down. I had new rituals now. I covered my face with my hands, inhaled deeply, then I screamed.

I screamed loudly for as long as I could, letting the awful sound scrape my throat and strain my muscles. It was a scream worthy of my mother, of my sisters in their final moments. It was the scream of the Chapel women.

When I finished, I stayed kneeling for several minutes, my hands still covering my face. I stayed that way until I could hear the birds again.

2.

I woke up the next morning with Zelie snuggled up beside me in my bed, her limbs threaded through mine, her face nestled in the nape of my neck. I wasn't going to be able to move until she woke up, so I closed my eyes again, feeling her heart beat gently against my back.

This was a habit she had, climbing into bed with me. She did it a couple of times a week; it's possible she wasn't fully awake when she did it. In the morning, she'd roll out of my bed and go back to hers, never acknowledging her visits. Although I knew she was too old for such things, I allowed her this indulgence. Zelie was the closest I'd come to having a child, I knew this even then, and I had to admit I found joy in being needed, in being held. It was the only physical contact I had with anyone.

Our bedroom was on the ground floor beneath the girls' wing. If there had still been girls there, we would have heard their footsteps, but now there was silence. In the days after Calla and Daphne died, we'd made the move downstairs, packing up our spacious room with the purple irises and witch hazel painted on the walls and relocating to an unused sitting room on the ground floor.

The sitting room had belonged to our grandmother in the years before her death. The "rose room," as it was called, had been renovated and redecorated in the 1920s with rose-patterned paper on the walls, roses on the curtains and sofas and rugs; the Tiffany lampshades were adorned with bright glowing roses; even the mantel over the fireplace was carved with thorny vines. It was as if our grandmother had anticipated Belinda and designed the space to repel her. As such, after our grandmother died, it was locked and we opened up the room only when we were on the hunt for new quarters.

The new bedroom was somewhat smaller than our old one, but it was big enough for two single beds placed on either side of the picture window along with the rest of our furniture. It wasn't ideal, but there was no question of staying on the second floor, and at the time we moved in, no question of separate bedrooms either. Even our father had relocated to the ground floor, converting an unused billiard room into a bedroom on the opposite side of the courtyard from us. Zelie and I would have preferred to move to a different house, but our father wouldn't consider it, explaining that the wedding cake was the Chapel family home and he would remain in it for the rest of his life.

I always woke up before Zelie, who lagged behind in most things. I'd bathe and dress, then sit at my desk and read to her from the newspaper as she got ready. "How about Prince Edward Island? This little house is adorable," I said, as I cut out the ad from the real estate section and put it in the old cigar box where I stored my clippings. "We could live like Anne of Green Gables," I added, which sounded kind of nice.

Zelie finished buttoning up her linen dress, which was a tangerine shade that didn't flatter her. "Does it snow there?"

"Yes, probably quite a lot."

"Then no," Zelie said. "I need a warm climate."

"Last week you were interested in the mountains of Colorado."

"Then why on earth are you suggesting an island?"

Zelie was being difficult, but we were just playing. We'd made a vow that when I graduated from teacher's college, two years in the future, we would leave Bellflower Village and start our lives somewhere else. I would find a teacher's position, and Zelie would . . . well, that part wasn't clear.

Belinda had told me to run, and this was the best I could come up with. It was incredibly ordinary, the future I'd envisioned for myself and my sister —a teaching position, a modest home, a couple of old maids and their cats. I planned to do my art as a hobby. I was sometimes disappointed in my lack of imagination and daringness, but survival was more important than excitement.

Our father had no idea what Zelie and I were planning to do; it was our secret. He gave us a generous allowance each week, and I always saved half of mine, depositing it in my account at the bank. Zelie was supposed to save half of hers too, but she never did, spending it instead on dresses and handbags she didn't need and that wouldn't fit into the Citroën when it came time to go. That was my criteria for any purchase: Could we get it in the Citroën?

I was still scanning the real estate section when Zelie piped up: "Have we ruled out California?"

"Northern or Southern?"

"Hmm," Zelie said, taking a pause from powdering her face. "Which is sunnier?"

"Southern, of course."

"Then I'd like to go there and buy a house with lemon and palm trees where we can sunbathe all day."

"You mean *you'll* sunbathe while I'm at work."

"Yes," she said, oblivious to my sarcasm. "At night we'll go to parties with movie stars."

"And I'll sit by the pool grading papers."

"That sounds about right."

I cut out an ad for a cottage on the Florida coast and put it in the box. "Zelie, if you want that kind of life, you'll have to start helping me save. Otherwise we're going to Nebraska or somewhere like that. Montana. Arkansas. Far away from the movie stars."

"*Pft.*"

We headed to breakfast. When we got to the dining room, Zelie walked in and said good morning to our father, and I continued on, heading up the stairs. This was another ritual. I'd nearly reached the landing when Dovey called to me. "Mrs. O'Connor has already served. The breakfast is getting cold."

"I'll only be a moment," I said, looking down at her from the landing, but she didn't move. I didn't like her watching me. *Leave me alone, Dovey,* I wanted to say. *Fly away.*

None of them — not Dovey or Zelie or my father — knew why I visited the second floor each morning before breakfast. None of them had ever asked. Once the center of activity, the second layer of the wedding cake was rarely acknowledged; if it could have been sliced away, no one else would have protested. But to me, that wasn't acceptable.

I continued up the stairs and walked past my parents' old wing, the doors all closed and everything dark. And then the girls' wing.

"Good morning, sisters," I said to the corridor of closed doors. Of course, they never said good morning back. Contrary to what the maids might have thought, there weren't translucent figures in flowing white gowns haunting the hallways, only ghosts of absence. My sisters left so much *nothing* behind them, objects and silence, and a suffocating stillness that could drive a person mad.

To be honest, I would have preferred translucent figures in flowing white gowns.

I thought for a moment about which room to enter. I had worn Aster's perfume the day before; Rosalind was next. I opened their door to a pop of morning light as rich and yellow as a marigold. I had asked the maids to leave the curtains open even though they always closed the doors. I liked to think of the bedrooms above my head filled with light, not shrouded in darkness. They weren't tombs.

All that remained of my sisters, the dearly departed, were the things they left behind: the bottles of perfume and silver hairbrushes, the jars of night cream and the wardrobes still stuffed with many of their dresses. Their beds were neatly made, their white crocheted bedspreads pristine and the quilts at the foot of each bed neatly folded. The flowers on the walls had begun to fade, to crackle in places, the only sign of time passing.

At Rosalind's dressing table, I looked over the things she hadn't taken when she moved out and the things Roddy's family had returned to us after she'd died. There was a gold tray of rings, and I picked out Rosalind's coral cameo, always my favorite. But before I slipped it on my finger, I picked up her hairbrush and pulled a strand from the bristles, careful to remove only one. I wrapped the strand around my ring finger as tightly as I could without breaking it. Then I slid the coral cameo onto my finger over the brown band of hair to keep it in place.

I returned downstairs, feeling the pressure of the hair against my finger, as if Rosalind herself were holding my hand. I turned the ring around so only the gold band was facing out, not wanting Zelie to notice it. I could hear her talking to our father and I paused outside the doorway. "I don't know why I can't go," she said. The Hellands, our neighbors in the village, were having a party that Zelie was desperate to attend.

"We're having an important guest over for dinner this evening," our father said. "And I need you and Iris to be here."

I took this as my cue to enter, however reluctantly. Our father sat at the head of the table in his brown work suit; it was Saturday, but he was heading to his office. Zelie sat directly to one side of him in Aster's old chair, and I would sit on the other side. They were nearly finished with breakfast by the time I sat down, fidgeting slightly with my ring. My father glanced at me only briefly, then folded his newspaper and set it down on the corner of the table between us.

"It's not fair," Zelie said, and I knew her protests would continue through breakfast and go on after our father had left for work when only I, who was powerless in the matter, would be left to listen to it.

"I'm eighteen, you know," she said. This was her latest tactic — a vague threat that she was an adult and could do what she pleased. She never pushed it, though, knowing the limitations of financial dependence.

The brown egg in the cup on my plate was waiting for me to remove the top, to reveal the soft white and yellow flesh beneath, but I hesitated to eat, not yet ready to set the day in motion. I thought of the activities that lay ahead, none of which I wanted to do.

Zelie kept arguing with our father as I buttered my toast, wishing as I did that the grating sound of the knife against the bread was loud enough to drown out her pleas. She looked so much like Aster, with her rounded figure and long dark hair. (I'd cut my hair years ago, and it barely reached my shoulders. Zelie didn't mind the extra work that long hair required, and she spent a great deal of time on her appearance, unlike me.) But while Zelie may have resembled Aster, she didn't act anything like her. Aster had always been the most obedient, and as the oldest, the most responsible. I didn't blame Zelie for her complaints, at least some of the time, but there was nothing I could do for her right now. *Two more years,* I wanted to whisper to her. *Just hang on.*

Finally, I removed the top of my egg and began to eat, spooning out some of the yolk and smearing it on my toast. "Don't argue, Zelie." I was in it now. The day had begun.

Zelie turned to me, the fresh powder on her face concealing the pink I was sure was there. I wasn't on our father's side; I hoped she knew this. I was on the side of a peaceful life and there were certain ways to attain it. In the years since our last sister died, I'd become the obedient older daughter, which sometimes surprised me.

"Why does Iris get to have a car?" she asked our father, but she was squinting across the table at me. "It's not fair."

"You don't have a license," our father said, and Zelie turned to him with barely suppressed rage.

"That's because you won't let me take driving lessons."

"Yes, well," our father said, picking up his coffee cup. "Maybe this summer."

"I'm so *bored* and you're both just being cruel." Zelie was obviously in a mood to complain. Our father, having had enough, set down his cup rather more forcefully than was necessary and appeared ready to change the subject. He was no longer part of a pair, sitting at the head of the table with daughters on either side and a wife at the other end. That's why he needed us at dinner, so he wouldn't appear alone.

He asked about the menu, which I had planned with Mrs. O'Connor earlier in the week. These things fell to me now. The role of eldest female in the Chapel family had been mine for six years, a record of a sort — only Belinda had been at the helm for longer. "Consommé to start, then broiled steak with mushrooms and a sherry cream sauce, mashed potatoes, roasted asparagus. Red wine to drink," I said, and my father looked pleased.

Mr. Colt was coming to dinner. I didn't know anything about him besides what his name revealed. It was one of the usual names I heard discussed in our house: Colt, Remington, Browning, Smith, Wesson — a name like our own. He was driving down from Hartford to meet with my father at the factory that afternoon, then he would join us for dinner. That's all I thought I needed to know about him. I didn't think Mr. Colt mattered, not then. It had been years since death had receded from our house, rolling out to sea like a dark tide. I had grown used to living without the specter of it; I'd grown complacent. I didn't see it swelling just offshore, waiting to come crashing down on us once more.

3.

"Come on, Zelie. It's not that bad, is it? Cheer up," I said, as she got into the Citroën and slammed the door.

Every Saturday we went to visit Belinda at the sanitarium, something Zelie never wanted to do. "Do you know what normal girls get to do on Saturdays?" she said, when I got in the driver's seat. She was primed and ready to come at me. "They go shopping and paint their nails and have their hair done; they go to parties and meet boys. But *we* have to visit our crazy mother in the asylum."

I handed her the bouquet of flowers I'd picked in Belinda's garden and wrapped in brown paper. "It's not an asylum, and Saturday is visitors' day," I said, as we pulled onto the main road.

"But why do we have to visit her at all?"

The drive to Andover-by-the-Sea took about an hour, but it seemed much longer thanks to Zelie's complaining, which was more barbed and urgent than usual. Once I turned onto the highway, she clammed up — this was part of her routine as well, refusing to speak to me. She looked straight ahead out the windshield, shadows passing over her face. I tried to be patient with her. The weekend before this one had been disastrous, and it had been my fault.

The previous Sunday I'd organized a picnic to celebrate her graduation from high school and invited a few of her friends from the village. I had thought it would be a nice thing to do, but Zelie had taken a turn after the picnic and I didn't quite know what to do about it.

We'd picnicked on the green in the center of the village near the white gazebo with its Revolutionary War cannon. Even though I hated being in the village, I'd wanted things to be convenient for Zelie's friends, Florence Helland and two sisters, Cathleen and Patricia something-or-other. As we spread out our blankets, I was aware that people were watching us, but I chose to ignore them.

Mrs. O'Connor had prepared a hamper with thermoses of lemonade, a platter of sandwiches, a bowl of strawberries, and a plate of sweets. For a while, I managed to sit on my blanket and feel something close to happiness, letting the sun bathe my face, looking at my car parked across the road near the church, the car that would one day bring escape. I was always happiest when removed from the present moment.

The afternoon took a turn after I passed around the bowl of strawberries and a plate of cookies, the cinnamon stars that Mrs. O'Connor loved to make. All the girls helped themselves except for Florence, who took off her dainty white gloves to reveal an enormous diamond-and-sapphire engagement ring on her left hand. There were squeals of delight when the ring appeared, with Florence holding out her hand to be adored as if she were a queen.

Florence was the first of Zelie's friends to get engaged and had done so before the ink on her diploma was even dry. Many of my classmates had become engaged just as quickly; the sudden appearance of diamonds was like a brushfire tearing through the class of 1955. Now the same thing was happening to the class of 1957.

The discussion turned to wedding dresses and honeymoons and Florence's imminent move to New York City, where her fiancé and his family lived, and the linens and dishware Florence would select for the apartment on Fifth Avenue that her in-laws were giving them as a present. I stopped listening before the conversation turned to the baby that would undoubtedly arrive, and the baby's schooling, and its own graduation one day, and its marriage and children and death from old age, which wouldn't occur until the twenty-first century, an unfathomably long time away.

Instead of listening, I watched Zelie. She was looking at Florence's ring as Florence drank from her glass of lemonade, as Florence reached for a cinnamon star and finally a strawberry, which she bit in half, leaving pink lipstick on the tips of her fingers. At first, the sapphire had been nothing more than a drop of blue, a captured splash of the Caribbean Sea purchased by Florence's fiancé at Tiffany's. But as Florence waved her hand about, as she smoothed her blond hair or reached for another strawberry, it glistened in the sun and seemed to grow larger, and one drop turned into an ocean.

Zelie was drowning. The talk of weddings and babies was like someone sticking tiny pins in her heart. Her friends should have known better, but they were careless and selfish, and Zelie *looked* happy, sitting with her legs tucked beneath her on the blanket, her lips curved into a smile, pushing her cheeks into the shape and color of tiny blushing plums. What they didn't notice was her right hand as she grasped a half-bitten strawberry, its juice running down her fingers onto her cream-colored dress and blooming into a red stain on her thigh, making it look like she'd been hit with something sharp, a bullet or an arrow.

Zelie and I would be invited but wouldn't attend the wedding — weddings were something we both avoided — but I could see the two of us on a shopping trip to New York, buying a wedding gift for Florence at Bloomingdale's, then having something to eat in one of the foggy tea rooms near Grand Central before taking the train back home with the mantel clock or serving platter we had bought.

I watched Zelie's face as she watched Florence, and anger swelled in me, overtaking me suddenly. I stood up, calling an abrupt end to the picnic. "Time to go," I said, brushing the cinnamon from my dress. The girls looked up, confused, but Zelie looked grateful. I tugged at the corner of a blanket, which Florence was still sitting on, and she crawled off onto the grass and stained her dress. I, annoyed at the future trip to the housewares section of Bloomingdale's, thought she deserved it.

I shook out the rest of the blankets and stuffed them into the hamper along with the empty glasses and platters and thermoses. My anger at Zelie's friends was mounting, but I was trying not to show it. She stood in the middle of her circle of friends, the red stain on her dress now unavoidable; I took the strawberry from her hand and tossed it onto the grass.

"Oh, I'm — sorry," Florence said, observing the strawberry stain and Zelie's stricken look, finally realizing the inappropriateness of the afternoon's conversation. Florence covered the sapphire with her right hand, Eve covering her nakedness. "I didn't mean to . . . it wasn't my intention to . . ."

"It's not your fault," I said, wanting to rescue Florence from her horrified mea culpas.

We dispersed, the other girls relieved to get away. I lugged the hamper back to the car; Zelie trailed behind. As I lifted the hamper into the back seat of the Citroën, I knew it would be impossible for us ever truly to escape. Zelie and I could move to the far ends of the earth, but there were things we could never outrun.

Nearly a week had passed since that dreadful picnic and Zelie still seemed deflated. The sapphire continued to cast its shadow.

"We could go to Boston in July, just the two of us," I said. "The swan boats, the glass flowers. You'd like that." I tried to entice her, but she merely nodded. I knew what she was thinking: *We would have fun in Boston, but then what?*

An ornate sign on the road announced that we'd arrived at the St. Aubert Sanitarium, but after the turnoff, there was still a two-mile drive up a winding road to the main house. Once the Gilded Age estate of a rich family, it had been converted into a sanitarium for wealthy New England women, some of them insane, some of them only unhappy. The main house, which had been built on a dramatic cliff overlooking the Atlantic, became visible suddenly after we rounded a bend, its turrets and gables castlelike in the noonday sun.

As we rounded the circular driveway, I steeled myself, not knowing which version of Belinda we would meet today. I hoped for the best, the Belinda who wanted to talk about gardening as if we were in her sitting room at home, but I feared the haunted one, the Belinda who was lost in memories, fixated on the past. Even more than that, I dreaded the sad version of my mother, who'd pleaded with us as we'd left a week earlier: "Take me with you, blossoms." I'd cried on the walk back to the car.

But today's Belinda was none of those. She was floating in a cloud of drugs, blinking slowly.

"Hello, Mother," I said. Zelie said nothing.

She'd been waiting for us at a table on the veranda as she always did on warm-weather visitors' days. The veranda was filled with round glass-top tables and wicker chairs with floral cushions. It could have been outside a plush hotel filled with day-trippers and vacationers if not for the abundance of not-quite-right women, women who'd been removed from society and left there like the wayward strands of gray hair plucked from a glossy chestnut mane and discarded.

The patients allowed out on the veranda were mostly well-behaved and civilized; the serious cases were locked upstairs, deprived of fresh air, and kept away from potential weaponry like cutlery and hot tea. There were occasional cries on the veranda, even outbursts, but these were mostly due to sadness, not derangement. Sadness could be managed.

Belinda didn't get up to greet us. Her eyes were lowered, her chin resting on her chest. We sat down without touching her. Our table for three was at the end of the veranda tucked into a corner, which allowed for more privacy.

One of the serving girls had placed a clear glass vase half full of water in the middle of the table, awaiting the flowers that I always brought with me. I unwrapped the lavender and chamomile from the brown paper and placed them in the vase and attempted to fan them out, but they wouldn't behave.

"Did you have a rough night, Mother?" I asked, when I couldn't extend the task of arranging the flowers any longer. "Did you have bad dreams?" The spirits of the Chapel victims hadn't followed her from the wedding cake, but she still had nightmares.

She didn't respond. She stared at her shoes, black leather with silver buckles, something a pilgrim might wear. Her dress was white, as usual, with her favorite gold and carnelian thistle brooch pinned above her right breast. The dress was buttoned up wrong; at the top, there was a single button standing alone.

"Maybe one of her Chapel victims hitched a ride over here last night," Zelie said with a laugh. She was reading the copy of *Photoplay* she'd taken off the table in the lobby.

"Shh, she can hear you," I said; although looking at her, I wasn't actually sure of that.

Lunch arrived: chicken croquettes and green salad, with gingersnaps and tea for dessert. A plate was placed before Belinda, but she didn't eat.

Zelie stabbed at pieces of croquette with her fork and ate them quickly, head down, engrossed in the magazine she'd rested beside her on the table. I nudged Belinda's plate toward her. Zelie looked up at the moving plate, at the yellow sauce over the croquettes that was beginning to congeal.

"We should leave," she said, closing the magazine, sensing the possibility for early escape. "She doesn't know we're here."

"Not yet," I said. "It's only been a few minutes."

Belinda received one visit from her daughters every seven days; it needed to be substantial enough to last. Our father didn't visit; he'd tried once and she'd stabbed him in the arm with a hatpin. She wasn't normally violent; her gold and carnelian brooch was evidence that the staff felt confident of that. Still, I thought it best he never return.

"My semester ended yesterday," I said to Belinda, aware of Zelie eyeing me like a spiteful child. "Two years down, two to go. I'm quite enjoying it." I cut into a croquette, pretending I was having a normal lunch with a normal mother.

"Zelie is registered at Darlow's Ladies College," I said. "She'll be starting there in September."

"No I won't." Zelie, who'd started on the gingersnaps, dipped the cookies in her tea to soften them.

"What do you mean?" I said quietly, departing from the performative conversation I was having for Belinda's sake.

"I never sent the check. I'm not going."

"That's not necessarily a bad thing," I said. I had wanted Zelie to attend a music college in New Haven, had been pushing for that. She was a good-enough pianist to pass the audition. "At Darlow's, all you'll learn is how to cook and perfect your social graces and —"

"And why would a future old maid like me need to learn those things, right?"

"That's not what I meant."

Zelie stood up and dropped her napkin onto the table. "I'm going for a walk along the cliffs," she announced.

"*Zelie*," I called after her, but she sulked away.

After Zelie left, Belinda raised her head for the first time. With her back to the ocean, puffs of wind blew strands of her white hair forward and back, up and down; they looked like the arms of a jellyfish moving in water.

"We watched a film last night," she said, as if she'd been waiting for Zelie to leave. She often spoke to me in the tone of a confidante, as if only I would understand what troubled her, a habit left over from when I was younger. Over the past year, when Zelie wasn't around, she'd told me many more stories from her life, filling in gaps from the past now that I was old enough to understand them. Some of these stories — like her trying to hang herself when she was pregnant with Aster — I wished I didn't know.

"That's nice. Which film?"

"I can't remember the title. It was about the war."

"Oh."

The serving girl cleared away Zelie's dishes and wiped crumbs from the table. "It gave me bad dreams. Battlefields, guns, blood — you know how I hate that."

"Yes, but the war's over now, Mother. There are no more wars." She regularly cycled through events of the past in which the Chapel rifle had played a role — the Civil War, westward expansion, World Wars One and Two. After what had happened in Nagasaki and Hiroshima, the Chapel rifle seemed quaint by comparison, although it had probably killed more people than those bombs combined.

I poured us glasses of water from the pitcher that the girl had set on the table. "Chapel Firearms didn't sell guns to the bad men in the war," I said, hesitating to defend the company in front of my mother. But maybe I could soothe her. "It was Americans who used our guns, and the British and the French. Not the Germans." *Our* guns. And they were, in a way. They paid for our clothes and food, for our mother's stay at the sanitarium, for everything in our lives.

"I could smell blood during the night."

"Please stop," I said. "Let's talk about something else. Have you been sketching?" I'd gotten better at steering the conversation away from guns and ghosts.

"Mother?" I asked, sipping my water. But she rested her chin on her chest again and fell asleep soon after.

I pushed away my plate of half-eaten croquettes and watched her for a while. I should have gotten up to leave, but I didn't have the energy to face my sister.

"I'm worried about Zelie," I said. Belinda didn't hear me, or at least it didn't seem so, but I needed to say it to someone.

4.

Whenever we had guests over for dinner, they were our father's associates — "gun people," we called them, an assortment of graybeards in unfashionable suits, sometimes with wives and unmarried daughters in tow. But even this wasn't a frequent occurrence. Visitors rarely came to the wedding cake, and we rarely went out to socialize. It wasn't for lack of invitations — we'd become a spectacle of sorts, and thus we were invited to dinners and charity events and summer picnics out of curiosity. *(First they get married, then they get buried.)* We usually turned down most invitations at our father's behest and to Zelie's dismay. There were too many risks in venturing far from home, too many young men about — our father had grown protective of his family now that there was so little left of it; and besides that, he knew people were curious about us and he refused to indulge them.

When the rare guest did come over, I could immediately see the effect the house had on them — no one, however old, outgrows the macabre allure of a haunted house. I would watch them as they scanned the outside, the entry hall, and the downstairs rooms with wide-eyed fascination, already planning what they'd tell their friends later: *It's only the three of them rambling around in that cold, cavernous house. I tell you, I'd have upped stakes after the first one died, certainly after the second.*

In contrast to that, our father's dinner guest and business associate Samuel Colt, who couldn't have been more than thirty, didn't appear daunted by any of this. That's the first thing I noticed about him when he arrived and parked his red Aston Martin sports car next to my father's staid black sedan. There was no hesitancy upon stepping out of the car, no looking up at the looming facade as its shadow enveloped him. He practically bounded into the house alongside my father.

After our father introduced him, Mr. Colt took my hand first, then Zelie's. "The famous Chapel sisters!" he said, and Zelie and I exchanged a quick look of disbelief. I thought he was being incredibly morbid, even offensive, but then he smiled, and said, "Your beauty and charm precedes you," and gave a playful little bow. I relaxed a bit, deciding to be generous; he probably would have said something similar to any pair of young women. He hadn't considered how his words might be received here.

Our father led us all into the front parlor for drinks before dinner. Zelie clearly had anticipated a dull evening — she wore a loose-fitting gray dress, square in shape, with dull little beads sewn into the neckline. It resembled a pillowcase, a dress she never would have worn if she'd wanted to impress. I could see her despair now that she'd realized our dinner guest was handsome and fairly young. She brushed the front of her dress with her hands, as if there were a better dress buried underneath.

The telephone beckoned our father to his den, so he was saved from having to make small talk. Zelie and I were left to entertain his guest on our own. We offered him sherry and tried to direct him to one of the sofas, but Mr. Colt couldn't seem to stay seated. He browsed around the parlor with Zelie at his side as he pointed out this and that, and asked questions. The parlor had undergone a slight redecoration over the years; the furniture remained the same, but with Belinda gone, there were more Chapel rifles hanging on the walls and a movie poster, which was tacky, but I didn't care enough to change it.

"Chapel House is as charming as I expected," Mr. Colt said, taking it all in. I nearly choked on my sherry at the word *charming* but said nothing. He was our guest, a loquacious guest with a light auburn beard clipped neatly against his jaw and chin, and a wave of auburn hair resting above his forehead. He was of average height and slender, with a compact body — no limbs astray, no hairs out of place; on a sunny day, his shadow would have been smooth lines and clean angles on the sidewalk. He wore a gray suit with a silk tie in pale lemon yellow, a tie he must have bought in New York. He was suave, but I wasn't attracted to him.

"We don't call it Chapel House," Zelie said. "Otherwise it sounds too much like the Chapel Factory on the other side of the village." She giggled and Mr. Colt laughed, not a chuckle born out of politeness but a spontaneous deep-throated roar, one it would have been impossible to suppress.

I decided to join in. "The Chapel Factory produces firearms and ammunition," I said, as Mr. Colt turned to me with interest. "Whereas this house, in its heyday, produced daughters." It was meant as a joke, but Zelie frowned; clearly it had come off poorly.

But Mr. Colt, still buoyant with happiness, turned to Zelie again. "There aren't enough ladies' names that begin with *Z*. How wonderfully dramatic."

"She's Hazel," I said before Zelie could speak. "With a sensible *H*." I sounded like a schoolmarm and cleared my throat before going to a sofa and sitting down.

Mr. Colt moved to the window and continued chatting with Zelie, his tone lively and gay as he remarked on the day he'd spent with our father. Mr. Colt, scion of the Colt firearms family, trafficked in death just like my family did. We shared that in common, he being one of us, one of the "gun people," although I was sure his daily life was far different from ours. I pictured him in executive boardrooms and traveling the globe for business, spending his leisure time at grand estates with debutantes, the high society girls of Manhattan. Zelie and I perhaps seemed shabby by comparison.

"Mr. Colt —"

"Zelie, please call me Samuel. Actually, I'm Samuel *the fourth,* but that makes me sound like a king."

Zelie made a joke about King Samuel, as I knew she would, and although my back was to them, I imagined that she'd curtsied. She was such a flirt, another reason our father restricted our social calendar. The one thing Zelie was truly good at had been taken away from her.

"I prefer to be called Sam, actually," he replied, whittling the name down even further. Soon there would be nothing left.

He found something about Zelie's dress to compliment. Even in the drab gray pillowcase, Zelie was a luscious flower. I was more of a stalk, neither curvy like Zelie nor slender like Calla had been but something in between, something solid, hard to snap in half, bamboo maybe.

"And what about you, Iris. What do you do?"

I startled at Sam's turn of attention toward me. "What do I *do*?" I swallowed some sherry.

"How does Iris spend her days?" he said, as he came over to sit near me.

"Oh," I said. "I help manage the household and I'm a student at Grace Street Teacher's College. Nothing much, really." How did he think I spent my days? Practicing neurosurgery? The options open to me could be counted on one hand.

"And what do you do, Zelie?" he asked.

"I only finished school recently," she said. She paused for a moment, a bit of gloom passing over her, then she continued brightly: "I love to play the piano."

"Delightful," he said. "Will I get to hear you play after dinner?"

I hoped not. I didn't want the evening to extend itself on account of Zelie's allure. I dreamt of hot tea, bed. But before Zelie could respond, Sam leapt up from the sofa. "Now look there!" He had spotted the framed poster from *Chapel '70: The Gun That Won the West* hanging in a corner behind the open door. It featured Jimmy Stewart in a cowboy hat, Chapel rifle in hand.

The sight of the poster in our front parlor made me cringe, but Sam was never to know that. The film was supposed to be a point of pride for our family and I had always played along. As far as I knew, none of the firearms made by the Colt's Manufacturing Company had ever been the subject of a major Hollywood film, and I enjoyed Sam's potential jealousy. I didn't like him, though I wasn't sure why.

"Did you enjoy *Chapel '70*?" I asked him, peering at Zelie over the rim of my glass.

"Do you know I missed it? I was in Europe when it was out."

"We've been to Europe," Zelie said, then launched into a long account of our travels. I stopped paying attention.

Zelie entered into flirtations from time to time, but that's as far as she was allowed to go. No one had ever expressly forbidden us from having contact with the opposite sex or sat us down and explained that dating and marriage weren't an option for us given what had happened to Aster, Rosalind, and Calla. Our father avoided talking about our older sisters entirely, and he'd never said out loud anything about their deaths that contradicted Dr. Green's absurd diagnoses. For him, I knew, my sisters' deaths had taken on the aura of something distinctly female and thus shameful. Discussing what had happened would have been like discussing sex or menstrual periods or other things one didn't speak about publicly or even privately very often, at least in those days. Thus the subject of what had happened to our sisters had become taboo.

But while our father never sat us down for any kind of talk, his actions told us all we needed to know. We weren't allowed to attend the dances our girls' school held in conjunction with a neighboring boys' school, nor were we allowed to attend any other social events where boys would be present unless our father was also there. We came home directly after school; home was where our father preferred we spend most of our free time. Local young men knew all about the Chapel girls and were too scared to come near us anyway, the general sentiment about us having been summed up by Roderick during his outburst at Rosalind's funeral: *you witchy girls.*

When we traveled together as a family on summer vacations, we encountered plenty of young men who had never heard of us — turns out, it's a big world. Our father was always there to dispatch anyone who asked us to dance or take a moonlit stroll, whether on shipboard to and from Europe or at the resorts where we stayed in Switzerland or on the Italian coast. "They're not interested," he'd say with a wave of his hand.

Despite our father's vigilance, Zelie managed to have a secret romance with a boy named Jørgen Gundersen. He was Florence Helland's cousin, and he came from Norway to stay with her family during the summer of 1954 when Zelie was fifteen. Florence only had sisters, which is why our father allowed Zelie to spend time at her house, which is how Jørgen slipped through the net. He didn't look as I imagined a Norwegian would, a blond icicle. His mother was from South America (Argentina, I think), and he had a shock of black hair that contrasted with his pale skin; at that age, he was all gangly limbs and looked like a marionette.

I saw him only once, when he appeared outside our bedroom window one Saturday morning. We were still in bed when I heard a knocking on the glass. "Iris, no," Zelie had said, but I pulled back the drapes anyway, and there was Jørgen in the morning sunlight holding a bouquet of roses. He was speaking, his mouth moving, but we couldn't hear what he was saying. I had no idea Jørgen even existed at that point — Zelie had kept him a secret — so I screamed in terror when I saw him, thinking I was having a nightmare.

At the sound of my screams, Dovey and our father came racing into the bedroom while Zelie pleaded and tried to explain. A terrified Jørgen ran away, leaving the roses discarded on the grass outside. Soon it all came out; Zelie tearfully confessed to their secret summer romance, which consisted of nothing more than a few shared milkshakes at the ice cream parlor on Main Street, holding hands under the table, and a stash of love notes Zelie had hidden under her mattress, which our father confiscated and burned in the stove.

Zelie was forbidden from seeing Jørgen again, and he returned to Norway without getting to say goodbye. There were tears, certainly, but mostly, once she got past the initial sting, Zelie was just glad to have had a romance; she hadn't been sure she ever would.

There had been no one since then — at least no one I knew about — but she took a fancy sometimes to the men who came into our orbit and lavished attention on them. It was Sam's turn tonight.

I, on the other hand, found our social restrictions a relief in many ways; my father's strict rules allowed me to avoid sorting out my feelings about men. I knew for certain that they didn't interest me, and I suspected it wasn't only because of my sisters, though what had happened to them didn't help matters. Like a person with a dairy allergy avoiding an ice cream shop, I avoided the topic of men. What would be the great tragedy of Zelie's life was easier for me to accept. I knew I was lucky compared to her, though this hadn't saved Daphne.

Zelie continued her talk of Europe (she was up to our hike in the Alps, "dreadfully boring" as she described it), with many more countries to go. France was next, and she launched into a discussion of the Louvre, explaining to Sam what it is. He cut her off.

"I've been to the Louvre, doll." He laughed at her in a pitying sort of way.

Zelie couldn't hide her embarrassment. "Of course you have. Silly me."

"Oh, don't feel bad," he said to her, and the awkwardness passed. "You're actually quite funny." They fell back into their flirtation, and I groaned loudly in my head. I longed for dinner and bed, but most of all for the time when I'd hear the sound of Sam Colt's car starting and heading down the drive. Until then, I would have to endure.

The dining room was lit up with candles. The men sat at the ends of the table, with Zelie and me sitting on either side like two sconces. Little was usually required of us during these dinners, and I luxuriated in the smell of steak and mushrooms coming from the kitchen. A good meal always passed the time more quickly.

We were nearly finished with the consommé before a word was served out to Zelie and me. Sam told us that his sister lived in Greenwich with her husband and children and that he was thinking of staying with them during the summer. At this news, I set down my spoon and looked at Zelie, who clearly assumed her pleasure wasn't visible in the candlelight.

"Why stay? You must be terribly busy with your work," I said in a tone so lacking in charity that I might have been offering to drive him back to Hartford myself.

"My sister has three little boys, and her husband is away on business for most of the summer. I figure the boys could use a man in their lives."

"I think it's a fine idea," our father said. "And it'll give us more time to talk."

"Talk about what?" Zelie asked.

"It's a business matter," our father said, since "Hush" would have been impolite.

Dovey came into the dining room with the main course, setting a plate before each of us.

"If you must know," Sam said conspiratorially once Dovey left, "your father and I have been talking about joining our two companies."

Zelie and I turned to our father, who frowned slightly at Sam's indiscretion. "We're having discussions, is all," our father said, cutting into his steak. "The postwar years have been difficult for all of us," he explained, not yet aware of the fortunes that Vietnam would bring.

"Yes, it's early days yet. The old man doesn't know anything about it," Sam said, then clarified. "*My* old man."

I knew Zelie was bursting with questions, as was I, but she glanced at me across the table and I signaled to drop it. Our father didn't like being questioned, particularly in front of guests.

The conversation continued on safer ground, with Zelie and Sam doing most of the talking, but it didn't take long for Zelie to return to the previous topic. "I've got it," she said. "How about Cholt?"

Sam, who was eating with gusto, stopped chewing and wiped his mouth. "Pardon me?"

"Cholt," Zelie said again. "Chapel plus Colt equals *Cholt*." In response, Sam slapped his knee and laughed that deep-throated roar again.

Oh Zelie, I thought to myself. *He's not worth it.*

Later that night, after Sam had finally left, Zelie deflated as she had after the picnic. She climbed into bed still wearing her pillowcase dress and curled up on her side, her back to me. I moved around the bedroom quietly, putting on my nightgown and finishing my cup of chamomile tea at my desk as I scanned the real estate listings in a magazine.

"Zelie?" I said, cutting out an ad for a house on Martha's Vineyard. I preferred to leave New England, but Martha's Vineyard, being an island, appealed to me. The house in the ad, like all the others, would be sold long before Zelie and I were ready to buy anything. And as an unmarried woman, I probably wouldn't even qualify for a bank loan. But I put the clipping in my cigar box with the others anyway, considering it research.

"I know you're not asleep," I said, as I closed the magazine and went to sit on the edge of my bed. "Zelie?"

"What is it?" She was annoyed, thinking about Sam. It wasn't him per se — he could have been engaged for all we knew, but I doubted it. It was more about what he represented, what a young man could promise — marriage, children, a home like the one at 64 Grouse Court, all the things Zelie knew she could never have.

"In another life," I said, and turned off the lamp.

"In another life, I might be happy."

I listened to her breathing quietly for a while, which slowly became the deeper breath of sleep. I pulled the covers up to my chin, imagining the coming days with dread. Our guest would be in Greenwich with his sister, but the memory of him would be more difficult to expel, like the scent of some rancid weed or the corpse flower of Indonesia that bloomed once every seven years and smelled like death. I assumed Zelie would sulk for a while, then she'd move on.

It was my mistake to assume. At the start of the summer of 1957, I thought I was in control of my life; I was halfway done with my teaching degree and making plans for the future. But I was going through my days that summer on a hair trigger. I just didn't know it.

Son of a Gun

1957

I.

Zelie sulked through the whole first week of my art classes. As I dressed for college each day, I tried to cajole her into coming with me. "It would be nice to get out, don't you think?" I asked on that first morning, buttoning up the new dress I'd bought at Bonwit's, a jersey shirtwaist dress in cream with brown polka dots. "You could play the piano in the music room or swim in the pool," I said, as I slipped on my pumps, but she didn't bother to answer. I had signed up for the Summer Art Intensive in part to get away from her, but I felt bad at the thought of her moping at home. "Zelie? You need to get out of the house."

"I don't want to go," she said from her bed.

I fretted over her each day, and each day played out the same way, with her grumpy refusals. On Friday, I prepared for a day in New York with my class — we'd spend every Friday in New York at museums and galleries — and I tried to convince her to join us, thinking my professor wouldn't mind, but she had no interest in going. So I went alone, driving to the station in Rye to catch the train into New York. The Greenwich station was closer, but I liked to minimize time spent on the train. I wasn't fond of trains or subways or buses. I didn't like being pressed into the train carriage with so many strange men, and I hated how they found ways to bump up against me and brush their legs against mine when they sat down. The other girls just seemed to ignore it; for them, it was apparently a minor annoyance, the price of venturing into a man's world. But I was too aware of the potential for danger.

My attempts to persuade Zelie had delayed me, and I arrived late to the Sandler Museum near Gramercy Park. My class was already deep into the exhibit on abstract expressionist painters. A large room in the exhibit was dedicated to female artists, much to my surprise, and that's where I found my class.

"You didn't miss much," said Susan, one of my classmates, as I made my apologies. She and the rest of the girls were standing behind our professor, who was seated on a bench in front of Helen Frankenthaler's *Mountains and Sea*.

"Don't you think this looks like finger painting?" Susan said. "A child could do it." The other girls laughed.

Our professor didn't react. His name was Nello — I didn't know if that was his first or last name; he insisted on simply Nello. "None of that bourgeois 'professor' nonsense," he'd said. Every summer they brought in a guest lecturer to lead the Summer Art Intensive; Nello was the second Frenchman in a row, but he wasn't dashing like the previous one. He hadn't shared much about himself, only that he'd immigrated from France during the war; he mentioned a fellowship and told us where his work had been exhibited, all of this rattled off quickly as if he were embarrassed to have achieved any kind of success.

"Keep an open mind, ladies," he finally said, not turning from the painting. None of the other museumgoers would have guessed that he was our professor. He gave the impression that he'd just rolled off a park bench. He wore baggy gray trousers and a wrinkled white shirt that wasn't buttoned all the way at the top or bottom. No tie, no jacket. His hair, an unremarkable shade of sepia, was wispy and sat atop his head like a bird's nest. I saw him as middle-aged, but he could have been in his thirties.

To prepare us for the exhibit, he'd lectured on abstract expressionism the day before, explaining the nonrepresentational nature of it. He'd explained that we wouldn't be seeing traditional landscapes and portraits in the exhibit — much of what we'd see wouldn't be recognizable at all. These painters didn't attempt to make their work appear three-dimensional either but instead embraced the flatness of the canvas. He shared with us some of the techniques that were used, giving us the example of Jackson Pollock, who set his canvas on the floor and dripped and splashed paint onto it. Nello said that abstract expressionism comes from the unconscious mind — like surrealism does — that it's about expressing emotions and what is often inexpressible. He said that after the devastation of the war artists needed to find new ways to represent the chaos of our minds and of our world during the atomic age.

But at the museum, surrounded by such paintings, most of us still didn't quite understand. "I don't get it," one of the girls whispered.

"There's nothing to *get*," Susan whispered back. "It's just a blob of paint." She mindlessly fingered the bumblebee brooch she had pinned to her tight blouse, trying to make sense of what she was seeing.

"It's improvised, like jazz," Nello said, still not taking his eyes off the painting. "It's magnificent."

"I don't like jazz," Susan said. "I prefer Buddy Holly."

"Buddy what?" Nello replied.

"Never mind." Susan and the other girls took advantage of Nello's distraction and dispersed while I remained with him, staring at *Mountains and Sea*. Nello's long legs extended before him; his feet, in worn leather loafers, were crossed at the ankles, making it difficult for anyone to pass in front of him. He wanted the painting for himself.

Mountains and Sea didn't look like finger painting, but I couldn't figure out how it was a landscape. Against a beige background were seemingly random patches of delicate pink, blue, and green. It was a pretty array of colors, even quite soothing, but it looked more like an accident than a piece of art.

Nello looked up at me. "How does the painting make you feel?"

"Confused," I replied too quickly, regretting my facile answer.

"Don't try to solve it. It's not a puzzle. Go find a piece that you like and sit with it."

I made my way around the room of women's paintings. The only female artist I'd ever heard of was Mary Cassatt. Our usual art teacher, Mr. Richardson, had told us that men tended to make art while women were the inspiration. I thought this might explain why so many of the women in the paintings we studied in our textbook were naked — Waterhouse's water nymphs among the lily pads; Renoir's voluptuous nudes; and Manet's bizarre painting of a picnic luncheon with two fully clothed men and a woman whose dress must have fallen off — it was unlike any picnic I'd ever attended.

But in this exhibit, the women were the painters — Lee Krasner, Elaine de Kooning, Helen Frankenthaler, and so on — not the models. What they'd painted wasn't what I would have expected women to paint — no flower gardens, no mothers and babies, no cozy domestic scenes. The works in the exhibit presented nothing recognizable but rather an array of colors in infinite patterns. I remembered what Nello had said, that the paintings represented the unconscious mind. So I figured that's what I was seeing all around me in that room — women expressing the otherwise inexpressible. I didn't quite know how to look at it.

Most of the canvases in the room were enormous. I spotted a vacant bench and sat down in front of a rather dark canvas that intrigued me. Only after I'd settled down did I notice the placard next to the painting: *Memory of My Mother* by Ruth Davidson Abrams. The canvas was covered in strokes of orange-red, blue-black, green and gold, and white, and the colors had movement, cascading down the canvas like a waterfall. I saw a hint of a face in the upper-right corner, or maybe I imagined that. The painting was written in a language I didn't know how to read, and yet it spoke to me somehow, this memory of the artist's mother. I tried to figure out why.

After staring at the painting, I realized that if I were to paint my memories of Belinda they would need to be similarly abstract. I could paint what she looked like, but how she made me feel, the essence of who she was — that was another matter; it would be like a perfumer trying to capture a scent in a bottle. As I thought of my own mother and whether I could ever truly represent her on a canvas, what I was seeing around me began to make more sense. I mixed a palette for Belinda in my mind — white for her dresses, her hair, and the wedding cake; violet for her favorite perfume; deep red for the roses; black for what I'd see when she woke me up with her screams; and ultramarine for the patch of sea that was visible from her window at the sanitarium. The colors were easy enough to come up with, but I didn't know how I could actually use them like the women featured in the exhibit had done.

After the exhibit, we went to a nearby luncheonette. Nello and my classmates chatted about the exhibit, but I found I didn't yet have words for it. I felt slightly woozy.

"I'm going to give you an assignment for your portfolio based on what we just saw," Nello said, as the lunch dishes were brought out. His plate was piled with Coney Island hot dogs, each one topped with meat sauce and chopped onions.

"This'll be easy," Susan said, twirling a piece of her dark hair between her fingers, her scarlet nails matching her lips. "I'll ask my little brother to do it for me."

"I suspect you'll find it's not going to be easy at all," Nello said, as we pulled out our notebooks to write down the assignment.

"I want you to think of an important person in your life," he continued. "Think about how this person makes you feel. Focus on a single emotion, the most dominant one."

"Can I choose Rock Hudson?" Susan asked.

"Someone in your life," Nello said, then our classmate Lois added: "*Not in your dreams.*"

Susan, sitting next to me, frowned for effect. I looked at her in profile, at the tiny black beauty mark above her lips, and I imagined leaning over and licking it off.

The exhibit, I worried, had put me in a sensual mood. I smoothed my hair back, putting it behind my ears, and cut into my avocado pear stuffed with crab and mayonnaise. My left arm brushed up against Susan; I scooted my chair over.

"After you've chosen the person and decided on the dominant emotion, I want you to think of what color that emotion is," Nello said.

"Emotions don't have colors," said Lois, eyeing Susan with a smirk.

"Of course they do," Nello said. "Your assignment is to paint the emotion you chose using only a single color."

I looked over the instructions in my notebook, making sure I'd written down everything important. My classmates did the same, and we all fell into thought as we ate. For the important person in my life, I had three choices: my mother, my father, or Zelie. I feared I wasn't yet ready for the complexities of Belinda and my father bored me, so the choice was obvious.

Zelie.

What was the primary emotion she elicited in me?

Exasperation. Fear. Love.

What color was that?

I closed my notebook, having no idea how I'd approach this project. Before that day, I hadn't known it was possible to paint feelings. I didn't know what my feelings looked like and I wasn't sure I wanted to find out.

2.

The Fridays I spent with my class in New York always left me with a hangover, a feeling of artistic exuberance. The next morning, I wanted nothing more than to sleep in, then spend the rest of the day painting, but Saturdays were never my own. Saturdays meant Belinda.

"Let's get going earlier today," I said, as I sat up in bed, trying to hide my dread from Zelie, not wanting to offer her an opening; she was always looking for an excuse to skip visitors' day. I thought that if we left early we could have a short visit and still get home in time to salvage the afternoon.

Zelie, reading *Peyton Place* in bed, didn't acknowledge me at first. She turned a page and kept reading.

"Come on," I said, standing up and stretching. "We'll get breakfast on the way."

"I'm not going."

"*Zelie*." My tone was mildly scolding, a version of Aster's "*Rozzy*."

"I'm eighteen," she said. "I don't have to do what you tell me to do."

There it was, the "I'm eighteen" routine again. She turned another page, but I knew she was waiting for me to argue with her, to give her a chance to complain about her life. I was in no mood to indulge her. I dressed quickly, went to the girls' wing, chose one of Daphne's books, clipped a few blooms from Belinda's garden, then drove off, my art supplies on the back seat.

It was a relief not to have to listen to Zelie's complaints on the drive. I stopped for a fried-egg sandwich and coffee at a café on the coast, and sat at one of the windswept tables outside to eat and read and feed the seagulls the crusts of my bread. I was soon pulled into Daphne's book about a group of army women sharing barracks. It bordered on sordid, to be sure, and the writing was poor, but the story was interesting in the way of a soap opera. The women sweated a lot (they glistened, they were wet, they were moist) and smoked and swore. Nothing explicitly untoward happened between them, but much was hinted at, leaving the reader to imagine. And imagine I did, much more than I should have.

Daphne's books inevitably made me think of Veronica, whom I hadn't seen since the funeral. I didn't dip into my memories of Veronica often — they were like a nearly empty bottle of a favorite perfume that needed to be spritzed lightly and sparingly. I didn't pine for her; I didn't even wish to see her again. But since that day among the cherry blossoms, I hadn't experienced anything similar, nothing that had brought up the same intense emotions in me, and for that, she lingered.

I read Daphne's book for much longer than I should have, enjoying the story and the sea air so much that I debated whether to be as selfish as Zelie and skip the visit to our mother. But duty spurred me on.

When I arrived, it was too early for lunch on the veranda, so I suggested we sit outside. A promontory jutted out from the house, a finger of rocky cliffs that was closed to patients unless they were accompanied by a guest.

Belinda eagerly agreed, having always loved the sea air. An orderly accompanied us, carrying two folding chairs and a blanket for Belinda since she was always cold. The blanket, in a lovely shade of garnet, had been knitted by Dovey, the only person besides Zelie and me who ever visited.

"How delightful," she said, once she was comfortable in her chair, the blanket tucked around her legs. She'd closed her eyes, letting the sunlight wrap around her, smiling at the quiet hum of the sea like a baby hearing a lullaby. The orderly left once I assured him I could handle things. Belinda was lucid and calm, the best way to find her.

I let her sit while I opened my pad and began sketching the cliffs and the ocean beyond, the flat-bottomed cumulus clouds, the scaly blue water stretching to the horizon. In my drawing, I hoped to capture the *neverendingness* of the sea, how it went on and on; *if only I could swim in it,* I thought, *and feel the seams that hemmed my life dissolve in the salty water.*

Belinda asked about my art class, and I told her about the exhibit of female abstract expressionists. She, still with her eyes closed, nodded and smiled as I spoke, imagining me in this other world so far removed from her own.

"Where's Zelie today?"

"She wanted to stay at home," I said, not in the mood to lie for my sister.

"Last week you said you were worried about her."

I looked up from my sketch pad to see that Belinda's eyes were fixed on me. "I didn't think you'd heard me."

"I did," she said. "Why are you worried?" She reached for her brooch, patting it lightly, a nervous tic of hers.

"She seems adrift since graduating. She'll be all right once she figures out her path."

"It's not going to be easy for her."

"I know."

"Did something troubling happen?" Belinda was calm now, but I knew how quickly that could change. I wanted to move on.

"A man came to dinner, one of the Colts. Zelie took a fancy to him, but we haven't seen him since that night," I said reassuringly, resuming my sketching. "Nothing happened between them, but she hasn't been the same."

"She's reminded of what she can never have."

"I thought she would have snapped out of it by now, but it's been a whole week."

"You can't possibly understand her, that's the problem."

I paused my sketching. "I'm the only woman on earth who *can* understand her."

"You don't know what it's like to be a young woman who craves marriage and children, and not to be able to have that."

I looked at my mother, confused. "But I can't have those things either."

"You don't want them. You're different," she said, and I was stung; my skin flared and burned. Belinda was watching my reaction, so I turned my face to the side, trying to hide it.

"We're alike," she said, reaching over and touching my hand as if such a comparison would be soothing. "My life was forced upon me, and I'm relieved that this won't happen to you. Your sisters freed you."

I focused on the sea, at the mothlike sailboats and thick rays of sun. Belinda rarely spoke this way, so clearly and assuredly. It was jarring to hear her, not only her manner but what she was saying.

"You don't realize what a gift you've been given."

A gift? It was difficult to think of what had happened to my sisters as a gift.

"You know I never wanted to marry your father."

"I know." I set my sketch pad aside and reached over to straighten her blanket. "Mother, please don't upset yourself."

"There are things you don't know about my life."

"Of course," I said, grateful that I didn't know. I didn't want to know.

"I never loved your father; I never even liked him. I didn't like his face, or the way he spoke, or the way he smelled, or anything about him. I cried for days before the wedding."

I knew this much and hoped she was finished. "Should I see if I can get us some sandwiches? You must be hungry."

But she wouldn't stop. "The wedding night, the honeymoon, every night he came to me, it was hell. When I asked him to stop, when I cried, when I told him he was hurting me, he said I'd get used to it, that I was his wife and I couldn't refuse him. He undressed me, he put his hands and mouth all over me, and I hated the way it felt, his tongue, and the way his breath smelled. What he did to me — he said it would stop hurting eventually, that the only way for it to stop hurting was for him to keep doing it. He said that soon I wouldn't feel it anymore, then I wouldn't hate him anymore."

I asked her again to stop. Her complaining about my father was nothing new, but this level of intimate detail was different. I couldn't stand to hear it.

"On our honeymoon, I didn't feel like myself anymore. I felt like a shadow walking around. I was surprised other people could see me."

"I really don't want to hear this."

She looked at me with her old fierce intensity. "Who's left to hear it but you?"

I worried she was going to have an episode and looked toward the building for the orderly, but she settled down. "Women don't talk this way, I know." She patted my hand again. "But what more can anyone do to me, blossom? This is the last stop."

A look of relief passed over her, as if she'd said something she'd long wanted to say. She pulled up her blanket, burrowing deeper under it. I thought of Zelie and me leaving in two years for a point unknown, the inevitable end of these visits.

"Maybe we can move away," I said. "You and me and Zelie."

"That's what I want for you and your sister. I know I'll never leave this place."

"You don't know that." I thought of our visit two weeks ago — *Take me with you, blossoms* — and how heartbroken I'd been. But this, her acceptance of her fate, was somehow worse.

"Zelie will be your burden now, not me. You'll have to stop her from doing anything reckless or she'll suffer the same fate as your sisters. You can't let that happen."

. . .

We sat for a long while without talking though I couldn't stop thinking about what she'd said. I carried the burden of her unhappiness whether I acknowledged it or not. I hadn't asked to be born, but somehow I was complicit in what her life had been.

I sketched a while longer, then saw an orderly walking toward us. "He's coming over," I said.

"That's fine; I'm getting tired. You don't mind, do you?" She picked up her blanket and stretched her legs. I said I didn't, but to my surprise, I did. Without Zelie hovering nearby, jittery with impatience, I didn't mind being with my mother; she may have probed into pain that I often preferred to leave unexamined, but even that had been clarifying.

"I don't want to see you again for a while," she said, as the orderly helped her out of her chair. "You and Zelie need a break from coming up here. I want you to focus on yourselves this summer. Zelie needs you — and you know I only upset her."

"Are you sure? It's not a problem for me," I said, knowing Zelie would be thrilled.

"I'm sure." She wrapped her arms around me and pulled me to her, whispering in my ear with urgency: "You have to take care of Zelie."

The way she spoke, it was as if she knew we'd never see each other again.

3.

When I arrived home, I expected to find Zelie playing something gloomy on the piano; Satie's *Gnossiennes* had been in constant rotation since her graduation. Instead, I was greeted by silence. I checked our bedroom and called her name, but she'd gone out. I assumed Florence must have picked her up and taken her to the Bellflower Cinema.

"God bless Florence," I said, as I ran a bath. I soaked for a while, then ate a sandwich alone in the kitchen. The house was startlingly quiet. My father was at some kind of golfing event for the day, with a banquet that night; he'd given Mrs. O'Connor and Dovey the day off.

I went out to the meadow with my watercolor set and sat in the grass, wearing a sun hat, and painted what I saw around me, the poppies and bee balm, soothing imagery that my professor probably wouldn't have liked. I didn't want to think about anything else, especially my worry over Zelie, which I'd passed on to my mother. I spent a lovely afternoon this way, with a nap in the middle, and when I went back to the house, I saw Zelie walking up the drive.

"Iris!" she called in a happy singsong. Her tone was unexpected.

"Where've you been?" I said over my shoulder, as I opened the side door off the kitchen. I hoped her sulk was over, but I didn't want to seem too eager.

"I've been out sailing," she gushed, as she ran toward the house to follow me inside.

"Sailing?" I set my pad and paint set on the kitchen table.

"With Florence and Edwin. He bought a sailboat." She filled a glass of water from the faucet and quickly gulped it down.

It was unlike Zelie to keep such an outing to herself. Whenever she received an invitation anywhere, she demanded my advice on clothes and hairstyle. "You didn't mention sailing this morning."

"It was last minute." She shrugged. "Florence called right after you left."

I took off my sun hat and pressed down my dampened hair. "Since when does Edwin own a sailboat?" Florence's fiancé worked in a bank and had the pallor of dough waiting to be rolled out. He was hardly the outdoorsy type.

She shrugged again. "What's for dinner?"

I stood across the table from her, perplexed. I was confused by her account of the day, but she was finally in a good mood, and I didn't want to send her spiraling back into melancholy.

"Let's see," I said, as I opened the icebox, needing to tread delicately. Since I didn't know how to cook much of anything, I made us a tray of Mrs. O'Connor's leftovers: roast salmon and salad, bread and butter, grape Jell-O for dessert. We took the tray to the library next to our father's den, where the television was set up, and enjoyed an evening together, engrossed in a variety of programs, beginning with *The Honeymooners* and ending with *Gunsmoke*.

4.

Over the next week, Zelie kept busy with Florence. When I arrived home from college each day, I no longer found her sulking in the house. Instead, she was out, and she'd breeze into our bedroom later, telling me about her day, which always included Florence and her wedding somehow — she'd helped Florence make out the guest list or spent the afternoon with her exploring potential reception halls. Each day there was some new wedding-related activity to keep them busy; it was as if Florence were marrying Zelie, not Edwin. While I was pleased she'd fought her way out of the gloom that had enveloped her since graduation, I found her behavior odd. Only weeks earlier, news of Florence's wedding had sent her into a depression, but now she was living and breathing it, and not only that, she seemed to be having tremendous fun.

That weekend our father was going to be in Boston on business. Mrs. O'Connor and Dovey were off until Monday, and Dovey had gone to Brooklyn to visit a cousin, which meant Zelie and I would have the house all to ourselves. I relished the promise of the weekend and had mentioned to Zelie the possibility of doing something together on Saturday since we didn't need to visit our mother. She'd seemed interested, but when I woke up that morning, she was gone. I found a note on my desk.

> *I*—
>
> *I'm going sailing with Florence and Edwin today. Please don't be upset!*
>
> *I'll be home late. No need to wait up.*
>
> *Love, Z.*

She'd made no mention of sailing the night before, but obviously she'd already made plans with Florence and Edwin. I couldn't imagine why she hadn't mentioned it. There was no reason for her to be so evasive. Our father didn't like us to socialize much, but Florence was an exception — Zelie could spend as much time with the Hellands as she liked.

I was suspicious and confused but decided not to let the situation ruin my day. I spent the morning going through the newspapers looking at real estate while listening to Billie Holiday's *Lady Sings the Blues,* which Zelie had bought me for Christmas. The Sunday papers had the most ads, even for far-flung places, so it took me a while to clip all the listings of interest, most notably a dramatic Greek revival in Louisville.

I saved the *New York Times* for last. When I was done with the real estate section — which had several tempting listings in Europe though even in my fantasies I thought that moving there was unlikely — I scanned the rest of the paper quickly, checking for any interesting news. Eventually, I landed on the wedding announcements. Normally, I skipped over them, and as I was turning the page, desperate to move on from the spread of black-and-white brides staring at me like space robots — I could never pretend that marriage was anything but terrifying to me — I saw a face I recognized in the upper-right corner, a headshot of a bride with the caption, Mrs. Clyde H. Bassett.

I knew who it was even before the headline on the announcement confirmed it.

MISS V. A. CREAM WEDS CLYDE BASSETT

I'd thought of Veronica only the day before, and now here she was again. Reading her news felt like a blow. I sunk back in my chair as if I were a girl who'd just discovered her former beau had gotten married, which was silly. I had no connection to Veronica, and thus no reason to be upset, and yet I was. I recalled her cries upon learning that Daphne had died, and they'd been evidence, I was certain, of true love for my sister. Yet here was Veronica, married to a man.

I opened the newspaper again, unable to resist reading about the man

Veronica had chosen, feeling stunned that she'd chosen any man at all. I knew the relationship she'd had with Daphne was forbidden, but it hadn't occurred to me that most women like Veronica married eventually. Daphne wouldn't have, but Veronica, I could see, was different. She was more willing to wear a mask.

The wedding had taken place the day before at a church in Greenwich, followed by a reception at the Hotel Cream. Veronica, according to the paper, had worn a gown of ivory silk and Chantilly lace with a portrait neckline and bouffant skirt; she'd carried a small prayer book down the aisle and a bouquet of lilies of the valley. Besides the fashion report, there was very little information about Veronica herself though the announcement was full of details about her father, her father-in-law, and her husband. The whole thing was upsetting to read, the last paragraph in particular.

> After their wedding trip to London and Paris, Dr. and Mrs. Bassett will set up house in Waterbury, Conn., where Dr. Bassett is a dermatologist in private practice.

I considered cutting out the announcement just so I could have a photo of Veronica, a souvenir of the past, but I decided I'd rather forget. The Veronica of my memories was about to become a housewife living in a center-hall colonial. She'd been a goddess; she wasn't designed for ironing and mopping floors and changing baby's diapers — that, to me, was all wrong. More than that, it felt like a betrayal, and I think that's what bothered me the most. I knew who the real Veronica was — I'd seen her with Daphne. Her new, unexpected life made me think of Godzilla. He'd been transformed during the war by nuclear radiation — Zelie and I had seen the movie the year before. Similarly, Veronica Cream had mutated, but into a distinctly female postwar monstrosity: Mrs. Clyde H. Bassett.

I tore the announcement out of the newspaper, wadded it up, and threw it in the trash can. I would have set it on fire if I could.

Once I calmed down, I went to my wardrobe, pushed aside my clothes, and reached all the way to the back. I felt a slim paper bag sitting upright there. I pulled it out and sat on my bed to open it, slowly removing the canvas inside, which I hadn't looked at in a couple of years. It was Daphne's painting, *The White Iris*.

In high school, a teacher had shown us a drawing that looked like a young woman from one angle and an old woman from another depending on how you looked at it. *The White Iris* achieved something similar: my namesake flower and also a woman's body — Veronica's body. But the juxtaposition of *The White Iris* and my mental picture of Veronica the bride, her name erased, unsettled me. I couldn't square those two images.

I banished the photo of the bride from my mind and ran my fingers across the white paint, the blushing pink of the canvas. I set it on my desk, leaning it against the wall, and stared at it for a while. My body felt alight. This didn't happen often, and when it did, I usually ignored it. Normally, I stayed tight and buttoned up. I worried that if I didn't everything would come spilling out.

But now I stood up and locked the bedroom door, though I was alone in the house. I began to undress in front of the mirror that was attached to the inside of the wardrobe door, unbuttoning my blouse and tossing it aside, then letting my skirt slide to the floor. I removed my underthings methodically, revealing one breast, then the other. I pulled down my underwear, feeling the satin brush against my skin, and I was naked at last. I gently rubbed my hands over my body, alive to my own touch, feeling aroused at the thought of how I might look to someone else if they were spying on me as I'd spied on Veronica all those years ago.

From the wardrobe door, I lifted the mirror off the nail and set it on the floor, squatting over it so I could see myself. I explored for a few minutes, opening up my layers, then I grabbed my sketch pad and pencil from the desk and began to draw what I saw in great detail, wanting to create a map of myself, this uncharted territory. I sketched for a while, producing several drawings and considering ways I could use these sketches as a template for my own floral paintings, for an iris, as Daphne had done.

The time I'd spent sketching hadn't quelled the desire in me, and I set the sketch pad aside and crawled into bed, enjoying the sensation of my skin against the cool cotton. I rolled gently from side to side, moving my hands all over my body, sensitive to every touch, as if I were pulsing with electricity. I glanced at *The White Iris* on my desk and imagined Veronica, my memories of her nearly naked body. She was watching me as I thought of her; she enjoyed seeing the pleasure she brought me. Then she crawled into bed with me, as did Susan from my class. I didn't know how Susan had gotten into my fantasy, but there she was, unfastening her bumblebee pin and taking off her blouse, climbing on top of me. After a little while, I let out the most exquisite scream.

Afterward, I took a bath, momentarily feeling — to borrow a word from Zelie — *dreamy,* the fragrant bathwater like gentle waves in a steamy spring. But soon that gave way to waves of disgust. I didn't know why I had those desires. I felt ashamed of what I wanted, of the way I'd touched myself. I'd sat in judgment of Veronica, but I knew that part of me was jealous that she was trying to lead a normal life. For me, that would always be impossible for a variety of reasons.

As I soaked, I thought of Clyde and Veronica together — there'd been no picture of Clyde in the newspaper, so I was left to imagine him. And as I did, Sam Colt drifted into my mind like a wisp of smoke. I'd avoided thinking about him since the dinner, but I knew it was foolish to push him — and the danger of him — out of my mind.

Like my mother, sometimes I knew things. And there was a suspicion growing in me that I couldn't ignore.

I got out of the bath, dressed, and went to make lunch. In the entry hall, on my way to the kitchen, I picked up the phone and called Florence's house. When Florence answered, I hung up.

After lunch, I went out to the terrace to work on the assignment Nello had given the class, which I'd been putting off. My expectations were low, so I decided to use a small canvas I'd previously ruined with an errant splash of green paint. I set the canvas on my easel and tied my smock around my waist.

Zelie was the person I'd chosen, and given how I was feeling about her, I settled on fear as the dominant emotion. I poked around in my box of paints to find the right color. Black was the obvious choice to represent the pit-in-the-stomach sense of dread I was experiencing, but I worried I couldn't make that work, so I settled on a tube of red-purple, a dark bruising red, the kind that haunts. I didn't bother with a palette but squeezed a glob of paint out of the tube directly onto an old brush and attacked the canvas with a few aggressive strokes. What is fear anyway but a rush, an attack? I moved the paint around, waiting for it to match what I felt inside, the fear about where Zelie was and the person she was with, since it clearly wasn't Florence.

I hadn't a clue how to represent my fear abstractly. It would have been easier in a representative way, which is what I was used to; I'd paint Aster in her wedding dress, Rosalind on the dance floor with Roderick, Calla getting ready for her date with Teddy. Moments of fear filled my past and marked the present, but an abstract representation was difficult to portray, that sick feeling, the terror of the unknown.

I brushed a slash of red-purple across the canvas, which looked like a wound, then I did another. I recalled the paintings at the museum, *Mountains and Sea* and *Memory of My Mother,* the sense of movement they'd achieved, the dimension and mystery, the emotion of the latter painting in particular. I channeled my fear into my painting, at one point setting it on the ground and dripping paint onto it like Nello said Jackson Pollock had done. I'd used most of the tube of red-purple, but it still looked nothing like fear to me.

I continued on with this for more than an hour, wanting to lose myself in the project — there was normally no better pleasure than immersion in my art. But this project was different. It made me uncomfortable, and it was bringing up unwanted emotions. I felt uneasy with every brushstroke, knowing that my sister was lying to me, until my fear and the red paint became one.

Zelie's note said not to wait up for her so I didn't. I was asleep before she arrived home, and in the morning, she was getting ready to go out by the time

I opened my eyes. Whatever she was doing had made her crepuscular. She moved in and out at the edges of my days, not wanting to be seen.

"Sorry if I woke you," she said, dropping her powder compact into her purse. "I'm going out for the day." She wore a halter dress that I'd never seen before, her bare suntanned shoulders on vibrant display.

I didn't bother to ask where she was going, but she offered up an explanation anyway. "I'm going sailing with Florence and Edwin again. It's just so much fun."

I sat up, taking in her appearance. I felt like a raisin in comparison, shriveled and shrunken.

"Did you hear me?" she asked impatiently.

"You're going sailing," I said, and set my head back down on the pillow.

That afternoon, without anyone around to bother me, I pulled out some of the sketches I'd done of myself and played around with drawing them as flowers. But it was much more challenging than I thought it would be, and after a couple of hours of working intensely at my desk, it seemed that to do what Daphne had done so beautifully with her iris painting one would need to have much more familiarity with female anatomy, the way a bird-watcher knows every inch of a kestrel or a waterthrush. I didn't know how I could obtain that kind of experience, and the thought of it bordered on indecent.

I stuffed my sketch pad in the wardrobe, not wanting anyone to see it, and thought I might take a drive when I heard the front door open. To my surprise, I found Zelie in the kitchen, scouring the cupboards.

"I didn't expect to see you," I said, and observed her closely, trying to determine whether she'd actually been sailing. She did look a bit sunburned.

"We were on the Sound for hours," she said, popping open a box of crackers. "It was lovely, but we were ready to leave."

"If you're hungry now, we could have an early dinner," I said, eager for us to spend some time together in the hopes she'd open up to me. "I heard about a new Chinese restaurant in Greenwich. Wanna try it?"

"Not tonight," she said. "I only came home to take a bath and get changed. I'm going to Florence's house for dinner with her and Edwin. She's making us the clams we got today."

"The Three Musketeers," I said with amusement. "Maybe they'll have to take you on their honeymoon."

She was chewing a cracker and paused, forcing a weak smile. I wanted to tell her that I knew she was lying, that I'd called the Hellands' house the day before and Florence had been home, not out on a boat with her as she'd claimed. But then she'd know I'd been checking up on her, and I didn't want to be seen that way — like I was trying to control her. That would only make things worse.

"I'll drive you to Florence's house when you're ready," I said. "I was thinking of going out anyway."

"That's all right, I'll walk." She took a few more crackers from the box and headed to our bedroom.

A little while later, she left, freshly bathed and wearing a beautiful wine-colored dress with a bowknot collar, much too elegant for a simple dinner at Florence's house.

In her absence, I didn't know what to do with myself and my anxiety. I decided to drive to Greenwich for Chinese food anyway, but when I arrived at the restaurant and opened the door to a delicious gust of steamy air scented with garlic and ginger, I felt out of place. Couples and families sat at every table, chatting and laughing, attempting to eat with chopsticks and slurping noodles. They made me feel lonely.

I ordered two egg rolls to go. They came wrapped in wax paper like a present, with a delicate red string tied around them. I drove back to the village and decided to cruise past Florence's house. My car was distinctive, but it was twilight and I hoped the semidarkness would conceal me.

All the lights were off at the Hellands' house; clearly, Zelie was not inside having a clam dinner with Florence and Edwin. I parked for a bit and ate my egg rolls, then drove away through the leafy residential roads that connected to Main Street. I stopped to make a right turn near the church, and a car zoomed by on the opposite side, as sleek and red as a candy apple. The car was an Aston Martin, the same kind of car that Sam Colt drove.

I stopped midturn and watched its taillights as it moved down the road and around the town green with its gazebo and Revolutionary War cannon; it was driving entirely too fast. A car behind me honked its horn, but I didn't move, wondering whether I should follow the Aston Martin. I hadn't seen who was driving or if they had a passenger and I wasn't sure I knew exactly where they'd gone. The car behind me honked again, so I made my right turn and headed toward home.

Once there, I left the lights off in the front parlor and pulled a chair up to the window to watch for Zelie as I ate a bowl of strawberry ice cream. If she was with Sam, he'd have to leave her at the door. It was nighttime; she couldn't walk home alone. But as one hour passed, then two, I began to feel uncomfortable with my behavior — calling Florence's house, parking outside, watching for a car to pull up. I couldn't regress to how I'd been when I was younger, creeping around in the dark and scheming — even if I'd always meant well. There was already tension between me and Zelie. It could easily escalate. I knew how stubborn she could be.

I was certain that Zelie was sneaking around with a man — I couldn't imagine any other reason for her to lie to me — and it seemed likely that the man was Sam Colt. Who else could it be? But if I'd learned anything, it was that I couldn't change my sister's mind for her. It would need to be Zelie's decision to break things off. And she'd witnessed what had happened to our sisters just as I had. Zelie wasn't always entirely rational — she was immature in many ways and unhappy with her lot in life — but that didn't mean she wanted to die.

5.

For more than a month, Zelie continued on this way. She claimed to be spending her days with Florence, wedding planning, sailing on the weekends. There were barbecues on the beach, firework displays, even a yacht race. I didn't believe her, but I still wasn't sure quite how to intervene effectively. Our father was away for business often and would be on the West Coast for the second half of July, so he was unaware of how much time Zelie was spending away from home. But even when he was home, he didn't complain when she missed dinner; she'd been so difficult after her graduation that he seemed pleased that she was keeping busy.

I stayed late at college most nights, working in the art studio until it closed at eight o'clock, focusing on my portfolio projects. I'd tried another abstract expressionist painting—an attempt at portraying how the ocean looked on the morning after Daphne died that I titled *The Sound*—but in the end, it was more of a realistic painting; I couldn't figure out how to portray the ocean as a feeling. And when no one else was in the studio with me, I worked on my flower drawings and paintings, but they usually ended up in the trash.

Zelie and I saw each other only fleetingly, which was a relief—I hated that she was lying to me, and it hurt to be around her knowing a gulf had opened up between us. I felt confident that she'd end things with Sam, but it was taking longer than I would have liked.

When we did see each other, usually at breakfast or when we were getting into bed at night, we exchanged pleasantries. "Another late night at the college for me," I said, when we spoke briefly one night, to which she replied: "I've been at Florence's all day. She's still figuring out her menu."

I pretended to accept her stories, and she was gullible enough to believe that I thought her happiness, uncorked and fizzing over, came from helping Florence decide between prime rib or salmon en croûte for her menu. "There are so many things to do," she said. "You know what weddings are like."

"Yes, I remember." I wanted to add, *Don't* you?

The end of July soon came, which brought with it the end of the Summer Art Intensive. August loomed, and I was bereft at the thought of spending it at home, where it would be harder to keep busy and block out my worries over Zelie.

On the second-to-last day of class, we needed to meet with Nello individually to review our portfolios. Class was essentially over, though the next day we would spend our usual Friday in New York, visiting a museum and a gallery together one last time. I was the last student scheduled to meet with Nello that Thursday, and as Susan made her way out of the studio, I went in. Nello asked me to shut the door, but I said I'd rather leave it open, claiming the room felt stuffy. I liked Nello and didn't feel uncomfortable around him — Susan said he was "light in the loafers" — but he was still a man.

We went through the pieces in my portfolio, more than twenty of them. He examined each one slowly while sipping his coffee, admiring my watercolor of a sunset, my charcoal drawing of an elderly woman who came to model for our class, my still life of a vase of daisies, and *The Sound*. He carefully considered the red canvas, my abstract representation of fear. He hadn't allowed us to tell him anything about the work as he wanted to form his own impressions.

Under the lights of the art studio, it looked like even more of a mess than it did at home, and I hated the sight of it — each brushstroke representing my fear over Zelie. Nello stared at it intently and I was embarrassed.

"When I look at this, I see rage," he said. "A red mist."

"Really?" I asked, trying to see it through his eyes. As I suspected, I'd failed to convey what I'd wanted.

"Oh yes. I see a rage that can't be contained, Iris." In his French accent, he said "Iris" like *I-reeze*. "It's quite striking."

I felt exposed suddenly and smiled faintly.

"Is rage not what you intended?"

I shook my head. "Fear."

"Well, sometimes the artist thinks she's conveying one thing, but in the end, she gives us something else entirely. It's what I love about art. So much of it comes from a hidden place in our mind."

"Like the paintings in the exhibit," I said.

"Exactly."

He set the red canvas on the table in front of us. When he briefly left to retrieve his cigarette lighter from his office, I set my sunset watercolor on top of it.

"If you want my honest assessment," he said, when he came back, sitting next to me again and lighting up a Gitanes, "I think you're wasting your time at this college."

"What do you mean? Is my work not good enough?"

He laughed and took a drag on his cigarette. "This isn't a serious place, is it?"

"I — I don't know. I mean, it's not Yale."

"Who needs Yale?" he said, waving his hand, trailing smoke around. "Most of the girls are just wasting time until they find a husband. But you have real talent. You should be in art school."

I was flattered and momentarily at a loss for words. I'd never had my work complimented by my usual art teacher, Mr. Richardson, who also taught swimming. I explained to Nello that before I finished high school I'd dreamt of applying to the Rhode Island School of Design but that my father said it was impractical.

"What does it matter what he thinks?" Nello asked. "You're an adult. You don't need his permission, do you?"

"He pays for my education."

Nello shrugged. "Get a job."

"That's why I'm training to be a teacher," I said. "To support myself and my sister."

"Is that what you want, to be a teacher? Or will you teach just for money, like me?" He gave me a sly smile and put out his cigarette in his empty coffee cup.

"I suppose I don't know what else to do."

He nodded, as if he understood. "Life isn't amenable to artistic pursuits. You have to fight for it." He picked up my sunset watercolor and the red canvas again. The two images presented quite the contrast.

"If I may, Iris, a word of advice?"

"Okay," I said uneasily.

"You have a gift, and I rarely tell my students that, okay? But you're capable of more. I think you need to push yourself harder and stop being so" — he paused for a moment to consider his words — "stop being so timid."

I felt insulted and was trying not to show it. "What do you mean?"

He stood up and set all of my pieces out on the table, ending with the red canvas. "This one was more of an exercise, I know, but it has a certain energy, a vitality that your other pieces lack. There's a mystery here; you should use your art to explore that."

"But . . ." I was unsure if I wanted to reveal what I was thinking.

"Go on," he said.

"I didn't like working on that one."

"Why not?"

"It made me uncomfortable."

"Ah," he said. "You see, that's precisely why it's the best piece you've done."

6.

The next day, my last day of class, Zelie surprised me by asking if she could accompany me to New York. She'd been working so hard to avoid me that this unexpected request made me immediately suspicious.

"Why?" I asked, bracing for some new tall tale.

"I want to go to Bloomingdale's. There are some things I need."

"Like what?"

"Just odds and ends."

"All right," I said, surprised at the simplicity of her plan for the day. Maybe this time she wasn't lying. "I usually get the 4:15 train home. Are you sure you can keep yourself busy that whole time?"

"What kind of person can't stay busy in New York?" she said, as she grabbed an outfit from her wardrobe, a swingy cotton dress in pink gingham. We were running late, so I put on a navy skirt and white blouse, and ran up to the girls' wing, slipping one of Aster's embroidered handkerchiefs into my pocket, my companion for the day. There was no time for breakfast, but I went to the kitchen for a piece of fruit to eat in the car. As I walked through the entry hall, the telephone on the table rang.

"Is this Miss Chapel?" a woman asked when I answered.

"Yes," I said, hoping whoever this was would be quick.

"This is Mrs. Greenberg from the Brandwin Travel Agency. I wanted to check to make sure you found your passport."

I had no idea who this woman was or what she was talking about. "I'm sorry, who is this?"

"It's Etta Greenberg, your travel agent. Isn't this Hazel Chapel?"

I had a sick feeling. "Yes, it is."

"Did you manage to find your passport? We'll need to reschedule your flight otherwise, and there isn't much time left."

I looked over my shoulder to make sure Zelie wasn't coming up behind me. "I found it," I said. "Will you remind me of the flight details again?"

"Certainly. Please hold on." I heard her shuffling some papers, and while I waited, all sorts of scenarios ran through my mind, none of them good. "All right, here we are. I've booked you and Mr. Colt on Pan Am, as we discussed. Your plane leaves Idlewild Airport on Monday at six o'clock in the evening. You'll land in Rome the following morning."

Zelie shouted from the bedroom that she'd only be a minute more; I didn't want her to see me talking on the phone. "I'll call you back," I said to the travel agent, and hung up. I rushed into the kitchen, grabbing an apple from the copper bowl on the table.

"We're not too late, are we?" she said, having hobbled into the kitchen with only one shoe on. She was waiting for an answer, but I found I was speechless. "What's wrong?" she asked, as she slipped on her other shoe.

"Nothing." I turned to the sink to wash my apple, grateful for a reason to look away from her.

"I'm going to the car, hurry up," she said. I knew I had only a minute or two to collect myself — I wasn't sure it was possible. I felt the red rage of my painting. Nello was right — it had been there all along.

I'd trusted Zelie to break things off with Sam. I'd been fearful, but I hadn't panicked because I knew that even if she didn't break things off what would come next — an engagement, a wedding — all took time, and I would have tried everything to stop her. But this — a trip to Rome after she'd known him for only two months? I didn't know what this was.

I needed to calm down fast. I was in no state to confront her. Shouting at her, threatening her — I knew that wouldn't change her mind. I needed time to think about what I should do, whether I should involve my father, though he was still in California. Zelie's flight wasn't until Monday, assuming she had found her passport. I had a few days, and I clung to the promise of them.

When I got in the car, I realized I was still holding my apple, which I no longer wanted. I handed it to Zelie and she took it, crunching into it as if she didn't have a care in the world. "What took you so long?" she said.

I turned on the car and stared through the front windshield, unwilling to face her. She was happy; she must have thought she was in love. Rome was ahead of her and she'd convinced herself there was a future beyond that. I had to force her to see reality, but I had to do that gently.

"Do you want to have dinner later?" I asked. "We could meet at Grand Central, then take the train back to the car and drive up the coast to that seafood place we went to last summer."

"The place with the clams casino? And the lemon chiffon cake? I'd like that." She smiled at me sweetly, and I tried to smile back to throw her off, but I couldn't. She seemed genuinely pleased by the plan to have dinner. She probably thought of it as a farewell. The question was whether she would even bother to tell me we were saying goodbye.

Lady Don't Leave Me

1957

I.

I spent the morning with my class at the Museum of Modern Art, looking at Van Gogh's sunflower paintings, a whole wall of striking yellows and golds not dulled at all by time. The exhibit had been touring the world, and there was more to it than just the sunflower paintings, but they were the ones that transfixed me. Van Gogh's paintings weren't entirely realistic, but they weren't like the abstract expressionists' work either; they were in between, a recognizable if slightly off-kilter reality. It was how I'd felt since the shock of the travel agent's call — I couldn't see clearly. So that morning I felt an affinity for Van Gogh and his distorted view of the world. I wanted to lose myself in his sunflowers, in his irises and daisies and poppies. Flowers had always brought solace.

After the visit to MOMA, I went with my class for a late lunch at a pizzeria. Everyone was enjoying themselves, talking about their plans for the month of August, while I wondered if Zelie was really at Bloomingdale's.

My rage had settled into surprise — she was so much more devious than I'd ever thought she could be — then into fear, my old standby. I wouldn't start an argument with her at dinner, wouldn't yell, and she wouldn't be able to avoid me. We could just talk, and I could try to understand why she thought she could run away with Sam Colt, or any man. Then I could decide how to talk her out of it.

After lunch, we went downtown to a gallery owned by a friend of Nello's from Paris. The gallery occupied the ground floor of a redbrick townhouse on Ninth Street near Washington Square Park. It was completely empty that afternoon, which was just as well since my classmates made the kinds of comments I would have been embarrassed for anyone else to overhear.

The paintings hanging in the main room were a world away from Van Gogh. They were all by the same artist, an up-and-coming French painter named Lucette Toussaint, who would later become quite famous. Each canvas looked similar, in shades of black, white, and gray; her work was stripped down, lacking Van Gogh's vibrancy and color. Lucette's mind, which we'd just stepped into, was a gloomy and terrifying place to be. Each painting focused on the same old woman's face, her ghostly visage emerging from a black batlike void. The old woman's wide eyes were foreboding, transfixed on something the viewer couldn't see, something that seemed to be literally scaring the life out of her. She looked at once monstrous and vulnerable, like a character from one of Goya's Black Paintings, *Saturn Devouring His Son*. I couldn't help but recoil. Lucette, it was clear, wasn't afraid to push herself to places of extreme discomfort.

I walked by painting after painting, seeing the same woman's chalky white skin and terror-filled eyes. I couldn't help but think of Belinda waking in the night to face the Chapel victims. I hadn't heard my mother's screams in many years, yet now they were ringing in my ears, the lullaby of my childhood.

"I might never sleep again," said Susan, wearing another tight blouse with a brooch pinned to it, this time a butterfly. "Lois went outside for a smoke. She said she felt sick looking at all this."

"I find it very compelling," Nello said, walking over to us.

"What's compelling about it?" Susan asked. "It's like a nightmare."

"So what if it is? Is it the artist's job to comfort us?"

"Pas de tout." A man's voice echoed through the gallery. Susan, Nello, and I turned around, and Nello exclaimed at the sight of his friend. They embraced, then the man introduced himself as Félix Toussaint, the brother of the painter. He was a short, round man with bouncy silvery curls.

Susan, obviously embarrassed, fled to join Lois and her cigarette.

"My students were just admiring Lucette's work," Nello said.

"That's not what it sounded like," Félix replied, and he and Nello shared a laugh.

"The paintings are striking," I said, hoping I sounded at least semi-insightful; I wanted to separate myself from the others.

Félix nodded gratefully. "I'm honored to share my sister's work," he said. "This woman you see in the paintings is our mother. She died in the war."

I wasn't surprised. I could spot a haunted mother easily.

Félix held out his hand. "And you are?"

"Iris Chapel."

"Ah, Chapel!" He made a gun with one of his hands. "Bang bang!"

"No," I said, shaking my head perhaps too adamantly.

"How interesting," Nello said. "I'd never made the connection before. Whenever I see her name, I think of a church. She's so quiet, solemn. It fits."

"Ah, I see, Chapel . . . *comme une église?*" Félix asked, pressing his hands together in mock prayer.

"It's just Chapel," I said, annoyed. I'd made it two years at Grace Street Teacher's College without anyone asking me about firearms.

Nello launched into another subject, guiding Félix to one of the paintings on the other side of the room and asking questions; Félix was eager to respond. I didn't follow them. There were other rooms in the gallery to explore, and since the rest of my classmates had gone outside to smoke, I'd be alone.

I could see a room at the end of the hallway that was full of color — much more to my liking. I headed back there and read the placard above the doorway.

ART OF THE AMERICAN SOUTHWEST
FROM
THE PALACE SCHOOL OF ART AND DESIGN
SANTA FE, NEW MEXICO

My only reference point for the Southwest was the garish Technicolor tableau of *Chapel '70,* a backdrop for men on horseback. But the work hanging in the room was nothing like that.

I saw an empty highway stretching into the distance under a stunning cloud-filled sky, the clouds like white marbles on blue carpet; pine trees and striped sienna stone in a place called Frijoles Canyon; an aspen grove in the Sangre de Cristo ablaze with autumn gold; the brilliance of the orange mesa at Zuni Pueblo during sunset; and yellow chamisa blooms on a cliff overlooking the Rio Chama. The landscapes were full of space and light, airy and sunbaked; it was brighter and more colorful than the world I inhabited, more open and expansive; New England was so confining.

There were cityscapes and people too: Santa Fe Plaza, with its adobe buildings and turquoise doors; an old Indian man sitting in a Ford pickup truck surrounded by pink and yellow hollyhocks; a woman with a long black braid sweeping in front of a roadside café. These weren't the cartoon characters of *Chapel '70;* they were people who weren't posing for outsiders or playing a part.

The last painting was different. When I reached it, I blushed before I realized I was blushing. It was a painting of a rose, or part of a rose. Against a background of deep medium red was a close-up of two petals in a slightly darker shade. It was nothing like the red canvas I had painted; it was delicate and understated, confident. I immediately thought of Daphne's painting, *The White Iris,* and all my attempts to copy it; here was a rose and also a woman most intimate.

It was a relatively small canvas. I leaned over to read the placard hanging on the wall next to it: *The Land of Enchantment* by "anonymous."

"What's with all this cowboy stuff?" Susan said, poking her head into the room. She was annoying but alluring despite herself. Seeing her near the rose painting made me recall the afternoon I'd taken to my bed, fantasizing about her. I blushed again.

"No cowboys here," I said, straightening up, unsure if I looked flushed. If so, Susan didn't comment on it. She came into the room and breezed by most of the paintings, then stood next to me.

"This one doesn't fit, does it?" she said, snapping her gum, exhaling spearmint. She could see my interest, and said: "What's the big deal? It's just a couple of rose petals." She squinted intensely at the canvas. "At least I think that's what it is. Right?" She turned to me with the expression of a person trying to recall a word she had forgotten, but I wasn't going to explain it to her.

"Nello wanted me to let you know he's ready to leave. We're all going to a café for a drink."

"I can't go," I said. "I have to meet my sister." Susan left, but I barely registered her departure, as transfixed by the rose petals as I'd been by the sunflowers earlier.

With fears for one sister, I imagined another; I saw Daphne in the radiant landscape of the Southwest, a student at the Palace School of Art and Design. I pretended for a moment that the painting was hers, that she had a promising future ahead of her. And for a few moments, it felt like that could really be true.

2.

Zelie was waiting at Grand Central when I arrived. I spotted her standing beneath the departures sign holding a small Bloomingdale's bag. She didn't notice me as I walked toward her through the pre–rush hour crowd. To see her from afar, in her pink gingham dress, white heels, and gloves, was to recognize that she had become a woman. It was hard to see that at home. She'd been a baby there, was still the baby of the family.

She waved when she noticed me but didn't move from her spot. Waving back, I breathed deeply to clear away the jumble of fears in my mind.

"You didn't buy much. No luck shopping?" I asked, as we embraced.

"No *time* for shopping," she said, her face lit up. "You won't believe what happened. I ran into Florence and her mother at Bloomingdale's. We spent the *whole* day together. There was some problem with Florence's bridal registry and they had to come into the city to sort it out." She was playing at being breezy, but she fidgeted as she spoke, letting her eyes fall on various passersby rather than on me. That's what gave her away.

All I could manage to say was "I see."

She chatted on about her afternoon, which she claimed to have spent at a tearoom with Florence and Mrs. Helland, followed by a walk in Central Park. I hated to watch her lie. "Such a beautiful day," she said, watching a man sweep up the trash. "I should come to New York more often."

I looked away from her and up at the enormous station clock, which was as round and white as the moon. "Our train's leaving soon. We better go."

"I can't." She handed me her Bloomingdale's bag, which I mindlessly accepted. "Will you take this home for me? It's just a pair of earrings."

The bag was so light that it felt empty. I guessed she'd run into Bloomingdale's and grabbed the first thing she saw — then went where? I wondered if Sam was nearby, watching us, thinking I was a fool.

"I'm really sorry," she said, "but I can't have dinner with you tonight. I'm meeting Florence and Mrs. Helland. We're eating early, then going to the theater. They have an extra ticket."

"But you promised to have dinner with me."

"I never promised. We can have dinner tomorrow."

I didn't want to confront her at Grand Central. I'd had everything planned out. I grabbed her wrist and tried to pull her along. "We better hurry," I said, but she snapped her wrist back.

"I told you I'm not coming."

We stared at each other in a kind of standoff. She must have realized then that I didn't believe her; she straightened her back, putting on a defiant expression.

"Why do the Hellands have theater tickets? You said it was an impromptu trip."

"I don't know," she said, flustered. I had caught her in a lie, which hadn't been difficult.

"Fine," I said. "I'll come along. I'd like to have dinner and see a play."

"They only have three tickets."

"I'll buy one at the box office."

"You're not invited!" she said in an angry huff. "We'll have dinner *tomorrow*. I'll see you later." As she turned, I took hold of her left arm, grasping her hard above the elbow and pulling her to me.

"I know you're lying," I whispered in her ear.

"Let go." She tried to pull away, but I tightened my grip.

I'd sounded angry, but mostly I was afraid and hurt. "Please don't leave me."

"Iris, let go!" she shouted, pulling free and stumbling back. Other people were staring at us, I knew.

"What's wrong with you?" she said, rubbing the pink on her arm where I'd grabbed her. If I tried again, she'd make a scene. So I let her go.

3.

When the train from Grand Central arrived at the station in Rye, I bolted through the doors and ran down the platform, then out into the street, running the two blocks to my car. Safe in the Citroën, I let go, releasing the tears I'd been holding on to.

I calmed down and wiped my eyes with Aster's handkerchief, then set it on the dashboard to dry, wanting to preserve its delicately embroidered AC. Once I felt steady enough to drive, I set off, my eyes red and glassy. I decided to go for a drive to clear my head; my confrontation with Zelie would come later, at home. Until then, I needed to stay steady.

I headed to the country club, an enormous green space that straddled a couple of other towns in Westchester County. After a day in the city, I longed for green, so I drove around the perimeter of the golf course with my window rolled down — once, then twice, inhaling the scent of imminent rain, the breeze cool against my swollen face.

I should have gone home then. I was really in no shape to be driving — fear and anger had their arms wrapped around me, squeezing me in a suffocating embrace, and everything still looked distorted, like a Van Gogh sunflower. But I didn't want to go home; I rarely did. So I turned down the road I thought would take me back to the center of Rye and to the highway, thinking about where I'd go next, up the coast as originally planned or out into the countryside. After a few minutes, I realized that somewhere I'd taken a wrong turn. The road I was on looked completely unfamiliar. I considered turning around, but Rye was small and I figured I'd eventually loop around to where I needed to go.

The first houses on the road were sprawling Victorians, but as I continued on, the houses grew newer and smaller, and soon I saw one I recognized. Then another. Then it hit me. I knew where I was. I gripped the steering wheel tighter, unsure how I'd ended up here. I pulled to the side of the road a few moments later and looked to my left into a cul-de-sac: Grouse Court.

Apparently, Appleseed Estates had a back entrance. I looked at Aster's handkerchief on the dashboard and tried to convince myself that ending up here wasn't a bad omen.

I was about to leave when a woman and three small children came out the front door of Aster's old house. My window, speckled with falling rain, didn't provide a clear-enough view from across the street so I rolled it down. The children scurried around the yard picking up toys, then took them into the open garage and set them down out of the rain. The mother, hands on hips, wore a green dress that was pleated and flared out like one of those colorful umbrellas that came with cocktails. She was giving them directions, but I couldn't hear what she was saying. She was a young brown-haired woman, as curvy in shape as Aster had been, and as I looked at her, I pretended she was actually my sister. Daphne, I'd dreamt that afternoon, was out in New Mexico, and here Aster was with her three young children.

They finished cleaning up and got in the station wagon that was parked
in the driveway, leaving the house without closing the garage. I rolled up my
window and leaned over so they wouldn't see me as they drove past.

A minute or so later, I sat up again. I took Aster's handkerchief off the
dashboard, still damp, and put it in my pocket. Then I opened the door and
crossed the road to Grouse Court, deciding on a short walk even though I
didn't have an umbrella. There was no sign of anyone around. I passed the
yellow colonial, the house where the gargoyle baby lived (*Look at that horrid
little creature,* I heard Rosalind say), although she wouldn't be a baby anymore. As I approached Aster's white four-over-four, the middle house of the
three in the cul-de-sac, the rain was changing from a sprinkle into something
heavier. I debated whether to run back to the car; summer downpours could
happen swiftly, almost violently, and I didn't want to be drenched. But Aster's opened garage was closer, and on impulse, I ran there, taking shelter.

It was a bad idea, but I did it anyway. The garage was full of boxes and
junk, leaving no room for cars. I stood at the top of the driveway just under
the overhang of the house, out of the wet. If the mother and children happened to come home, I could say that I was taking a walk and ran for cover
when it started raining. Surely they'd understand that. I didn't look suspicious in my neat blouse and cotton skirt.

I took Aster's handkerchief from my pocket and wiped my face. Aster's
handkerchief, Aster's house, Aster's sister.

The rain grew harder and louder, sounding like the sizzle in a frying pan.
I could barely see my green Citroën across the road. I turned around to look
at the garage; there were boxes labeled CHRISTMAS and CAMPING, and
behind those, some skis and fishing poles. And next to all that was the white
door that led into the house.

I'll just take a peek.

I twisted the brass knob and found the door unlocked. It opened onto a
small mudroom with an adjacent laundry room to the right. Colorful items
of children's clothing were piled on top of the washer, a few tiny socks litter-
ing the floor. To the left of the door, there was a short hallway and I tiptoed
down it.

The kitchen, still as yellow and bright as a lemon-drop candy, was extremely tidy, in contrast to the garage, and it looked as if no one lived there at all, certainly not a family with three young children. The countertops were wiped clean and everything was put away; two matching tea towels with a sunflower pattern hung from the oven door; next to the sink, there was a bud vase with a single pink carnation. I smelled something, a whiff of peanut butter and sugar. I touched the oven door, which was slightly warm. The mother had made peanut butter cookies.

It had been seven years since I'd stood in that kitchen with Aster and Rosalind while Zelie played outside with the white cat, but it seemed longer; the past was far away but also smaller somehow. I felt disoriented, the rain beating against the windows, the walls of the kitchen too yellow.

I'd made a mistake entering the house. I walked quickly back to the door that led to the garage, running my hand along the wall for support.

Outside, I rushed down the middle of the cul-de-sac to my car, no longer pretending to be a woman on a casual stroll. I was desperate to get out of there. Back in my car, feeling dizzy, I closed my eyes and rested the back of my head against the seat. This would be my last visit to Grouse Court and Appleseed Estates. I needed to look forward, not back. The past didn't want me.

I opened my eyes, the burst of rain having reduced to a patter. As I reached for the keys, I saw in the rearview mirror that a patrol car had pulled up behind me. An officer opened the door and got out, and at first I thought he must live in the house I was parked in front of, but he came to my window and rapped on it with one of his knuckles. I rolled the window down.

"Miss, will you please step out of the car? I need to ask you a few questions."

"*Me?*" I asked rather stupidly. It seemed impossible that a police officer would want to talk to me.

"Step out and show me your identification, please."

"But why?"

He gazed down at me, his cap casting part of his face in shadow. "I don't want to have to ask you a third time."

I reached for my purse and got out of the car. Up close, the officer, whose badge said SGT. QUINN, appeared to be a young man, perhaps only a few years older than I was. I handed him my license.

"Iris Chapel?" he asked, and I nodded. "Miss Chapel, would you like to tell me why you were trespassing inside that house?" He turned and pointed to Aster's house.

"I wasn't," I said, patting down my wet hair. My words were shaky and not entirely convincing. I cleared my throat. "I only stepped into the garage to escape the rain."

"A neighbor saw you go into the house. She called the station, said she's seen you parked out here many times."

"Oh." I looked to the house of the gargoyle baby; her mother was at the mailbox, surreptitiously glancing over at us.

"Well?" he said. I squirmed under the officer's downward gaze; he was at least half a foot taller than I was and much larger than he'd originally seemed, thick and muscled, with a sunburned neck and sprouts of blond hair on his neck.

"The truth is that my sister used to live in that house. She died, and I — I don't know; I suppose the house makes me feel close to her." I hoped that would be the end of it.

"Did you steal anything from the house?"

"What? No."

"Can I look inside your pocketbook?"

I hesitated for a moment, unsure if I could refuse. But if I did, it would only make me seem guilty. I handed it over, hoping he'd decide to let me go once he saw there was nothing suspicious inside, no silverware, no tangle of expensive jewelry. He pawed through the bag and handed it back to me, then went around to the other side of the car and opened the doors, then the trunk. The front and back seats, completely empty, reminded me that I'd left Zelie's Bloomingdale's bag on the train. *Serves her right,* I thought. *If she'd come with me, I wouldn't be in this mess.*

"Can I please go home?"

Sergeant Quinn shut everything, a series of slams, then came back around to my side of the car. "Afraid not. Trespassing is a serious offense. I need to take you down to the station. We'll contact Mr. Wheeler. He owns the house and will decide whether to press charges."

A half laugh of disbelief escaped from me. "Are you serious? This is all a misunderstanding. I can assure you —" I paused, since Sergeant Quinn had turned and walked back to his car, not willing to engage in conversation with me. He barked orders and I was expected to follow them obediently. "Sergeant? I can assure you this was an honest mistake." I considered mentioning my father, but I didn't want to bring him into this yet; I still thought I could wrangle my way out of it.

The officer opened the back door of his patrol car and waved me over. "We can talk about it at the station."

"I'd rather talk about it here." I stood next to my car, handbag dangling from my arm, hands clasped politely in front of me.

"You've committed a crime, Miss Chapel."

"*A crime?*"

"You can't just break into a stranger's house. It's against the law."

"I didn't *break in.*"

"If you resist coming with me now, I'll have to arrest you."

I had no choice but to follow his command. I got into the back seat of the patrol car, and he drove me out of Appleseed Estates as if I were a common criminal. My composure loosened a little as we made our way downtown, my confident facade crumbling out of fear, the fear of being arrested, of what my father would do when he found out, of being completely in the control of a strange man. I reached for the door handle, just to rest my hand on it.

Sergeant Quinn led me inside police headquarters, a drab building made of uneven pewter-colored stones, with an American flag out front soaked through with rain. The building was next to the train station, and a train was pulling away from the platform so I kept my head down in case one of my classmates had just arrived back from the city. Inside, there was no one sitting in the small waiting area, and the receptionist didn't look up as we passed by. I walked deeper into the station at the sergeant's side, and there were only a couple of men sitting at the cluster of desks in the middle of the squad room.

Down a hallway was a series of closed steel doors, and Sergeant Quinn opened the door to one of them and motioned for me to follow him inside. It looked like an interrogation room, the kind I'd seen on *Dragnet,* with a simple wooden table in the middle and a chair on each side. "This is all a mistake," I said. A person like me didn't belong in a room like that.

"Take a seat," he said, shutting the door behind him. The windowless room was dingy, the cinder-block walls painted over with white that was chipping off, the floorboards dirty. It was as chilly as a cellar.

"Are you going to arrest me?" I asked, sitting down on the freezing chair. I set my handbag on the table and pulled Aster's handkerchief from my pocket, squeezing it tightly in my hand.

"Not yet," he said, picking up the chair on his side of the table and setting it down next to me. I didn't know why he did that. He took off his hat and set it next to my handbag, then he sat down, his leg bumping mine. My leg jerked away from his involuntarily. He smiled.

"Are you nervous?" His pale blond hair was shaved at the sides but thicker up top and tousled, thanks to the removal of the hat. His face was ruddy and clean-shaven, his eyebrows blond to match his hair. "People get nervous around police," he said. "I understand." Taking off his hat had been like taking off his armor. His posture relaxed. He turned his body toward me, resting one of his arms, bent at the elbow, over the back of his chair as if we were at a bar.

"Sergeant Quinn, I want to call my father." I didn't know where my father was, but I thought Dovey could track him down.

"Chuckie," he said.

"I'm willing to sign a confession or whatever needs to be done, but I really need to speak to my father first."

"Iris — can I call you that?"

"All right."

"You don't need your father here. I can contact Mr. Wheeler, and I can probably get him to understand the situation since you seem like a nice girl.

But if you really want to involve your father in this, I'll have to take you back to the cells for now." He left the word *cells* dangling for a moment. "Do you know what kind of *ladies* we have back there? Whores. Drunks. No one classy like you. But if you want to be locked up back there with that trash, we can do that."

"I don't," I said, pleading.

"Good. That's a wise choice. You did a bad thing, and I don't want you to get in trouble for it, but I can't just let you walk out of here." He had full lips for a man, the bottom one jutting out slightly.

"I know what I did was wrong, but I was upset about my sister. I wasn't thinking clearly." There was a handprint on one of the cinder blocks, brownish, like a coffee stain in the shape of a human hand.

"I'm sorry about your sister," he said, and put his hand on my knee. At first I thought, rather foolishly, that his hand was an awkward attempt at comfort.

"I have an older sister," he said, still with his hand on my knee. "She lives with her husband and kids in Yonkers. Her husband owns a butcher shop. They live above it and it smells, you know? That metallic smell of blood."

"Chuckie," I said, about to ask again if I could call my father. I wanted to move his hand, but I worried about how he'd react. Waiting in the cells would be preferable to this. But before I could say anything, I felt his hand slide partway up my thigh. I didn't move but glanced down at the dark blue fabric of my skirt, now bunched up behind his hand. He was watching me, I could feel it, waiting to see what I'd do. When I did nothing, he began to rub his thumb back and forth over my stocking, his fingers gripping the interior of my leg.

"Maybe I won't even call Mr. Wheeler," he said. "I bet you and I can work something out."

For a moment, I froze. But then I looked in his eyes and gripped Aster's handkerchief. His eyes were a pale swimming-pool blue, translucent and clear. Beyond them was an abyss, a place where I would go and never escape. I'd disappear into the same place my older sisters had. I needed to get out. I leapt up and ran for the door, crying out for help.

"Hey, hey!" Chuckie shouted at me, as I opened the door and ran out into the squad room. An older officer, standing at the coffee station, rushed into my path.

"What's wrong, miss?" He reached out to me, but I shrunk away, stumbling backward and falling into a chair at one of the desks. I couldn't catch my breath and held my hand to my chest, trying to calm myself.

"Chief," Chuckie said. "I brought her in for trespassing and she went bananas."

"He's lying," I said, pointing a finger of accusation at him. I was still breathless, spinning, still gripped by fear. "My father is Henry Chapel. Chapel Firearms? When he finds out what you've done to me —"

"We ain't done nothing to you," Chuckie said.

"Chuck," the chief said, moving his head to the side as if to say, *Go away.* Chuckie resisted at first, his face reddening, but he did as his boss had directed.

I bent over to pick up my handkerchief, which had fallen to the floor, and put it in my pocket.

"Do you want a drink of water?" the police chief asked me.

I shook my head. "I just want to go home."

He offered to drive me back to my car, but I refused. There was no further discussion about the trespassing charge. I was free to leave.

I walked down Main Street in the rain without an umbrella, and I must have appeared a pitiful figure. A woman driving a station wagon pulled over and offered me a lift; from the back seat, two curious children peered at me through the foggy glass. I got in, generous with my thanks, and the woman drove me to my car.

Zelie wasn't at home. Dovey was distressed when she saw me, drenched and shaken from what had happened at the police station.

"Car trouble," I said politely. "I'm okay."

Dovey brought a tray to my bedroom: a glass of water and two aspirin, a bowl of soup, a mug of milky tea. "This'll warm you through," she said, and left me alone to eat at my desk. I couldn't stop thinking about Chuckie's blue eyes, the memory of which blew through me like a shivery wind. The danger Zelie was in felt more acute now; it felt closer. But I knew I couldn't allow myself to unravel as I had when my mother lived with us. I'd worked too hard to hold myself together, and for six years, I'd done it. I needed to keep vigilant so I could reason with Zelie when she came home.

But she didn't come home. Midnight passed, then one o'clock. Exhaustion overtook me and I fell asleep not knowing where she was.

4.

In the morning, I awoke with Zelie in my bed, snuggled up behind me. I sighed with relief at the warmth of her body and the touch of her hand at my waist.

She was alive. She had come home.

Since Sam had entered our lives, I could no longer take these things for granted.

I rolled over so that we were face to face. She was still asleep, her makeup from the previous day still visible but muted — black eyeliner faded to gray, a touch of pink on the apples of her cheeks. I recalled her behavior at the train station under the enormous white clock, how she'd lied to me and pulled away, how she'd been lying for almost two months. I thought of the evening I'd had after our fight.

After a few moments, she woke up and looked at me with a cold, deliberate stare, which I matched. She seemed disappointed that she'd crawled into bed with me; she usually had no memory of doing it. We were about to have a fight; I could tell by the look on her face. I waited for her to speak.

"This is how our future together would be," she said in her strained morning voice. "It's not normal."

"What's not normal?"

"Two sisters sharing the same house, the same bedroom, even the same bed." She looked at me with an expression of disgust, then rolled over and got up. She sat on the edge of her own bed, still looking at me but now with more space between us. She'd made it clear in so many ways that she craved space.

"It's better than the alternative," I said, sitting up myself and throwing off the blankets.

"Is it?" Her voice was clear now, at full volume. "What's so great about simply living? I'd rather be alive."

"Does Sam make you feel *alive?*" I couldn't avoid mentioning him any longer. "I know you've been seeing him."

"Ooh, good for you, Nancy Drew," she said, then seemed to regret it. "I'm sorry I lied to you, *I am,* but I knew you'd react poorly."

She spoke as if she'd borrowed a pair of my shoes without asking, utterly clueless to the danger she was in.

"We're just dating," she said.

"Is that so? I talked to your travel agent yesterday. She wants to know if you found your passport. You better look for it — you don't want to miss your flight to Rome on Monday."

I'd stunned her, her face revealing her shock. For once she was unable to come up with some tart response, but I was only getting started.

"What's wrong with you?" I stood up and paced angrily about the room. I ranted at her for a while, accusing her of being reckless, of being stupid.

"Are you so unhappy with your life that you'd rather die?" She was still too taken aback to respond, too startled that I'd learned of her secret plan. She just stared at me.

"*Well?*" I said, but she only looked down at the floor. I thought she might cry, but that wouldn't make me back off.

Finally, without looking up, she said, just above a whisper: "What's a life without love?"

I startled. I'd thought she would lash out and insult me. I couldn't answer her question, had no way of consoling her. I'd never been in love and never expected to be. "We'll find other ways to be fulfilled." It was all I could think of to say.

"You don't understand because you don't want what *normal* women want. It's easy for you."

"What does that mean? I'm normal," I said, even though I knew I wasn't.

"You don't seem to have any interest in men." She looked out the window. "Maybe you're like Daphne. She was never interested in men either."

"I'm not like her," I said, rather too defensively. "I just haven't allowed myself to want what I can't have." I knew, of course, that this wasn't really true. But it was what I told myself. "Normality is deadly to us. You know that."

She fell silent again, which was more irritating than if she'd screamed at me. I put on my robe, tying the sash around my waist. I enjoyed the feeling it gave me, the feeling of tightening up, of steeling myself. In reality, I felt as wobbly as gelatin. "It has to end. You know that."

"Do you ever feel like it was all a dream? Like maybe our older sisters never existed and it's always just been the two of us?"

"You know that's ridiculous," I said, though in a way I knew what she meant.

"I know it wasn't a dream, but it feels like one. It was so long ago — a different era. Maybe what happened to them won't happen to us. Mother is gone. She's the one who caused all the problems."

"She'll never be gone. She's in our blood."

Zelie bellowed a dramatic, irritated sigh. "Why do you always act so sure of everything? You don't know that what happened to them will happen to us. We don't even know why they died. You just always expect the worst. You really are the gloomiest person I've ever met." She laughed, her solemn mood from moments ago disappearing, replaced by something spiteful. "I told Sam that if I were a painter like you I'd make a portrait of you as a big gray storm cloud blocking every last bit of sunlight."

She laughed some more, and I could see the two of them together, making fun of me. I could see Sam kissing her, leading her away like Orpheus — and her falling down into the dark.

"If that's how you feel, have fun on your vacation. It'll be just like *Roman Holiday* except for the tragic ending." My rage was turning into that bruising red-purple, the kind that haunts. It scared me, and I needed to get away from her. I went to my wardrobe, put on a skirt and blouse, then looked for an overnight bag.

"We're not going on a *vacation* to Rome," Zelie said. "We're staying there."

This time I laughed. "You really are out of your mind," I said, stuffing a dress into the overnight bag. "Not to mention indecent. You want to run away with a man you've known for two months? What kind of man would ask you to do that? Did you even tell him what happened to our sisters or is that part of the thrill for him?"

"You'd like him if you got to know him."

"I'm sure. He seems like a man of great moral character."

"He's tired of Connecticut and the gun business. He wants to move to Europe for a fresh start. Can't you understand that? It's what I need too," she said, as I continued to pack, too upset to speak. "I've thought about it a lot, and I know I'll be safe with him far away from here. It's this house, this *place,* that's the danger to us. You'll see. When we're settled in Rome, you can visit us."

It scared me to hear her talk this way. She had convinced herself she'd found a loophole in her fate. "It doesn't matter where you go," I said. "It'll follow you."

"No it won't," Zelie said, her voice pleading. "Where are you *going?*"

"Upstairs to the girls' wing." I zipped my bag closed and walked out.

"Iris," she called out, annoyed. "You're not my mother!"

In the entry hall, as I headed toward the stairs, the front door beckoned. *Go,* a voice said to me. *Get out now.*

5.

It took a while for me to cool down after my argument with Zelie. I spent a couple of hours in the girls' sitting room railing against her with the windows wide open. Our whole lives I'd taken care of her. Any sane girl would have fled this place the minute she graduated high school. But I had stayed for Zelie, planned a future for us, worked toward a profession that would support us both while she did whatever she pleased. My only concern had been keeping her safe; I had never prioritized my own happiness.

Now I wondered if she'd ever planned to come with me at all or if she'd just been leading me on, placating me. I'd been in a tailspin thanks to her, and I didn't like the feeling. I couldn't control her anymore, I had to face that, but I didn't need to be at her mercy, sitting around and waiting for her to decide what her fate would be — and thus mine.

I refused to be the last sister left in this house.

The bookcase under the Annie Oakley painting was still crammed with my sisters' books, folders, and other odds and ends. I could see Rosalind's road map of America sticking out from beneath a dictionary, folded haphazardly; she'd never had any patience.

I spread it out on the coffee table as Rosalind had done during those giddy days when she was consumed with planning her honeymoon. She'd marked the route in red pen; down the East Coast all the way to North Carolina, then over to Tennessee, across the Mississippi River, through Arkansas, and finally to Texas. Midland was marked with a big red circle.

She'd had such big plans even if they were only for marriage, which was all she could imagine. But she was outside in the family plot instead.

Daphne had big plans to run away, but she drowned in the sea.

My mother had wanted a different type of life — a quiet existence with her greenhouse and her cherished plants. But she'd ended up in this house instead, married to my father with six daughters.

Why was it so hard to run away? I'd promised Calla I'd become an artist, yet I'd decided to follow a safer route by becoming a teacher — a safe, respectable profession — while doing my art on the side as a hobby. Nello said I had to fight for my art, but that's not what I was doing. I hadn't even tried to run yet, but I'd already allowed my dream to shrink.

My eyes moved across the vast continent, right to left, north to south. I didn't know a soul outside of New England, no one to take me in or lend a hand. It was daunting. Vowing to run away was easy but actually doing it was another matter.

I considered closing my eyes and pointing to a random place, like someone opening the Bible at random and looking for a message. But my eyes were drawn back to the red circle on Texas, and to the left of that, I saw New Mexico. I thought of the paintings I'd seen in the gallery the day before, those brilliant landscapes that glowed with light. I thought of the rose-petal painting, how it had looked so much like Daphne's work. The "anonymous" painter mentioned on the placard was undoubtedly a woman, and my fantasy of that artist actually being Daphne returned; I smiled for the first time that day. I loved imagining her in that life.

If any of my older sisters could have survived, it would have been Daphne, who'd had no interest in weddings or babies, which seemed to be how things went wrong for the women in my family. She and Veronica were the only two women I'd ever known who led a different type of life — *subversive* was the word, though I wouldn't have known that term then. But Daphne was gone and Veronica had become Mrs. Clyde H. Bassett — in a way, she was gone too.

My own planned future — modest, pocket-size, working as a teacher and living as a spinster with my sister, who would be perpetually unhappy but alive — was slipping away from me as well. But I didn't know if I would miss it. Zelie was trying to cut me out of her life, and perhaps she was right — it would be better if we each forged our own paths. But I had never really contemplated other options. As a Chapel girl, I knew I could never lead a normal life, yet I'd been aiming for as close to normal as I could get. The more I thought about that, the more I started to wonder why it was necessary. Why not be bold? Nello saw something in my work. What if I believed in myself as he seemed to believe in me?

Daphne may have died, but maybe, just maybe, the life I'd imagined for her could be mine.

The idea was too big, too exhilarating, to be considered in the girls' wing. I drove to the beach, craving the *neverendingness* of the sea, which in a way was like a highway leading anywhere in the world. I mingled with the summer crowds, holding my shoes as I walked across the sand, weaving through blankets and colorful striped umbrellas. I tried to carry myself like someone else, the "anonymous" who'd painted the rose petals. Maybe that was the secret to running away, to freedom — becoming someone else.

Under the shadow of a lighthouse, a towering red beacon, I ate a fried-clam sandwich and drank lemonade and thought about packing up the car and leaving for New Mexico. I'd have to pay for my own schooling and everything else, something I'd never had to worry about before, but I was willing to take on the challenge. It seemed now that my whole life had been leading to this moment — it seemed inevitable. Just thinking about leaving had lifted a burden from me, as if the wedding cake and everyone contained within it, even Belinda's ghosts, had been sitting on top of me my whole life, and now, miraculously, I'd dug my way out. I could breathe.

When I got back home, I couldn't bear the thought of going inside straightaway, of being enclosed again. I never could. It was still light, so I headed to the meadow with the saltwater taffy I'd bought at the beach stuffed into my skirt pockets. I sat in the grass for a while, shoes off, unwrapping candy after candy and eating them until there were none left. I couldn't sit still, so I began pulling up daisies and mindlessly braiding the stems together.

Eventually, I walked back to the house with the daisy chain in hand. The bedroom I'd shared with Zelie was empty. I knew she was out with Sam, but I hadn't given up hope that she would change her mind and run away with me instead of him. I tied the daisy chain into a crown and set it on her pillow. Then I went back upstairs.

6.

That night, lying in my old bed in the room with the irises and witch hazel painted on the walls, I remembered how difficult it was to be in the girls' wing. Zelie and I had moved out years ago with good reason. After what had happened to our sisters, it was an impossible place to be. Although I visited briefly every morning, my visits were precisely that: brief.

As I attempted to sleep that night, I felt as if I were in a museum, and it smelled that way too, slightly musty. There were artifacts everywhere, evidence of the people who had left them behind. The evidence of who I'd been was there too — being in the girls' wing brought up all those feelings again, those memories. I felt a darkness enclose me, a black bird tucking me under its wing. Something was tugging at me, trying to pull me back to the haunted girl I used to be. And it managed to succeed.

I heard footsteps in the hallway and a laugh coming from the girls' sitting room. I swear I could smell Aster's English lavender, then, more troubling, the scent of roses. I wanted to flee, to run back downstairs to the bedroom I shared with Zelie, but I wouldn't give her the satisfaction of that. And so I endured, hour after hour, drifting to sleep only to be woken up by some startling sensation. I thought I heard someone call my name: *Iris.*

But no one was there.

At dawn, having finally fallen into a deeper if not restful sleep — I felt I was clinging to a rocky cliff at the edge of a waterfall, and in my mind, I kept repeating: *Don't fall, don't fall in!* — I woke up.

"Hello?" I said, certain that someone was there. The girls' wing was completely quiet, penetrated only by the dimmest morning light through the curtains, yet I sensed a presence.

"Hello?" I said again, but there was no one. I set my head back down on the pillow and closed my eyes.

Then I heard it, a voice whispering in my ear.

Something terrible is going to happen.

7.

I raced through the darkened corridors of the second floor, reaching the stairs and taking them two at a time. The front door was wide open, and I welcomed the light after my torturous night — the bright, blazing sun.

"Zelie!" I called out, hoping it wasn't too late to save her. Outside, wearing only my nightgown, no shoes on my feet, I turned to my right and saw her. She was loading suitcases into the trunk of the old Hudson. She was freshly coiffed and scented, her hair pinned up with tendrils falling artfully to her shoulders. She wore a dress with daisies embroidered around the hem, a strand of green beads around her neck.

"I wanted to be gone before you were awake," she said, when she saw me, clearly annoyed by my being there. "It would have been easier that way."

She'd left the keys on the roof of the car, and I walked over while she was busy with her bags and grabbed them. "Your prince can't bother to pick you up?"

"I told him not to come here. Sam's sister will have someone bring the car back later."

"You can't even drive."

"I can drive well enough. Give me the keys."

I refused to give them to her, clenching them tightly against my chest. "Why are you doing this?"

"I love him."

"You love him the way Rosalind loved Roderick. He's just an excuse to get away. But you won't actually get anywhere."

"I'm going, Iris." She'd shut the trunk and was holding out her hand for the keys.

"You never planned to run away with me, did you?"

Her normally expressive features were pulled tight, as if by a drawstring. "You're impossible. You're always telling me what to do, spying on me. I know you mean well, but I can't live that way."

"Without me, you won't live at all." I was grasping. "Please. I told Mother I'd take care of you."

"Sam will keep me safe. What happened to our sisters isn't going to happen to me."

"You can't actually believe that," I said, but she seemed to have convinced herself. This was the moment I'd always feared would come, but now that it was here, it didn't seem real. She'd said I was the gloomiest person she'd ever met, but I was, at heart, an optimist. She'd clearly given up on herself, but I hadn't. "Zelie, no," I pleaded.

"Nothing you can say will change my mind."

It still didn't seem real. It couldn't be. "Is this how you want things to end between us — the two of us arguing over a man? He's not worth it. You might as well point a gun at your head and pull the trigger. There's no difference."

She showed no visible emotion. The dream of a man, which for her was the key to the future she longed to have, had her firmly in its grip. I could have stood there arguing with her. I could have thrown myself in front of her car, or tried to drag her inside the house and lock her up. But I knew, in the end, it wouldn't matter. Despite the warning I'd heard that morning, weariness washed over me. If she stayed, I could see what our future would look like. I'd have to chase her relentlessly, like a hunter; we'd fight all the time, growing increasingly bitter and resentful; and I'd always worry that I was going to lose her. Every day I'd gulp down anxiety as if it were air.

"You're willing to die for him, so just go," I said. It hurt to say it. "It's time we went our separate ways anyway. See how well you do without me." I dropped the car keys in her hand.

"I'll do just fine," she said.

"If you come back, I won't be here. I'm leaving today." By the end of the week, I'd be in New Mexico, in the vibrant landscapes I'd seen in the gallery.

She pressed her lips together, holding in whatever she wanted to say. And that was it.

I can recall the next moment so vividly that it's like I'm watching it in a film — the driveway lined with daylilies and zinnias and a vast purpling of vervain; a chorus of warblers in the trees; the darting silhouettes of passing butterflies and birds; and above our heads, a tint of white and cerulean without a cloud to be seen.

And I see myself from the outside, standing in front of the house, watching Zelie's car as it heads down the driveway and disappears from view.

8.

In the bedroom we had shared, I dressed quickly, then opened the wardrobe and took out several outfits. There wouldn't be much room in the Citroën even without Zelie. I packed a couple of bags, squeezing in as much as I could; I'd have to buy whatever else I might need in New Mexico. This reminded me that I needed to stop at the bank on my way out of town to empty out my account.

My departure had taken on great urgency. I placed *The White Iris* in the front pouch of my largest pocketbook, a brown boat-size leather contraption I'd bought on sale at Bonwit's. I carried the purse to my father's den and took a framed photograph of our family off his desk. We were standing outside the hotel on Terrapin Cove in July 1949, days before Aster met Matthew. It was a rare photo of the eight of us together, and I set it carefully inside the bag.

My next stop was Belinda's rooms. She had her most treasured possession, her brooch, with her at the sanitarium, but I took the stuffed wren off her nightstand and wrapped it in one of her handkerchiefs, which was embroidered with a little bee. In her sitting room, I pulled one of her spirit journals at random off her shelf.

As I entered the girls' wing, I recalled my mother's voice from earlier that morning, warning of the *something terrible*. "I tried," I said, as I looked over Aster's vanity. "Honestly, I did."

I took a small bottle of Aster's English lavender perfume and her hairbrush, which still had some strands of her hair tangled in it. From Rosalind, the coral cameo ring and the tortoiseshell combs. In Calla and Daphne's bedroom, I took the book that Calla had written her poems in as well as the moonstone ring we'd bought together at Bloomingdale's, which she'd been wearing when she died. I'd already taken Daphne's painting, but I grabbed one of her pulpy novels from her shelf: *Lady Don't Leave Me*. It seemed fitting.

I turned around at the end of the hallway before I went back downstairs. *Don't look back,* the adage went, but I knew this place would never be truly behind me. This was our Elysium, as Calla had said, or maybe it was the place one goes beforehand.

We'll wait for you.

I practically tiptoed through the entry hall with my suitcase and handbag. Dovey and Mrs. O'Connor had started their day and I could hear them chatting in the kitchen. I didn't want them to notice me leaving. I shut the front door quietly behind me, not looking back this time.

As I pulled away from the house and headed toward the main road, my eyes were wet with tears. I rested my hand on my bag, feeling my sisters, trying to calm myself. I wasn't leaving them; they were coming with me.

I approached the end of the driveway, which connected to the main road; I slowed down before the left turn but didn't fully stop. No one was coming from the left; the view to the right was blocked by trees and a slight curve in the road. We usually inched out before making a left turn, but that morning, in my haste, I didn't. I barreled along, foot on the accelerator, wanting to put the wedding cake far behind me. *Run!* my mother had said, and I was finally doing it; I didn't want to slow down now.

I was in such a rush that I didn't see the truck until it was about to crash into me.

About the aftermath of the accident, I remember only one thing: The sound of strange men talking and shouting. The last thing I thought I would hear in this world was the sound of their voices, and it somehow seemed wrong that this was how I should end.

Night-Blooming Iris

1957

I.

It's easy to lose track of time in a hospital when you have a bandaged head, a braced neck, and veins heavy with narcotics — everything goes fuzzy and out of focus — but it had been at least twenty-four hours since my accident and Zelie hadn't come to see me.

"Where is she?" I asked my father, when he finally arrived, fresh off the plane from San Francisco. He sat by my bedside and patted my hand gently, an unexpected thing for him to do since he was rarely demonstrative, physically or otherwise.

"Is Zelie coming?"

I wasn't thinking clearly, and some aspects of the accident and its aftermath were a blur, but I remembered everything that had happened before that. Unfortunately, I remembered it all quite clearly.

"Did you track her down?" I asked him. "Tell her to come visit."

"You're not allowed any visitors besides me. Rest now." He stayed until I fell asleep and didn't return for days.

• • •

As far as car accidents go, it could have been worse. I suffered a concussion, bruising all over but no broken bones, and a laceration in my left arm that spilled so much blood I needed a transfusion. The doctors said I was lucky, that given the speed and size of the truck, I could have been killed. They didn't know at first how serious my head injury was so I was kept under close observation.

When I wasn't sleeping, I watched the door. Anytime someone came in, I was disappointed it wasn't her. I was hazy from the drugs, but I could feel myself being examined and prodded; I lay there passively as my blood filled glass tubes. A candy striper brought me a vase of sunflowers one morning, which reminded me of the Van Gogh exhibit. There was a card with the flowers.

Dear Iris,

We hope you're restored to good health soon!

Sincerely,
Your friends at Grace Street Teacher's College

The candy striper set the flowers on my bedside table; it hurt to turn my head to look at them, but knowing they were next to me made the room feel brighter. I appreciated the care from my classmates and professors, but I couldn't help but feel abandoned by my family. My father hadn't returned and Zelie hadn't sent word, not even a card. If something had happened to her, I was sure my father would have told me. I supposed she was still mad at me, which seemed petty given my accident. But Zelie could be petty.

"Do you know where my father is?" I asked a nurse a couple of days later. "Have you seen my sister?"

"I'm sure you'll have visitors soon," she said, smiling out of pity. During visiting hours, I could see people walking in the hallway with flowers, teddy bears, brightly wrapped packages.

"I'd like to make a telephone call."

"Maybe later," the nurse said. "The doctor wants you to rest now."

I slept for a while, and when I woke up, a candy striper gave me a canvas bag that had been dropped off for me. Inside, I found a change of clothes, a tin of Mrs. O'Connor's cinnamon stars, a few magazines, a jar of my face cream, and a well-worn copy of *Jane Eyre*. I knew Dovey had left the bag, though I wished she would have stayed to visit. I opened the book and saw the name Calla Chapel written inside the cover. It reminded me of Daphne's old joke about Joan Eyre, the unhappy housewife of suburban Connecticut. I laughed, the first time I'd truly laughed in weeks.

One afternoon — I'd completely lost track of the days by this point — a police officer came to see me. He wanted to ask me about my accident. I didn't like being alone in my room with him even though he was old and jowly and seemed slow. I kept my hand on the call button the whole time he was there, just in case.

"Do you remember the accident, Miss Chapel?" He had a pad of paper and a tiny pencil in his hand, poised to write down what I said.

"I remember the truck crashing into me. After that, I must have blacked out."

"The truck driver said you turned out in front of him without even looking. Do you remember that?"

I did remember but didn't say so. I didn't want to be declared a reckless driver and have my license taken away. "No, I have a head injury."

"Yes, your father told me," the officer said, and he wrote something on his pad. "There was a man on a motorcycle behind the truck. He was a medic in the war, lucky for you. He confirmed the truck driver's version of events."

I hadn't seen the man on the motorcycle, but he must have been one of the voices I'd heard. "I'm a very careful driver."

"Is that so?" the policeman said sarcastically, closing his pad and putting it in his pocket. "I'll be writing you a citation, Miss Chapel. Feel free to appeal." He touched the brim of his hat, then walked to the door.

"What about my car?"

"Damaged beyond repair," he said. "It's a shame; it was a pretty car. Best to be more careful from now on."

When he left, I mourned the Citroën, my shiny green goddess car. It had never been just a car to me; it had been my means of escape. I recalled those fleeting moments heading down the driveway when I thought I was finally free, then — well, I only had to look down at my bandaged arm to remind me of what happened next.

Running away, as I had suspected, wasn't an easy thing to do; if it was, more women would do it. I wondered if my accident was a sign. If so, I was afraid to know what it meant.

2.

At noon the next day, I waited for my father to pick me up outside the hospital. I'd been cleared for release, the doctors concluding that I'd experienced only a concussion and not a more serious head injury. The candy striper had pushed me out in a wheelchair and offered to wait with me, but I assured her I was all right on my own. I sat on a stone bench to the right of the entrance next to a bed of petunias and marigolds, and for the first time in days, I was able to inhale the earthy air and clear my lungs of the sterility of the hospital ward.

My father pulled up in his black sedan almost twenty minutes late. He left the car idling, not bothering to get out and assist me. I arranged myself in the front seat next to him, the canvas bag at my feet, and we drove off in silence. Returning home, I couldn't help but feel defeated. My plan to run away had failed and I didn't know where Zelie was.

The hospital was located in Upper Seward just blocks from the Seward School for Girls, which my sisters and I had attended. We passed by the school, with its expansive lawn and red-sandstone building, a clock tower looming over the entrance. Then we descended into Lower Seward down a steep hill; my father still hadn't said anything. Whenever we stopped at a traffic light, he turned to look out his window.

"Is something wrong?" I asked, when we were stopped on Main Street in Lower Seward. I wondered if he knew I had been in the process of running away when I had the accident.

"It's been a difficult week," he said, as if it hadn't been for me too.

It was a peculiar journey. He seemed agitated, and I was apprehensive about returning home. On the road outside the wedding cake, I flinched at the scene of my accident. There were tire marks on the pavement and a few small bits of broken glass in the dirt at the side of the road.

"This is where it happened," I said to my father, and he nodded. He turned up the driveway, and when the house came into view, I inhaled a quick, sharp breath.

My father guided me up the steps and through the front door into the parlor; it was exactly how he used to maneuver Belinda around. "Don't make a fuss, I'm fine," I said, jerking my arm away from him.

"Sit down." He pointed to the sofa. "There are things we need to discuss."

He didn't explain and excused himself, telling me to stay put. When he returned a little while later, Dovey came in behind him carrying the silver tea service.

"Thank you for packing that bag for me," I said.

She nodded and smiled as she set the tray on the coffee table, but she didn't look at me. After she left, my father took his seat and poured us each a cup of tea, setting mine on the table in front of me.

"Is Zelie at home? She can't still be with Sam?" I asked, becoming anxious.

"Sam Colt is dead."

I was too shocked to say anything at first. "*Dead?* That's impossible." I recalled Sam in the parlor, admiring the *Chapel '70* poster, flirting with Zelie.

"He was a dishonorable man who chose a coward's death."

My father always referred to suicides as cowards' deaths despite manufacturing and selling an instrument that made killing oneself remarkably easy.

"But why?"

"He wasn't what you'd call a responsible man. A bit of a bon vivant, according to his family." My father pursed his lips in disgust. "Let's not dwell on him. Suffice it to say, he decided to take his own life."

"I can't believe it," I said. "Zelie must be devastated. Where is she?"

He stared down at his tea and attempted to say something, then paused. He appeared upset, and it didn't seem to be about Sam.

Something was wrong, I realized then. I stood up quickly, holding the arm of the sofa to steady myself. "What happened?" I asked, but as I watched him, I suddenly knew. I rushed out of the parlor to the front door, ran down the steps, and went around the side of the house while my father shouted at me to come back inside.

I reached the gate of the family plot and held on to the iron bars. There were the four white stones lined up in a row: Aster, Rosalind, Calla, Daphne. Next to Daphne's stone was something else, a fresh mound of earth. No headstone, just a wooden stake stabbed into the ground surrounded by a panoply of fresh flowers.

In the words of Emily Dickinson: *The Horror welcomes her, again.*

3.

I have no memory of what happened immediately after that, but I must have carried on and made quite a scene. An ambulance eventually came, that part I remember. I was strapped to a gurney and drugged. I woke up back at the hospital, eyes fluttering open in confusion over where I was and what had happened. People were talking to me — men's voices — but I didn't understand what they were saying. They might as well have been birds, warbling and screeching, only communicating with one another.

Finally, something broke through.

"Your sister is dead," a doctor said. He was staring down at me; behind his head, a burning orb of light. "Do you understand that your sister is dead?"

"Which one?"

4.

I won't relive the next few days, what I can remember of them. There's far too much grief here, and I fear that continuing to write about it cheapens it in some way, as if it can be described, as if the twenty-six letters of the alphabet can contain it, make it presentable for consumption. I've never been fond of letters, and writing in this diary hasn't changed that. They're a terrible way to express oneself.

The pain I felt over Zelie was worse than the pain I felt over my other sisters combined. This might seem unfair — a sister is a sister, after all, and I loved every one of mine dearly — but we were *IrisandZelie*. When we were being split apart, I'd been unaware, lying in a hospital bed bandaged and drugged, oblivious to the fact that the worst thing that would ever happen to me was unfolding out of view.

After a few days, once I'd grown calm enough to be unstrapped from the bed, stable enough for them to ease me off the tranquilizers, I was transferred to another part of the hospital.

An orderly pushing me in a wheelchair delivered me to my room in the women's quarters of the psychiatric unit. I was perfectly capable of walking myself, but I didn't mind being wheeled around, an act of physical surrender. I didn't scream or protest when we arrived at the locked unit, but felt a sense of acceptance, as if this had been my destination all along.

My room was even more spartan than a regular hospital room, with a single bed, a desk and chair, a bureau, and a small two-seat sofa near the window. There were no pictures, no decoration, just the white walls, the scuffed brown of the worn wooden furniture, and the pale peach fabric of the sofa. My father was waiting for me there, sitting at the desk, but I didn't acknowledge him. I climbed out of the wheelchair into bed, curling on my side away from him. When he spoke to me, I ignored him, and he eventually went away.

I was angry that he hadn't told me about Zelie as soon as it happened, that he hadn't waited to hold the funeral until I could be there. He deprived me of seeing her one last time, of placing a crown of daisies on her head; there'd been no one there to mourn her except for him and his mourning had never been enough. He claimed that he hadn't wanted to upset me while I was recovering from my injuries and that the doctors had agreed, but I knew it was because he didn't want to manage the burden of my grief. He'd put me off until later, and the bill had come due, and I didn't want to talk to him.

5.

"How about Lorraine?"

A woman's voice woke me up. I opened my eyes to see a nurse opening the curtains and brightening the room. On my desk was a tray with steaming coffee, scrambled eggs, and toast. "My name isn't Lorraine," I said. "I'm Iris."

The nurse came toward my bed. She was heavily pregnant, her belly stretching the white fabric of her uniform. "I'm considering Lorraine if it's a girl," she said, tapping on her tummy. "What do you think?"

"Lorraine is fine," I said, not caring what she named her baby.

"Fine isn't good enough," she said with a sigh. "She'll be called this name every day of her life. I need something better than just *fine*." She pulled back my blanket and motioned for me to get up. "If it's a boy, he'll be Leroy Brewer Jr. That's not *my* choice, but my husband is insisting. You know men. Always wanting a little clone of themselves."

"Uh-huh."

"Need any help?" she asked, as my bare feet touched the cool linoleum. I shook my head.

She waited as I went to the bathroom. When I came out, she was arranging the breakfast items on my desk. "Hurry before it gets cold," she said, then she sat on the sofa and watched me eat. She had olive skin and dark hair pulled back into a tight bun. I couldn't tell her ethnicity and stole glances at her as I ate, trying to figure her out.

"You can call me Brewer," she said. "Not Nurse Brewer, I'm only an aide. They say I have to quit soon because of the baby." She rested her hand on her belly. "How about Elizabeth, like the queen? Lots of nicknames there: Liz-zie, Betty, Betsy, Beth."

"Elizabeth is fine," I said.

She frowned. "You're hard to please." She saw that I was finished with my breakfast and stood up with great difficulty, coming over and stacking the dishes on the tray. "If you don't mind my saying so, you don't look like you belong here, honey." She lifted the tray, balancing it on her belly. "If I were you, I'd get along nicely so they'll let you leave."

A psychiatrist arrived a while later. I was sitting on the sofa reading *Jane Eyre,* having picked up where I left off, though my whole world had turned upside down since I'd begun reading it. Someone, Dovey or my father, had delivered the canvas bag with my books and magazines, a fresh tin of cookies, and art supplies this time, clearly assuming I'd be here for a while.

The doctor came in without being invited and closed the door behind him, a privilege only he had — I had to keep it open at all times. The door had a window in it, with a view to the hallway, and the lack of privacy was re-assuring. I didn't want to be shut in a room with this man.

"I'm Dr. Westgate," he said, and I reluctantly set down my book and allowed him to shake my hand. He set himself up at my desk, spreading his files and papers around, scanning various documents before saying anything else to me. I'd never met a psychiatrist before, and he wasn't what I'd pic-tured — younger, blondish, and clean-cut, wearing a tweed suit with a dark green tie. He offered up the kind of well-mannered handsomeness that Aster and Rosalind would have brought home on a date.

"So, Miss Chapel," he said, turning the chair from the desk toward me on the sofa so we were face to face. "Iris." He crossed his legs, a pad of paper balanced on his lap. He spoke with a low, soft voice rather than the usual au-thoritarian tones of a doctor. "How are you feeling today?"

I felt like a fish cut open, its guts spilling out, but I only said: "Fine." He nodded and smiled, trying to put me at ease, but that wasn't going to hap-pen. I didn't like psychiatrists despite having never met one. Psychiatrists had taken my mother away from me. My father might have delivered her to them, but it was their choice to keep her locked up, punishing her with a life sentence.

"You've had a rough few days and I'm sorry for that. Tell me, have you had any thoughts of hurting yourself?"

I could have refused to answer his questions, but Brewer's advice had stuck with me. I'd be better off if I tried to get along.

"No."

"I want you to be completely honest with me. Anything you tell me is confidential."

"I don't want to hurt myself," I said, which was the truth. I didn't have the energy for it besides.

"Good," he said, appearing to trust my word. "Your father was very worried about your reaction to Hazel's death."

I must have shrieked and screamed just like Belinda, and that would have terrified him. I could imagine him running for the telephone, eager for me to be taken away.

"He'd lied to me about her, and when I found out the truth, he couldn't control me," I said. "He hates not being in control."

"Do you think that's why he wanted you admitted to the psychiatric unit — as an act of control?"

"I don't know why I'm here."

"He worries that you might not be able to cope with this latest tragedy. He fears that you might become —"

"As crazy as my mother?"

"Do you think your mother is crazy?"

"No, but everyone else does."

"I don't think you're crazy, Miss Chapel, and I don't like that word. But your father feels — and I agree — that you should be evaluated. You've suffered tragedy upon tragedy, and that's too much for anyone to bear."

"He seems to be doing fine."

"I doubt he's fine, but in any case, you're a young woman. Women experience things differently. And given your mother's history, I think being here will be beneficial to you. All right?"

I shrugged. I didn't like being in the hospital, but I knew being at home — being the last sister left in the house — would have been worse.

After he left with a promise to return again in the morning, I sat very still in my room until Brewer brought in my lunch. She didn't linger this time as she was busy with other duties, and I almost missed her nonstop chatting. I ate my sandwich standing at the window and looking out at the lawn and the grove of trees just beyond it.

When Brewer came to collect my lunch tray, she convinced me to join her and a group of patients in the TV room. We walked together down the wing to a sitting room with sofas and chairs. The interior was as austere as my room, with the same colorless tattered furniture, including a few hulking sofas faded to gray.

There were about ten women in the room watching television. Many of them were older, but there was one girl my age, who I would later learn from Brewer had drowned her baby in a toilet bowl. They all watched the television quietly, and I could tell they were lost in a haze of medication. Brewer pointed out an empty chair for me, but I waved her off and returned to my room.

If I'd been at home, I would have taken a walk in the woods or gone to the meadow. But in the hospital I was trapped. From the canvas bag, I removed a sketch pad and charcoal pencils. I stood at the window again, pencil in hand, hoping for inspiration from the nature I could see. But with a pane of glass in between, I got nothing.

I turned and looked at the blank white wall to the left of the desk on the opposite side of the room from my bed. An enormous canvas. Without really thinking about it, I began to sketch a branch of blooming witch hazel on it. From memory, I copied the one Belinda had painted on the wall in the bedroom I'd shared with Zelie, the room we'd abandoned after Daphne died.

The branch kept me busy; the wall was much more difficult to draw on than a sheet of paper; it required more pressure and the patience to go over every line several times. When I finished the witch hazel, I drew an aster, then a rose, then a calla lily and a daphne flower, and finally an iris. Each flower was about the size of my head at eye level. I enjoyed sketching so much that for a while I forgot where I was.

"I don't think they're going to like what you're doing," Brewer said, when she came in with my dinner. I thought of what Belinda had said during our last visit: *What more can anyone do to me, blossom? This is the last stop.* It seemed there was plenty more they could do to *me* — padded rooms, straps, electroshock therapy. But in that moment, I just didn't care.

The next morning, Dr. Westgate arrived not long after breakfast. He dashed right to the desk, dropping his papers and files onto it; he was in such a rush to sit down that he didn't notice the flowers on the wall. The desk faced the adjacent wall, and he turned the chair sideways so he could face me as I sat on the sofa. He was wearing his tweed suit again and another green tie, this one a lighter shade. There was a stain on his shoulder, what appeared to be a bit of baby spit-up. I looked him over, eager for other details that would reveal his domestic life, but aside from the stain, he was freshly pressed and spotless. He must have had a wife who was fastidious, a doctor's wife, like Veronica had recently become.

"Iris, I'd like to explain what's going to happen over the next few days," he said, leaning toward me slightly, hands on his knees, an attempt at acting casual. No crossed arms and stern gaze for him. "We're going to have a series of conversations so I can assess your mental health. When I have all the information I need, I'll make a decision about what should happen next, whether you'll be released to go home or whether you'll stay here or be transferred to another facility. Do you understand?"

I nodded. Each of my possible fates was behind a closed door, and I didn't know which one I wanted to open. It wasn't up to me, anyway.

"Very good." He sat back and crossed his legs, picking up his pad and pen. "The loss of your sister Hazel, taken on its own, is a serious traumatic event for you, as it would be for anyone. But this is the fifth death of a sibling you've endured and that's —" He shook his head, a pained look on his face. Perhaps being a father to the spitting baby had made him more sensitive to the thought of losing a child. "That's —"

Words, letters — they were insufficient at times like these.

"You have my condolences," he said finally.

I nodded for him to move along. Years of medical school, and he spoke like a card stuck in a bouquet from a flower shop.

"I'd like to discuss what's just occurred, Hazel's death, in the context of what happened to your other sisters. I think it's important to start at the beginning. Who was the first to die?"

I was about to say Aster, which seemed like the obvious answer, but then I wondered if it was more accurate to say that my grandmother Rose was the first to die, or her mother, or her mother's mother? I realized that I didn't know where the story actually began. I didn't even know what the story was, not really. None of it had ever made sense.

As I thought about whether I wanted to open up to him, the feeling I'd had the day before returned: I didn't care what happened to me. Maybe being completely honest with him would make my situation worse, or maybe the truth would somehow free me. Either way, I was ready to let it all out.

"Aster was my first sister to die," I said. "But I don't know if what happened to her was the beginning." I told him it really began with Belinda, and Rose before her, and Dollie and Alma.

"I'd like to hear it all," he said, so we spent the whole day talking about Belinda and the women who came before her, all those motherless daughters. We talked about how Belinda had heard her mother screaming from the moment of her birth and still did — a distant roar that had never left her. I told him that she'd never wanted to be married and about the rose smell; I explained her visions of the Chapel victims and her prediction of the terrible thing that no one believed but me.

"Why do you think you're the only one who believed her?" Dr. Westgate asked.

"Everyone always said it's because I'm like her, but I don't think that's it. We aren't alike, really, at least in our personalities. We're actually quite different."

"Then what's the reason?"

"My sisters never listened to what she had to say."

"But you did?"

"Yes."

"And you believed her?"

"I came to believe her because I saw things. Experienced things. And then she was right, so why shouldn't I have believed her after that?"

"What kind of things have you seen?"

I told him about the voices and the headless bride. "I don't know if it was real or —" I didn't want to say that I'd imagined it. I didn't think that was true. "Maybe seeing or hearing things is a form of intuition."

"Tell me more about that."

"Sometimes I know things, like my mother does, and maybe seeing or hearing things is my mind's way of making sure I don't ignore them."

"Did any of your sisters ever see or hear things?"

"I don't think so. They closed off that part of themselves." He asked me to explain what I meant by that, so I went further. "I told you, sometimes I know things, like my mother does. She passed this on to me, and maybe to them as well, but they were never open to experiencing it. As I said, they never listened to her."

"Why not?"

"My mother can't communicate in a normal way. She doesn't have the language to say what she needs to say. So she expresses herself differently and they didn't understand her."

"Your mother communicates by screaming at spirits and sharing premonitions?"

"That's not exactly how I would put it." I thought for a moment about what I should say, how I should describe it. "Women aren't always believed."

"That's true."

"It's easier to say that women like my mother are crazy. Then you don't have to listen to them. And so maybe in a way she became crazy. Maybe she could communicate only by screaming."

I thought of the abstract paintings by the women in the exhibit, the colors and shapes and strokes meant to represent emotions, the unconscious. That's perhaps what my mother had been trying to do — to express the inexpressible using the only kind of language that was available to her, a more feminine kind of language that women were forced to use. I tried to explain this to the doctor.

"I see," he said. "And this is a language your sisters ignored?"

"Ignored and belittled. My father told them not to believe her. Everyone in my family saw her as an embarrassment."

"But not you?"

"Not when it mattered, no."

"And now you're the only sister left. Do you see a connection there?"

"Yes."

"How so?"

"I believed her when she said we were in danger."

We talked through lunch and quit just before dinner, which left me exhausted. That evening I continued to draw flowers on the wall, sketching more blooms and connecting them to the earth with branches and roots. I drew a snake in the grass for Belinda, like the snake she'd painted on the wall behind her wardrobe. Dr. Westgate didn't take note of my drawings again the next day; he continued to sit with his back to them. We spoke about Aster, and Matthew, and Belinda's warning. I told him how I'd tried to stop the wedding and been banished from the ceremony, about the way that Aster had died, the howling and laughing, the broken glass. That night I drew ten more asters on the wall, and when the doctor came in the next day, we talked about Rosalind. I told him about *Chapel '70* and Roderick in his cowboy hat, Palomino Road, Belinda's renewed prediction of the *something terrible,* the disastrous Easter dinner. I stressed to Dr. Westgate that both Aster and Rosalind had hated me when they died.

"They saw our mother as a madwoman, and by extension, me too. But we were only telling them the truth."

"People often resist the truth," he said, and I nodded in agreement, thinking back to my last conversation with Zelie on that terrible morning.

That night I drew roses all over the wall, garlands of roses, the forbidden flower, and the next day we talked about Calla. I told Dr. Westgate about my day with her in New York, and how we'd tried to find her that night she'd gone out with Teddy but couldn't save her.

I shouldn't have been so unguarded with the doctor, but once I started to tell the story, I couldn't stop or censor myself. My father hadn't allowed us to talk about what had happened to my sisters; it had become taboo, and while Zelie and I shared memories with each other, we only discussed their deaths vaguely, in side steps. The truth had lived inside me for years, and it had festered. Talking to the doctor was like expelling something, like having the poison sucked out of a snakebite. Aster and Rosalind hadn't died of the flu, I told him, and Calla's cause of death wasn't unknown. We all knew how and why they had died, and that was why my father had kept Zelie and me away from young men — harder to do with Zelie than it had been with me, clearly.

Daphne's story, of course, was different. I told him how she had died of a broken heart, intoxicated and swimming out to sea until she was lost. That night I continued drawing flowers, standing on the chair to reach up toward the ceiling. When I had only one charcoal pencil left, I drew the forest in the corner, just as my mother always had.

I was finished. The next day, the last day of my assessment, we were going to talk about Zelie.

After breakfast, I read *Jane Eyre* until the doctor arrived. When he came, he finally took notice of the flowers on the wall. "What's this?" he asked, and I wanted to chide him for his lack of observational skills.

I told him about the walls in the girls' wing, which Belinda had painted with flowers to match our names, and the dark forests always lurking in the corner.

"Do you miss home?" he asked.

I shrugged. I wasn't sure what *home* meant to me anymore. Without my sisters, the wedding cake was just a building. I couldn't imagine going back there.

He arranged himself at the desk again. "Today is going to be difficult," he said, turning his chair to me.

"Every day has been difficult."

"Yes, of course. What I mean is that I'd like to discuss Hazel today. And you don't have any distance from her and her death as you do with your other sisters."

Hazel. Calling her that just showed that he didn't know her, that she might as well have been a historical figure in a textbook, like Joan of Arc or Cleopatra.

"I'd like to discuss her death, Iris, if you're able to."

We'd worked our way through my sisters, starting with *A* and arriving at *Z*. It wouldn't have been fair to leave her out despite how much I didn't want to talk about her.

"Where should I begin?"

"Tell me about the months leading up to her death."

I started at the obvious place. "Everything changed when she graduated from high school."

I told him about the picnic where Florence had revealed her engagement, how Zelie had become depressed after that, facing a future that was the opposite of what she wanted. "Moving away with me, living as two old maids —I thought she'd accepted that as our fate, but it turns out for her that this was a fate worse than death."

"How did that make you feel?"

"Hurt. I worked so hard for years to plan a future for us, and she had played along, but in reality, she'd never been planning to go away with me."

"I can understand why you feel hurt."

"It doesn't matter how I feel. It was my job to take care of her and I failed."

"And whose job was it to take care of you?"

"After Aster died, there was no one."

"That's quite a burden."

"I managed it until the accident. I'm not the broken person you see here."

He assured me he didn't see me as broken, but I doubted he was being truthful. We took a break, and when we resumed talking, I told him about the dinner with Sam Colt and how Zelie started lying and sneaking around soon after that. I explained how I'd discovered the secret trip to Rome, how that had pushed me to the edge with fear. I recounted my trip to Aster's house and what had happened with Chuckie.

"I was desperate to keep her from running away with Sam, but I couldn't. She chose him over me."

"And what happened after she left?"

"I'd already decided that I wanted to move to New Mexico. There's an art school in Santa Fe that I'm interested in. As I explained, I've been planning to move away for years and I was only waiting for Zelie to graduate. When she left, I was desperate to get out." My plan probably seemed like a whim, and maybe it had been. "I was upset and in a hurry. I didn't see the truck. That's it." That day was the end — the end of Zelie. I looked down at my arm and rubbed my wound.

I knew only what my father had told me about what had happened to Zelie. After she left our house that morning, she drove to Sam's sister's house in Greenwich to meet him. Zelie and Sam went to a hotel in the city where they intended to spend the night before their flight. They shared a room and a bed, and the end came quickly for Zelie. By early evening, she was dead.

"Sam killed her," I said. "And then he killed himself."

"Is that what you believe, Iris?"

"It's what I know."

"Well, Sam killed himself, that part is certainly true." Dr. Westgate reached over to the desk, rummaging through some of his papers and pulling out a newspaper that was folded to reveal an article several pages in. He handed it to me. The paper was dated from that day.

INQUEST BEGINS INTO COLT DEATH

The Connecticut State Police have begun an inquest into the death of Samuel Colt IV, 28, of Hartford. The Coast Guard recovered his body last Wednesday after his family reported him missing. Mr. Colt, found in a sailboat floating adrift on Long Island Sound, was dead from what appeared to be a self-inflicted gunshot wound to the chest. His death comes just two days after the death of his girlfriend, Hazel Chapel, 18, of Bellflower Village. No foul play is suspected, but the inquest continues.

I read it, then tossed the newspaper onto the desk. "He deserved to die for what he did to my sister," I said without a hint of emotion.

"What did he do to your sister?"

"I already told you. He killed her."

"How did he do that, exactly?"

"The same way Matthew killed Aster, and Roderick killed Rosalind, and Teddy killed Calla."

Dr. Westgate stared at me more intensely than usual. "Iris, it concerns me that you think these men killed your sisters."

"They did. Aster was in excellent health until her first night with her husband; the same is true for Rosalind. Calla was fine until she spent the night with Teddy. Same with Zelie and Sam. What other conclusion would you draw?"

He shook his head. "What you've told me is impossible."

"Dr. Westgate, everything I've told me is true." I had the sudden urge to run away, a bad habit. "After Aster died, my sisters claimed our mother had poisoned her somehow—"

"Poisoned?"

"Not with actual poison, but just—" Dr. Westgate didn't like the word *crazy,* but I knew that's how this all sounded. "Our mother had a troubled history, she and the women before her. Marriage, children — it killed them, either literally or, in my mother's case, figuratively. My sisters thought she'd passed that to us somehow. But it wasn't my mother's fault. It's the men. I admit I can't explain exactly *how* these men killed my sisters, but they did."

Dr. Westgate stared at me in disbelief.

"Ask my father," I said. "He'll tell you." Though, of course, I had no confidence that he would.

"I spoke to him at length. He told me Aster and Rosalind died of the flu. Calla's cause of death is unknown. The full results of Hazel's autopsy are not yet available."

"Autopsy?"

"I know this is upsetting. I'm sorry."

I was on the brink of becoming weepy, but I braced myself and continued on. This was almost over. "My father never allowed Zelie or me to go out with boys. Did you ask him about that?"

"No, but he had lost four daughters, something no father could imagine in his worst nightmare. I'm not surprised he'd grow protective of the two he had left, given the circumstances."

"You don't understand. That's not why he did it." He was twisting around the things I'd said. "He's against women getting a college education, but he allowed me to attend teacher training because he knew I'd never be able to marry and have children, and I'd have to do *something* with my life. Don't you see?"

"You're interpreting your father's behavior in a very distorted way."

"You're the one distorting things," I said. "You weren't there when all these things happened. *I was.*"

"You're a deeply traumatized young woman, with good reason. I'm not sure I could have withstood what's happened to you. What you've been through — it's comparable to what a soldier might go through in a war."

I hated what he was doing. Pretending to empathize with me while disbelieving me. "You say that my version of events is wrong, yet you have no explanation for how my sisters died."

"Not every death can be explained. Medical science doesn't have all the answers, but I can assure you that what you think happened to your sisters didn't actually happen. I'm telling you this as a doctor who graduated from Harvard Medical School: You can't trust your perception of things."

I wanted to keep arguing, but I could see there was no point. Yesterday I'd told him that no one believes women and that everyone prefers to think we're crazy; now he was doing that exact thing to me without apparently seeing the irony. I'd been *Belinda'd*. In that moment, I knew my mother in a way I'd never known her before.

"Tomorrow you're going to be transferred to Fern Hollow. It's a psychiatric clinic for women near Greenwich."

"I know what it is." It's where Belinda had gone the first time she'd been sent away after Aster's death.

"They weren't able to help your mother, but I think they can help you. It's a quality facility, and I'll be checking in on you from time to time. I've taken a great interest in your case."

A case. That's what I'd become.

"Do you have any questions about what's going to happen to you tomorrow?" I shook my head, looking at my wall of flowers instead of him. "Very well, then. Your father would like to take you there himself and I've agreed. He'll pick you up in the morning."

I could see it all: I'd stay at Fern Hollow for a while, then I'd eventually be sent off to St. Aubert's. My mother and I would sit in chairs along the cliffs, our legs wrapped in matching blankets, staring out at the sea.

Haunted mother, haunted daughter.

6.

Brewer came into my room that afternoon, and to my surprise, she announced that I had a visitor. "Miss Edna Dove would like to see you."

I sat up, not wanting Dovey to find me sprawled on the bed. My final session with Dr. Westgate had left me depleted, unable to move.

"There you are, dear Iris," she said, as she came in and kissed my cheek. "I needed to see your face again." She smiled at me wistfully, at the impossibility of me, an only child.

She wore a white blouse and an oatmeal skirt, with a cardigan, as always, even in the summertime. Her crown of blond curls had grayed over the years, and she looked older to me than she had even a few days ago.

She settled on the peach sofa while I sat in the desk chair turned so I could face her as Dr. Westgate always positioned himself. She'd been carrying two handbags, which she set beside her on the sofa. I thought that was odd, but then I realized one of the handbags was mine. It was the boxy brown leather bag filled with treasured objects that I'd taken with me when I'd tried to run away.

"I'm surprised to see you," I said, although I was grateful to have a visitor. Anything to take my mind off the last session with Dr. Westgate.

"It's been an awful business, and for what it's worth, I don't think your father should have waited to tell you about Zelie."

"Yes," I said, surprised she'd criticize my father in front of me, something she'd never overtly done before.

"Mrs. O'Connor and I are heartbroken over Zelie. It had been so long since Daphne died, and I suppose we thought" — she paused to pull a handkerchief from her purse and dab her eyes — "I suppose we'd hoped it was all finished."

"I told the doctor what happened to my sisters, how they died, and he doesn't believe me."

Dovey frowned. "He came poking around the other night. Spoke for quite a while with your father, but I don't know what was said."

"But you know what happened to my sisters." I needed her to confirm it.

"I certainly do, and don't trouble yourself too much. My mother always said doctors don't know much about the lives of women."

I wished that Dovey could talk to Dr. Westgate on my behalf, but if she did, he'd probably send her away too.

"I see you've been busy," she said, pointing to the wall behind me.

"They'll probably paint over it when I leave."

"Your father told me you're going to Fern Hollow tomorrow. That's why I'm here. I rushed right over when I heard." She picked up my brown handbag and set it on her lap, her hands resting on top of it. "I went to see your mother recently to tell her I'm leaving. I've decided to return to Ireland. My sister was widowed last year. She and her husband ran a restaurant in Galway, so I'm going home to help her with that. I'm quite looking forward to it."

It had never occurred to me that Dovey might leave. She seemed a permanent part of the wedding cake.

"Mrs. O'Connor is going too; she's handed in her notice. With Zelie gone, and you . . ." She was searching for a polite way to describe my situation.

"In a psychiatric hospital."

"Yes, well, neither of us wishes to stay on any longer. It wasn't an easy house for me to live in at the best of times, and those days are long behind us."

I thought of the house with only my father in it, the graves outside. He'd be outnumbered by the dead.

"When I went to tell your mother that I'm leaving, she asked for a favor, which is why I've come to see you so urgently. Your mother gave me her brooch, the one she always wears."

"Rose's brooch."

"That's right. She asked me to take it to a jeweler in New York and sell it, which is what I did last week." She leaned over and whispered the next part since my door was open. "There's an envelope in this handbag that contains one thousand dollars in cash."

"For me?"

"There's a letter inside from your mother that explains it." She stood up and gave me the handbag, then collected her own. I was sad she was leaving so soon and wanted to reach out to her.

Instead, she leaned over to embrace me as I remained sitting in the chair, then she gave me a quick kiss on the cheek. "I'm not your family," she said. "So I'm not going to claim I loved you like my own daughter. That's not my place." She cupped my face in her hands. "But I want you to know that not a day will go by that I won't think of you and your sisters."

After she left, I felt bereft. She'd seen it all. Her knowledge of what had happened to the Chapel girls was inside her, all those little pieces of us. It was a story no one else would believe, yet she was taking that precious understanding across the Atlantic.

My sisters held most of the pieces of me, and those pieces had been buried with them. With Dovey gone too, I worried all that was left of me was fragments.

I could see it clearly for the first time — the end of Iris Chapel.

The question was: How would Iris finally come to her end?

7.

I didn't read Belinda's letter that night. I knew she was saying goodbye, and after everything that had happened, I wasn't capable of reading that. Still, I opened the bag and looked through it. Two envelopes, one with the letter, the other full of cash, then all the things that I'd taken from my sisters — the bottle of English lavender perfume, the jewelry, Calla's poetry book, *The White Iris,* the framed family photograph, and everything else. Inside one of the inner pockets, I found an envelope with Zelie's name written on it in Dovey's distinctive handwriting, a lock of Zelie's chestnut hair inside, tied with a dainty white ribbon.

I pulled out *The White Iris* and set it on the desk, propping it up against the wall so I could see it. It was small, but it added some color to my otherwise sterile room. I'd been longing for color.

That evening, Brewer sat on the sofa in my room, entertaining me with her baby-names book while I ate dinner.

"How about Donna?" she asked. "Do you like that? The book says it means 'lady.'"

"Sure," I said indifferently.

She gave me a playful, exaggerated look. "Some people are hard to please," she said, and returned to flipping through her book.

I didn't know if there'd be anyone like her at Fern Hollow; I'd miss her. She continued to rattle off names — Leticia, Rachel, Gertrude — as I ate my dessert: canned peaches in syrup.

"How about Sylvia?" she asked.

"That's pretty. I like that."

"At last!" She was delighted. "The book says it means 'from the forest.' I thought you might like that." She gestured to my mural and the forest in the corner.

I turned to look at my artwork. Belinda had intended the forests on our walls to be dark and mysterious, a contrast to the beauty and brightness of the garden. I'd been scared of that when I was a little girl, scared of the unknown. I'd spent so much time wandering around the forest near our house, a place of adventure but also of haunting and loss.

But that evening, thanks to Brewer, I realized the unknown of the forest was where I lived now. I'd left the garden and was surrounded on all sides by tall trees with no idea how to make my way out.

8.

My father arrived at noon, parked outside the entrance in his black sedan. Brewer accompanied me out, handing my suitcase and canvas bag to my father, who'd gotten out of the car to assist me this time. He didn't seem to know quite what to make of Brewer, with her protruding belly and indeterminate ethnicity, and he mumbled his thanks, steering me toward the passenger's-side door and leaving me to get in on my own while he went back around to his side of the car.

I rolled the window down all the way and waved to Brewer as we drove off. It was a boiling day in early July, and my father had his window down as well, his forehead damp with sweat. He'd taken off his suit jacket, his shirtsleeves rolled up to the elbows. We pulled onto the main road outside the hospital, and after a block, the two lanes of traffic on our side came to a complete halt.

"There must be an accident," he said, and sure enough, sirens soon began to blare around us. He frowned and checked his watch, but I was in no hurry.

We crawled along, my pink linen dress stuck to my skin with sweat. My father hadn't said anything since he'd remarked on the traffic; I knew this extra time in the car with me was excruciating for him. I reached into my handbag to see if I'd placed a handkerchief in there, and I had, to my relief. I'd wrapped Belinda's wren in it. I touched the soft feathers of the wren, which always felt soothing, then used the handkerchief to pat my face. I opened the bottle of Aster's English lavender perfume and dabbed a bit on my wrists, filling the car with her scent.

The letter from my mother remained unopened, and next to it was the envelope of cash. I wondered if they'd confiscate my things at Fern Hollow. I feared that they might, so I pulled Belinda's letter out and quietly opened it.

Dear Iris,

You must be suffering tremendously in light of what happened to our dearest Zelie. I wish I were there to comfort you, but they won't allow me to see you. I've struggled with my health since I received the news, but I feel a sense of urgency in reaching out to you now.

We shall never see each other again in this life. This you must accept. I'm sorry for the kind of life you've had — this causes me tremendous regret and haunts me as much as any of my spirits ever did. I failed your sisters, but things can be different for you. This I see very clearly, so please pay attention to me now: You can't let your father put you in an institution and you can never go back to that house. The money Dovey gave you is my money, not Chapel money, not blood money. I want you to use it to start a new life somewhere far away. It might seem impossible, but it isn't, not for you.

You're the only one left, and your continued survival isn't something you should take for granted. Through me, your sisters whisper

in your ear: Run, dearest Iris. Run away as fast as you can and never
look back.

With much love,
Your mother

I put the letter back in the envelope, swallowing the symphony of emotions that threatened to overwhelm me, the notes sharp and intense. I knew I couldn't visibly react to what I'd read, but it was hard. I appreciated my mother's heartfelt advice, but I had no reason to believe another attempt at running would turn out any better than the first. After all, if running away was easy, she would have done it herself.

I couldn't run again — could I?

"Are you all right?" my father asked. I arranged everything back in the handbag and zippered it closed.

"Why didn't you tell the doctor what really happened to my sisters?" It was, at least in part, his fault I was in this situation. I wanted to hear what he had to say for himself.

"I told him what I know. Aster and Rosalind died of the flu, Daphne died in the water, and as for Calla and Zelie — we don't know."

"We *do* know what happened to Calla and Zelie, and what really happened to Aster and Rosalind too. Why can't you admit it? The doctor thinks I'm delusional thanks to you."

"Iris, don't upset yourself."

"I'm not upsetting myself. *You're* upsetting me."

He stayed focused on the road ahead even though we weren't moving. "We'll be at Fern Hollow soon. Just relax." He was nervous. He had to keep me calm.

As I stared at his profile, I thought of what my mother had told me on our last visit: *I never loved your father. I never even liked him. I didn't like his face, or the way he spoke, or the way he smelled, or anything about him. I cried for days before the wedding.* I was a product of that union. It was the fabric that had made me.

A certainty returned — that my life as I had known it was over. This was the end of Iris.

I reached for the door handle. He didn't notice, still focused on the line of cars in front of us. In one swift motion, I climbed out and slammed the door behind me. I leaned over to look at him through the open window, my handbag gripped tightly in my right hand, the other arm still wounded and bandaged.

"Get back in this car at once," he said, finally bothering to make eye contact with me. I considered saying something to him, but what? There was nothing left to say.

I took off running. People in the other cars peered through their windows at the curious sight of the young woman in the pink dress running for her life. I ran faster and faster — heeding my mother's advice.

"Iris!" I heard my father shout.

It was the last time anyone would ever call me that.

The Violet Notebook

It used to happen just once or twice a year, but since I've been writing in the blue diaries, it happens every night. *Tap tap.* It goes on for hours, the tapping on the windows, the rattling of the doorknobs, growing louder and louder until dawn. I've become like Belinda, haunted in the night, only I know the tapping I hear doesn't come from Chapel gunshot victims. I know who taps, who wants to be let inside. I ignore her and keep writing.

Yes, *her.* Is it any surprise my ghost is female?

Since I haven't been able to sleep much at night, I've stayed up and worked diligently for the past two weeks, writing all three volumes of the blue diaries under the cover of night. During the day, I wander around dazed, not a person but a conduit for memories that I feel a compulsion to record. At last I've finished, having written the final words just before dawn this morning: "It was the last time anyone would ever call me that."

In the sixty years that have passed since my father shouted my name — *Iris!* — no one *has* called me that again, a remarkable achievement on my part. It's not easy becoming someone else, but it worked out quite well for me until recently, when I was forced to remember the past and Iris Chapel clawed her way back in.

The emotion of completing the diaries this morning propelled me from my desk and out the back door of the house into the red hills, where the moon was still faintly visible. I didn't rush outside so I could scream like Iris used to do, although I was tempted. Sudden swells of emotion aren't uncommon to me. When one has buried so much, it builds up beyond containment. Imagine a volcano.

Racing up the hill, which at my age is no easy feat, I ignored the pointy rocks stabbing the bottoms of my tender pink feet and pushed on, determined for some reason to reach the top. (A desire to ascend this earthly plane?) I arrived breathless and wobbly, taking in the view of the village, with the red cliffs in one direction, and in the other, the low, sloping hills covered in the muted gray-green of piñon and sagebrush that was broken up only by yellow patches of chamisa. After a moment, I toppled over. I lay crumpled in the dirt, worried that I'd caused myself irreparable damage, that various bones might have broken or internal organs bruised. I was afraid to move for a while, but I eventually found the strength to roll over onto my back.

Above me, the underbelly of the night sky was softening into a delicate blue still sprinkled with stars that were faintly glowing. Its beauty caught in my throat. Beneath the sky, I felt like nothing but a tiny speck in the universe; I'll eventually blow away, a particle of dust. I enjoyed that feeling of smallness. After weeks of writing, the heaviness of it all and the toll of what I've come to understand is "survivor's guilt," I welcomed the idea of my eventual obliteration. I've finally become Calla's night-blooming iris. My reunion with my sisters is moving ever closer. We've been separated for such a long time; I am an old woman while they will always be young. I've spent years pushing their memories aside, the only way I could survive. If I had a chance to talk to them now, to defend myself, I'd tell them that Iris died back in 1957 — she's been with them this whole time.

• • •

I'm not sure how long I lay in the dirt this morning. I began to worry I wouldn't be able to stand up and get home, that I'd perish in the August heat and decay slowly, become food for wild animals. They'd tear me apart limb by limb, and that's how I'd end: a woman in pieces, scattered over the landscape.

I was tempted to shout for help, but it seemed such a melodramatic thing to do, and I didn't want to give in to panic. Then I heard the voice of the angels, my young neighbors calling my name.

"Miss Wren, is that you?" Diego shouted.

And then Jade's voice. "Miss Wren?"

I wanted to cry with relief. "Up here!" I called out.

Diego reached the top of the hill and rushed to my side, kicking up a cloud of dirt that sent me into a brief choking fit. "Miss Wren, are you all right?" I hated that he and Jade persisted in calling me Miss Wren like I was some dowdy old maid.

"For the love of God, Diego, call me Sylvia," I said, as he hoisted me up. I'd never made much space for men in my life, but they're useful to have around when heavy lifting is required. I wrapped my arms around Diego's neck and let the burden of my weight sink into him. He carried me down the hill the way a groom carries a bride across a threshold. Jade was waiting at the bottom, the ever-present baby strapped to her chest.

"You could have died up there, Miss Wren," she said in her scolding, nasal tone.

"Let's not be dramatic," I said, as the baby gurgled. The baby was why they'd been up so early and had spotted me. I patted the little creature on the head gently once we were inside the house. It was possible that she'd saved my life.

Diego and Jade fussed over me for a while. Normally, I would have fought them off, but fussing over the elderly makes people feel useful, so I allowed

it, their reward for helping me. Jade made me tea, and Diego fetched the
first aid kit. He cleaned my wounds — minor, only a scrape here and there,
though I imagine the bruises will come later.

"No need to tell Lola about this," I said, once the initial kerfuffle was over.
They'd settled me into the comfy chair in the living room, and I couldn't
help but moan with pleasure whenever I sat in it. Lola and I had given up our
stylish modernist furniture once we hit our mid-seventies, replacing it with
grotesque recliners and fluffy sofas that looked to be upholstered in teddy
bear fur, but I secretly loved it all.

Diego and Jade sat on the sofa across from me, watching me drink my tea.
They wore innocent expressions on their faces, as if they didn't know what I
was talking about, but I knew Lola had been calling them to check up on me
while she was gone. Lola and I are the same age, but she has no qualms about
flitting off to another continent on her own. Then she worries about me the
whole time she's away. To be fair, she has good reason to worry, but it irritates
me nonetheless. It's her way of showing that we aren't the same, that I need
to be doted on and surveilled.

"Are you sure you don't need to see the doc?" Jade asked. Her blouse was
wide open as if we were on a beach in the French Riviera. I didn't mind,
watching the baby.

"I'm unscathed," I said. "No need to worry." This wasn't true. My body
ached from the fall, and every time I moved my teacup to my lips, I had to
hide a wince.

Jade and Diego glanced at each other, then back at me. They were an
odd-looking, mismatched pair. Jade was as white as white, not much darker
than chalk in complexion, a real feat in the sun of New Mexico. She wore
bleached-blond dreadlocks, and some sort of fabric headwrap, and a nose
ring through her septum. Her entire look appeared to be appropriated from
other cultures. Diego, meanwhile, had brown skin and shiny black hair he
wore tied back in a ponytail and a scraggly beard that he braided and fastened near the tip with a green rubber band (always green). His arms were
covered in tattoos, which looked like the long sleeves on a colorful shirt.

The fashion and grooming habits of the young are a mystery to me, but they're a nice-enough pair. Diego is the grandson of my former neighbors, the Guerreros. Mr. and Mrs. Guerrero died within three months of each other earlier this year, and Diego inherited their house. Having a young couple nearby has turned out to be useful even if they hover too much.

"Miss Wren," Diego said, "we can drive you to the doctor. It's no big thing."

I screamed internally at his persistence in calling me Miss Wren. He'd served in Afghanistan and I supposed it could be a military thing, the deference. I wondered what Belinda would make of him, this former warrior. For the first time in decades, Belinda had begun to penetrate my daily thoughts and she didn't belong here in my Sylvia Wren life.

"I can drive myself if I need to go," I said, fearing that I *would* need to go. I ached terribly. "The two of you better get going. I'm sure you have things to do." Diego kept bees and sold honey at farmers' markets; Jade was a potter.

I nodded at them in assurance that I was all right, so they stood up to leave at last and I felt myself relax. With the exception of Lola, I can never fully relax when other people are around.

"If you need anything, give a holler," Diego said on his way out. He often says this, assuming I find comfort in the protection inherent in his maleness. I've never had the heart to tell him that men have never been the ones to protect me.

(This morning notwithstanding.)

When Diego and Jade had finally left, I hobbled to the kitchen for ibuprofen and more tea, then went to my study; the evidence of what my life had been for the past two weeks was spread across my desk: three blue diaries and correspondence from Eliza Mortimer.

After Eliza's initial letters and my postcard kindly telling her to get lost, I didn't hear from her for about a week. Then she made up for lost time. Every day for the past week I've received something new from her. She's sent me packets that included copies of my sisters' obituaries from the *Greenwich Observer;* an article from the *New York Times* about Zelie's and Sam's deaths;

and a pamphlet from the modern-day reinvention of the old Colt's Manufacturing Company that showed off their corporate retreat — the house I grew up in.

The packets have continued to come, most certainly more news clippings chronicling my family's traumas, which Eliza casually ran through a Xerox machine and sent off to me with notes that say: "I'd love to discuss this with you." But I haven't opened the most recent ones. As the saying goes, Fool me once . . .

I suppose she wants to draw me out, to break down my resistance. Little does she know, her tactics have been very effective. I had never — and I mean never — contemplated writing the story of my sisters until her intrusions began, and I can't yet decide if I'm better or worse off because of it. Yet even before she contacted me, I'd begun to look back at my artistic career, so you might say I was primed for the backward glance. Lola and I had been discussing creating a museum dedicated to my work, a small one, given that so much of my art is on display or in private collections. Lola even scouted places in Santa Fe with a real estate agent since, of course, it would be located somewhere in New Mexico. But when they asked me to visit some of the potential sites this past spring, I hesitated. It turns out I didn't like imagining the afterlife of Sylvia Wren after all, and I told Lola I needed more time to prepare myself.

Now I've written these diaries, and I don't know what their fate should be. After I filled up the first blue diary, Jade went to the bookstore in Santa Fe and bought me two similar ones in slightly different shades of blue, so the three diaries, when stacked on top of one another, create a lovely ombré, a movement from dark to light. I'm not certain, though, that this is how the story actually ends. I've had to search for the light each and every day of the past sixty years, and only sometimes do I find it.

It's lunchtime and I've taken a drive to Española in our old Outback, achy bones and all. Driving helps me think, as it always has. I was hungry, so I pulled into the drive-thru lane at Lotaburger and ordered two double cheeseburgers with extra green chiles and a Coke. I drove to an abandoned lot across the street to eat, not daring to take the food home with me. Thanks to Lola, I've been a vegetarian for most of the past sixty years except when she's out of town. She won't eat what she calls "death," won't even allow it into our house. She says that if we eat death we'll absorb it into ourselves and the negative vibrations and toxicity will harm our creativity. I don't necessarily subscribe to this view. I am, however, convinced that Lola and my mother would have liked each other if they'd ever been able to meet.

As I ate in my car, a most ecstatic experience complete with burger grease dripping down my chin, I thought more about the diaries. Before I wrote them, what had happened to my sisters was buried so deeply that it had fossilized like amber. I could have worn them — Aster, Rosalind, Calla, Daphne, Zelie — like gems on a chain. But these diaries are far too heavy to wear around my neck, and I worry that they are far too heavy to hold on my own. I must do something with them.

I considered my options as I ate my second double cheeseburger. I could burn them, but that would make the project of having written them nothing more than an exorcism. And when I die, the story of Iris Chapel and her sisters would die with me, and while that's the way things were headed before, now I'm not sure I could let them suffer that fate a second time.

I could place the diaries in my archive at the University of New Mexico for researchers to find after Lola and I are dead (what a jackpot that would be).

Or I could publish them now. I don't even know if my manic middle-of-the-night ramblings from the past two weeks are good enough to be published; I haven't read through them and I don't intend to. I'm hardly the Leo Tolstoy of northern New Mexico, but I did my best. Regardless, it's foolish even to entertain the idea of publishing them. I've spent decades hiding, and it would make little sense now, at eighty years old, to open my veins to the world.

On my way home, I stopped at the post office, not in the mood for my ritual walk to collect the mail. There was, no surprise, a letter from Eliza Mortimer

—just a letter, not a puffy packet of newspaper clippings to hit me like spinning headlines from a Depression-era movie. Once I was back in my study, I tossed it onto the tray where I'd set the others, then sat at my desk and looked out at the view, the hollyhocks, the red hills, the same view that's been there since I first visited the house in 1957. Lola had rented it before she met me, wanting a quiet place to work with a garden to grow the flowers and herbs she used to make her perfumes. Later on, we bought it and moved here full-time; Lola had someone else take over running the shop. The view hasn't changed, but the house certainly has. Once Lola and I made some money, we renovated it and added a wing, and over the years, we've kept it up, adding modern touches. When the house is turned into a tourist attraction, as it certainly will be after we're both dead, they won't have much work to do. I can already see a bored man sitting on a folding chair in the living room, saying, "Please don't touch" when someone reaches for Lola's Navajo vase or the framed photograph of Taos Pueblo.

It's a horrible thought, really. I should forget about it and go relax in bed for the afternoon, read a book, take a nap. My body needs to heal from my fall and I shouldn't push my luck. I keep wondering, though, about the letter from Eliza Mortimer. The slenderness of it after all those packets. What could she want now?

Dear Ms. Wren,

You haven't responded to any of my letters, and I can certainly appreciate that, given your desire for privacy. Please understand that while I do feel conflicted about pursuing this matter, since it's obvious my investigations are unwelcome, I am a journalist and you are a public figure, one of the most important artists in American history. I believe your story would be a valuable addition to women's history as well as to our understanding of feminist and contemporary art.

I've recently spoken to Fredrika Helland Branch, Florence's younger sister. Fredrika still resides in Bellflower Village, but sadly, Florence died last year. Fredrika tells me that Florence was a close friend of Ha-

zel "Zelie" Chapel, and that she and the rest of the Helland family always felt certain that you and Iris Chapel are the same person. One of the other sisters in the family, Frances, owns an original Sylvia Wren painting that she bought at a gallery in New York City.

Fredrika has been very helpful to me in my investigations and has supplied me with photographs of Iris Chapel, which further confirm the theory that she is you. She said that after Mr. Chapel died many of his family's belongings were sold since there was no one left to take them, and she bought a number of items (a silver tea service, for instance) that she'd be happy to give to you if you'd like them. Fredrika and I were allowed to explore the Chapel family home one afternoon, and my understanding of Sylvia Wren deepened after I saw the flower murals on the bedroom walls. (The bedrooms are used for storage now. I can go back and take photos if you'd like.)

While Fredrika and the other elderly residents of Bellflower Village have been helpful, there are limits to what they can tell me, and I still have no clear understanding of how Aster, Rosalind, Calla, and Zelie died. No one does.

As you can see, though questions remain, I've compiled compelling evidence that you and Iris Chapel are the same person. An editor at Vanity Fair has contracted me to write this investigative piece about you for the magazine. I would welcome your participation for this article, as much or as little as you'd like. You know how to reach me, and I promise that I will treat you and your story with the utmost respect.

Yours sincerely,
Eliza L. Mortimer

I tossed the letter aside. I wasn't surprised Eliza had interested a high-profile publication in her story about me, though I'm not sure I like the idea of Vanity Fair being the venue, a magazine that features "serious" journalism inside but usually has a starlet on the cover with her tits hanging out.

Eliza's letter hasn't panicked me like her earlier correspondence did, at least that which I've bothered to open. I suppose I've already accepted that I'm going to be exposed, but there are limits to what she can find out as she herself acknowledged. She can write about flowers and firearms, but she'll never discover the true story of my sisters.

While I'm not panicked, I'm angry at the thought of Eliza and some glossy magazine exhuming my sisters, metaphorically speaking, without my consent. I picked up the pamphlet Eliza had sent of the wedding cake, now a corporate retreat for gun executives (the horror of that is beyond words), and looked at all the pictures with a magnifying glass. I've done this several times before to see if I can spot the graves, all seven of them, including those of my parents, but if the graves are still there, they're obscured by trees.

Before I could really think through what I was doing, I picked up the phone and dialed my lawyer in New York since I didn't know anyone else who could possibly help me. Without Lola, I'm out of my depth with these matters.

As always, Rebecca took my call right away. "I want to buy a house," I said. "Do you know someone who can do a real estate transaction for me?" I explained to her about the house in Bellflower Village, now taken over by gun executives. That's how I phrased it: "taken over."

"Why?" Rebecca said with surprise.

"That's my business," I said, as snappy as a turtle. Then I felt badly. "I'm sorry, I'm having a stressful day." I hoped she would savor the only apology she would ever receive from me. "My grandparents were the original owners of that house," I explained. I didn't see the need to hide it anymore. It would all come out soon in the starlet-saturated pages of *Vanity Fair* anyway. "I'm their only living descendant. You could say it's my house and I want it back."

"How fascinating," she said, eager as always for any tidbit about me. "Are you going to live in it?"

"*Of course not.* But maybe—" Then I was startled by the idea that had suddenly come to mind. "Maybe it could be a museum one day."

"You're full of surprises lately, Sylvia," she said. "I do have a colleague here at the firm who handles real estate. I can talk to him for you."

"Yes. Please do."

"I'll reach out to Kenji and see what he thinks. I'll get back to you."

After I hung up the phone, I sat in disbelief over what I'd just done. Eliza Mortimer had a knack for spurring me to action. Why stop now? I picked up the phone and called Diego, asking him to come over and do a job for me.

"Are you sure, Miss Wren?" Diego asked.

People have always questioned me my entire life.

"Yes, I'm sure," I said, standing with him in the far corner of the backyard. "Don't worry about the bushes. Just dig until you find a wooden box. All right?"

"I'll try to dig around them," he said, grabbing the shovel. I watched him for a while, then limped back to my study (the soreness from this morning lingers); by the time I sat down at my desk, the telephone was ringing. It was Rebecca, providing an update before she left her office for the day.

"My colleague Kenji was fascinated by your request—his daughter is a *huge* fan of yours—so he made some calls right away. It seems you might be in luck. Colt has actually been interested in selling the old house for a while even though they haven't listed it. They manufacture those god-awful AR-15s, and let's just say they aren't too popular in Connecticut nowadays."

"So it's for sale?"

"Not officially, but they're open to an offer. It'll be expensive. Kenji says to offer two million to start—"

"Fine. Tell him I want a quick sale, all cash." The thought of doing business with Colt was distasteful. The Colt family no longer owned the company, but the name alone inspired dread in me.

After my call with Rebecca, I watched Diego dig for a while. I wondered what Lola would make of what I'd asked him to do. Lola, bless her, would be facing a number of shocks when she arrived home from Brazil at the end of the month. She'd been laid low by a bug for several days, and since her recovery, she'd been busy catching up with her perfumery students, so our telephone conversations had been brief and not as interrogatory as they normally are. But I'm certain Jade and Diego have filled her in on my odd behavior. One morning, Diego came over and saw me through the window, asleep in my recliner, holding the rifle we keep stashed under the bed.

There'd been no place for Lola in the blue diaries and I'm unhappy about that. It's like a family portrait with one person standing just outside the frame. I spent twenty years as a Chapel girl, but I've spent sixty years as Lola's partner. Will I have to write another diary that's just about her? Maybe now that I've started recording my life — my formerly private, out-of-sight life — I'll have to keep going.

I met her the day I arrived in Santa Fe, still wearing that pink dress and clutching my enormous handbag. I'd taken a bus from New York to Chicago, then to Denver, then on to Santa Fe, having become Sylvia Wren on the journey. I'd left Iris in Connecticut; Sylvia had been born in Illinois. The bus had stopped at a filling station in a small farm town for a comfort break. I bought a Grapette soda and a bag of peanuts, and sat in the adjacent field while the other passengers queued to use the single restroom. I watched the sun rise over the cornfields, the first time I'd seen the sun since we left the East Coast the evening before, and I realized that I'd managed to do what no other woman in my life had done — I'd run away. I knew I needed to transform myself, to disappear; there was nothing left of Iris but fragments, but those fragments could destroy me. That life, that past, was unbearable.

Sylvia Wren from Illinois — that's who I became and how I would introduce myself to Lola within an hour of my arrival in Santa Fe. The bus from Denver dropped me off near the Plaza in the middle of one of their summer monsoons; I saw nothing that resembled the vivid colors of the paintings from the gallery as I stepped into a murky gray landscape. I ran to the nearest diner, ordering a plate of scrambled eggs and toast; there were green chiles mixed into the eggs, and I spent a great deal of time trying to pick them out before giving up. I scanned the classifieds in the local paper as I ate, which is where I saw Lola's ad for a room to rent. I'd later learn she owned the perfumery in the Plaza, which she'd taken over from her aunt after she died. There was an apartment above it; her aunt's former bedroom stood empty, and Lola hated that emptiness.

I was embarrassed to meet her, my potential landlady, having rushed over from the diner in clothes I'd worn for days, my hair soaked through with rain, my arm still bandaged. The perfumery sat between a shop selling Indian jewelry and an art gallery. The walls were lined with wooden shelves, and around the perimeter was a waist-high glass display case in a U shape with just enough space behind it for a salesclerk to stand. Each shelf was lined with perfume bottles, which I smelled upon opening the door, a pungent wall with no particular fragrance standing out, the way too many paint colors mixed together turn black.

Lola was the only person there and she was standing behind one of the counters looking immaculate in a midnight-blue dress with a gold belt around the waist, dainty gold hoops in her ears, and manicured nails with clear polish. She wore her black hair pulled back into a low bun, her face clean of any makeup. Cat-eye glasses hid her eyes, but I noticed her full lips, with a prominent cupid's bow, which I wanted to draw. My first impulse toward art upon my arrival in New Mexico was to attempt a landscape — the peaks and valley of her mouth.

"I look a fright," I said, after I'd introduced myself, feeling incredibly shabby in comparison to her. She merely stared at me with a faint smile; it wasn't possible for her to disagree, and as such, a smile was the greatest kindness. The saying "Begin as you mean to go on" comes to mind since that moment in many ways exemplified what our relationship would be: Lola the steady, calming presence, and me — the mess.

"I just arrived on a bus from Illinois," I said. "That's where I'm from."

"Like a tumbleweed just blown in?" she said, and this brought a real smile. "The rains are terrible today; would you like a towel?" She didn't wait for a response but opened a door at the back and returned with a white hand towel. I gratefully accepted it and dried my face.

"I've never been to Illinois," she said, as she watched me attempt to dry my hair. I wanted to reply: *Nor have I, not really.*

"What town are you from? Chicago?"

"No, Bellflower Village," I said without thinking, folding the towel and setting it on the counter. It would be this way for a few years to come, Iris's tentacles holding on to me however they could.

"Not every flower can be used in perfume making," Lola said, and I noticed a hint of an accent. "Bellflowers are one of them."

"Okay," I said hesitantly; I wasn't sure why she was telling me this.

"But we can go about it another way. What does Bellflower Village smell like? In other words, what does *home* smell like?"

It was such an odd question, asked with such authority, that I answered it without inquiring why she needed to know. I didn't yet have a new home, but I thought about my old one. "In the summer, it smells green. Is green a smell?"

"Yes, of course."

"It smells like earth, like wildflowers in a meadow," I said, noticing as I spoke that, rather unexpectedly, I was a tad homesick. "It smells like violet perfume and English lavender."

"Yes, and what else?" She reminded me of Dr. Westgate probing my psyche. I didn't know what was going on, but she intrigued me.

"Like an old Victorian house."

"Hmm," she said. "No one has ever said that before. What does that smell like?"

I thought for a moment. "A wedding cake and secrets."

"Interesting," she said. "What else?"

"Definitely not roses."

She raised her eyebrows. "Why not roses?"

I'd gone a few days without sleep. Nothing made sense. When I didn't answer her, she pushed me: "Can you explain about the roses, Sylvia?"

It was the first time anyone had called me Sylvia, and I felt a momentary thrill. I certainly didn't want to be talking about roses, but I could understand her surprise — roses, to a perfumer, are like onions and garlic to a chef. "I'm sorry, but why are you asking me these questions?"

"For your perfume," she said, picking up a small white notepad and pencil from the counter. "I assume that's why you're here." She wrote a few notes, then looked up and noticed my puzzled expression.

"People come in here and tell me things about their lives," she continued.

"I make them a bespoke fragrance. I can do one that smells like Bellflower Village unless you'd like something else." She wrote another note on the pad and I read it upside down: NO ROSES. "But I think this one has a lot of promise. I can have it ready in a couple of days. Does that suit you?"

I explained the mix-up, that I was there for the room. "Oh," she said, taking in my appearance more carefully, presumably imagining what it would be like to share her home with this messy stranger.

"I plan to enroll at the Palace School of Art and Design," I said. "I'm very quiet. I won't be any trouble." (Not all of that would turn out to be true, but I would enroll at the school and I am fairly quiet.)

She introduced herself to me then, realizing she hadn't done so, and offered her apologies. Her full name was Dolores del Bosque, but she went by Lola; it wasn't until many months later that I learned del Bosque means "from the forest," just like Sylvia does. By then, we were already intertwined in every way, physically and emotionally. Like me, Lola was untamable, and like me, she had run away, leaving her conservative family in Mexico City as a teenager and moving in with her bohemian aunt in the United States, who had herself run away on the eve of her marriage at seventeen.

I can still summon the exhilaration of those first few years in Santa Fe, a time for me that was pure magic, especially considering the first twenty years of my life. Although Lola and I needed to keep the true nature of our relationship secret from almost everyone, within the walls of our home — one that wasn't haunted by anything but the memories I fought to forget — we were high on freedom, two young women in love, beholden to no one and able to live how we wanted.

In those days I had a small circle of friends from school, young women like me who had come from elsewhere in the country to reinvent themselves, to devote their lives to making art. None of us were on the prowl for a husband, which was radical at the time, like being part of a secret society. We'd stay up all night painting and talking and listening to music, and with their encouragement, I pushed myself to go deeper into that place of discomfort that made me a better artist. My professors at the college were startled by what they called my "explicitly female" work. They said that if I continued on with that kind of painting I'd never be taken seriously as an artist. (Ha!) Their criticisms eventually drove me away from the college. In hindsight —

I'll leave it there. Diego is calling for me. I think he's found my treasure.

It's only 7 p.m., but I'm going to bed soon since I suspect I'll be up in the night. (I hope I'm wrong.) I don't have much of an appetite, so I'm having a light meal of toast and tea. The wooden box that Diego dug up is outside on the back patio. I gave him his check and sent him home hours ago, but I haven't been brave enough to go outside and open it.

Middle of the night

I have indigestion from the two cheeseburgers I scarfed down. Lola had warned me against eating death, but I hadn't been able to resist, and now I'm burping them up, those dead-cow spirits.

The indigestion isn't the reason I woke up, unpleasant as it is. I woke up for the same reason I've been waking up every night: *tap tap*.

I should just ignore my visitor, but that's difficult to do. My mother screamed when her visitors came in the night because she witnessed the horror of what had happened to them. I don't believe now that my mother actually encountered any ghosts. Rather, I think she was highly attuned to the suffering of others — she had, perhaps, an excess of empathy, a woman who would hear her mother's dying screams for her entire life, a roar early on that grew much quieter but never went away. When she moved into my father's house, she remained attuned to suffering but also to injustice, to domination and violence; they haunted her.

I could be wrong, but this is what I came to believe while writing in the diaries — that she never really actually saw any ghosts. That doesn't mean they weren't real.

I've never seen my ghost either, but I know she's out there.

Tap tap.

Many years ago, around the time I went through menopause, Lola and I made friends with a married couple from Denmark here for the summer. To be more accurate, Lola made friends with them; by that time in my life, I didn't much concern myself with other people. They were a straight couple, and the woman, whose name was Margit, went into the perfumery one afternoon and ordered one of Lola's bespoke perfumes. She requested one that smelled like a Gothic cathedral, like Notre Dame and Canterbury, since they were her favorite places to visit, cold and gloomy and dark, she said, with history burned into the walls. She was depressed at being stuck in relentlessly bright New Mexico while her husband, whose name I can't recall (husbands rarely stick with me), had come to research something to do with the atomic bombs developed in Los Alamos, Little Boy and Fat Man.

Lola, wanting to impress Margit, who was quite glamorous, agonized over the perfume for weeks, much longer than she took to make my Bellflower Village fragrance (which I refused to smell, resulting in our first argument — I eventually threw the bottle out the window of a moving car, racing away before its fumes could follow me). When it came time to deliver the perfume, Margit invited us to dinner at their rented house on Canyon Road and Lola insisted that I go with her despite my attempts to get out of it.

I wore what I always wore, a long black dress, no frills, just simple linen, with my hair in a braid down my back. When we arrived at the house, I felt practically Amish. Margit, who must have been in her early sixties then, had the most gorgeous white-blond hair that fell to her shoulders. I can still see her as she greeted us wearing a tailored blouse and trousers with silver jewelry in just the right places. As carefully tended as a bonsai, and just as elegant and understated.

The rented house was nestled in the trees, a bit of darkness for Margit, but it was also ablaze with candles set on every surface. She made it known right away that she knew who I was, that she and her husband had seen my work at museums in London and Paris. I didn't like being recognized, scrutinized. Margit could tell I was uncomfortable and steered the conversation away from me as much as possible; I came to like her. The dinner conversation ultimately was monopolized by talk of atomic bombs and white floral perfumes, but the whole time Margit and I engaged in a silent conversation, glancing at each other with knowing looks as our partners talked nonstop and peppered each other with questions about their work, both of them endlessly curious. It was a fun sort of flirtation.

When the meal was finished, I went to the kitchen with Margit to make coffee. "Fat Man has found an audience," she said. "You and Lola might be here all night."

"Fat Man?" I said.

"Let's not talk about bombs. If I hear any more about bombs —"

"You'll explode," I said, and she laughed.

"Precisely. Let's talk about art." She asked me about one of my paintings. "*Sea Asters*?" she said. "That's one of yours, right?"

I nodded and turned away. If Lola had been there, she would have said, "Oh, don't mind Sylvia, she hates talking about her work." She had a knack for smoothing over the ways I disappointed people.

"You portrayed such a feeling of loneliness in that piece," Margit said. "The asters on the salt marsh all by themselves. It made me cry, but I don't know why."

"Is that a good thing?"

"I think so," she said. "I don't cry easily. It touched something in me. The painting is beautiful and melancholy. Which is probably how I'd describe you too." She winked at me and led the way out of the kitchen with the tray of coffee things. I couldn't help but think that's how most celebrated artists were regularly treated, flirted with and flattered; it can't be good for their art. Still, a little bit is nice.

A couple of days later, Lola left for a week in Montréal to attend a conference and visit a cousin. The second night she was away: *tap tap*. It was impossible to sleep. Back then, the tapping was quieter, as if a piano key were being struck in some distant corner of the house, but still I couldn't sleep, knowing my visitor was out there.

The next morning, Margit called to invite me over for lunch. She apologized for the last-minute invitation and asked if I'd mind driving to see her since her husband had taken the car. Normally, I would have said no, as I did with nearly every invitation, particularly since I was exhausted, but I said yes immediately to Margit's. I was lonely without Lola, and more than that, I had enjoyed Margit in a way I rarely do other people.

The house smelled of the fish stew Margit was cooking for our lunch. "It's just Lola who's the vegetarian, right?" she asked, and I nodded, transforming in the way that I did when Lola was away, becoming a carnivore. I wondered how she changed when she was away from me.

Margit and I sat on oversize pillows in front of the kiva fireplace in the living room while the stew cooked, holding cups of tea. The house didn't sparkle as much during the day, but the trees outside filtered the sunlight, which landed on the walls and furniture in pretty patterns.

"You look tired today, Sylvia," Margit said. I appreciated her directness.

"I didn't sleep last night. Sometimes I don't sleep well when Lola is away."

"Oh? Why is that, do you think?"

I shrugged. I didn't want to tell her the reason why.

"Come on," she said. "Let's explore it together."

I laughed. "What are you, a psychiatrist?"

"Yes — I am, in fact."

I wondered if maybe she was kidding, but she wasn't. She explained that she'd closed her practice for the summer to travel with her husband but that she missed her work and was bored.

"Tell me why you can't sleep when Lola is away. Give me something to do."

I worried that this was why she'd invited me over, to assess me. She looked eager, sitting across from me in a white sundress with a white crocheted top over it that hid her shoulders.

I didn't want to talk about myself, but at the same time, I didn't want to disappoint her. I still felt drawn to her and wanted to keep enjoying the charge of her attention. If I was being completely honest with myself, I would have had to acknowledge that's why I'd accepted her invitation, so I could feel desired by her again.

"Well," I said, feeling cornered. I was normally quite direct, but she'd left me flustered. The last psychiatrist I'd spoken to had been Dr. Westgate when I was twenty years old, which at that point was about thirty years earlier. I'd never opened up to another doctor or anyone besides Lola as I was unwilling to expose the underworld of my mind and let the so-called medical professionals pick through it. I'd managed to get by without professional help. *Get by* but perhaps not thrive. I've been successful, sure, and I've managed not to crack up completely, but there are the panic attacks, severe anxiety (sometimes debilitating), periods of agoraphobia, and (as evidenced by this diary) chronic irritability.

Margit was waiting for me to respond, so I finally said: "Do you believe in ghosts?" I was willing to play along as we waited for lunch, tossing her a bone or two if not the meat. She'd be leaving at the end of the summer and I'd never see her again.

"What do you mean by *ghosts?*"

"When Lola is away, a ghost visits me."

"How fascinating," she said, narrowing her gaze, examining me like she must have examined *Sea Asters* at the museum in London. "In what way does this ghost visit you?"

"She taps on my bedroom window during the night."

"*She?* Does that mean you know who it is?"

"Maybe."

"But you don't want to tell me?"

"No."

"All right," she said, getting up from her pillow and sitting in a chair, putting herself in her official position. "What does Lola say about the ghost?"

"I've never told her. It's the only secret I have from her." It felt wrong to be sharing it now with Margit, more a betrayal than any flirtation.

"Sylvia, have you seen the ghost that haunts you?"

"No, she stays outside. I can only hear her."

"Have you talked to her?"

"No."

"Why not?"

"She's angry with me. I'm afraid of her anger."

"I see. And how long has she been visiting you?"

"Almost thirty years."

Margit was incredulous. "An angry ghost has been tapping on your bedroom window for thirty years and you've never talked to her? Never asked her what she wants?"

"I know what she wants. I don't need to ask."

"And what is it that she wants?"

I thought about how I should describe it since it was something for which the right language didn't exist. "I guess you could say . . . I can only think of one way to put it: She wants to devour me."

Margit looked at me with thirst, eager to explore this bizarre statement. "*Devour* you?"

I hated the way she was looking at me. Whatever appeal she had was withering away, a shriveled morning glory on the vine. I set my teacup on the coffee table and climbed up onto the sofa. "Forget I said anything," I said, attempting nonchalance. But the embarrassing revelation had changed everything between us. "Is lunch almost ready? It smells good."

"Sylvia, I can't help you if you don't tell me the whole story."

"No one ever tells the whole story," I said, closing the door that had, for a few minutes at least, inched open.

But now the door has swung open completely. I fear I have little chance of shutting it again. It's letting in a breeze — no, a veritable *mistral* — and I don't like it.

Tap tap.

If I plug my ears, I can still hear it. That must mean something.

Tap tap.

I'm sitting in the living room, in my comfortable old person's chair, with this notebook balanced on my lap and all the lights off except for the lamp on the table next to me. It's still the middle of the night, the house smothered in blackness inside and out. The wooden box that Diego dug up is outside on the patio, freed from its grave. But I didn't dare go get it.

The doorknob rattled. I knew it was only a matter of time before she got in.

"Go away," I said. I've never spoken to her, but it felt good to take Margit's advice after all these years.

"Leave me alone," I growled at her. For a moment after that, everything went quiet. But I didn't think she'd actually left me alone. I think that her sudden silence was due to her surprise at being acknowledged. Maybe, for her, that was a sign.

The women in my family have always looked for signs.

August 18, 2017 — Abiquiú, New Mexico

The phone rang at 7:30 and woke me up. "Sylvia?" said Rebecca. "I just spoke to Kenji. As I suspected, Colt won't accept two million."

"Go to three million," I said, and hung up. Rude, yes, but you can't wake a person up from a deep sleep and expect them to be nice about it.

With great effort, I extricated myself from the living-room recliner, where I'd sat all night. My body was even achier the day after my fall, and I had large bruises on my right arm and leg. I made a mug of coffee, then limped outside to the backyard and sat in one of the rattan chairs, with its plump, ivy-patterned cushion. I've always loved this yard. The stucco wall around the perimeter with the gate at the back makes a clear demarcation between the civility of home and the wildness just beyond it. There are shrubs around the perimeter that Lola and I planted, Arizona rosewood and boxwood, and then, of course, there are flowers — the rosebushes and hollyhocks, the latter like something out of a fairy tale, with stalks as tall as I am.

But this morning there was something out of place — the wooden box Diego had dug up. It sat next to me on the patio. He'd cleaned it off so it wasn't covered in clumps of dirt, but it was grungy from being buried for so long. I lifted my left foot, clad in a light summer slipper, and pushed on the box just to make contact with it. Nothing came jumping out at me, not that I expected it to, but I spook quite easily, hence the rifle under the bed.

I finished my coffee as I worked up my nerve, then I stood up and undid the latch on the box and opened the lid. The way I gasped and turned away, there might as well have been a little body nestled inside. And I suppose there was, in a way.

I picked up what was in the box, the handbag from Bonwit Teller, all I'd had with me the day I left Connecticut. The leather was dull and crackly, but it was remarkably well-preserved. In sixty years I hadn't touched anything that had belonged to Iris Chapel, yet here, as if by magic, was her handbag. I carried it inside and set it on my desk.

As soon as I sat down, the phone rang. It was Rebecca. "Sylvia, they said no to three million."

"Go to five and call me back. I've got to go," I said, and hung up.

I reached for the zipper to open the bag but pulled my hand back, suddenly afraid, wondering if I should have left it undisturbed. Lola and I had buried it together, and at the time, she thought it was an odd thing to do. I'd told her about my past within weeks of our meeting, and she said she believed me and I never pushed her on that — if she had doubts, I didn't want to know. She said she understood why I'd become Sylvia, but she thought a mock burial for the person I'd been was morbid. I tried to explain to her that I didn't need a *burial* per se; the problem was that I couldn't keep the items with me. I needed a clean break, but I also couldn't throw them away. In the end, though, I was glad of the burial — the end of Iris deserved to be marked in some way with ceremony.

I put my hand on the zipper again, but the phone rang again, startling me. "Gee, Rebecca, that was fast," I said when I picked up.

"Sylvia?" It was Lola.

"Oh," I said, and laughed, feeling as if she'd walked in on me doing something I shouldn't have been doing. Which in a way was true.

"Why are you expecting a call from Rebecca?"

"It's nothing," I said, but I knew Lola wouldn't believe that. "I'll tell you when you get home. Don't worry about it."

"I'm definitely going to worry about it now. Are you all right?"

"I'm just tired, sweetie."

"I have a class in a few minutes, but thought I better call to remind you that the man from the National Gallery of Art is coming this afternoon."

"What man?"

"He's coming all the way from Washington, D.C., to pick up Abigale. Did you forget?" she asked, but she already knew that I had.

"Yes, but I'll be home."

"I called Diego and asked him to come over to be with you."

Lola, always thoughtful, knew I didn't like men to come into the house when I'm here alone. I only trust Diego because he's a Guerrero.

"Sylvia, I'll be home soon. I think this'll be my last long trip. I'm exhausted."

"Good," I said. "That's good. Not that you're exhausted, but I don't like it when you go away." I wasn't religious, but I prayed she wouldn't die before me. I couldn't bear it.

"You sound strange," she said. "Tell me what's happening."

I agonized over what I could tell her in these moments before her class. I wanted to tell her something, to give her a hint about what was happening, but I didn't want to scare her. Finally, rather too cryptically, I said: "I worry Sylvia Wren is slipping away from me."

Lola was quiet for a moment. "What does that mean?"

"I'm not exactly sure, but I feel like I'm losing my grip on her."

"On *her*? You are Sylvia. She's not some other person."

"Is she, though? I mean, is Sylvia really me?"

Silence, rather too much silence, then I heard clicking on a keyboard. "I'm coming home."

"You don't have to do that," I said, though I desperately wanted her to.

"The airline website says there's a flight at eight tonight to Houston. From there, I can get home by around noon tomorrow. Will you be okay until then?"

"I'll be okay," I assured her. But how can anyone ever assure anyone else that they'll be okay?

I sat for a little while with Lola's voice still fresh in my mind, not willing to let it go until I felt ready. Then I unzipped the handbag, and without looking inside, I stuck my hand into its silky interior. I pulled out the first thing my fingers grasped, a glass bottle, and I knew what it was before I pulled it out: Aster's English lavender perfume. Next came Aster's hairbrush, still with her strands of hair; Rosalind's coral cameo ring and her tortoiseshell combs; Calla's book of handwritten poems and her moonstone ring; one of Daphne's lurid novels; Belinda's spirit journal and the wren, still wrapped in the handkerchief. I removed the little brown bird from its shroud and felt its still-soft feathers. "My namesake," I said, and kissed its forehead, setting it on the windowsill.

In one of the interior pockets, I found the envelope containing Zelie's hair, which I didn't open since I couldn't handle seeing it. From the front pouch, I pulled out Daphne's painting, *The White Iris,* which had flaked in places but was still surprisingly beautiful. So much of my life, my success, could be traced back to this painting. To see it unearthed after all these years was incredibly moving in a hard-to-breathe kind of way.

There was one more item in the bag; I had felt my hand graze it, but I couldn't bear to look at it, not yet.

When all the objects were set out on my desk, minus one, I looked them over as if I were an archeologist and they were a collection of tiny bones. Looking at the objects, up from the depths for the first time in six decades, I feared I'd become overwhelmed with emotion and fought the urge to run up the hill again. (I knew that if I did I might actually kill myself.)

I considered a cup of tea (a poor substitute) but then the telephone rang and I nearly jumped out of my skin.

"Sylvia?" It was Rebecca.

"What is it?"

"Colt will accept five and a half million."

"Done."

"Don't you want to talk to Lola about this?" she asked, and I sighed audibly. Why does everyone always question me?

"Lola isn't my mother," I said, while working to maintain my cool. "I don't need to ask her permission."

"Okay then," Rebecca said. "I'll tell Kenji to close at five and a half million."

We talked about paperwork for a few minutes. When I hung up the phone, I brimmed with a nervous, shaky energy that I didn't know what to do with. I picked up Calla's moonstone ring and slipped it on my finger, taking several deep breaths.

My sisters were closer now. I could feel them.

In preparation for the man from the National Gallery, I went to Lola's study at the other side of the house to collect Abigale Calisher. The walls in Lola's study were packed with framed art, posters, and photographs with barely any white space to be seen. At the center of one wall was a relatively new addition: a large framed poster from a MOMA retrospective that had run in February to mark my eightieth birthday. *Sylvia Wren at Eighty: An American Icon* it said in bold black lettering above my most famous flower painting, *The Purple Iris.* I refused to hang the poster in my study, the word *icon* making me cringe with embarrassment. But Lola, of course, loved it. "A man wouldn't be embarrassed by it," she'd said, as if that mattered.

On another wall was *The Land of Enchantment,* the rose petal painting from the gallery in New York I'd seen those many decades ago. It was a complete fluke that I encountered this painting that day, and yet my seeing it was largely responsible for my moving to New Mexico and thus, in a sense, responsible for the last sixty years of my life.

The painting hadn't sold at the gallery show in New York, and so it was returned to the Palace School, where it was put up for sale in their shop. I saw it the day I enrolled. It cost only five dollars or so — it was, after all, by an anonymous student — and I bought it immediately upon seeing it. It was the first item that Sylvia Wren ever owned. A professor later told me that the "anonymous" who'd painted it was a woman named Grace, who hadn't signed her name because she was afraid her husband would see it, figure out what the rose petals were meant to signify, and become angry. I never met Grace; her husband joined the army and they left for Texas in the weeks before I moved to Santa Fe, but I dedicated *The Purple Iris* to her. FOR GRACE, I wrote on the back with a pencil: NO LONGER ANONYMOUS.

I tended to avoid Lola's study even when she was away and I was missing her desperately because it was like a museum of my life. I scanned the walls, looking for Abigale Calisher before finding her to the right of the desk. The full title of the painting is *Abigale Calisher's Last Look at the Sky,* but Lola refers to it as simply Abigale, as if they're old friends. Abigale Calisher was a real woman who was hanged at the Salem witch trials. Young and unmarried and living with a woman friend, she sold herbal concoctions — ointments, salves, and cordial waters — to survive, which is what led to accusations of witchcraft. Lola had read a book about the witch trials and remarked to me about Abigale, with whom she felt a kinship as a fellow maker of potions, as a woman with a lifestyle that other people found threatening. Her interest led me to paint the scene, my only New England painting, exhibited once in a museum in Berlin in the 1980s.

Abigale isn't actually in the painting — it's from her point of view, standing at the gallows. There's a crowd; one can assume they're watching what's about to happen to her, but the painting only shows the tops of their heads. Her focus is on the sky, which is in a vibrant shade of hyacinth blue that I like to imagine matched the flowers growing in her garden.

I removed the painting from the wall and blew the dust from the top of the frame. I don't know why Lola agreed to let the National Gallery exhibit it, but she's the one who discusses such things with my representatives, and I don't question her decisions. I'd like to exhibit the painting in the museum that will be dedicated to my life and work — no longer an abstract idea but a place I've just purchased for more than five million dollars.

I'll likely never see the wedding cake again. I haven't left the state of New Mexico since 1987 when Lola and I went on a camping trip to Yellowstone. But I can see Lola inside the house, and I like seeing her there, wearing a hard hat, telling the workers what to do as they renovate my family's home, repairing the damage the Colt executives probably caused and restoring it to the way it should be.

I've begun to imagine this museum, walking through it in my mind, thinking about which paintings would go where. The bedrooms in the girls' wing will hold the florals. Some of them are erotic, some aren't, but it's the viewer who gets to decide what they're seeing. I'll include *The White Iris* as well to give Daphne her due. In the girls' sitting room, I'd like to exhibit a series of my paintings of women's bodies, their reproductive organs made of flowers. In one of the paintings, there are dahlias as ovaries, and a bearded iris as a uterus, and daisy chains for fallopian tubes. In the sixties, this was considered daring (these are the paintings that led to my leaving the college) and raised my profile as an artist; in the seventies, one of these pieces was featured on the cover of *Ms.* magazine.

In my mother's rooms, I could hang my Headless Bride paintings. There are six paintings in the series, an evolution from woman to landscape, from a bride to the Cerro Pedernal, the mesa near my house that looks like a neck without a head. One of the Headless Bride paintings was featured on the cover of a novel, one of those seventies feminist novels that sold millions of copies, and as a result, the image was everywhere for a while, not just in bookstores but in airports, supermarkets, and drugstores, and it entered the public consciousness in a way few pieces of contemporary art ever do. My flowering as an artist coincided with the rise of the women's movement, which accounts for my subsequent fame.

This earlier work, the work that made me famous, is what Sylvia Wren had drawn from the deep well of the Chapel girls' shared experiences even if

I never consciously acknowledged that's what I was doing. Iris was still much closer to me then — I'd been Iris for much longer than I'd been Sylvia, unlike now, when it's the other way around. When I was painting back then, I allowed myself to acknowledge what haunted me; the past didn't come as memories but as images that I transformed into art. Painting those memories was similar in some ways to my conversations with Dr. Westgate — I felt as if I were expelling something. Eventually, I was able to move on to other subjects for my work, and I became Sylvia completely. Or that's what I thought anyway. Until recently.

My early work is viewed as a liberatory and progressive celebration of women's bodies and sexuality, but there's a great deal of pain in it when you know what lies beneath — the undercoat if you will. I'd thought I could purge the past through my art but the past is still there. I've never, in any real sense, reckoned with it. I ran away from Connecticut to New Mexico, but in a way, I never arrived anywhere — I just kept running.

I went back to my study, Abigale Calisher in hand. I sat at my desk and pulled the last object out of the handbag, the framed photo of my family at the hotel on Terrapin Cove during the summer of 1949. Since I'd buried the only photo I have of them, I hadn't seen their faces for so long that I wept. Sylvia Wren isn't known for crying — she has hard, impenetrable edges.

The family photo is black-and-white, but I see my father in his brown suit and my mother in her white dress. My sisters and I are wearing our colorful sundresses; Aster and Rosalind are already women, Calla and Daphne look resentful at having to stand with us for posterity, and I, still innocent, hold Zelie's hand and smile.

In the photo, my parents are both much younger than I am now — neither of them lived to be as old as I am. About three months after I arrived in New Mexico, I awoke to a wren tapping on my bedroom window and I knew my mother was dead. I called the St. Aubert Sanitarium that morning, pretending to be her friend, though she didn't have any, and the nurse told me she'd died in the night. ("Her heart failed her," the nurse said, which was an odd way to phrase it. I replied: "It's not surprising, given how much it had endured.")

My father's death came six years later. Lola returned from a trip to Boston and handed me a copy of the *Boston Globe* that she'd bought at the airport, opened to the obituary page. At the top, a large headline announced my father's passing: CHAPEL FIREARMS TYCOON DEAD AT 70.

"What does it say?" I asked her, unwilling to read the piece myself. I was in my studio working on one of my Headless Bride paintings; I continued with it as Lola read.

"Cancer," Lola said. "It says: 'Preceded in death by his beloved wife and five daughters.' No mention of his remaining daughter."

"His remaining daughter has been written out of history," I said with an air of cynicism, though that's not how I felt inside. I didn't know how to feel.

"Sylvia," Lola had said that day, setting the newspaper aside. "Why don't we go for a walk?" I must have seemed monstrous to her, a woman who didn't cry over the death of her parents. But Sylvia Wren didn't have parents. All she had was hard edges.

"I'm fine, really," I said. "I just want to work." Art was the only language I had, the only way I could express the emotions I felt, but it's not sufficient for what I'm facing now.

On the back of *The Purple Iris,* I'd written: For Grace, no longer anonymous. But isn't that what I've been all these years — anonymous? Maybe Sylvia Wren is just a synonym for anonymous. After all, I've never signed my real name to any of my work. I am, as Eliza Mortimer reminded me, a ghost.

I got up from my desk and went to my bookshelves. It took me a moment to find what I was looking for, a memoir by Johnnie Marquis that I had recently read. He's an artist roughly my age, though not as famous, and was known in his youth (which in male years extends until at least forty) for his antics as much as for his artwork, partying in Manhattan nightclubs, tearing up hotel rooms, and even once, in the 1970s, attempting to hijack a plane with what turned out to be a water pistol. Once he reached old age, he decided to settle down and marry a girl young enough to be his granddaughter, producing a string of children made with old gray sperm well past its "best buy" date. That's what passes for being edgy these days.

I flipped the book over, wanting to see the name of his publisher, which I couldn't recall. I spotted the familiar H&V symbol at the bottom, then I remembered: Harth & Vaudrey. They're the most prestigious publisher of books by and about artists in the United States. I imagined their publishing my diaries, which would be a departure from the lives of Marquis and his ilk. My story would be something quite different.

Reflecting on this, and the possibility of sharing my story, reminded me of lines from a poem about the artist Käthe Kollwitz, a favorite of mine, written by Muriel Rukeyser.

> *What would happen if one woman told the truth about*
> *her life?*
> *The world would split open.*

I've spent my life running from my past, fearing that if I acknowledged the truth, the world — not the world at large but *my* world — would split open. I feared that facing my past would cause a chasm in me so deep that I'd never be able to climb out of it. And I was right in a sense. I wrote the diaries, and now I'm in that chasm, swallowed up whole. But to my surprise and relief, there's light in here.

In the light, I can see quite clearly what I must do now. I must share the truth about what happened to me and my mother and sisters. My art tells part of the story, and the diaries will finish it. Then I'll be complete; then I can climb out of this chasm.

I dialed Rebecca in New York, knowing and not caring that she was probably sick of me by now. "I need you to do something for me," I said, when she answered. "I've written my memoirs and I hope that Harth & Vaudrey will publish them."

"You've written your life story?" Rebecca asked with disbelief.

"My life until age twenty."

"Your life before you were famous?"

"It still counts, Rebecca," I said, as snappy as always. "If people want to know me, what happened to me in my childhood is a good place to start." That, of course, was true of anyone.

"I'm quite literally bowled over," she said. "You're so private. Your memoirs will be worth an absolute fortune."

"I suppose so," I said. "But I don't care about the money."

She laughed. "Oh Sylvia. I never hear that from my other clients. You're a delight. Truly."

"Highly doubtful," I said.

"What exactly is it you'd like me to do?"

"I've been going through something lately," I said. "You might have noticed."

"Yes, well." She was serious now.

"I've written my memoirs in three diaries. Lola can work with my agent to arrange publication. You know she handles all that for me. What I'd like you to do is keep the diaries safe for now."

"I don't quite understand."

"If something were to happen to me, I need to know that they'll be published. It's important for me to know this."

"I hope you're not ill?"

"No, it's just" — I hated to put my fears into words — "if I weren't around for some reason, I worry that Lola wouldn't honor my wish to publish the diaries. She'd fear that I'd made a rash decision, that I wasn't thinking clearly. She wouldn't want my reputation to be ruined."

"*Ruined?*" I heard the concern in Rebecca's voice. "But how —"

"I haven't done anything awful. Don't worry, I'm not a serial killer."

"Of course not," she said, but she probably wouldn't have been completely shocked if one day it was revealed that there were bodies buried in my backyard. I'm a recluse, so I must be hiding something.

"You never know what someone might do if they're upset," I explained. I could see my blue diaries ablaze in the fireplace. "I'd prefer that you have the diaries for safekeeping, with a letter from me stating that I would like them published so there's no misunderstanding. All right? You and Lola can talk when she gets back from Brazil."

"Copy that," Rebecca said. "They'll be safe with me."

After our call, I didn't pause to think about what I was doing. I wrote a letter stating my wish that the diaries be published and that Harth & Vaudrey was my first choice as a publisher. I added a paragraph about my newly acquired estate in Bellflower Village and how I would like that to become a museum dedicated to my work and a learning center for disadvantaged young people. I packed everything in a small box and addressed it to Rebecca at her law office. Then I held the box in my hands for a few moments, feeling the weight of my truth.

The man from the National Gallery didn't stay long. He was all business and didn't fawn over me, which was a relief. He packaged Abigale Calisher with Diego's help and loaded the painting into the van.

"Be careful with her," I said, not liking the thought of Abigale on the United shuttle to Denver and then on to D.C.

The man left, and Diego came into the house with me. He'd brought with him two loaves of zucchini bread, which he and Jade had baked that morning. The loaves were wrapped in parchment paper like presents, but he hadn't had time to unwrap them before the man from the museum came. With that task done, he settled me into a chair in the kitchen.

"Have you been eating okay?" he asked, as he pulled out one of the loaves. In fact, I hadn't eaten all day. Somehow, he had a sense for these things.

"I'm surviving."

"I see the bruises on your arm. You sure you don't need a doctor?"

"I'm sore, but there's no damage," I said, pulling down the sleeves of my black dress. I hadn't remembered to hide my injuries; the man from the museum must have thought I'm a battered old woman.

Diego cut me two slices of zucchini bread, and while they were toasting, he made me a cup of tea. I let him. I needed, even for a few moments, to be taken care of — though I never would have admitted that.

"If you don't mind my saying so," Diego said, "you don't seem like yourself."

"I'm not myself," I said to him, gratefully accepting the cup of tea. "You have no idea." I wanted to laugh.

I practically inhaled the zucchini bread, and he sliced me more. "I knew you hadn't eaten," he said, as he watched me from across the table and played mindlessly with the green rubber band at the tip of his beard. Lola and I paid Jade and Diego well for the jobs they did for us, but we didn't pay them for all the worrying they did. I'd find it touching if I didn't get so annoyed at being fussed over.

When I finished my snack, I asked Diego to go with me to my study. I handed him the box of diaries and asked if he'd drive to Española straightaway and send them via overnight mail.

"It's an urgent job," I said. "I'll pay extra."

"No problem, Miss Wren. I'm headed there anyway to run an errand for Jade."

"Thank goodness." I felt relieved that the diaries would be on their way to New York by tonight.

We walked back toward the living room, and on a whim, I took one of my paintings off the wall, a deep purple petunia, one of my erotic flower paintings.

"Here," I said, handing it to him. "It's for the baby."

He took it from me and studied it. After a moment, when he realized what he was looking at, he shifted uncomfortably. "Uh," he said, seemingly at a loss for words. The young didn't like to think of older people as sexual beings. It horrified them. "It's nice of you, but the thing is, Jade decorated the baby's room with ducks, and I don't think this matches."

"No, Diego, it's not meant as *decoration* for the *baby's nursery*." I stiffened. Like most people in the village, his grandparents had never much concerned themselves with my artistic fame, which I'd always found refreshing;

I thought it possible Diego didn't fully grasp who I was, which was fine, but on this particular matter, he was testing my patience. "This painting is worth an obscene amount of money. So just take it and sell it one day after I'm gone when it'll be worth even more."

He seemed stunned, looking down at the petunia, probably wondering how it could be worth money. "Are you sure?"

"It's for the baby's future," I said, patting him on the shoulder. After a few more minutes of talk about the painting, with me repeatedly assuring him that I wanted him to have it, I ushered him out of the house. I was eager to be alone, as I always am, but as I watched Diego walk to the front gate carrying the painting and the box, I dreaded the aloneness that awaited me and the night to come.

With the house to myself, I crawled into bed and thought I might take a nap, but my mind was too frenetic for sleep. So I lay there on my back staring at the large painting on the wall directly opposite the bed — *The Purple Iris,* which I'd never surrendered to a museum though it had toured widely. I painted it when I was around thirty. Lola was my model. She's the only female body I've known besides my own, my favorite landscape. She and our love affair are displayed in museums around the world.

As I lay in bed this afternoon, unable to nap, staring at the iris, I could see Lola coming into the bedroom looking as she did when we'd met. It was in this bedroom that we were first together. It was Christmas, when everything outside was covered in snow, the burning red of the hills temporarily extinguished under a blanket of white. We'd been inseparable for months, but we were both young and completely inexperienced, and the desire we had for each other left us ashamed and conflicted. It seemed such an unnatural thing to want to do with another woman, and yet we both wanted it.

"Are you afraid?" she asked me that first time, kissing the scar on my arm — my desperation to flee the life I'd had was written on my body, would always remain there.

"I'm not afraid," I said, knowing I'd be okay. Somehow, I just knew.

When I'd run away, I thought New Mexico was my destination, but it had been her. I'd finally found my place.

That afternoon with Lola, I felt things I'd never felt before, her skin touching mine when I was so rarely touched, her body warming mine when for so long I had been cold. I felt happy and fulfilled, and I wondered for the first time whether the torment that was seeded so deeply inside me could be quelled.

When we were both finally quiet and still, watching the snowfall, a voice came into my head, one of those voices I thought I had buried.

What's a life without love?

Zelie. She had asked me that question only months earlier, and at the time, I couldn't answer her, hadn't even understood the question. But in Lola's arms, I understood why Zelie couldn't bear to face a life without being touched, without the warmth of another. Love was no longer an abstract idea.

I wept for my sister that afternoon — I'd never properly grieved for her, and she'd deserved more than that — but after that day, I rarely allowed myself to think of her again.

It's my last night alone, and I decided to make a black-bean stew for dinner. Diego had reminded me that I'm not properly caring for myself, so I walked to the market for the ingredients, and back at home, I chopped the onions and garlic and celery with my sore arm, reflecting on the events of the day.

When my stew was ready, I took a bowl outside to the patio to watch the sun setting, the light reflecting off the landscape in ways that continue to fascinate me. But I wasn't tempted to grab my paints as I wasn't feeling any impulse toward art. I've been consumed with writing, that's the problem; what I see and feel now seeks expression not in color and imagery but in letters. These dreaded letters.

In the hours since I last talked to Rebecca, I haven't regretted my decision to publish the diaries. I am, however, experiencing a degree of mourning. It's not any kind of profound mourning, not the kind where you hurl yourself onto the grave and wail but rather a quieter, anticipatory grief for what's to come. I'm sure that when the diaries are published my biography will forever overshadow my art, a fate that befalls so many women in the arts. That, to me, is the worst part of it.

I know the reaction to the truth I share in the diaries will be disbelief. I hear the voice of Dr. Westgate all those years ago: *I can assure you that what you think happened to your sisters didn't actually happen.* That disbelief, that rebuke, is why so many women prefer to stay silent. It's why I fear that Lola, if I'm not around, might choose to burn the diaries. Lola, always my protector, would want to spare me from being viewed as a madwoman, like my mother was only very publicly. Globally.

But I think I've finally come to realize that it's my destiny to be one of the madwomen. One of the women who speaks the truth no matter how terrifying it might be. One of the women who stands apart from the crowd, focusing not on their angry faces and disapproval but looking above them at the sky, which is in a vibrant shade of hyacinth blue that matches the flowers growing in the garden.

Middle of the night

This will be my last entry in the violet notebook. I carried it into the living room with me, having woken up for the usual reasons. Only the lamp is switched on. I'm wrapped tightly in my robe, a lovely emerald-green silk one that Lola bought me on a trip to Japan. She'd gone there to accept a prestigious award on my behalf, as usual representing me while I stayed hidden away at home, in this house where I've spent most of my life.

My visitor is here. She's been knocking on the windows and rattling the doorknobs, making more noise than she ever has before. She knows I'm in here, sitting in this dimly lit room, and that I'm ignoring her. I'm inside, and she's out there. That's the way it's been for a long time.

I look around the living room, trying to ignore the noises she's making.

Despite the renovations we've done to the house, the evolution of furniture from stylish to comfortable, the living room looks similar to how it always did. I can see Lola's collection of antique perfume bottles, the painting of Ghost Ranch, and a Chapel '70 rifle she bought before she knew me, which hangs above the fireplace looking like a bent finger. It's as if I just arrived, back in 1957, in love and with a life of possibilities in front of me.

I was young then, and now I'm old. Looking back, I made the most of the life I fought so hard to have. I knew it needed to matter.

[Lola, if you're reading this, please know that you're what mattered most. Zelie was right — a life without love isn't any kind of life.]

Now the house is shaking. This isn't a surprise — the earth has been quaking for weeks, cracking open all around me. Iris is tired of being ignored. She's angry at being left outside for so long. I thought that if I wrote about her she'd be satisfied, but she wants more. She wants the life that is rightfully hers.

She's coming for you, my mother might have warned. But I'm not afraid anymore.

It's time to set down my notebook and open the door —

AUTHOR'S NOTE

The title of this novel is borrowed from "Cherry Robbers," a poem by D. H. Lawrence, who lived for a time in New Mexico.

As will be obvious to some readers, Belinda Holland Chapel is very loosely inspired by the life and legend of Sarah Winchester. Mary Jo Ignoffo's *Captive of the Labyrinth: Sarah L. Winchester, Heiress to the Rifle Fortune* was useful to me in learning about the real life of Sarah Winchester. No other character in *The Cherry Robbers* is inspired by any real person, past or present, in the firearms industry.

I did not write Iris Chapel/Sylvia Wren to be a fictionalized version of Georgia O'Keeffe, but O'Keeffe's influence is obviously significant in the novel. While the life of my protagonist is vastly different from O'Keeffe's life, and they would be fifty years apart in age, I have nevertheless drawn inspiration from O'Keeffe's flower paintings and her home in Abiquiú, New Mexico. In the world of *The Cherry Robbers,* Georgia O'Keeffe does not exist, and Sylvia Wren occupies (some of) that space. As a fiction writer, I reserve the right to rearrange the world as I see fit, and in doing so, Georgia O'Keeffe's work and her New Mexico life gave to me many gifts that I would like to gratefully acknowledge.

In writing about Iris Chapel as an aspiring artist in 1950s New York, the following book was tremendously helpful to me: *Ninth Street Women: Lee Krasner, Elaine de Kooning, Grace Hartigan, Joan Mitchell, and Helen Frankenthaler: Five Painters and the Movement That Changed Modern Art* by Mary Gabriel.

As I was writing, I thought a lot about Richard Yates's novel *Revolutionary Road,* and the film adaptation. In particular, I thought about April Wheeler, patron saint of white suburban housewives in 1950s Connecticut.

Two poets were essential in helping me create the world of the novel — H.D. (Hilda Doolittle) and Emily Dickinson. I cannot imagine how different this novel would be without their influence and their words. As such, I would like to acknowledge the following books: *Collected Poems 1912–1944* by H.D., edited by Louis L. Martz; *The Complete Poems of Emily Dickinson* by Emily Dickinson, edited by Thomas H. Johnson; *The Gardens of Emily Dickinson* by Judith Farr, with Louise Carter; *Lives Like Loaded Guns: Emily Dickinson and Her Family's Feuds* by Lyndall Gordon; and *My Emily Dickinson* by Susan Howe.

ACKNOWLEDGMENTS

Many thanks to my editor, Naomi Gibbs, for her diligent and thoughtful work in helping me transform *The Cherry Robbers* into the novel I had always hoped it would become. Thanks also to everyone at Mariner Books for doing so much to support my books.

My sincerest gratitude to my literary agent, Alice Tasman, who is a fierce champion of my work, and to Jennifer Weltz and everyone else at JVNLA for all that they do. Thanks also to my international coagents, publishers, editors, and translators.

For helping me in so many different ways, I offer my heartfelt thanks to: Jenna McGrath, Susan Scarf Merrell, Helen Maryles Shankman, and Michelle Walker, all of whom provided invaluable feedback on the novel; Alice Mattison, who drove around New Haven with me and showed me the old Winchester factory and Betts House; Anita Taylor and William Vandegrift, for always checking in with me; David Hough, my copy editor; and Lauren Wein, for acquiring the manuscript. I must also acknowledge Shirley the cat, who curled up on my desk every day as I revised this novel during the bleakest, loneliest months of the pandemic.

My parents — the loveliest parents anyone could ever hope to have — deserve my immense love and gratitude for everything they do to support me.

Finally, although I once abandoned this novel in frustration and despair, the Chapel sisters continued to haunt me until I finally figured out how to tell their story. For that, I'll always be grateful.